The Come From Aways

A Romantic Adventure

By

Nanette Asher

Sweet forbidden love, murder, secret identities, and high romance on and off the waters of Long Island and Newfoundland in the early '60's

1663 LIBERTY DRIVE, SUITE 200
BLOOMINGTON, INDIANA 47403
(800) 839-8640
WWW.AUTHORHOUSE.COM

© 2005 Nanette Asher. All Rights Reserved.
Originally published as Loving Teachers by Nanette Asher

No part of this book may be reproduced, stored in a retrieval system, or transmitted by any means without the written permission of the author.

First published by AuthorHouse 07/01/05

ISBN: 1-4208-4753-8 (sc)
ISBN: 1-4208-4752-X (dj)

Printed in the United States of America
Bloomington, Indiana

This book is printed on acid-free paper.

DEDICATION

*To our American classroom teachers.
Long may they endure, inspire, and
appreciate.
Thank you to all our teachers.
With love, the author*

Deepest Thanks to the following friends who have given helpful advice to the author:

*Eva Arce, Jerry Borg, Sarah Colton, Patrice Ryan, Peg Slaven
And especially
Jack Bilello, and Al and Betty Gold*

And finally *Mike Asher*, whose loving support and insights have sustained both the project and the author, and *Dawn and Justin Asher* and *Sol Rey Vashez* who, among other favors, help me to remember my humanity.

****

All these events happened in one way or another. None of the characters have ever existed.

THE CHAPTERS OF THE COME FROM AWAYS

Prologue xiii

Chapter One: Suppogue, New York, 1959 1

Chapter Two: Swimming Lesson 13

Chapter Three: Into the Breech 26

Chapter Four: The Communist and the Owl Prince 40

Chapter Five: Heavy Petticoats 53

Chapter Six: Henry, Bound 63

Chapter Seven: Winds From Abroad 71

Chapter Eight: Into the Potting Shed 87

Chapter Nine: Nigger-loving Teacher 104

Chapter Ten: Sam, Kurt, and Harper 122

Chapter Eleven: Murder, My Love 140

Chapter Twelve: Marge Gone 159

Chapter Thirteen: Henry's Solution 172

Chapter Fourteen: Harper, Noah, Unbound 190

Chapter Fifteen: The Come From Aways 204

Chapter Sixteen: Jeanne 221

Chapter Seventeen: Short Cruise 229

Chapter Eighteen: Miss Mackenzie 235

About the Author 241

PROLOGUE
1936

*"Hereafter, in a better world than this,
I shall desire more love and knowledge of
you."* Le Beau, in *As You Like It*
by William Shakespeare

The Convent School of St. Mary of the Mount of Halifax stood in granite splendor against the brilliant, soft green hillside. Autumn flowers blazed in formal beds surrounding this bastion of harsh discipline and high learning, for the sisters of Holyrood prided themselves on their obedience to God's thoughtful work. The October winds fluttered the tissue leaves of the poplars, scattering a prayer of peace to this outpost of great natural beauty.

Blessed Art Thou Among Women
Blessed is the Fruit of Thy Womb
And I Shall Dwell in the House of The Lord
Forever, Forever, Forever

The raven-haired acolyte embroidered her favorite phrases onto the linen with flourishes around "The Fruit of Thy Womb" and "Forever, Forever, Forever."

Oh, to be Our Lady. To be so blessed as she. To have God within. But we are mortal. We cannot know such a gift, ever. Why can we not feel at least some approximation? At eighteen years of age, this bitterness was too great to bear. Ah, but Sister Mary Rose saw in Jennie all indications of being the most perfectly suited of all the novices for the rigors of the convent. A wondrous instrument of the Lord, the most elevated function for women, admitting no other, in humble service of the priests and bishop; already she was demonstrating only the kindest way with the young orphans; she might be even an administrator someday.

She spent the longest time in prayer, in devotions leading the children, in studying with the sisters; and she asked the most profound questions which the sisters often had to refer to the fathers. There was no doubt that Jeanne Du Bonne would rise quickly into a position of significance as she grew within the church.

Someone else was watching Jeanne grow. Someone, younger than she, for whom the gentle home discipline of earlier years also protected him from the rowdiness of the institutional orphans. Someone who, though tenderly reared and lovingly inclined, had not the same avocation for holy vows. One who had not the same aspirations to stay In the House of The Lord Forever. Brought to the convent as a boy in his early teens, he had seen his family broken apart by tragedy, this boy who now dreamed of worlds far apart from the strictures of the convent, and who looked upon the young Jeanne with her long-lashed eyes and exciting mind as the loveliest creature he had ever seen.

She had not the firm resilience of those who had taken the final orders, the self-control that grew around the Sisters of Hollyrood like the bark on an oak tree. Her young willfulness was inclined to respond to the sensual messages of both God's and Man's worlds, all of which she felt acutely. And it was often a mystery to her puerile mind how to separate one world from the other. How could the aged sisters know what she felt? They celebrated her questions and her abilities with enthusiasm and praise. Did she not have the right to explore the joys of life as God saw fit to gift her?

Inside in a long hall called the art library these two latter-day orphans, who had lately become inseparable, spent their time by either studying or sketching, working side-by-side, and had neglected to answer the call for supper.

The young man, encouraged by this slightly older acolyte, spent long hours with the lives and histories of the masters, living in his dreams, blotting out the sadness of his rejection in the rocky world of his origins.

The pretty acolyte helped. This late afternoon, alone in the library, Jeanne was sketching in charcoal a sculpture of a runner. As her pencil outlined the smooth sinews of the runner's thigh, a deep thrill rose through her torso and out to tingle her fingers as she drew. And she was not surprised when the young man, after months of worshipping her mind and body from an academic distance, lifted her headscarf and pressed his hand against her neck.

She turned to him, and in the lonely need of a cloistered eighteen-year-old, threw her arms 'round his neck and drew her body and lips against his. How perfectly her lips fitted to his; how wonderfully warm his body felt, his hard firmness against her softness, which seemed to melt into his chest. These strong throbs of feelings were new to both, and so delighted, so overwhelmed them, that when, after a minute or two, they parted, feverish, they agreed to meet at a discreet time after vespers when the sisters would be employed with the youngest members of the school.

They were old enough to know the perils that lay in such disobedience, but their knowledge that the world had cheated them both of their due affections discharged an effective measure of guilt and shame. Alone in a sheltered wood, high on the hill beyond the poplars, they drew each other to the bed rug the young man had brought from his room, and after only a tentative wandering of hands and mouths, sought each other's flesh under their heavy autumn garments. But this first time she pulled away before they could enter the phase of lovemaking that admitted no recourse. "My mind tells me that we must stop, stop now, and think, think exactly what we are about to do, how terribly desperate we are."

They had both read ardently, not only the holy writings of the martyrs and saints of their studies and the literary tomes meted out for them in the convent school, but also the periodicals that the young men and women smuggled into their quarters, romance magazines which whetted their already voracious appetites.

For the next few days they tried to tell themselves that this forbidden passion must be subdued. But finally the young man could contain himself no longer. "Jeannie, please, let's just walk out after vespers, just to talk, Jennie, just talk." And she did not draw back. Now they both had to take more, and without much talk of anything, they were soon sitting on the rug at the edge of the woods, this time hugging each other tightly as if to prevent a profane movement, as if to protect each other from what they knew was an inevitable coming to pass.

The fading summer skies over the hill had turned to an autumn gray, but the setting sun curving down behind the horizon streaked the dome over their heads with silver, then glimmers of gold. A bird, disturbed by their steps into the woods, protested with startled chirps, and then settled back into its nest again. They could hear at a distance the crashing of the ocean waves against the palisades far below, which came to them as a muffled roar. This exquisite natural beauty only heightened the promise of the pleasures of their forbidden love, and the sharp chill in the air drew them to cling together for another natural need.

Finally he released her gently, and kissed her fervently where her laced collar met the soft curve of her throat as his hands slid slowly around her waist under her wool jacket. Powerless to call a halt, she turned to his eager mouth, and as they locked together, they fell back upon the blanket, hidden from view by the heavy brush behind the tall poplars. A new depth of passion aroused her now. It was a passion bred of a resentment that she didn't know she had been feeling. It said, "Take what is yours. Take what has come to you. Do not question this wonder, this beauty. This rapture was given to you to enjoy."

"Please, please, it's good, it's fine, please try now," and as she was hugging the breath almost out of him, he finally dared to enter into a tender act of love.

He was suddenly frightened. They were so young, so unprepared; but he could not stop now. He could not leave her like this, even if he could stop himself. Please God help me go slowly and not hurt her I love her so.

Afterward he was the first to move, "God, Ye'll catch terrible cold lying here," and hurried to fetch her garments that lay hurled about them on the rug. After they dressed, they lay speechless against each other and began to fondle each other's bodies again. This was a passion that could not be quenched. Without knowing sophisticated techniques of love, they spent themselves again feverishly, and it was a long time before they could end.

"No more now," she cautioned. "We will have more time,.and soon."

And there were many more times that autumn, and later, when they discovered that they could be together in the little art library after hours when no one would think of going there, and on weekends when most of the senior nuns went on holiday.

They grew bolder in their expressions, and because Jennie was so respected among the sisters, and because she never once neglected her duties to her charges and her devotions but seemed to work with an added zeal and commitment, was given more and more freedom. In her hours off from her work, they could love nearly as often as they chose. They now loved more wisely and with more care and concern, but the careless passion of their earliest couplings showed all signs of bearing precious fruit. In late winter, Jeannie cried against him. "I'm going to have to go away. There's no hope for it."

"You can't. We must stay together. I'll take care of you. I'll find some way," pleaded the brave sixteen-year-old. But early one morning he heard sounds under his window of an engine at the entrance to the convent, and three nuns escorting Jeannie into a long wagon. She pulled back for a moment to look up at his window with a drawn face, and even though he raced down to the monitor's desk, then to the Mother Superior, no one at the school would give him any accounting or explanation. He wept many nights though and grew thin and listless over his work. But he finally drew away from the habit of looking out his window at the empty place where he had last seen the beautiful face looking back longingly at him. And when he was so tempted, turned away to the window opposite, toward the sparkling sea instead of into the empty air.

Finally, in the summer, he was enjoined to take work at a nearby farm, and the long hours of the early morning harvesting led him to sleep deeply and begin to allow his stabbing pain to mellow and fade.

On weekends, the boy workers would go into Halifax for evening entertainment, and although the school made them keep some notice of hours, they spent a bit of time at some of the more carelessly run pubs where the establishment never questioned age. He met girls there who struck his fancy for an evening or two … some careless kisses and one or two fumbling liaisons which were hardly worth the trouble, but they helped to pass the summer after his sadness, and, as is the wont of youth, interested him in other possibilities. He thought of those days now, but often, when in the act of love, his body and enthusiasm tired even before he could be through with lovemaking. Now only in his imagination was his life real again, and full, and loving. Many years later, nine hundred miles and over twenty years away, he was unable to think of Jeanne Du Bonne without wanting to weep. He longed to regain some of that youth. He wanted it all with a desire that exceeded all other fantasies that plagued his waking moments.

SUPPOGUE, NEW YORK, 1959

Chapter One

*"But come what sorrow can,
It cannot countervail the exchange of joy
That one short minute gives me in her sight."*
Romeo *in Romeo and Juliet*
 By William Shakespeare

On a blistering hot August morning Lucy Mackenzie alighted from a Long Island Railroad coach at the Suppogue station on the Jamaica-Patchogue line. She pranced across the tracks in her slender, healthy body, high in the heels of *1959*, disciplined in tight girdle and hose under a proper seersucker suit, auburn curls fluffy from fat rollers, framing a piquant face, whitely powdered and punctuated with the pink-pink lipstick of the day.

The heat baked morning shoppers into their clothes as they rushed to escape the sultry afternoon. Summer increased the population twofold in this bayside town, and the new year-round dwellers were changing the old scenes. Most of the elderly folk, descendants of early New Englanders, still talked with wide A's and strolled with wide gaits. But the scurriers in the crowd represented the newer immigrants from the city. The town was unique. It had not been absorbed by its neighbors or by an all-county attitude or economy. A few purebred dogs on leashes trotted with proud owners, but the majority, leashed or not, were nondescript mongrels. Perhaps the mild climate of this south shore village encouraged a casual mood. There were none of the self-conscious boutiques of north shore towns, rather the storeowners here took pride in their vinyl storefronts, and here and there, a little touch of neon in the night.

Lucy consulted her eighteen-jewel graduation watch, adjusted her pencil-thin skirt, and toed gingerly up to the sidewalk of the town's broad main thoroughfare, on her own in search of her first real job---at least part of a life of her own.

Her mother's dreary admonitions of the morning eddied forth from the back of her mind, taunting her illusions: the ritual warnings to remind her adult daughter of teeth brushing, suit pressing and "if-you-will-be-late-call-me-or-I'll-worry-myself-sick" she forced down behind her pleasure at the sensation of freedom of the day.

This was a time before the Beatles but during the full pelvic thrusts of Elvis after the heyday of Joseph McCarthy when simple minds were still stalking closet communists; and it was just before the election of John F. Kennedy. The Beat Generation was being called "Hip" before the anarchists appeared called "Yip," and it was before the *Fugs* appeared on McDougal at the *Cafe Wha*. Hats and gloves were required for ladies' luncheons and all religious services, and people still believed in flawless Presidents and heroic American gladiators. It was a long time before Woodstock and the flower children, and it was even months before the Buddhists burned themselves in Vietnam.

Great Bay Avenue spread itself north to the Long Island Expressway and beyond to the hills and coves of the North Shore of Long Island, south to Montauk Highway, then narrowed onto a peninsula into the wide ocean bay. The school was to be in the middle of the third block from the train station on the east side of the street.

She checked her watch again---ten fifteen---she couldn't be early for her eleven o'clock interview, and glanced around the business block to see a small luncheonette on the opposite side of the street. As she crossed across a small park to save time, she paused at a colonial scaffold with the perfunctory head and arm stocks and a plaque underneath, dedicating the park to one Thomas Goodwell, who had settled and farmed the area and made himself something of a local manor lord and arbitrator with the Indians in 1743. Her mother would appreciate this piece of town history, she knew, and so she attempted to memorize the names and dates for dinner conversation.

She hurried to a counter stool in the restaurant, wanting quick service, as the jukebox blared "A Summer Place."

"Is the high school far down this street?" she spoke loudly over the music to summon a muscular man in an apron, who poured her coffee.

"Yes... no... two blocks down," he shouted back, and the creases of his mouth smiled all the way back to his graying sideburns. "You teach? You look like a teacher."

"I hope to teach somewhere soon," she responded with a short, nervous laugh that caught in the back of her throat.

He folded his muscular arms. "This is a good town. Nice place. Nicer than city. Not so crowded. People more polite---take time with you." He paused and seemed to reflect at her particular presence. "Teachers come here to eat. Maybe I see you again."

"I hope so," she smiled at the ploy for business.

"You come far?"

"Just from Jamaica,"

"Jamaica," he repeated softly. "Bet I know where you go to college."

She smiled at him playfully. "Where?"

"Saint Johns. You go to Saint Johns. You're a Catholic girl. Catholic teacher. Good girl. Nice town here. You should come to teach in this town."

She was suddenly uncomfortable with herself and with him. She was so easily identifiable --- her white gloves, summer suit and hat all called out to the world that here was yet another School of Ed product moving out for public consumption. The costume worked too well. She opened her purse, removed her cigarette case, and extracted a cigarette, brazenly tapping it on the counter and lighting it slowly for courage. Was this growing up? Was her life as a teacher going to restrict her world? Was she going too fast with her fears? Was her destiny shaped into that tight girdle and suit?

She left the luncheonette at a steady clip. As she stepped into the next block, Our Lady of Perpetual Help Roman Catholic Church, a pastel mélange of Baroque, Rococo, Moorish, Georgian and Gothic design rose on her left, shocking contrast to Lucy's granite cathedral in Jamaica. What sacred lessons could this new spiritual home teach her? She could yet be obsessed with the banalities of traditional religious forms: the old icons still thrilled her, protected her, she wanted to believe. She had lately escaped from so many temptations: that weekend in the ski lodge. A near moment-of-truth with George on Canarsie Pier.

Stepping delicately down Great Bay Avenue, primal warmth pleasantly aching from a seriously guarded erogenous zone, she knew she should protect herself against the frightening challenge of the fully sexual world. But what of the miracle which would transform her childhood? How long should she wait?

In another mood she practiced her approach: businesslike, her mind and body an unblemished example replete for developing young minds, newly hatched from Saint Johns English department, bent for high adventure in the classroom, guided by morality and a sense of fair play. She believed.

At the curb before the Catholic manse she paused. A tall, slim figure in flowing black robe was floating down the steps, young, spirited and graceful. God help him, she mused. No priest should be that beautiful. With longing eyes on the Father, she twisted her ankle off the curb into the gutter, flipped over into the side street in a pained heap of crumpled suit and splintered spiked heel as her white pillbox hat rolled round and round like a failing top before shuddering to its collapse in a black puddle.

*　　　　*　　　　*

Jimmy Duffer was not expecting Miss Mackenzie for at least twenty minutes, but still he stared down the corridor toward the front door of Suppogue High School and jingled coins in his pocket as the steady breeze from the bay blew pleasantly through the shaded yard and into the corridor. Jimmy had played Captain Queeg in a community theatre production that his first wife had encouraged him to join, and he had found it fun, a happy departure from the terrors of the war he had left in the then too recent past. He jingled the coins lovingly, a comforting reminder of a pleasurable time of escape and accolade. The audience had liked him. They had thought him a fine actor---had believed that he had gotten formal training. He picked the coins out of his pocket and stacked and restacked them in his hands as he glanced out of the corner of his eyes at Mina, straightening his desk.

"You're expecting a Miss Mackenzie this morning," she reminded him.

"Yes, and she comes with excellent credentials: Saint Johns, cum laude. Mackenzie, Mackenzie," Jimmy mused on, and to himself. "Queens …Saint Johns … might be related."

"Not an exotic name, Mr. Duffer," smiled Mina.

Suppogue High School looked from the outside like all other public high schools built in the early 1930's. Of solid Georgian style, its mannered appeal comforted Lucy as she limped her way around the corner of the drive, one shoe on, the other in her hand with her crushed hat, her suit besmudged on both jacket and skirt. As she glanced around the far right wall of the old building, she spied an affront to an aesthetic eye: the new addition, built in the late '50's, to accommodate the hoards of immigrants from Brooklyn who "grabbed up," as the saying went, the little frame houses in the development north of the old village and settled down with young families to work at nearby airplane factories or commute to jobs in the city.

The aluminum new addition housed the science and home economics wings and all the newly hired teachers in English and social studies. The glorious old building was reserved for the olde garde of the school. It was cooler in summer and warmer in winter than the new wing and had great beams, parquet floors, and real black slate chalkboards. The wooden desks were inscribed with thousands of historical witticisms, phone numbers, and filthy gutter talk, much of it carved so deeply that it remained as a perpetual monument to students and teachers alike. One day soon, on the eve of Parents' Night, a student, enraged with a C- on a book report, would carve deeply, with passion, *Miss Mac wears 28 NO CUP.*

Now the heavy oak doors at the far end of the corridor clunked shut, and then a strange thud, click, thud, click of a rhythm drew near. Jimmy glanced briefly at Mina and hurried to look around the corner of the hall. He stood motionless, forgetting to jingle his coins.

She came limping toward him, a wry smile contorting her flushed gamine face. "I know I'm not quite what you had in mind to interview today, Mr. Duffer, but I had a crazy accident out there in the street. I fell off a curb, right in front of the Catholic rectory, and it took me awhile to get to my feet…so disgusted with myself but there wasn't anything to do but come on down here just like I am. Please forgive my appearance---I usually walk more carefully."

"Oh, dear, are you hurt?" worried Mina, who, by this time, had scuttled to the door of the office, put her arms comfortingly around Lucy's shoulders, and drew her into the front office and into a chair.

The pretense that accompanies a formal job interview was erased by Lucy's bizarre entrance. Jimmy, apprehensive with all attractive females, relaxed in the presence of this waif who, distraught as she was, conjured up his fatherly ambitions. Mina was pleased with this young woman who was not too vain to be destroyed by a temporary disfigurement, and Lucy had lost the tension one feels from fearing that not all is perfect, in a mood one feels while returning from the beach when the hair is too heavy with salt and sand to be smoothed, and a feeling of well-being comes from knowing that nobody can expect anything better for the time.

Jimmy was now a youthful thirty-seven and had just begun to put on some extra pounds, which added to his boyish appeal. If school had been in session, a tension would have aged his demeanor, but as he did not yet have to come to grips with the pressures of teachers, school board, parents and careening youngsters, he was able to delight in this bedraggled girl.

"We'd like you to teach three classes of sophomore and two of junior English," and then he rushed to his new idea, "I guess you'll need some kind of replacement for those shoes. The only thing we might be able to offer you here is a pair of used sneakers. The kids leave them in the lockers every year, and sometimes the custodians save the best of them downstairs."

"James," Mina chimed in, "you can't expect this lady to walk home like that."

"Please, sneakers will be fine. I'm obviously desperate," Lucy sighed with relief, "and the class schedule sounds decent too. Did you receive my transcripts?" She was surprised that this man was so hasty to hire her without discussing her records or giving her an interview.

"One of our assistants did, and Mrs. Colerman recommended you, and that's quite enough for us for the present. Mackenzie. I had an old Navy buddy named Mackenzie who lived in Jamaica, but there's probably no connection. I understand he's a judge somewhere in Queens now."

"Peter Mackenzie, my father, is a judge."

Jimmy took a step backward and reappraised the young woman. He was overcome with a profound confusion. That face. He imagined that he could see something in those blue eyes that he had seen before. They looked like the eyes of someone long gone from him, as if in a dream. Was it Peter? It must be. She thought she knew the source of his puzzlement and wanted to help, but hesitated to reveal family intimacies. "Did you know him?"

"Peter Mackenzie was the finest officer I knew," Jimmy explained with delight. "Think of that. Your father. Unless there is another Peter Mackenzie, Judge, in Queens..." his expression slowly altered into a frown. War memories that he wanted to keep deep within had arisen at mention of his old comrade's name. Then he quickly remembered his audience and went on. "But he must be one and the same. Please give him my very best and tell how pleased I am to have you here."

"Excuse me, is anyone ready for lunch yet?" interrupted a specter who came so silently into the room that no one had heard. A tanned, slim figure of a man in white ducks, sneakers and a sailor T.

"Come in, Noah, and meet Miss Mackenzie," demanded Mina. "She's going to fill one of our English positions."

The man paused at the office door, elbow resting on the doorframe, taking in Lucy wordlessly, glancing first at her feet and then smiling, then meeting her eyes and not looking away. Lucy's composure, so even with Jimmy and Mina, began to falter.

"I ... lost my heel on Great Bay Avenue..."she began.

"And found it back on old Broadway," sang out Noah, breaking into a soft shoe, circling around Jimmy and bumping into Mina on the way around, ending with a deep bow to Mina, then to Lucy with a flourish to Jimmy.

"Lucy, this is our other assistant principal, Noah Leonard," smiled Jimmy with a faint ring of apology. "Noah always has a little entertainment to offer us around here."

"I'm really the wizard of curriculum development," Noah offered. "They pay me to sit in my office and clip articles. I only get called out when things get rough. How are you getting home?" And his stare was so direct that Lucy looked away.

"Mr. Duffer is finding some sneakers for me from the lockers."

"I don't believe this ..." and, as a custodian appeared at the door, holding a pair of scuffed Keds, "Ye Gods, those would fit an elephant." He grabbed them, hung them on his ears, and knelt before Lucy, "Take poor Jumbo home with you tonight," he crooned. "Jim, these are awful. My lady, I would be thrilled to drive you over to our shopping plaza to see you properly shod for your journey back to the Metropolis."

"I'll try the sneakers," she offered quickly, reaching for them. "And after that silly spill I took out there, I might be smart to wear them back in September."

"So young and yet so wise. Do we deserve this lady here, Duffer?"

Jimmy grew uneasy with Noah's presence. Here was the daughter of an old friend, and Noah was already on his customary edge of thinly veiled ridicule. Jimmy would protect her. He would give the world for such a daughter. Noah, he suspected, could not be trusted with anyone's daughter.

His entrance had spoiled Jimmy's discovery of Lucy's relationship to him, all fine sentiment. Noah, at other times his trusted confidante, now represented the difficult, unmanageable present to Jimmy.

"I've got to go, and thank you so much," announced Lucy as she rose. "Those old things," as she gestured to the size ten sneakers on her feet, "will do just fine." Like Jimmy, she sensed some discomfort in the moment and was eager to leave. Noah Leonard was one of the most startlingly attractive men Lucy had ever seen, but he had appeared on the wrong set. When he stared at her, there seemed to be volumes of suggestions behind his eyes, and his inappropriate burlesque spoiled any desire she might have had to hear more from him now.

Mina came forward then and interjected, "If you're looking for a place to stay out here, we have a list of cottages for rent. The owners of summer places give reasonable rents to teachers here for the winter."

"Oh, I just might like that list, please," smiled Lucy in surprise. She hadn't yet thought of moving out of her parents' home, but the idea was intriguing ... a place of her own.

Jimmy and Noah stood at the corner of the hall and watched her go. "Beautiful girl," began Jimmy. "Daughter of an old friend. Big surprise today, having her stop in like that. She's got a lot of gumption, just like her old man. She'll make a great teacher; even be able to handle these hoods here."

Noah said nothing but watched Lucy all the way down the hall. Jimmy saw his particular interest and grew annoyed, but said nothing more. He didn't care to risk fueling an unwelcome attraction.

The progress Lucy made north on Great Bay Avenue contrasted sharply with the steps she had attempted while traveling south some forty-five minutes earlier. She had found a scarf in her handbag and tied it around her head. With the scarf and sunglasses, she hoped that no one would be able to keep a clear picture of her in his head and relate it to the person who would appear at the high school September seventh.

The young priest was again outside, this time sweeping the steps in front of the manse, but now Lucy peered cautiously around the edges of her glasses. He glanced briefly at her face, down at her flapping shoes, and then retreated. Perhaps he too was embarrassed, she thought. During her journey home on the train to Queens, her thoughts turned to her new job and what the daily hours at the school would mean in traveling time. It might be better to take a place in Suppogue. Can I continue to live at home and listen to my mother's ideas for the rest of her life? I really don't know what I feel most of the time anymore. The interview with the broken shoe had given her a new self-confidence. It wasn't much, but it mattered. Perhaps I don't have to make myself over into a pristine goddess either, she mused. I wonder…could my mother control my thinking so much that I can't separate my own desires from what she wants of me? Like the child she was mostly still, she clunked the heels of the Keds together. It's great to begin a new adventure. I wonder how many single teachers there will be in Suppogue. I wonder if Mr. Duffer is married, or Mr. what's-his-name beautiful Leonard. I wonder where that priest came from. I wonder where I'll live.

As she continued traveling, she consulted the list Mina had given her and made notations in the margins. She would call a few places tomorrow. Her mother would be furious.

*   *   *

Jimmy Duffer sat at his desk behind the stacks of schedules Mina had arranged neatly for resorting the next morning. Noah and Mina were gone. He usually stayed behind the others any night when Selma had not announced a special evening engagement for them He was trying to think of something important he could do in his office to justify spending just another fifteen minutes there, perhaps thirty, to postpone facing Selma's nerves. He could phone Peter Mackenzie. Yes, he must do that. All these years. What should he say had prevented his calling before? He had already revealed to Lucy that he had known where her father was. He had gotten himself into a kind of social jam here and would have to find his way out of it. Be honest. Say, *Look Pete, I don't like to phone up old friends. Never know what you'll find. But seeing your daughter, I knew all was very well with you, fella.* And then there would be the awkward pause while each decided whether to invite the other to his home. Selma was good for occasions. She could rise to any company, thanks for that. But it was after they were gone ... Jim felt a mild sickness. Either way ... he decided.

"Of course ... we'd love to come, Jim," roared Peter. "Say, I'm glad Lucy will be in such good hands. This call makes my day. And Laura will be happy too. I never dreamed you'd be here on Long Island. We have a lot of catching up to do. A week Saturday, then. Great. I'll get to Laura right away, but I believe we're free that night. She usually has my calendar here marked...very efficient, my wife, and I see no notes yet. So... we're on! Fine going 'till then."

Jim smiled broadly as he replaced the receiver. He didn't have to worry about this plan. Peter would come out and be the same wonderful friend he had always been. Peter might even understand about Selma, without being told about Selma. Peter was perceptive. But Jimmy would tell him about Selma because Jimmy needed to. Because Jimmy had never told anyone and needed to so badly. And maybe Peter would tell Jimmy the truth about his wife ... (what did he say, Laura?) and then they would both feel better and Selma and Laura would manage with each other. Selma could manage with most women, and it would be an evening he could look forward to and look back upon with pleasure, an evening he had needed for a long time.

*   *   *

Noah Leonard walked with his dog Sludge down South Eighth Street along garbage can after can. The dog walked with a slight limp caused by a bite from a fight with a shepherd last week. Sludge was a puzzling amalgamation of medium-sized breeds and colors. Black, brown and speckled white hairs covered his bulging, tubular frame astride spindly legs. He carelessly pulled Noah's arm as he trotted back and forth in front of him although Noah, in discomfort, occasionally jerked at the leash to tighten the choker collar around the dog's beefy neck. A stranger passed, and Noah had to reign the dog to his side. Sludge had never been trained to refrain from sniffing stranger's crotches. After the dog lunged unsuccessfully toward him, the man glared at Noah.

"Common Sludge, baby, be-have," joked Noah for the stranger's ears. "Let's get a-going pal. It's time for Margie's stew. Let's go, kid."

The dog squatted in the grass beside the curb of the most carefully manicured lawn on the block. "Good God, Sludge, you uncouth cur. Can't you see where you are?" he muttered. The dog finished his job, loped a pace or two, and dug with all four paws into the turf to cover the fault. A gray head protruded out of a front window. "Get that mutt out-ta here."

The father of Veronica Lipswitch. Christ, thought Noah. Thank God he doesn't know me, and he pulled the dog along the street and away down the block toward his house near the tip of the peninsula.

Marge was waiting. She stood stirring her lamb stew and did not look up as Noah entered with the dog. He did not speak, but released the animal who stretched lazily alongside a low couch, hung the leash on a hook by the door, and came over to Marge in the kitchen. He lifted her thick, curly ponytail and softly bit into the ample flesh on the side of her neck.

"Owww, ye gods," she swatted at him. "What the hell are you trying to do" releasing her day's resentment into her words. She rubbed her neck and leaving the stew to sizzle on the gas burner, collapsed into a chair, breathing heavily and wiping her forehead with a napkin, having just finished her third martini.

"Hey, I'm sorry," he really was.

"Goddam it, Noah, what are you trying to do? It's hot and miserable."

"Take a shower, kid. Cool down. Then we'll eat."

"Naw, I'm just too tired," she crooned. "Let's get dinner over with." She shuffled back to the stove, extinguished the burner, and reached to the cupboard on the left of the stove for two plates and mugs, placing them carefully on the mats; but she suddenly tripped on the floor and clattered the second plate against the table, while steadying herself with the other.

"Sorry," she was embarrassed. She turned to the sink to fill two water tumblers as Noah regarded her well-formed torso and ample hips, a strongly sensual woman still, a woman in her prime.

"How was your day?" he tried hopefully.

"Nothing much. Was shopping, cleaning. No one's on the block this summer. All oldies, from the Bronx mostly, with grown kids."

"Did you call Sy Feldman yet? I though he sounded interested in your experience." She turned with the tumblers. " I don't want to do anything in Hempstead," she pronounced the town's name dolefully. "They're mostly amateurs without any training at all. It would be depressing---and it's a long drive."

She placed the tumblers on the mats, steadier now. "Can you wait just one minute. I want to wash up." Disappearing into the bathroom, she emerged a minute later looking brighter. "Please, I don't know why I'm so jumpy."

"Hey, kid, if it's O.K. Let's eat."

"Marge," he tried again after she had dished out the stew. "Do you want to go back to the city?"

"Oh, Noah," she leaned her head in her hand and smiled sadly, "I think I'm too old now. And what about you, and all we have here?" She gestured with a sweep of her hand to indicate the house. The small legacy she had inherited from her physician father in Minnesota had been spent on this ultra-modern-hi-tech-driftwood-stained waterfront house. The three rectangular levels were set upon one another irregularly, the geometric pattern in shocking contrast to the other two-floor, conventional beach houses on the several peninsulas which stretched out into the bay. A deck, sprawling around three sides of the lowest level, was reached through the kitchen and living room entrances.

Marge had decorated the house with multicolored prints, stripes and plaids she had taken several years to collect from stores around the Island. Against the white walls the colors made bright splashes at the windows and on the couches.

"I love all this, you know that," admitted Noah, "but it's not worth ..." he was going to say a drunken wife, but quickly checked himself; "when I just want to, to make love to you."

Her eyes filled with tears, and she rose from the table, her meal half-eaten, and walked to the sink to look out at the bay, hiding her face from him. "Look, let me take that shower, now, O.K? You finish dinner. I'll be out in a few minutes."

He heard the pelting of the water as he finished his meal, rose, went to the refrigerator and pored himself a generous glass of Chablis. The shower stopped. He was sticky and hot himself. The meal had made him drowsy, but he couldn't relax in these clothes, in this heat. He gulped a mouthful of the cold wine and padded through the hall into the bedroom. She had wrapped a shrimp-colored towel around herself and was standing in front of the mirror, unsnarling her curls. He came up beside her and kissed her shoulder at exactly the point where her bathing suit strap cut across her shoulder blades.

"Be with you in a minute," he stepped into the shower and ran the cool water full into his face, over his back, splashing soap and shampoo lavishly. Wrapping himself in a towel, he returned to the bedroom. Marge sprawled on her back on the low bed, towel loosely flung over her torso, her curly hair spread around on the pillow, her arms and legs at odd angles to her body, eyes closed, breathing the heavy breath of sleep. He knelt beside her and reached tentatively under the towel to lay his right hand lightly upon her softly rising and falling abdomen. She stirred slowly, legs and arms readjusting, arms reaching out, knees rising with eyes still closed. He pressed his lips against her mouth, her tongue, seeking an answer which he found in a rhythmic joining with hers, and she shuddered with desire as their bodies met and churned against each other; and it was better than he had known in a long time.

Afterward, they lay apart with arms linked. He began to imagine a trip they might take together, perhaps to the East next year, perhaps India, Thailand, and Nepal. She shuddered in her sleep, and drew away from him onto her right side. Later her heard funny little whimpering and wondered if he should awaken her to end her nightmare, but decided it might frighten her further. He didn't want to hear her, and he had trouble sleeping so early in the summer nights anyway, so he got up and walked through the living room, out and onto the deck. The new moon fell shimmering out across the water and a huge fish lunged into the air and fell with a generous splash back into the black water of the bay. He could see the tiny lights of the beach houses strung along the shore of Jones Island at Oak Beach, over two miles to the south. He was naked and drowsy now, and he leaned back against the cushions of the chaise and began to fall asleep. His last vision was of Lucy Mackenzie, sitting in the sneakers in front of Jimmy's desk. When she tied one sneaker to her foot, her tight skirt slid three-quarters of the way up her leg, and he could see the firm, white flesh of her inner thigh above her stocking top. She was so robust, so keen and happy. She was...fine.

SWIMMING LESSON
Chapter Two

*"It might be lonelier
Without the loneliness"*---Emily Dickinson

"If ye should lead her into a fool's paradise, as they say, it were a very gross kind of behavior, as they say, for the gentlewoman is young; and therefore, if you should deal double with her, truly it were an ill thing to be offered to any gentlewoman, and very weak dealing." Nurse *in Romeo and Juliet*
by William Shakespeare

Suppogue, New York is a town some sixty-five miles from New York City on the southern shore of Long Island. The "ogue" of that name derives from the mollusk quahog whose shell the Algonquin Indians of that area used for money. The origin of the "supp" prefix seems to be anybody's guess. Minnie Fervor of the town's historical society, equates it with "suppose" as in "suppose we dig here . . ." for clams. Irma Phinxt, town librarian, advises us that it relates to supper, for a good mare could clop from Manhattan to Suppogue and arrive just in time for the evening meal, and so on. We must remember, teaches Tony Nappa of the Suppogue High School Social Studies Department, that at best any Indian name is a euphonic translation from the sounds the Dutch settlers thought they had heard, and that later the British attempted to make these sounds more musical, that is, more English, and shifted consonants as they preferred. Noah Webster wrote in his American Spelling Book: "Nor ought the harsh gutteral sounds of the natives to be retained in such words as *shawangunk,* and many others." Does Noah mean gutteral Algonquin or Knickerbocker? The historians only assume that the ugliness is Indian.

But out of some deep sense of either guilt or revolt, romantic sons and daughters of the settlers who had time to record names in the 1800's, favored Indian words, however then preserved. So we are left with Suppogue, which everyone west of Hempstead mispronounces "Sup-pog-we." Suppogue is the last town anyone with any sense at all who works in New York City will live in and commute from. Of course some fifty or more senseless inhabitants a year move further east to the more isolated, quiet lands of the Shirleys and Hamptons for more property and class. It takes them several weeks to discover the potato farmers and the tedious fate of two hours each way on the Long Island Railroad.

The older, more entrenched residents, mostly geriatric English and German stock, watch the annual population shifts with whimsy, and oft are heard exclaiming succinctly, "Wall, it takes many a year to be a rael Suppogiaan, but these new folks are lively and charful."

Half the town south of Montauk Highway is developed on fingers of peninsulas sided by both natural and man-made canals from the Great South Bay. The boats docked there are modest crafts, small fishing dories, dingys and motor cruisers in this Long Island middle-middle class combination summer playground and year-round home, the poor cousin to Bayshore, and the smaller, twin sister of Patchogue. North of Montauk Highway the streets branch out from Great Bay Avenue where the avenues are wide, the lots large with spacious lawns surrounding eight-to-ten room homes built mostly between 1920 and 1950 and still owned by the original families.

The southern peninsulas bustle all summer, smaller houses filled with younger families of eager boaters and bar-b-quers. Come fall, a quiet, hazy lull steals over the area, commercial fishing boats drift out and in, morning and evening, and the other year-rounders go to businesses and schools all day.

The house Lucy Mackenzie rented wasn't much to describe. It was a simple frame summer bungalow set between two other identical structures in a row of one-floor dwellings on low stilts beside the body of water, which Lucy laughingly called the Grande Canal of Suppogue. The front of the house, which faced the street, was paneled in windows and the long L-shaped living room, which faced the east, was done in shades of gold. The two small bedrooms on the northern side of the house opened on to the living room; the kitchen and bath were behind these rooms, and an enclosed sun porch opened onto the backyard, which bordered the canal, the glory of the place. This stream, wide and deep enough for the largest pleasure boat in Suppogue to pass through to the Great South Bay, was a dredged river which brought the only freshwater which flowed into the Bay underground from Connecticut. On that canal streamed fishing boats, canoes and wild ducks. The lady owner of the house had remained through early September this year before returning to the Bronx for the winter, but was renting to Lucy until the end of June.

Lucy moved her belongings into her new home on the Saturday before school was to open, the bulk of her possessions consisting of twenty cartons of books and records, which she spent most of the day sorting and shelving lovingly by century, genre and author. She moved slowly and enjoyed scanning old favorites and perusing the unfamiliar pages of books she hadn't yet had the chance to explore. By three o'clock she was sweaty from all the lifting in the warm living room, which had absorbed all the morning heat through the windows and held it in the carpeting and draperies. Her hands were sore from scraping against the bricks as she stacked them to support the shelving. As she rose from the floor, her knees nearly buckled from kneeling so long. She was ready for strenuous movement.

The neighborhood was quiet. Few of the summer people had been able to find winter renters, and since it was well into September, had left for the winter. She walked toward the rear of the house through the kitchen where she contemplated the as yet unattached telephone, to the small sun poarch. Out the window of the door the water in the canal sparkled in the afternoon sun. In this mild September of southern Long Island it might be warm enough to swim still. Her bathing suit must be in the large duffel where she had stuffed all the clothes she had not intended to use till spring. Now that she had determined that she was indeed going to immerse herself in that mysterious body of water behind her new home on this sticky day in a most mystifying season of hot, hot afternoons, she found herself flinging the clothes out of the duffel onto the floor of her room with wild abandon. "I'm going swimmmmmming," she sang aloud in a childlike croon.

It was so grand to be alone at that time. To be in your own house with no one to care. To be able to belt out a song with only you to hear and know how grand you sounded, how terrific you looked in that shimmering black sheath of a suit. To have no deadlines of meals to dress for, chores assigned by someone else to help with, untidiness to excuse. She could leave her stacks of books unsorted in the middle of the living room and take her swim, and when she came out of the water she could go out and buy a sack of groceries or she could skip down the road to the burger house, however she felt. How exquisite, for the first time in her life. How marvelously free.

The edge of the grassy yard, which opened on the canal, ran off to one side into a cemented boat launch, and was built up into a bulkhead on the other. Lucy had seen the grandchildren of the owner diving from the bulkhead, and decided that the water was at least seven or eight feet deep underneath. She tested the temperature at the edge of the boat launch with her toe. It was pleasantly cool, not chilling, and she was uncomfortably warm from her heavy lifting and sorting in the sun-filled living room. There was no apparent life across the river at the boat yard there. There were no neighbors in backyards beside her house, no children's cries, no lawnmowers humming. She could hear no cars on the street in front of the bungalow. All she could hear was the hum of cars from Montauk Highway, the intersecting artery a long block away to the north, and an occasional gull's cry. The canal rippled lightly from a gentle mid-afternoon breeze.

She dived into the dark green depths. An unexpected thrill, this outdoor treat in autumn. She delighted in the shock of cool weightlessness, the utter freedom of the young, healthy, pain free body adrift from need, responsibility, and particular hunger. No calls had to be made, no books had to be read, no beds had to be made, and no apologies were required by anyone.

She had said goodbye to her mother that morning early. What kind of goodbye was she supposed to have said on that occasion? She had been moving out of her parents' house, but neither she nor her mother had acknowledged the fact. After all, the move had been only a matter of a journey of thirty miles. Was that really an occasion for a goodbye? Well, the goodbye had been something to take care of a stay longer than a day's journey. For Lucy it was the goodbye so sweet to the child who is financially able to leave home at last, but so difficult for the parent who is marking an ending more than a beginning. The goodbye of the child is a goodbye of relief, but the goodbye of the parent refuses to let go. It is accompanied with a "You'll be home Sunday?" It seeks closeness and ownership still.

Lucy had packed all her belongings the night before into her car so that she would not have to dash back and forth, to and from the house after breakfast and listen to more of her mother's questions which exposed Lucy's haphazard departure. "I don't know how you'll manage to keep any decent food in the house with your busy schedule … How will you ever do your laundry? Don't forget to get enough sleep."

Most of these innocent warnings had been offered from time to time during the past week. Her mother was aching for an invitation to see her house. Her mother was too proud to beg, and Lucy took advantage of that pride and refused to offer. Her mother would view her little rental with disdain, and would not refrain from acid comments. She knew too that she herself would be disturbed. Although Lucy understood well what her mother was about, her opinions still affected Lucy deeply. Her judgments hurt Lucy metaphysically; she feared her mother's judgment. She was happy in the little house, and she did not want someone to tell her that she should not be.

She had recently ended a romance with an assistant physical education instructor from Hofstra University. He had, unfortunately, never been able to make any kind of what her mother liked to call "good smart talk," and her mother also believed that he would eventually resent Lucy's superior intellect. He was not interested in certain ideas which Lucy had memorized and believed herself to hold close: great phrases in literature, "opulent and magical" moments in art, or a phrase from the *Saturday Review* which she had taped to the door of her closet "equanimity in the face of tragedy." Although she had never seen Spud face anything near tragedy, she believed that were he to come across it, he would somehow have great difficulty maintaining his equanimity.

However, it had been a difficult affair to end. It had been Lucy's first close-to-fully-physical experience, but because of her rigid puritanical training and her mother's urging, she was able to summon up lists of rationalizations and, on a steamy July afternoon on the Hofstra football field, say a final farewell to her "hairy beast," as her mother insisted on calling him. She had been frightened but overwhelmed and excited by what she had believed to be his obsession with sexual needs---without a doubt beyond the feelings of any normal twenty-two-year-old male. Her mother attributed what she recognized as excessive carnal longings to a "lower-class hormone."

That Spud didn't talk much around Lucy's granite-souled mother in their gentle Catholic home in Jamaica Estates was no reason for Lucy to doubt his intelligence. And after working out with the guys on the field all day, coming to contemplate an evening with Lucy left Spud in something of a stupor. In their relationship it was difficult to judge who was the more urgently obsessed.

Paddling lazily down the canal, she had long since passed her own bulkhead, and her little house was no longer in sight. She floated past backyards of other little summer shanties on one side and tall grasses lining the edges of the canal on the other, keeping afloat on her back, paddling her hands and feet up and down in a rhythmic splashing motion, practically suited for progress down the cooperative current of a canal of warm, brackish water.

Her musings turned to a classic moment in drama, to particular lines she had once memorized:

> *"There is a willow grows aslant a brook*
> *That shows his hoar leaves in the glassy stream.*
> *There with fantastic garlands did she come*
> *Of cornflowers, nettles, daisies and long purples,*
> *That liberal shepherds give a grosser name,*
> *But our cold maids do dead men's fingers call them.*
> *There on the pendant boughs her coronet weeds*
> *Clamb'ring to hang, an envious sliver broke,*
> *When down her weedy trophies and herself*
> *Fell into the weeping brook. Her clothes spread wide*
> *And, mermaid-like awhile they bore her up;*

Which time she chanted snatches of old tunes,
As one incapable of her own distress,
Or like a creature native and inbued
Unto that element; but long it could not be..."

She smiled at memories of the bizarre Ophelias she had seen in second-rate productions of *Hamlet*, more like clowns than mad women, and at the banal treatment in the story by Dreiser. Would that this more perfect moment of hers be preserved somehow in perfect cadences and original rhymes and metaphor.

Suddenly there were no more houses. The canal was beginning to widen, but as yet the tall grasses hid the vista of the bay from her view. She wondered if she were to swim to the tall grasses if she could stand there, or if the waters extended so far beyond the grasses that she could find no foothold and would have to cling desperately to the rushes until some boat came down the canal to rescue her. She had neither seen nor heard any boat traffic at all today except for a few early fishing boats, and she did not know when they were to return, as it was past the season for regular hourly excursions.

She grew fearful. The current was too swift to swim against. She did not know anything about the location of the mouth of the canal. She tried to swim toward the eastern edge of the weeds so threw her body over into a crawl position, and tested to see if she could touch the murky depths with her toe. There was a soft, muddy response to her probing as she submerged to a foot over her head. Nothing to stand on, but yet something firmer than air or water. She began to swim on toward the weeds, and her efforts and the current carried her on a diagonal, past where she wanted to go, but yet gradually closer and closer to the vegetation, those dead man's fingers, and after a minute her toe scraped more mud as she was kicking. The water was shallow here, but she still feared that awful soft bottom that might easily swallow her whole.

All at once over the edge of the weeds she spotted a house. It was at least twenty yards from where she swam, but it did mean something wonderful. Some dry land. She could not swim through the weeds. Could she stand there, near to where they began? She would have to try. The tall grasses were tough, long rushes. She met the first rows of them and began thrashing away with her feet. Nothing but soft, deep mud encircled her ankles as her feet sank. In a frantic splashing, thrashing and grasping she pulled herself along amidst the weeds in the direction of the house which she had seen for that moment but which she had no time to pause and consider now in this battle to keep above the muddy mass below and still make progress through to the hoped-for dried edge of the swamp. The mud was almost up to her knees when she allowed her legs to go straight down into the water. She was gasping so hard now in her efforts that her lungs ached, and her body was nearly spent and ready to float down into that black, soft grave of muck. She thrashed madly against the weeds in a last attempt to progress on her stomach with her legs as horizontal to the water as she could keep them. Her arms and legs were cut from the sharp edges of the rushes. And it was finally that her eyes spotted the opening.

The rushes opened out onto a little pond, and on the other side was the hard edge of land. And on top of that mound of gently sloping, welcoming land was the little house. It wasn't even as much of a house as Lucy's, but it was or had been a dwelling from some time ago. Lucy was spurred on to wider thrashings through the thicket, and soon plunged into the little pond. The bottom of the pond was shallow and firm, and she soon stood up to her waist on hard soil, panting and shuddering and crying out loud as she began to scrape the mud from her body. The air began to dry her wounds from the weed cuts and welts, but they now began to smart and sting. She washed herself all over with the clearer waters of the little pond and plunged her head under for one last cleansing immersion, the finale of her autumn swim.

Swashing painfully out of the little pond to the edge of the hill, she lumbered up to the house, a white frame dwelling which seemed to enclose no more than two or three rooms. It could have been constructed a hundred years ago. She reached the top of the hill and saw that a gravel road connected the front door with some passage that led north into the tall reeds.

The gentle breeze that had delighted her in her own backyard some forty-five minutes earlier had increased to a cool wind from the bay. She shivered, weakened by her experience, and looked to her right, the south, and saw the splendor of the Great South Bay of Long Island spread out in the late afternoon sunlight. She could see the sands of Jones Island two miles across the water and on it the dune houses and specks of boats tied up at their moorings. The water was shimmering gold. A few sails wafted out to the east, and she could see two fishing boats headed, one behind the other, directly for the canal. She had been only fifteen or so yards from the opening to the Bay when she had chosen to enter the weeds. Had she not thrashed through the weeds at that point and had floated into the Bay, she would have had a strenuous swim to any other dry land. There looked to be at least half a mile between the opening of the canal and any other solid promontory besides this one that the little house stood upon. And this peninsula was hidden from the Bay by the weeds themselves. She looked away and down the gravel road. It was growing too cold to consider the landscape further that day. But as she turned once more toward the house, she noticed a plaque by the front door. It was an impressive brass-plated marker, a pretentious ornament for so humble a dwelling, and she moved to consider it more closely:

> *Restored by the Suppogue Preservation Society, 1953. Childhood Home of Annie Oakley.*

Lucy's tired face spread into a wide grin. I'll be damned. Good old Annie, a trailblazer of the first rank. I guess if I'm going to meet the memory of anyone here on this godforsaken swampy spot, dear Annie might be a pleasant enough character.

As she was speaking to the wind, she turned to the path down the little lane. A light fog was beginning to close in and wrap itself around her ankles. As she moved on, she could not at first see beyond the edge of the rushes. Then suddenly another house appeared, and she could see where the lane met a wider road which led to an intersection of two other branches of roads and beyond to the streets, which led past the little bungalows like hers on the west end of town and joined with Montauk Highway on the north. Her pace quickened in anticipation of a warm house and dry clothes. At the fork, she chose the road to the far left, expecting that the canal had to flow off to the west of this peninsula, and she soon saw that she had been correct as she could see her own car parked down the block.

The sunrays were slanting up from behind the marsh grasses now and reflected against the enveloping fog layer in an almost blinding sparkle. Suddenly a dark colored dog bounded out of the tall grasses still at her right. It whirled around as it saw her, and facing her from several paces, began barking furiously. She could not advance, and froze, hoping the dog's barking would eventually stop, and she could try to soothe the animal into letting her pass. She noticed that it had a loose choker collar around its neck as though it had slipped free. It kept barking. She was beginning to tremble from the chill and the increasing darkness and the dog. It began to seem as if it had been an eternity since the dog had leapt out of the grasses. She knew she couldn't turn and run; that at best the dog would bite at her heels. She began a soothing "now puppy, nice puppy. Be nice and friendly nice puppy. Be quiet ... oh so quiet," but her voice shook, and the dog prevailed.

She suddenly thought of something different to do that she remembered from somewhere. She knelt and folded her hands on her knees. Instantly the dog stopped barking and sat back on his haunches, turning his head to one side, then the other. "Good boy. Nice boy. It's O.K. fella." The dog jumped toward her, all friendliness, panting, tail wagging, a miracle of a transformation. Still kneeling, she patted him on the head and he gave her his right paw. Now what was she to do with the dog?

"Sludge, come here, old boy. Commere, kid," and she heard the jangling of a chain. The dog picked up his ears, but did not budge from Lucy's side. She had made a fast friend, even though his owner was nearby.

It was almost nightfall, and the fog obscured her view down the road. She could no longer see her car, but she now felt secure in at least knowing that she could find her way to it, even in the dark.

A form clad in light-colored clothing approached slowly through the mist from the direction of the right fork, and the dog's tail began beating wildly against the ground as he sat beside Lucy. As the human form approached, and Lucy recognized him, she stood up, aghast. "Mr. Leonard, how did you get here? What are you doing here? Is this your dog?" came the chain of embarrassed, foolishly arranged questions.

"I don't believe it, is this Miss Mackenzie?" Noah smiled in amazement and delight..."or is it a mermaid? What in God's world are you doing here at this time of the evening in a bathing suit? You know you really shouldn't be down here alone at all."

"I had...an adventure in the water," she stammered, but with her legs smarting and her arms aching, she felt terribly tired, so tired that she knew she couldn't stand here much longer. "I've really got to go home," she began to walk slowly. "I got caught in the current of the canal and barely made it up on shore. I had no idea how swiftly that water ran."

"You didn't try to swim down that river, did you? That's for boats, not people, and you were going out with the tide. You're lucky you're alive," he followed along with her. "Are you actually living in this neighborhood? Hey, I'm sorry about my dog. I had no idea a person was behind those reeds. I thought he'd found a rabbit when he slipped out of his collar, but he seems to like you well enough now." The dog padded along close beside Lucy, who was limping slowly down her road, not even looking up to meet Noah's eyes as he talked. "Can I do something for you? Can I bring something to you? I'll at least walk you to your door, wherever it is."

"O.K., fine," Lucy managed. "I'll be perfect as soon as I get into the house and rest."

She remembered that she had left the house unlocked all this while, never expecting to float away for the afternoon, but as she opened her back door and threw the switch which flooded both the rear porch and kitchen with light, she could see nothing amiss. Noah waited in the backyard with the dog beside him. She turned to him, "Please, please, I'll be fine. Thank you for walking me home."

"Take good care," he responded, and vanished between the houses.

The smooth tiles of her kitchen floor felt wonderful to her tired feet. She padded into the softly carpeted living room, thence to the bedroom, and jerked her robe from the closet hanger, then returned to the bathroom and opened the hot water tap full. As soon as the steam began to rise, she flung her muddied suit on the floor and stepped into the shower, her head under the full pounding of the hot, steaming water from the spray above. She could have stayed there for hours, except that the cuts from the rushes were barely tolerable in all the warm massage. Finally she had had enough, the water was burning and her skin was reddened. She turned off the taps and grasped her bath sheet. She could not rub, so she patted her firery skin and sore slashes dry. There were long, red welts on her arms and legs and neck. But she was revived.

A bell was ringing somewhere. She couldn't think of where. She had no telephone yet. She had not yet heard the sound of her own doorbell. Could it be someone for the ONeills, thinking they were still in town? She did not know how to go to a door in her own home on a Saturday evening. Could she go in a bath sheet? No. Could she go in her robe? She was going to have to do that if she wanted to catch the caller before it went away. Her hair was stringing down around her shoulders, impossible to comb, and her face was still beet red from the shower. She had nothing to put on her feet, but her curiosity forced her to answer.

The bell had rung only twice and then halted for awhile, and she hoped that the visitor was still there as she suddenly was anxious to end her solitude in the house. She could see someone tall behind the venetian blinds and carefully slipped the chain lock into place before she turned the knob to open the door to Noah.

The odor of onions, pickles and fried potatoes reached her through the crack in the door. "I don't mean to intrude, but I brought you some things I thought you may need right now."

"Please come in," she laughingly assented. She was starving, not having eaten since early morning, and after all, how could she refuse this generous courier, her professional superior?

"And if you don't drink this, you can use it on all those awful cuts and bruises," as he handed her a bottle of Irish Mist.

"Oh, this is marvelous, but if you don't give me what's in the other bags first, I'll scream. I'm starved." He laughed and held the other bags away out of her reach.

"And here I am again, looking like a drowned rat," she fell into the sofa. She was going to treat this visit casually, but she felt so alone and unprepared. I must give the orders in my own home, she decided. He's so much older than I am. No telling where he's coming from.

He spread the burger wrappers out upon the coffee table and arranged the food carefully as she excused herself to get some glasses and returned to curl her feet underneath her in the far corner of the sofa, making a right angle with Noah's seat in the club chair, and began to entertain him with a slightly embellished account of her maiden adventure in the treacherous waters of her grande canal. Noah, appearing to be enchanted with her description, filled and refilled her glass, and Lucy gulped the sweet, thick brew in between the excited phrases of her descriptions.

Through her jumbled speech from the drink and the hour she whiffed Noah's woodsy cologne, felt the allure of his bronze features against the white cotton of his sweater, admired the firm, muscular legs under his tight ducks.

"It's nice of you to come back tonight," she finally broke in from her account of the swim. "You see, I really haven't done anything here yet except worry over my books and records."

"And attempt to commit aquatic suicide," Noah laughingly broke in.

"Oh, yes, I wonder if I had tried to stay in back of the cottage, if the current would have been difficult."

"I don't imagine it picks up until near the mouth of the river at the Bay, but you should wait till Spring to find out. It's not going to be as warm tomorrow as it was today, and the weather's likely to go downhill from now on. This is the month of September, the month of old fools. There are thousands of us out and around."

"Hey, don't destroy all my illusions. I thought summer was just breaking. We're in a different weather system out here from the climate of Jamaica. I'm just so glad to be alive and free and finally in my own house," she ignored his pointed irony.

"You look it. You really do. It's good to see someone happy for a change"and his voice had suddenly such a lugubrious quality that Lucy sobered for a moment through her glow.

There was a silence, awkward for Lucy, but Noah, as he appraised her, seemed to be working it, using it, looking at her and making her feel almost foolish.

"You have a good many books here for a start," he finally glanced away from her to the wall. "Light on the moderns, I see, but you've got Camus. I met him. Spent an entire evening with the man. Fascinating. I'll tell you about him one day. He stayed in the Village for awhile when I lived there... in my salad days." he paused again. She showed her awe, as he had hoped. "Why don't you show me around the place?"

Lucy was flustered at the idea of giving up her cozy, safe, wrapped-up position in the corner of the loveseat. Besides, she had noticed when she paused for breath after her lengthy account of her adventure that her body was numb. Could she stand? Could she, indeed, walk? She uncurled one leg timidly and lowered her foot to the floor, grasped the arm of the loveseat as firmly as a cripple, and pushed off to stand successfully but stiffly between the seat and the coffee table.

"I'd be delighted, Sir," she was heady enough from both the drink and her fright to effect a comic air, at the same time thinking that she should be staying right where she was and asking him to leave. She was beginning to think of Noah dangerously, almost as close as an old friend. She was afraid her guard was coming down. She saluted.

Noah guffawed. "How charming. Let's see her walk."

Lucy turned militarily on her heel and proceeded in a goose-step toward the kitchen, in some pain. She could hear Noah following behind, and didn't stop until she reached the back door, open to the screen and a gentle, cool breeze. She could no longer feel her sores as she contemplated the beauty of the hour and the air and her sense of freedom.

"This is it; this is all there is," she stopped, facing the yard.

"It's lovely," Noah whispered, his hands stealing around her waist.

She had no energy or desire to push him away. His hands felt so comforting, pleasantly warm in the cool breeze, and, she imagined, so good and gentle. His mouth came onto her neck, making slow, warm kisses as it brushed aside her damp hair. She did not seem to be standing under her own support, but her mind made a supreme effort to try to notice what was around her to bring her to her senses: the lights from across the canal wiggling their reflections in the water as though shaking long, bony fingers of caution. Noah's hands were caressing her breasts. She turned to him and began to give herself up to him, to his anxious body.

But all at once she shuddered with a pang of disgust at her own eagerness, and at the untimeliness of this meeting. With every sensible effort she could muster she shoved him away and fell against the back door. He did not resist her refusal.

"I really am sorry, really I am. I'm taking advantage of you, and you're keen enough to know it; but you've charmed me ever since I set eyes on you in those sneakers and frowzy suit." He dropped his eyes to the floor. "I'll go now. Please forget this, if you want, but," as he looked deeply into her eyes, "it was wonderful."

She could not reply as he turned and left through the front of the house. She heard the front door close firmly but quietly, and his footsteps fade into the street. She felt suddenly that he must be going home to some kind of family, and she felt alone, weak, and utterly defenseless, standing in the little kitchen, her right hand leaning her full weight on the sturdy pine table where a few hours before she had skipped through in a burst of grateful freedom to her swim. She was finding that freedom comes in sublimely transient moments, but that those moments have hidden within them treacherous dangers.

She had escaped two grave dangers today, her first great day of escape, and she could have laughed had she not been so sore and weak and afraid of herself. But I'll swim that canal again, albeit right around my dock. God help me from ever being alone with Noah Leonard again. I've got the freedom to risk my life and the freedom to love, both of which may amount to practically the same thing.

Suddenly she remembered the approval of the luncheonette man, "Good girl, Nice town for good girl. Good girl for nice town." So here I am, she muttered weakly as she turned toward her little bedroom to throw herself on her bed.

"Jerk," muttered Noah to himself as he shuffled toward home. "You really blew it."

But as she drifted into a deep sleep, his odor was still on her hands, his flavor on her lips.

INTO THE BREECH
Chapter Three

Suppogue, Suppogue, you are our home.
We love you, not Athens or Rome,
Moscow or London, Paris or Dubrovnik,
Venice or Dublin, we could have our pick,
But here is where we'll keep our port...
In Suppogue, New York.

Composed by students of Miss Mackenzie's Sophomore English class, September, 1959

"You've come to the little town with the biggest JD rate in Suffolk County," laughed Saul Razzler of the Social Studies Department to Lucy and a crowd of well wishers in the faculty room on opening day.

"Naw, in both Nassau and Suffolk," chimed in Phyllis Slavin of English.

"I'd bet on east of the Brooklyn Bridge," added Nina Cordoza. "Grab your car antennas tonight, folks. Rumor has it there's going to be a rumble this weekend in Amityville."

"What do they do?" Lucy turned to Saul.

"I've never seen a rumble. How should I know?"

"They fence with those antennas they steal," spoke up Elsie Cunningham of Home Ec. "But sometimes one or two get killed."

"Can't we phone their parents to keep them home?"

"If you think those kids are hard to reach, try getting through to their parents," continued Nina. "The children are left on their own. It's only the worst in the school who are involved. A very small group, but they make themselves visible." And then as she remembered, "You'll see some of the younger ones in that sophomore section you have at ten o'clock."

How could she do it, and so soon? She wasn't much older than they were. Was her skirt too tight, her hair too fluffy? Would she look foolish? She had taught some tough kids in practice teaching at Jamaica High, but that was with supervision, protection. Now she was on her own, and she had been warned that a teacher who asks for help is considered weak and unworthy of tenure.

The bell sounded for the homeroom warning, and it was time to get to her door. Everyone gathered up papers and cases and crowded out. "Take it easy, kid, it's not so bad out there," soothed Saul who had seen her fright. "If you have a problem, just let me know. I'll come in, and it won't go any further."

"Thanks so much," Lucy swallowed. "I may need you before the day is over."

He smiled reassuringly. He was just a little taller than Lucy and had a flat, brown crew cut, twinkling dark eyes, and a wide grin, not handsome, but pleasant. "They're afraid of me," he confided proudly. "I never touch them, but they don't like me to get on to them. I find and phone parents. I never give up. I know all the cops in town. If they know we're friends, they'll behave. I'll walk you to your door."

The kids were entering the building from all the doors, coming down all halls. Lucy's first feeling was of warmth and cheer. They were glad to be back with each other after the summer. She was happy to be with them, with these happy kids.

Suddenly a boy who must have been at least six feet five blatantly jostled another, smaller one laden with new notebooks and pencils. The equipment went flying; the taller of the two laughed and called, "Welcome back, Slocum," and sprinted down the hall. The smaller grabbed his belongings and tore after his friend.

"What'll we do?" Lucy turned to Saul.

"Nothing. They're gone. They're out of our end of the hall. Whoever they meet when they collide again will have to handle them."

"And what will they do with them?"

"Separate them and give then detention."

"That's it?"

"What else? They haven't maimed each other yet or been insubordinate, or had time to flunk anything. They're just horsing around like normal kids."

Her homeroom was filling up. Saul turned to leave. "Good luck, kid. It's a good place to work. A great job. The pay's lousy, but we've got all the holidays and summers and nice people around." He winked again and was off to four doors down the hall.

Lucy stationed herself against the doorframe, facing outward to the hall with a faint, calculated smile. The children in the room were visiting noisily, all summer spilling out, an heterogeneity of textures, races, colors, New York style.

THERE WILL BE A LENGTHENED HOMEROOM PERIOD THIS MORNING SO THAT STUDENTS WILL HAVE TIME TO FILL OUT PROGRAM CARDS. THANK YOU. The loudspeaker blared.

How long is LENGTHENED, thought Lucy.

"They give us an hour to do this idiot work," one of her boys from the first row offered pleasantly, as though he had guessed her question. She lifted the stack of schedule cards off her desk. "I am Miss Mackenzie, and you know what we have to do now, I'm sure."

"Can you spell your name for us, please?"

"Certainly, it's M-a-c-k-e-n-z-i-e... but here ..." and she printed it on the board, suddenly realizing that writing on the chalkboard was an awesome skill to be mastered. She knew instantly by the groans that the kids in the back couldn't read it. She erased and tried again, certain that she was giving her lack of experience away. Such duties might comprise a significant portion of her days, she reflected.

The bell shrieked.

PAY NO ATTENTION TO THAT BELL. STAY IN YOUR HOMEROOMS. (Were they all in Oz?)

The nasal voice was familiar to Lucy. It had to be Mina's.

Some of the students were shuffling about and making comments to their friends who hadn't finished yet. Most of them seemed to take little notice of her, so busy were they with impressing their peers, except for one girl in the second row who stared and stared at her. No matter where Lucy stood or walked, this child propped her chin in her hand and stared.

STUDENTS WILL NOW GO TO THEIR FIRST PERIOD CLASSES bleated Mina again.

Now the big stuff begins, thought Lucy. My serious students are coming.

The first English R class, R for the Regents, entered more slowly and more seriously. They were to bring notebooks every day to class, and they would be going on at least three trips to plays, and they would learn to read the front page of the *New York Times* and how to pass the New York State Regents Exam in English. The girls tossed their freshly washed curls about insouciantly; the boys leaned back casually against their seats and met all of this news with deadpan expressions. They sniffed the glue in the new texts with a show of mock delight.

"No homework tonight," smiled Lucy. "Just bring both books with you, and your notebook tomorrow."

"Will you be our teacher ALL year?" asked a tiny blonde girl in the back of the class.

"I'm supposed to be," answered Lucy, puzzled at the question.

"Last year we had a lady who left after winter vacation to have a baby," offered one of the boys, in a subtle dare.

"I'm not planning a maternity leave just yet," snapped back Lucy.

It was an easy, quick joke. The kids laughed in appreciation of her daring.

The loudspeaker blared them into second period. In bopped the *G*'s for General.

The *G*'s, as Lucy had been told, had "all the problems." Replete with black leather, silver staples, thumbs-in-belts bravado the boys swaggered about to one desk, then another. The girls all scurried together to one corner and sat, checking makeup with pocket mirrors, hair, stockings, whispering about each boy as he entered. Their black skirts, well above the knees, were as tightly seamed as they could move in. One was giggling, unable to cross her legs.

Lucy's heart sank. Where would she begin?

"Hi, teach," a male voice rang out brazenly from nowhere. Giggles.

"Good morning," Lucy responded with as much strength as she could muster. "Please find seats anywhere for the present. We have just a few minutes together." She smiled at them, covering the room with her gaze. She was going to meet them more than halfway.

"I hate school, teach," someone else bawled out. She stiffened, but told herself, don't fall for it.

"Well, then, for the time being, pretend you're not here." A great laugh. They liked that one. As the laughter died, she rose to speak again before the "hey teach" could think of another quip. She wished to end the exchange on the upbeat. "I have some new materials for you and a lot of news about what our year will be like. We're going to write our own books, we're going on trips, and we're going to see some plays."

"Hey, she's got the wrong class. Nobody takes us G's on trips. She thinks we can write books. She's crazy."

"Isn't this 10 G - 13?" she asked innocently.

"Yea, that's us. You make a mistake or somethin?"

"No, no mistake. What's your name please, sir?"

He was taken aback. "Joe, Joe Glunt. 10 G - 13. It says right here on my card, Miss. We G's don't go noplace. We don't write so good, and not too much gets done in our English class. They usually tries to teach us grammar. You know, verbs, nouns and stuff. That's what you're suppos' to teach us, you know. I think you're makin' a big mistake."

The impudence was out of his voice. He was trying to make a helpful suggestion. She was beginning to realize that although she was trying to show them her confidence, they might just consider her gestures foolish. But she had to risk a little more.

"Well, Joe, this year may be a little bit different for you. We are going to go on trips, and you are going to write a book, and I'm not so sure about nouns and verbs for the present anyway. You just bring me notebooks tomorrow, and we'll take it from there. Now, it's almost time to go, and I've got to check all your names and then get up to the old building for my next class."

It seemed that at least for today the jeers were over. The group dispersed slowly and silently, and one girl who had not mingled with the rest shyly approached Lucy with her hand outstretched. In it she clutched a paper. "I wrote something for you. I hope you like it."

The girl towered over Lucy, long brown hair falling around her thin, bony shoulders, large doe-eyes wistfully scanning Lucy's face.

"How nice. In this short time? Did you put your name on it?" Lucy took it eagerly.

"No, I forgot, but I'll be back tomorrow, and you'll know me then," she stammered rather confusedly. And then as an afterthought, "I'm Susan." and then vanished around the door.

What a lovely girl, thought Lucy. And she doesn't fit in somehow, with any of them. But that group could be a lot of fun, if I can just keep my wits about me. There's a different kind of challenge there.

"Any problems?" queried Saul, bouncing heroically into the doorway.

"Nothing major yet," she shrugged. "This last group is a riot, though. It'll take some fast talking, but I think I might even enjoy them."

"Hey, that's one of the worst groups in the school going. Watch yourself, Lady. Those G's can be very bad news."

"O.K., I'll be careful." But she wasn't at all as worried as she had been now that she knew that this class was the worst she had to face today. *After all, they're just kids. What can they do to me?* she asked herself.

"I've got to run to M24 now," she waved goodbye to Saul. "See you later, and much thanks. Please stay close by. Never know when I'll have to push the panic button."

The Come From Aways

    Halfway down the hall she met Mina, hastening toward her. "Oh, Miss Mackenzie, I'm so glad I caught you. There's been a change in your schedule. Mr. Schawnessey is taking the class you were to have this period. You'll be free until 11:30 and then you'll take a new group...an Honors 11 class. Stop into the office with me now, and we'll discuss it."

    Lucy was surprised. An honors section---great---but why the sudden shift?

    "We just learned a little while ago that one of our teachers won't be with us this year." Mina stopped as she bit her lip and her eyes filled with tears. "Oh, you'll hear about it before the day is out anyway. She had been with us for over fifteen years --- lovely person. Well, she was just found by the police --- dead in her house. Terrible. Single woman...had just her dog there. She's been with us for so long." Mina was upset.

    "Well, now here we are. We have to talk business. This is a good class. You'll enjoy them---a nice change of pace for you, but you'll have three lesson plans now. Hope you don't mind."

    "I'll do my best," smiled Lucy bravely. "I do like the other classes too." She felt that she could show no disloyalty to her other students. She was protecting them already.

    "These are a bright group, Fawn's class," continued Mina. "Some smart-aleks there, but exciting. Here's the class list, and you'll find all the texts stacked and marked in the classroom M16. It's up in the old building too. If you have any problems, get in touch with Joshua. Oh, you haven't even met Joshua yet," she remembered. "He's in 211, and you'll see him at your meeting today. He's your English Department chairman."

    In her unexpected half-hour of free time she decided to return to the teacher's lounge, which would be on the way to her next class.

    The room was electric with the tragedy.

    "A terrible way for school to begin." she heard as she entered. She connected the comment with Mina's news that she would "hear before the day was out."

    "Did Noah say anything to any of you about it?" one of the women spoke. They were all strangers to Linda in the room now except Phyllis Slavin, and were all women except for a horn-rimmed, pipe-smoking gentleman reading by himself in a corner. The southern windows were open to a warm breeze, which wafted green draperies to and fro, hardly a somber setting for a discussion of a recent death.

    The women all turned and looked at her as she entered, and the tall brunette closest to her at the end of a long table extended her hand. "Hello, I don't believe we've met. I'm Sylvia Blake, guidance." She grasped Lucy's hand warmly as her glasses fell from the tip of her nose to her chest where they were restrained by a gold chain around her neck.

"Lucy Mackenzie, new in the English Department," she explained quietly. "Please don't let me interrupt your conversation," and turned to sit in a lounge chair outside the group's circle at the table.

"No, Lucy, please sit here at the table and get to know everyone," continued Sylvia.

"Hi again, Lucy," smiled Phyllis Slavin under her curly red mop. "This is Dawn Peters from the Art Department, and Rhoda Stein in Social Studies." The two others nodded and smiled. "We're talking about Fawn Whitney. We just learned about her death a few minutes ago, and we're really a big family here, you see. It's touched all of us in a big way."

"Had she been ill?" queried Lucy carefully.

"Not that we know. We'd heard that she's just returned from a summer in England last week and was planning to come back to work today."

"I've been given one of her classes, next period, as a matter-of-fact."

"Oh, that's such a great group. She was looking forward to working with them," said Phyllis poignantly. "You're lucky there, but it's too, too bad."

"Fawn didn't come to school this morning, and so the office called and called her house, but they got no answer, so Dr. Duffer sent Noah Leonard over to see if anything was wrong. He could hear the dog barking, and her car was in the driveway, but she wouldn't answer the door," Dawn Peters summarized the account for Lucy that everyone else seemed to know.

"Noah had to call the police," she continued. "They found her face down in the bathtub."

"No one knows how she died?"

"Her body is with the medical examiner now. That's all we know. I guess Noah must have had to identify her, but no one has talked with Noah directly, I don't believe."

So that's why she hadn't seen him today. What a grisly duty.

"It would be nice to talk about something else today," began Rhoda. "but I guess it's hard with this so fresh in all our minds. Lucy, where do you hail from?"

"St. Johns. I'm brand new," she smiled shyly. "I hope I can handle this group you're telling me about, but I don't know how to begin with them. I guess they're all expecting Miss Whitney. I'll be quite a disappointment."

"They're great kids," comforted Phyllis. "I had some of them last year, and even though they'll run you ragged, they're a fair bunch. They'll meet you halfway if they respect you---if you're honest with them and don't resent them for their intelligence."

"Why, what do you mean, Phyllis?" snapped Sylvia. "They all think they're so great that they can get away with murder. You'd better find a way to put them down, or they'll walk all over you. I don't like them, those H kids. Their parents have gotten them to think that they're better than any of us. They think they're all going to Yale and Harvard. Well, not without my recommendations, they're not."

"Oh, Sylvia, really. How can you generalize like that about a bunch of kids? Who else in this school is going Ivy if not they?"

"I guess you love those kids because of your drama group, Phyllis." Sylvia went on with her sarcasm, "They'll brown up to you because they want to get into the plays. Well, I don't have any plays, and they just find a hundred ways to aggravate me."

The bell sounded.

"Anyway, good luck, Lucy. Don't take anything crazy from that gang now."

Phyllis just smiled warmly and shrugged. Sylvia turned and smiled, "We'll see you soon again, I'm sure."

"Thank you all. This is a warm, friendly school," spoke Lucy sincerely as she turned to go. But what mixed signals about the students. The gentleman in the corner kept on reading.

As she proceeded in the direction of her next classroom, the thought struck her that the students, in all likelihood, had not yet heard of Miss Whitney's death, and that she would have to be the one to tell them. She had no idea what these particular students had felt about Miss Whitney, whether they would have liked her or hated her. Whether her death would bring any strong reaction at all from them.

Room M16 was just around the corner, filled with a stunning silence from twenty-eight sixteen year olds. Suddenly a girl began to sob, as though Lucy's entrance had shaken her into the stark reality that Miss Whitney would never again appear. Several others were weeping silently. Lucy looked all around the room---no variation of expression from this despair.

"I see you've all heard," she began "As I was walking down the hall I wondered all sorts of things about what we should say to each other---how you had known Miss Whitney. I guess you're answering all my questions without my asking anything." She was surprised at her own easy honesty with them.

"A lot of us had her last year," blurted out one of the girls. "It's just terrible. She ... she ..." and the girl could scarcely get the words out, "was my very favorite teacher." From the other's looks Lucy could see that many shared their classmate's conviction. Lucy could not have imagined that there could be such feeling from these high schoolers over a teacher---an English teacher at that. It was an enormous responsibility---the influence this person must have had. The same she might have someday.

"I'd distribute the books," Lucy spoke her thoughts aloud, "but I'm sure you won't feel much like reading anything tonight."

"No, let's get started," one of the boys interrupted. "We have a lot to cover this year before the Regents." They all nodded assent. She was amazed. Where were the wisecracking brats that Sylvia had warned about?

"Well, fine," she eagerly consented. "We've got to start off with William Bradford and the 'History of the Plimouth Plantation,' so let's get those anthologies from the table back there and write your numbers and names on the book cards for me."

They busied themselves with the books and cards, still solemn, but no longer grief-stricken.

"What kind of writing will we be doing this year?" asked a tall, thin lad in black.

"All kinds---essays, fiction, poetry, journalistic articles … we'll keep busy."

"Great. Do you know you've got most of the staffs of the *Pontevechio* and the *Argo* in here?" continued the tall student.

"Looks like we're going to have an exciting year," laughed Lucy, delighted that the sad mood had been broken.

"Oh, look, her cat's dish is still here," one of the girls gestured to a white china dish on the wide windowsill.

"I don't understand," began Lucy.

"Miss Whitney fed a stray cat there everyday," offered another. "She wouldn't turn anything or anyone away. Even the pigeons came to beg, and she had crackers for them."

"I wish we could do something appropriate. We must think tonight of what we can do, as a class. Does anyone know of her family?"

"I think she said her parents are still living in Virginia," offered one girl. The bell interrupted.

They moved politely and quietly into the hall.

They could be met without artifice. They didn't seem to resent her yet, and their affection and loyalty at the shock of the news of Fawn Whitney's death had helped her to one conclusion that day. Somehow her work, like Fawn's, could mean so much to so many children. More than she had ever imagined.

"My name is Harper Jaffee," a small, dark boy gazed up at her as she counted the record sheets on her desk. "I'm in your fourth period 11 H class and I wrote some things over the summer. I really don't know if they're worth much or not. Would you read them for me, please?"

"I'd love to, Harper, thank you. I'm flattered that you ask."

"I'll bring them to you tomorrow," he announced solemnly. "I have a feeling I can trust you with them. Have a pleasant evening."

Was he daring her to appreciate them, or should she be flattered? At least there are two students I won't have to plead with for assignments.

She had lunch next, then another R section, and then the department meeting.

She was starving. On the way she met Saul Razzler again.

"Going to lunch? Come on. I'll introduce you to some more characters."

The tables in the faculty lunchroom were filling up as they entered with their trays. Saul steered her to a seat beside a little man in a paint-smeared white coat and across from a tall, blonde, disarmingly handsome man and Phyllis Slavin. He introduced her around, and the little man named Nick began to go into a wild routine.

"Nick always does this when he meets a pretty woman. It's all on automatic reflexes...and you won't believe the finale," the tall man joked. The room hooted and howled. Nick rose out of his chair, twisting his arms behind, then beside his body, hands locked together, eyes crossed and tongue hanging out. He stamped and danced around the table, arms now flapping, knees knocking until he came to rest on his knees beside Lucy. "I adore you, you beautiful creature. Will you marry me instantly?"

"Right here in the lunchroom," agreed Lucy, up to the lark.

"Yowwwwwweeeee," he bellowed as he rose and burlesqued a kiss on the top of her head, then sat neatly down again and began to cut his meat as though nothing at all unusual had occurred.

"You've just gotten the super supreme Nick Bruno welcome," announced Phyllis. "But I've never seen this version, Nick. You must save it for only the best of us."

"It's only for those brave enough to sit next to THE PRINCE," he announced. And Lucy could think only, R-U-M-P-L-E-S-T-I-LT-S-K-I-N.

"Phyllis," suddenly Nick was starkly serious, "What are we all going to do about Fawn?"

"No one knows anything definite yet. No one's talked to Noah. Jimmy has been in the office with him ever since he returned, and we just don't know what's going on except what Mina's told us."

Another party joined them; the same tweedy gentleman Lucy had seen in the faculty room that morning.

"Lucy, meet Sam Rose, another English colleague. Sam's a more serious intellectual than the rest of the clowns here," Saul joked. Sam blushed and looked down at the table.

"You missed Nick's welcoming dance, Sam."

"Please don't beg me for a repeat performance," sang out Nick. "That was an impromptu production for only Lucy here."

"It's not formally choreographed?" mocked Phyllis.

"I was Gower Champion's prized pupil," continued Nick with great mock humility, "but no, I'm a one-dance-a-day man."

Sam looked up from his soup. "I hope you'll enjoy yourself here," he smiled warmly at Lucy. "We have some fine folks around."

"Oh, Sam, 'fine folks' indeed. Can't you ever get out of Ohio?" Phyllis teased.

"I will when you stop adding 'R' to the end of America," Sam rose to her taunt.

"I never ..." she began ... "well, only when I'm not really careful. O.K. Sam, you've got me. You're a good guy, Sam, but you're still in Ashtabula."

"They're all showing off for you, Lucy," Saul laughed. "Behave yourselves, or Lucy will want to go back to Queens on the next train."

"Fat chance," Lucy fell into the mood. "I couldn't get much of a job on September seventh."

"Oh, you'd be surprised at what happens at schools on opening days ..." Tony Nappa, the tall man, began and then everyone, including Tony, thought of Fawn at once. "Sorry, I wasn't careful of what I was saying." They all fell silent.

"We'd better go---it's almost time for sixth period," broke in Nick finally. Sam accompanied Lucy down the hall. "Are you staying in town, Lucy?" He asked in a casual way.

"Yes, I am. I've rented a little house on South 9th Street for the winter. Are you here too?"

"No. I've got a place in the City. I really like being in there close to everything."

"That's funny. I though the commute from Queens would be too far for me. .Don't tell my mother."

He laughed. "You should stay where you're happy. Do you like your house?"

"Oh, it's great being out here on my own. I grew up in the city, so I don't mind being away from it for awhile."

"If you're from Ashtabula, the West Village looks like Valhalla," laughed Sam. "I've got to run now, but we'll see each other at the department meeting."

Lucy was impressed with the smooth sophistication and gentle speech of this man. His immaculate grooming and perfectly tailored jacket and trousers set him apart from the others, less carefully turned out. High school teachers were not known for their fashion, but she noted with pleasure Sam's British tailoring and Tony Nappa's Italian flair. And Sam moved with the grace of a dancer.

Her sixth period R's were livelier than the early morning group, and asked all kinds of personal questions about her life --- where she went to school; if she were married; how old she was, a question from which she carefully demurred and changed the subject quickly to their own experiences. But they were friendly, open and patient, considering that the warm day was almost at an end.

The English Department meeting was held in another room of the old building, and the mood of all was solemn as they entered, speaking in low tones---all about Fawn, Fawn, Fawn.

Joshua Perkins finally entered, and Phyllis gestured to Lucy that it was indeed he as she mouthed his name, for Lucy had inquired earlier about him. He was nearly as fair as an albino--- pale, straight hair so colorless that it was impossible to determine whether it had turned from blonde to white, or whether this was the color he had been born with; his skin stretched taunt across finely chiseled features, eyes so deep set that their color was indeterminate under heavy white eyebrows. He moved about quickly, youthfully, stacking handouts, shaking his straight, pale hair, long in front, away from his forehead as he moved.

After the room had filled, he came to the side of the desk, folded his arms, and looked out across the fifteen members of the English faculty.

"We all have one thing on our minds right now. I have to give you some more terrible news about Fawn, and then we'll have to get down to business. Noah Leonard and Jimmy Duffer have spent most of the day with the police. What you don't know is that Fawn was found in the bathtub with a kitchen knife under her breast. Her parents are flying in from Virginia tonight. There will be services Thursday at First Unitarian, and many of us will probably be called by the police for questioning before the end of the week. Of course I join you all in mourning for Fawn and I thank you for taking all those last-minute schedule changes without complaint. We all must be amazed by the sadness that has stricken the student body. We never know how we affect these children until something like Fawn's death occurs, and, well, I've had second thoughts about a good many things today---I'm certain all of us have. We all shall have our own ways to mourn. If there are any other particular questions about this matter of Fawn, please hold them off till after the formal meeting now, for we've got so much to go over, and I'll stay for awhile afterward."

His manner was at once businesslike and impersonal, but charming. The meeting was lengthy with instructions and information about curriculum changes, textbook availability, audio-visual aids, meeting and vacation schedules. Sam smiled once or twice at her across the room, and, as the group dispersed, some to leave, some to crowd around Joshua with questions, he caught up with her by the door.

"You'll join me for dinner Friday?" he nearly announced rather than queried. Lucy was surprised at his lack of elan in making the proposal.

"Love to," she agreed instantly.

"I don't go out much around here, but I hear there are some fine restaurants along the docks. I'll bring my car along on Friday. For now, I've got to rush to catch my train. Delightful." and he was off, his case swinging jauntily.

A torrid, crowded, poignant day.

Phyllis fell in with her, walking back toward their homerooms. "How'd it all go, gal? Have it all together? You look like you do. That was tough, walking into a tragedy like this."

"Those kids are wonderful, though, Phyllis. I can't imagine anyone not loving them----every one, but you know I like those G's too. I think a lot can be done to catch their attention."

"You're hooked at the game, gal, I can see that," smiled Phyllis. "We really need people like you around here for all these kids. There are too many here---and more elsewhere, I suspect, who can't wait till their days in the classrooms of America are over. To me---well, I hate to sound like Pollyanna---but even though I'm thoroughly exhausted at the end of the week, and sometimes I think I can't read one more essay or I'll go stark, raving loony, I wouldn't think of trading this job for one that paid me twice as much. Come to think of it, I must have been driven mad already to think this way," she laughed. "The tension is terrible, but I guess I'm one of those souls who thrives on stress. O.K. gal," she waved and turned off away from Lucy to reach her end of the corridor. "Have a good evening. See you early in the A.M."

They met again briefly at a distance in the parking lot, Phyllis gesturing toward her empty antenna cylinder. "Hey, look at this. Mina was right---no antenna!" Lucy looked for hers and saw that it, too, was gone. "Mine too," she shouted, and they both shrugged helplessly, then drove away simultaneously in opposite directions.

Lucy entered her little house, dropped her notes and books on the nearest table, collapsed on her sofa, and fell into a deep sleep. When she awakened several hours later it was almost dark, and She decided to drive out for a light supper. The house felt lonely again. I think I'll consider getting a roommate, she mused. It would be nice to share a meal with someone else at the end of the day, and there's certainly room here for another.

She showered and changed into slacks and casual shirt, and, as she had for most of that week, continued to see and hear and feel a little touch of Noah Leonard as she moved about the house.

THE COMMUNIST AND THE OWL PRINCE
Chapter Four

*On those rough edges between twelve and twenty
When home becomes a place to hang your head
And the hatred of mother's plastic beads
Regurgitates the guilt in your disgusted throat,
Before reason comes frozen truth
Wedges into that chasm of loneliness
Between the last mustard plaster
And your first love affair
That they are not gods who own your food,
Your clothes, your way of laughing,
'Till they become the object of your laughter.
They do the unnatural, human thing:
They build the edges of the nest still higher
'Till that first step takes all the strength of youth. (N.A)*

"The greatest intellectual capacities are found only in connection with a vehement and passionate will."
Arthur Schopenhauer

During the whole of a dull, dark and soundless day in the early autumn of the year when the clouds lay oppressively low in the heavens and the first passenger flight from Chicago into Idlewilde airport got lost in ground fog and ripped the radar equipment from atop the physics lab at Suppogue High School; that first Wednesday of September good, kind Dr. James Duffer, who now that school was in session was sometimes found to be incoherent, was discovered running down the hall to the nurse's office with a bloody nose. No one but Noah Leonard and Sylvia Blake know what happened. Noah, the arch co-conspirator of all misadventures, will never tell, and

Sylvia, while never revealing the truth, will forever take full advantage of her knowledge over Dr. Duffer.

Since September began Jimmy had undergone a transformation. From the relaxed day of his interview with Lucy he slowly withdrew to a world of foolish imaginings. During the summer months Jimmy could tolerate his primary stress, his marriage, but with the opening of classes, the return of staff, children and teachers, phones ringing with irate parents and disgruntled board members, his pleasant, rational demeanor disappeared and a jittery shell remained. The shock and subsequent investigation of the Fawn Whitney affair added to his consternation. Behind his own eyes, adolescent-like bewilderment replaced middle-aged wisdom, at least in school.

Last term he had developed a mindless habit of ogling legs through the bottom of his venetian blinds as students and faculty passed by on their ways to the entrance in the morning. Strangely enough, only the ankles and calves interested him. One might pause here for a moment to elaborate on Duffer's fear of the female knee, if one were interested in his biography. Noah Leonard, who boasted of several sessions with Wilhelm Reich, assured Jimmy that he could explain most sexual neuroses, and was certain that his penchant may have had something to do with the knee as a hated symbol of maternity, as with the elbow, of friendship, stability, and strength. All these qualities Duffer deigned to trust in the human female, and thus perhaps his ankle fetish.

The day Noah was appointed assistant principal he was introduced to one of his most pressing and punctual duties, that of identifying for Dr. Duffer the custodian of the most shapely appendages. Noah would stand above Jim, squatting on the floor beside his desk early in the morning, and separate the closed blind at his eye level.

"That's Sylvia!"

Right again, Jim. You're going to have a perfect record on Sylvia this week. Now who's coming up the walk with the purple pumps?"

"Ah, behold the Empress Josephine herself."

"Right again." It was Jo Hanky, the librarian, on mincing toe, bedecked in purple ruffles and multiple pink scarves and broaches.

"Now try the green sling backs getting out of the Chevy."

"Wait a minute. I don't think I've seen those saddle shoes before. Is that Marian Crawford?"

"Hey, now, Jim, you're slipping a bit; that's Shelly Clawson."

"Well, now, the new student council president. We'll have to call her in for an interview soon, Noah. Make a notation of that, will you? Now here we really go!"

"Yes, Jim, it's Kathy. The Queen has arrived." Noah noted with deep pleasure the generous endowments of their special secretary for curriculum. "Enjoy, enjoy. Then let's have our coffee. Ye Gods!"

Beside the office door stood Sylvia Blake. Noah let go of the blind that he had been propping several inches above Jim's nose. "Owwwwww." Crash! The blind caught Jim and sent him rolling back toward his desk. Noah thoughtfully stepped aside to accommodate Jim's shuddering roll and gave a dramatic shrug with dancing eyes to Sylvia, scintillating with discovery.

Jim slowly picked himself up. "Damn blind will have to be fixed, Sylvia. You'll see to it, won't you? If you see the custodian soon ... Noah and I don't seem to be doing too well with it ... awful mechanics."

"Dr. Duffer, your nose is bleeding." and indeed it was. All over his suit.

A new day of higher academics in Suppogue had begun. The joy of these moments showed in sharp contrast to the impending police investigations that Jimmy knew would be ongoing until Fawn's murderer was found.

* * *

Macbeth stumbled into the center of the class, ketchup-bloody, raving of sleeping grooms and sorry sights. "Hark, I heard a noise!" Pat, pat, pat came at the classroom door. Giggles.

Rats, a stupid interruption, and the kids are so intense.

"Mr. Love would like to ask you, did Benjamin Franklin ever write any poetry? He said you might know."

At least twice a week a little messenger came to Phyllis Slavin, English teacher, from Al Love of American History to seek information. Al usually knew the answer, but when his kids challenged him, his trick was to get another teacher to provide support, or, better for his ego, be wrong, so that he could once again flaunt his superiority. It was his only sorry method for enlivening the hopeless boredom of his classes, the most predictable of the school.

Each student in Al's groups did nothing but copy questions from the blackboard into his spiral notebook. On the following day the answers would be corrected and a new set of questions copied. Each year the questions were the same. The kids couldn't even cash in on their notes because Al had become quite a handwriting expert over the years, so the copying had to be done. When the brightest kids complained, Al would find some subtle error in the wording of their answers and flunk them. Even a genius could flunk American History II under Al Love out of sheer boredom with the insulting work. Al couldn't stand invention, which he labeled "duplicity."

Phyllis Slavin refused to play his game in a way which provided him with some entertainment and eluded his insight. "Ben didn't do much rhyming that we know, but one of his French mistresses published an X rated novel which we now think might have really been Ben's work...and then there's the speculation that Ogden Nash is really Ben Franklin reincarnated." The kids were giggling again.

"Hey, Miss. S. Tell him that Jane Austin was Ben Franklin in drag!"

"Enough of that filth around here, Greg. Get back to your murder."

The murder and porter scene thoroughly over-dramatized, complete with ketchupped letter-openers, the kids filed to their next class. Tony Nappa strolled by Phyllis' door.

"Where are you now, Tony?"

His eyes sparkled. "Guess what's happening today. We're going into The Soviet Union."

"That whole bit again?"

"Yes," he grinned widely. "Don't say a word."

"Never, ever," she vowed.

Tony Nappa stood a lumbering six feet four, sported a heavy tuft of ash blond hair over his high forehead and sapphire blue eyes chiseled into a face of a sun-warmed olive, all in all a precious relic of the Viking invasion of Sicily. He was by nature a rebel, and by birth an intellectual, and a rarity among high school political scientists for believing that no social, religious, or economic program or ideology could be flawless, a skepticism that made him suspect by most of his department. Most of the other social science teachers held some innocent faith in one or another philosophy or supernatural being.

Tony and Noah were the only real libertarians in the school, a bit feared and misunderstood, and perhaps envied for their intellectual panache and ability to burlesque the behavior of the rest of the world.

Tony was happy with his wife and family, very kind to old people, animals, and children; and even though the eleventh grade curriculum he taught included a brief review of the development of the philosophy of Humanism in Europe in the Thirteenth Century, no one ever thought to apply any of its tenets to Tony's ideas. And Tony never thought of giving his attitude a name. Not in 1959.

He had developed his Communism lesson into one of the greatest classroom hits of the school, and, for some reason, every year it seemed to work even better. The older kids were sworn to secrecy, and no one ever ratted. Tony began the class by lowering the blinds, putting a paper over the window of his door, and turning off all the lights. Then he stealthily crept to a front row desk and bent his six-foot-four frame out over the group.

"Before I begin this class today I feel it necessary to make a profound confession. I've been awake all night, tortured by my hypocrisy to you all these weeks, but you must swear to me and to each other that you will never, ever let my words go beyond this classroom."

"We swear, we swear," the chorus rolled. Little Sammie Butt in the second row right under Tony's nose began to bite his lower lip. "I gotta be excused!"

"Not now ... oh you can't leave now, Sammy, no matter what happens"

"I'm dizzy. I can't see."

Tony whipped out a spirits of ammonia capsule from his desk and shoved it under Sammy's nose. "Feel better?"

"Ahhh ... cough, cough ... yes" He sat rigidly, too afraid of Tony now to whimper or move.

"Fine. Now we must proceed."

All eyes were glued on Tony. He settled back on the desktop, smoothed his hair, adjusted his tie and took a long, tortured breath. "I have a philosophy which few, perhaps none of you Americans will ever embrace and which some of you may even find abhorrent, but remember, we live in the United States where each of us is free to choose his own religious and political belief without persecution or prosecution." The class showed frowns of uncertainty here.

"No one can be tried or sentenced for being an admitted ..." a long pause here, "communist. Still and all, you know the mistakes some people make when they think of American Communism. (Audible shudders.) They think that communists still steal secret government ideas and send them to Russia. They think that communists pray to the devil. They think that communists are sorcerers and burn churches and temples, and they believe that communism is out to destroy all America. Now, let me tell you that they are wrong, because I, I AM a communist, and I shall now tell you what we really believe."

The class was aghast.

"I gotta be excused."

"He locked the door."

"Shut up. Let him finish."

"We've got to get out of here."

"Sit down and listen to him."

Oh God, thought Tony. This year even nearer to Brando. I am a charmer.

"What's he going to do?"

"You see you are already proving what I've just said. That you are so frightened of communism that you refuse to sit in a perfectly safe American classroom with a gentleman who you all know treats you with the greatest respect and who would never harm you in any way ... I even took the trouble to have smelling salts ready for Sammy here... please don't be afraid. I guarantee that when the class bell rings, all of you will file out to your next class, deeply enriched by what you have heard and just as healthy and happy as when you walked in. Now, am I free to proceed?"

"Yes, yes, go on."

"Don't stop. We want to hear all of it."

"It all began with my father and grandfather in Italy. They, as I have mentioned before, were what we call Fascists and believed that Hitler and Mussolini were great men ... almost gods."

On and on he built the story of how he had worked in an underground youth movement during the war.

"I hid out in an Italian refugee camp and ate grapes. So many grapes that I couldn't fight."

"What did the grapes do?"

"He shh. He got WEAK, stupid."

And then the story of stowing away on a refugee boat to New York, meeting other communist refugees, forming a cell on Long Island, and then, the philosophy.

"But that sounds like what we believe."

"You're trying to tell us that communists want everyone to share equally. That's not true. That's what Democrats believe, and Democrats can't be communists, I don't think."

"No, there are lots and lots of differences between them."

The class hour was speeding to a close. Tony slowly raised each blind, punctuating his last phrases.

"Now some of what I've told you today is very, very true..."

first blind up, "and some lies." second blind up. "My father was a fascist. I did come here in a refugee boat, but I was like most of you at that age. Politics meant very little to me. I only wanted to find a good job, buy my own house, raise my family quietly and safety, so instead of being a communist..." third blind up... "I really am something very very different." Last blind zipped up with a crash. "I (over to the light switch) am a REPUBLICAN." The room was flooded with light. The bell screeched. The kids sat motionless.

"You really must be getting to your next classes."

Spasms of relieved laughter swept the group. "Tell us, why did you do this to us?"

"Why do you think, stupid. He wants to teach us about com-mu-nis-m," sung with much sarcasm.

"Maybe he's lying now about the Republican bit because he's afraid. Old Duffer is a Republican."

"How do you know that for sure? Maybe Duffer's the real communist."

"What are you going to be tomorrow, Mr. Nappa?"

Tony smiled softly. "Well, once someone blamed me for being a Thespian."

"What's THAT?"

"Go ask your speech teacher. You're late for class."

Phyllis met Tony in the hall again. "You know I hope that none of these days that beautiful lesson of yours backfires."

"Will you defend me, Phyllis?"

"I sure will, Tony. It will be great fun working on a case like that. Now how would you explain your split level house and Mercedes to the local cell?"

"My wife gets her housedresses mail-order from GUM. Oh, you know I forgot to remind them that Eisenhower's awfully soft on Communism these days."

*   *   *

The lunatic, the lover and the poet
Are of imagination all compact:
One sees more devils than vast hell can hold,
That is, the madman: the lover, all as frantic,
Sees Helen's beauty in a brow of Egypt:
The poet's eye, in a fine frenzy rolling,
Doth glance from heaven to earth,
From earth to heaven;
And as imagination bodies forth
The forms of things unknown, the poet's pen
Turns them to shapes and gives to airy nothing
A local habitation and a name.

Theseus *A Midsummernight's Dream*
By William Shakespear

The Owl Prince was holding court in his art lab. There were gathered around him a motley collection of the school's outcasts: bearded wizards, banes of the academic departments but of great artistic motivation; a tall, skinny brunette with a face much like the child Jacqueline Bouvier, swinging her long bare legs from a perch atop a drawing table and gazing enraptured at the Prince; Sweet Simon Finch in black turtle neck and tight black chinos, standing by the door to protect the flock from administration-of-prey, his foot mounted on a chair against the door, admitting latecomers only after careful scrutiny, taking notes on a clipboard balanced on his knee; a few more students lying on their sides on mats, heads propped with folded arms, eyes focused on an enormous paintbrush in a white orderly's coat atop a table.

The paintbrush man stood five feet five in elevator shoes and including his long brush haircut atop an over-sized, oval-shaped head, the dark brown eyes set lower than usual on the face and close together over a small pointed nose and cupid mouth. The close-set ears rode close to the oval head, the only dimension of this face which saved it from being wildly comical. The figure parodied a soulful paintbrush, yearning for a willing pallet.

The paintbrush man moved and swayed to the music of Shostokovitch's Symphony #1. "Today is Shostokovitch Day," announced the paintbrush man in deep, resonant tones. "Today we shall listen and then paint in purples, reds, and just a tiny bit of yellow. Today is the mood of Shostokovitch and we shall do everything to honor that mood. We shall have no faint strokes or colors. Everything must be in flashes of excitement or despair. Everything in Art Elective IV shall be in Shostokovitch. MAKE IT HAPPEN. Shostokovitch. MAKE IT HAPPEN!

A small hand from the floor raised upward, "Sir, may I speak privately?"

"Of course, of course, anything within or without reason is allowed."

The small head rose again, and the paintbrush man bent down to listen to the whisper.

"Sir, I see Shostokovitch in red and coral only."

"Absolutely fine, fine, for you it is different ... but only for you," the prince chuckled. "Only for very special people do I listen to a whisper. Today Harper Jaffee is that special person. Tomorrow, who knows, A-ha!"

The students who participated in this strange interlude called Art Elective IV were given encouragement to unleash some of their wildest imaginings with paint and affect any speaking style that moved them.

The owner of the long bare legs asked for attention.

"What is it, my beautiful one?"

"Only your permission, kind Mr. Bruno, to use blood if necessary."

"Permission most enthusiastically granted, O wonder of my sights. But be certain that the blood is drawn from only the very tip of your finger, else our artistic frenzy might be transformed into a folly of the very largest proportions, and the Owl Prince might be called before the local Board of Education."

At mention of the Board all students mocked the word by dropping low on the floor and tucking their heads in to their chests in perfect kowtows. Among this eager group knelt Allen Freid, son of the Board President, with the tightest kowtow in the crowd.

"Splendid, splendid, splendid. Now UP and PAINT." There was a flurry to the closets, which lined both east and west walls of the classroom. The lady of long bare legs took her time. She was in no hurry, ever, to leave the art room.

"Where should you be right now?" the Prince approached her.

"Dr. Zimmerman's."

"Ye mighty Gods, Susan. You are consistently incredible. Leonard the Enforcer will be here any minute for you."

"I know," she breathed. "That's why I'm going to stand by this closet door."

She positioned herself with paints and canvas in front of the Owl's Magic Closet. This was an enclosure that none of the students had ever seen, even though it was never locked. The Prince told them that they would be welcomed to see the contents of that closet after they graduated, and out of great respect for the Owl, no one had ever peeked.

"But you are standing now before the Magic Closet," the Owl protested. "This is a part of me which you should not see until you are a graduate, until you are no longer a part of this school"

"Mr. Bruno," Susan began weakly. "I will undoubtedly never graduate from this school, and both you and I know this. In an emergency why can't I go into the closet? Besides…" and Susan's dark eyes dropped to the canvas, "besides, I love you." The huge eyes rose from the canvas to regard Mr. Bruno's features, frozen by her words. The Owl Prince was now unable to keep his composure. But turning his energies into a mock rage, a rage that was almost real, he screamed, "No no, you must keep away from the magic closet."

The whites of his eyes turned red and his body contorted into the form of a wizened dwarf. Susan turned her back and began to sob quietly. The Owl turned on his heel and went directly to a group of students, brushes already in hands, who were staring at the pair, dumbfounded.

"Alright, a little passion for the moment off the canvas. Now apply yours in all reds, purples and that tiny touch of yellow. Once more, with deep feeling for the Shostokovitch mood. This is HIS day. But, don't forget your chiaroscuro!"

The Come From Aways

Bare, long-legged Susan Morand lived in the art and English rooms. She held a mixed status of senior and freshman, took senior English and art courses and was still registered for freshman algebra, social studies and gym, none of which she ever passed and rarely attended, except when she was escorted by an administrator. By a court order she had been removed from the home of her parents and brought to live with an older cousin. Both parents had been judged unfit; the tawdry details of their atrocities had never reached students or faculty, and no one really seemed to want to know the whole truth. Nonetheless, Sylvia Blake of the guidance department wanted to know how Susan had "the nerve to cut all those classes, and never even keep her guidance appointments with me."

Zimmerman of the math department snorted, "That child insults all our attempts to bring order and discipline to the school."

But in the art room she was a creature of fantasy, bringing pure joy to the Prince and Simon and Harper and Bailey and Conchita. She immersed herself in the arts and the artistic and ignored that which was to her not only emotionally untenable but superficial. She had found her separate peace. She found the rewards she had herself defined.

"In the beginning was the Owl Prince and the Prince was with Susan and Simon and Harper and Bailey and Conchita and the Prince was Susan and Simon and Harper and Bailey and Conchita. In the Owl Prince was life and the life was the light of the art room and the light shineth in the darkness of the administration and the darkness comprehendeth it not." So wrote Simon Finch, for *The Pontivechio*.

Dark, slender Simon sat in his long-sleeved black turtle-neck and his tight black chinos and short leather boots, his straight black pointed sideburns and a shock of black velvet hair over an almond rectangular face; shoulders square, back always straight, but somehow leading this image with a determined square chin, another of those tall, slender children surrounding the short, stocky Owl Prince, the fallen angel of art education, in worship. From this determined child came a deep-throated murmur with the faintest hint of a lisp---so incongruous to the picture and he character of Simon that it was immensely attractive, the beloved flaw.

Simon was fond of writing and illustrating derived epigrams:

"Joseph slew a thousand Philistines with the jawbone of an ass. Everyday teachers kill the self-images often thousand students with the same weapon," in *The Pontevechio*. His illustrations looked something like this:

How can you beee so stupid?

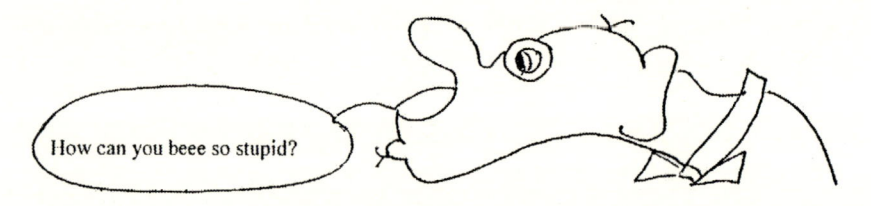

But Simon Finch was uncensorable. He never chided children, old people, or the religious, and he was never verbally profane nor his drawings pornographic.

In the art room this day the Prince approached him, Simon was using a tiny wisp of a brush for tiny, grass-like lines, and his elbow for rectangular smudges. The smudges were purple and red, the lines, yellow. "Excellent, excellent," the Prince ejaculated. "Now since you insist on using part of your body in your technique, I suggest you try an even better tool." With that he took a long plume and dabbed the end of Simon's small, pointed nose bright red. The crowd howled. Simon rose to a fury, and then looked into the bewitching eyes of the Prince and dissolved into a laugh, a nervous laugh. No one else could make Simon laugh like that.

The Prince returned to his desk. There were stacks of records to be marked, attendance reports and grade lists. The objects on his desk mocked all the tasks:

Owls. Birds of feathers, clay, metal and plaster. Birds of color, gray, white and speckled. Birds laughing, birds looking wise, and foolish. Objects which looked like birds and objects which looked as though someone should make them look like something, and perhaps someone would make them look like birds with minor effects. Owl birds, that is, all owls. The sort of wisdom that this collection inspired was counter to the prevailing notion of the owl as scholar. Scholarship was not the motivation that drew children to the art room. Love, hatred, and need drew them together, and a wisdom developed which transcended these feelings. The wisdom became possible out of a new sense of self-importance.

Nick Bruno, the Owl Prince, looked another way at his stack of records. He could attend to these at three o'clock. He could see that Susan was still blubbering in the corner by the closet, so he stood and returned to wait beside her. She heard him coming and remained with her head in her elbow, propped on a table.

"Can we talk?" he spoke softly.

"Yes, let's," she assented eagerly, weary of lonely grief.

"Let's go next door," he motioned to Allen Freid, who had some clout with the class, to take charge, as he often did, and pointed in the direction of the auxiliary classroom where he intended to go with Susan. Allen shook his head in understanding, and Susan rose and walked with chin on chest out and through the door with the Prince.

"Do you want to tell me why you can't stand math?" he began when they were comfortably alone.

"It's not Mr. Zimmerman," spoke Susan dolefully. "He thinks it is, and gets insulted, but it's not. I can't begin to understand numbers. I can't add higher than five plus eight. Why can't he see that? I just sit there and feel sick. Did he tell you that I really did throw up one day all over an algebra test? How can I take algebra? The letters could mean anything---one hundred---ten thousand, what's the difference to me?" She sadly put her chin in her hand again, her straight, long auburn hair falling over her right shoulder. She made a kind of childish sense that Nick understood.

"And history?"

She bristled. "History? All the past? I HATE history," and she shuddered with such malice that he was amazed at her depth of feeling. "No, no I can't go to history." She played with a carving on the table, running her little finger into and around the grooves. "You know, they ought to have a course called 'Planning the Future.' If Mr. Leonard would teach that course, I'd go in a minute. You could plan how parents ought to act with their kids and how teachers ought to do things and how the President ought to run the country. Then maybe we'd all get someplace. People might be happy. Things could improve."

"O.K., tell me about biology." He knew he'd hit upon yet another disaster as he observed her face.

"Worms and spiders and snakes and dead leaves ... and ... all your insides ... laid out in all those diagrams ... so ugly I can't stand it. So ugly... how they can look at all that, I don't know. Then you have to draw it and memorize all the names for it. And they talk about sex like it's all matter-of-fact and everyone and everything does it and it's all like in a laboratory and everything's all spoiled. I hate biology too. I really hate sex too, if you want to know the truth," and she had said what she had to say, but she was embarrassed and she looked toward the window to try to hide her tearful eyes. Nick was devastated.

"Are you still staying with Julie?"

"Yes. She's nice. She's really sweet. She doesn't hassle me. She's O.K. I really like Julie."

"You go away sometimes, they told me, and no one can find you. Everyone gets concerned."

She started. She hadn't known that he knew. She had been absent from the home of her cousin, where the court had assigned her to stay, for as many as five days at a time, and no one could find her. When the police had been summoned, they could do nothing. The cousin never knew where she had gone, and there were no legal parents to fine. Her legal guardian was now the state.

But then one day she would return, to school and home, with no stories, no apparent changes in her. Just the same soft, wide-eyed wonderment. And she was beautiful. She floated through the halls in flat-heeled ballerina pumps, flared skirts and peasant blouses, a willowy five-feet-ten with shiny clean straight chestnut hair softly falling over her shoulders from tapered bangs across her high ivory forehead. And the doe eyes.

"Please don't say anything," she strained out in a whisper. "Please. It's so important" and she thought a moment. "I've got this friend. It's O.K. He's wonderful," and then after seeing the skeptical look creeping into Nick's face, "He doesn't touch me... honest. I think he may even have a girlfriend for that ...I don't know, but he just comes with me and we go away to this place where we can eat and sleep and read all day, and in the summer we can sit by the ocean and it's perfect. He brings lots of food and books. It's the greatest thing that's ever happened to me, Mr. Bruno. Please, please, don't say anything." She was growing frantic, realizing that Mr. Bruno had adult responsibilities.

"How old is ... is he older than you?"

"A lot older," Nick started."He's in coll ... You say you won't tell? "

"I won't tell a soul. No, I won't tell anyone, Susan. Susan ... please just be careful. Don't tell anyone else what you've told me."

"No, no, of course not."

"People in this world are warped and crazy. They follow laws that aren't always good for everyone. I've forgotten your story already. But try not to worry your cousin. Try to get to her, O.K. Tell her something ... that what you're doing is all right, because the police are on to it, and if they find you, your friend will be in trouble. Do you understand? If you can talk just a little to Julie, maybe she'll not send the police, because if it's really all right, you don't want him in trouble. Do you understand?"

"Yes, Yes, Mr. Bruno."

"I really just want to help."

"You're really O.K. Mr. Bruno. I think ... I want to go back to class now."

"We will." He was grateful that the moment had come to a conclusion. He had done what he imagined his duty to be, but his own desire was becoming a difficulty.

HEAVY PETTICOATS
Chapter Five

"A little song, a little dance, a little seltzer..."

Lucy had to go to Fawn's funeral. This woman's spirit pervaded her H classes all week. The students' mourning still evident, each one exhibited singular reactions, from Victoria Lipswitch's bold challenge to Lucy to "do as well with our work as Miss Whitney would do," through Harper Jaffe's solemn wish to write a class poetic tribute to "the teacher who will never teach again," to Kurt Sutherland's snide ridicule of the "sentimental fools who will never let her spirit rest." Lucy drove to the Unitarian fellowship for the service with Phyllis Slavin, who had asked to go with her when Lucy announced her intentions that morning over coffee.

"Fawn was never very close with anyone, but we all admired her. She kept to herself in her little house with her dog and her books. Beautiful woman, loved the kids, came here from Virginia at least ten years ago. She had a low, soft voice, Masters from U. of Virginia, always went to the theatre on weekends with friends from the city and was involved in civil rights activities---but---quietly. She tacked up notices about meetings and rallies on faculty bulletin boards but never pushed them in conversation. Have her students mentioned her interests?"

"Not at all. All their reactions have been personal---about her mannerisms, her feeding stray cats, her poetry club and her help with their writing for publications and contests."

"I think she was wise not to try to use the students politically. Some teachers take advantage of the kids that way for their own causes. I'm not certain that's part of our job. We're not supposed to indoctrinate."

A throng of students was massing in front of the door to Fawn's church. Lucy and Phyllis joined Joshua, Sam, and Ed Shawnessey by the steps.

"There are her parents getting out of that limousine," remarked Joshua. Jimmy Duffer and Noah Leonard and Mina Leighton met the elderly pair. They made a striking couple, both gray-haired and slightly stooped; the mother, tall, and handsomely thin and fair; the father, a portly, exquisitely groomed and tailored black man.

"Fawn's mother is an English professor at St. James, a Negro Episcopal college in Roanoke, and her father is Dean of Students."

The ceremony was led by a minister who had known Fawn well and now dwelt on her work with civil rights organizations and causes and her devotion to her career. Fawn's ashes lay in a pewter urn in front of the chancel surrounded by flowers. "Seems too short a service for such a great life," remarked Phyllis, "but then I'm too Catholic."

Lucy found the personal, though secular, elegy attractive. She sensed strength in Fawn's belief that fought injustices without cant and incense.

Fawn's parents, who had been joined by a younger woman whose face matched Fawn's fathers in hue and features, sat stoically in front of the urn. Fawn's photograph was displayed near the urn, and Lucy noticed, as she joined other guests after the service to pay respects, that her face and features seemed almost entirely Caucasian, though her eyes were widely spaced and deep-set like her father's.

"Was there ever any comment at school about Fawn's parentage?" asked Lucy of Phyllis as they rode to Lucy's house, a wholly natural question, given the temper of the times.

"Nothing racial. Even though Fawn was active in so many civil rights programs outside school, she never mentioned her personal identification with any racial conflicts. She seemed wholly dispassionate about any prejudices she may have experienced, if there were any---certainly there were never any here. She was a deeply respected colleague, and a love. I'm glad you told me you wanted to go to the services, Lucy."

"I wanted to be part of something that is so important to the kids, and to have them see me there. Wish I could just hug her parents and tell them how the kids reacted, but because I don't know them, I was shy about being officious."

"They will know how her students felt by their attendance and their solemn behavior. Teenagers don't attend funerals so readily. Well, these ceremonies are good to have. They make a statement of finality for us. Now we can go on."

"But I guess the investigation will go on too, for some time."

"You know I hope that the whole thing was an accident. She let in an addict looking for drug money who stabbed her in a fury after he found that she was a poor schoolteacher. What are you doing tomorrow? Like to take in a movie?"

Lucy smiled, a little chagrined. "I've got a date ... with Sam."

Phyllis looked really surprised. "Sam? He dates? No kidding. Well, have a fine time of it. Let me know when you have a free evening, and we'll maybe drive in to a concert or play. I try to leave at least one night a week for myself after all the papers are marked."

"Thanks again. It was good to be with you."

Lucy was glad she didn't have the weekend entirely to herself, and that there were now options for other weekend evenings with Phyllis.

There was no one Lucy would rather have seen that Friday night than warm, comforting Sam Rose. She opened the door that evening at six with a Cheshire grin, and there stood Sam with an equally silly grin and a box of Fanny Farmer candies in one hand and a spray of daisies in the other.

Lucy led him on a quick tour of the house, ending in the kitchen where she procured a magnum of Piper Heitzeig from the depth of the refrigerator. "To christen my house," she proclaimed, "but we're not going to bash it against the foundation. Twill be a simple toast."

They pored their first drinks and carried them back into the sitting room. Sam sat modestly in the club chair, knees crossed, sherbet-turned-champagne glass perched daintily on his knee. He was, as in school, immaculately groomed from his then stylish blonde crew cut over an oxford-cloth buttoned collar shirt under a wool Shetland on top of corduroy slacks and shiny brown penny loafers. His broad shoulders looked comforting. His horn rims over deep-set dark brown eyes flashed a different kind of challenge than had her rejected Hofstra coach.

"You look lovely tonight," smiled Sam to the floor, suddenly shy. Lucy, voraciously hungry, gulped the champagne guiltily, imagining him savagely mussing her ringlets, down on the sofa where they would entangle themselves, steaming, groping ... but this did not seem to be the routine she could expect from Sam for awhile.

He commented appreciatively on her book and record collection and asked a number of questions about her days at St. Johns.

"Where did you go to school?" she tried.

"Wisconsin...then Columbia. I want to go back, but right now I'm lazy and having good summers. In this part of the country there are too many playful alternatives to scholarship."

"What sort of things do you do in the summer?"

"Oh, plays and concerts in the Berkshires, visiting friends in the Hamptons and Fire Island. Some years we've rented a place for a couple of weeks on the Cape. Summer's gone quickly, and there's so much to do."

"I guess I'll have to continue my grad work soon," she said vaguely. "But I want to take at least a year to get started in the classroom. I think three lesson plans a day will be enough for awhile."

Sam continued, "I understand the police say they have no leads at all on Fawn's murder, and I expect I may be called Monday. There are only three or four of the faculty who haven't been questioned yet. We know of no enemies she had, certainly no one at the school, but there was no evidence of forced entry. Whoever the killer was, she let him in. Him … Ah …I suppose it could have been a woman as well as a man, but when there is a knife, one generally suspects that she was overwhelmed … or perhaps surprised?"

"Did she have a male friend?"

"That's difficult to say. Fawn was a singularly private person. Of course there is always talk, if you put much credence in gossip. She had a sadness about her as though she had some secret, but then we all have a secret or two, eh? But hers seemed, well, more like a burden. She was a beautiful woman, but private. Too beautiful to be living alone like that. I suspect there will be quite a mystery to unravel here, with a few false leads to blind alleys. How did her students react?"

"Tragically. They will be seeing that lady's ghost for a long while, let me tell you. She certainly captured their imagination,. and their hearts."

"I expected as much. She charmed us all. Well, then, we'd better be off. I have to drop off a book at Noah Leonard's on the way to our restaurant. I made a reservation at Cap'n Joe's, if that's alright."

Lucy was not answering.

"You seem to be thinking of something else. Did I depress you too much, talking of Fawn? How's Cap'n Joe's for dinner?"

"Oh, sorry. Yes, Cap'n Joe's is great. You say you're stopping at Mr. Leonard's?"

"Yes, he's out here on the street next to yours, don't you know. I'll be just a minute there."

She had been finding Sam more and more attractive with every sip of the champagne: his woodsy cologne, the soft allure of his Shetland sweater and those deep, dark eyes; but the mention of Noah Leonard's name and the sudden prospect of being taken to his home, even if they were merely to park by his curb, stunned Lucy. She was furious with her feelings as she went for a sweater.

Sam guided her gently toward his quietly designed sedan, helped her formally into the passenger seat and turned the car toward the end of the block where the two roads met and where Lucy had first encountered Sludge, then Noah.

"Have you seen Leonard's house yet?" Sam wanted to know.

"No, I really don't know exactly where he lives." She had felt that she didn't dare to investigate.

They turned the corner by the tall reeds and headed back north down the street adjoining hers. On the right the startling white geometrics of the Leonard place rose up before her.

"That's it," announced Sam with admiration, as though pleased that he could show her this architectural phenomenon. "I don't even know if they're home ... Oh, there's a car. I'll just run up and drop this off; for he doesn't know I'm coming." Sam slid out of the car and ran in his dancer's leaps to the door. Lucy could see Noah's form outlined by a bright light; then Sam leaping back towards the car and Noah waiting.

"He says we must come in for a few minutes at least," Sam smiled and opened the door for her to embark. She was trapped. How was she to look Noah in the eye in what was, for her, a highly charged social situation? How inexperienced she knew she was. But she must be the silliest baby. She had no idea what sort of family he had. Did he live with his mother, or wife and six children, or was he divorced or living with housemates or ... and the most frightening ... living alone?

"Lucy, so good to see you again," the charm went on, this time without the mockery. "I told Sam you really have to come in for just a few minutes so I can show you around our castle, and then you can be off for your dinner."

"Our" ... so there was someone else here.

As soon as she entered she sensed the woman living in this home. The wide expanse of hall, living-dining-kitchen areas which were all exposed on this first level were meticulously, decorated with such an exotic blend of textures and color that someone had given full time to this project; someone who had hours to shop for fabrics and knick-knacks and paints and woods. Someone who did not work nine-to-five and who did not throw all this together on a summer vacation.

"This is the faculty dream-house," smiled Sam. "Lucky Noah Leonard to be living in such beauty."

"Marge thanks you," Noah bowed. "Let's go out on the deck a minute." He opened the glass doors off the far southern end of the sitting-room area and beckoned for them to follow, coming between them and putting his arms around both their shoulders, so at ease with his body as with his words. "See those crazy sailors out there? They don't care that there are gale force winds building up. If we watch, we'll see some of them go over in a minute or two."

As he spoke Lucy saw the sail of one of the smaller crafts hit the water. "There's a show of one kind or another out here every night," Noah laughed.

57

The warm breeze swept Lucy's hair straight back, and her eyes smarted from its force.

"Do any sailing, Noah?" asked Sam.

"God, no. I'm scared to death of the water. I just love to look at it---at others on it. You both look ravishing tonight. First Date?" He teased.

Sam was up to him. "Actually we've been lovers since the first day of school, but don't tell Jimmy Duffer. He's sensitive about his young women teachers. Tries to protect them, you know, or that's what he says."

"Yes, Duffer makes it hard for all of us," Noah relaxed his arms and moved to perch on the railing of the deck. "Hey, you're in a hurry for dinner. Let me show you upstairs, and then you two can get going."

"All Long Islanders give you the house tour," taunted Sam. "Rat pack of nuveau riche, don't you know?"

"Hey Ashtabula, who are you, telling her about Long Islanders?" Noah continued.

"Because I find your habits quaint---lovely, often, but quaint." They mounted an exposed spiral staircase at the northern side of the semi-circular seating area, "And we ascend into the library," continued Noah, "where you will find that the pages of all the books have been clipped and turned. Marge, hold on tight to that paint can. We have visitors."

Lucy's first glimpse of Marge Leonard was of a nondescript shape clad in men's overalls, huge shirt with rolled-up sleeves, hair tucked under a painter's hat perched atop a seven-food ladder which also supported a paint tray and roller. "Hi, there," she warbled. "Sorry I'm not ready for guests, but Friday's my work night," her voice warbled. "Michaelangelo always worked weekends too, I've read."

"If she doesn't finish the ceiling by eight-thirty, she doesn't get dinner," pronounced Noah heavily, " and if she doesn't do a good job, her soul goes straight to hell."

"But this is NO chapel," she laughed. Lucy could see underneath the hat, wisps of hair and dabs of paint, a golden face, remarkably pretty.

"Presenting the erstwhile star of Heavy Petticoats to entertain you from seven feet in the air," sang out Noah.

Marge answered in a Gilbert and Sullivan-like impromptu, "I want a violet ceiling very much, very much, But our master here has cursed me with this blue, this blue."

"I think we should maintain the hues of the natural colors around us---blues, grays, and whites---but Marge is in love with these lingerie colors."

"You like my stuff downstairs!"

"Yea, but whoever heard of a library with a violet ceiling?"

The Come From Aways

"Do you know why he said he married me, guys?" came from the ladder. "Listen to this one... he said I could burlesque the universe... ha ... now that's he's in super-suburbia, he don't appreciate me act na mor. Well, look at this, old library-worm," and she rolled out a band of bright blue paint across the ceiling as far as she could reach. "How's that for intensity and passion?"

"Let's leave. I don't think I want to see the rest of this," laughed Noah, proudly.

"Bye all, nice meeting ya," yelled Marge, waving to Sam and Lucy with one hand and touching the handle of the roller to the tip of her nose in Noah's direction with the other.

They descended and padded through the heavily carpeted sitting room.

"Come back when you can stay awhile. We're always home on Friday and Sunday. Anything can happen on Saturdays," he winked at Lucy, who suddenly remembered that it was Saturday when she had met Noah and Sludge out for their walk. The dog all this time had been curled up on the sofa, and came over slowly to say goodbye. He nuzzled Lucy's hand.

"He behaves as though be knows you," remarked Sam.

"I'm fond of dogs," offered Lucy, but she kept walking through the door, eager to be out of that house. Sam held back to speak to Noah. She heard him say, "I know you've had a bad week. Hope it's over. Your part of it."

"I don't want to talk about it, please." Noah answered, only cordially now, and then quietly closed the door in back of them.

It had all ended on a downbeat, and the cerebral energy in that house had tired her mind. Her head hurt, and she was glad to be in Sam's car, driving slowly down Montauk Highway toward Capn' Joe's. She was glad of his civility, his care, tact and warmth. She was glad for the soothing clam chowder. But all Sam wanted to talk about was the Leonard's.

"Aren't they fascinating?" he went on. "They really are stimulating for each other. They've had an interesting time of it, those two."

"Oh, how so?" She wasn't at all certain that she wanted to know. Fascinating, stimulating, interesting.

"Witty ..." Sam was saying. "Noah Leonard is more full of wit than all the rest of the faculty put together."

"Nick Bruno does a good turn, I've noticed," Lucy put in, wanting to shift the subject, but Sam in his tedious admiration was not to be deterred.

"Oh, yes, Nick. He's wonderful. He's the clown to Noah's prince."

"Witty as two fools and a madman" my father is fond of saying.

"Clever man, your father. How about 'wit kills the soul as argument kills reason?' That's Balzac. But now Marge was a musical comedy star of some significance fifteen or so years ago. Ever hear of *Heavy Petticoats*?"

"Not until a few minutes ago at the Leonard's."

"Well Marge, her stage, and I think, her maiden name, Marge Duprey, was a singer---beautiful, husky contralto out of Minnesota direct to New York to audition and star in this satire of Sigmund Romberg Off-Broadway, that was the Off-Off Broadway of today. You remember you could see shows then for two or three dollars a night---from classical to experimental theatre --- directed by talent ranging all the way from rank amateur to polished professional. In those days often an angel financed an entire production, and guaranteed them a minimum run. This show of Marge's was innovative but popular, a hit--- sellout crowds. Marge made the show, in more ways than one, and when she left, the show closed. I saw it---wonderful. It should have gone uptown, and everyone thought it would."

"Well, then why didn't it? What happened?"

"Noah happened---to Marge. Get them to tell you about it sometime. It had to do with Marge's relationship with the Angel---the guy who backed the show---and how she left him for Noah," Sam laughed. "The business folded, and Marge followed Noah out here to become the wife of a suburban schoolteacher."

"What was Noah doing when he met Marge in the city?"

"Finishing his MA in history at N.Y.U.---just a kid, young grad student. He had a wife up on the West Side. He used to joke that he and Marge had to wait to get married until his father-in-law finished putting him through college. He used to call his first wife the Queen of the West Side J.A.P.S. I never met her," Sam added, almost apologetically for having missed this chapter in the saga of Noah Leonard.

Lucy's young sense of moral justice was shaken. She had read about people who lived like this, but until now, had never met them, and these people were her colleagues. And here was her escort for the evening, hithertofore so respectable, entertained by the sad history of these two and admiring it all. She had to think a long while about all of this ... and Marge so beautiful, Noah so attractive. She bit her lip to suppress her feelings and felt herself wriggling in some painful trap.

They were finishing their dessert. Lucy tried to turn her attention to Sam himself. He had seemed so steady, so reliable to her. His foolishness over the Leonards had put her off, but she tried to erase her disillusionment. He had only a childish admiration for the flamboyant.

He drove her home slowly, engaged in a long monologue, a description of a difficult graduate professor at his old school, Wisconsin. He seemed so formal with her ... still almost shy. Lucy liked that, but she had been lonely. This meeting tonight with the Leonards after all the champagne had exhausted her emotionally. She needed someone to lean on for awhile---some kind of affectionate response.

At her door he cleared his throat and stated, "It was such a lovely evening. Thank you," and was about to turn, but Lucy was chagrinned at his abrupt departure.

"Sam," she thrust the words out boldly like a missile in a shooting gallery, "I like you very much."

Sam started. He had ventured a great deal in asking Lucy to dinner. She could not know how much. He had met Noah's jibes successfully, and his confidence was high. Lucy seemed so young, so fresh and virginal, like his sister, safe and pleasant. But maybe this time there was something more. He decided to take a great risk, and as he reached for her and she came to him he felt a warm flush spreading from his ankles up and through his body. She fit perfectly into where his arms had been placed to surround her. He was on fire, and when their lips met, he was filled with urges that he had never before allowed himself with a woman.

A girl from a Minnesota choir had once aroused him pleasantly, but not demandingly, for he was yet a boy. But this beautiful mature woman, Lucy, was tearing him apart, was going to make him do things that he would hate himself for doing, would make him dependent, fawning, foolish.

He broke away, "No, no, Lucy. It was nice, you are lovely, you really are." He didn't want to insult her, hurt her. "I, I just really must be going." He turned suddenly as he was horrified by the tears that were welling up in his eyes, and ran to his car, jumped in, and sped away up the road toward Montauk without glancing back at the bewildered girl on the steps of her little house.

"What is this?" Lucy demanded of the air. "Is this my humiliation? I'm really sorry I came on to him that way. My God, I wonder what's wrong."

Two confusing men, Sam and Noah. And their rapport puzzled her even further. Her feelings for Noah shamed her. She was, as yet, disinterested in sophistry. She felt, married is married. The truth is simple, and it doesn't vary. Responsibility means one thing. If I touch my finger to that flame, it's going to burn. There are certain things I just can't do. I know what I can do and not lose my self-respect. I know that there are people, nice, sensitive creatures, who have lost their self-respect because they have done something that they knew they should not have done. I will never be one of them. Of course there are those who have done terrible things and not cared, but they have no self-respect to begin with. I never want to permit myself to have cheap thoughts.

At the same time the knowledge came to her that whatever fortresses she could build against the temptations of Noah's attentions, they could crumble if she were thrilled again with the power of his words. What frightened her most was Noah's mind. This mind held respectable power and could make much more than the good smart talk her mother cherished. She thought that she had neither the ideas nor the words to extend her world to within a mile of Noah's.

Entering her house slowly, saddened by the evening, she consoled herself that this time most of it had been out of her control. Noah's last words were puzzling too. There seemed to be much to learn about the Fawn Whitney case. She was glad that she wouldn't have to go through an interview with the police. It was difficult enough working in her room every day and hearing and seeing the sadness that continued among the students. She leaned against her living room wall, suddenly bone tired and glad that all was quiet and that she was again by herself to collapse in her bed and not wake until the sun pierced the light curtains in spikes late the following morning.

HENRY, BOUND
Chapter Six

Minus times minus equals plus~
The reason for this we need not discuss.
W.H. Auden

The Rocky Road class of the school was Algebra One instructed by the infamous Henry (from Heinrich) Zimmerman. There was no way to avoid Henry's class if your I.Q. read out over 90.

Nobody else taught algebra, and Henry taught four straight classes of it to all the Suppogue freshmen. He also taught Algebra II to the unfortunates who couldn't schedule themselves into Sy Fleigel's or Helen Jasperson's more jovial sections.

Henry was a stickler for promptness and exactness. Every number on every paper had to be positioned into a predetermined position on the page, or the entire problem was wrong, and one wrong problem failed the entire exercise. Only perfection was acceptable. Everyone had to conform to pass. There were no pleas of illness, forgetfulness, or acts of God to be considered. Once locked into these expectations, once one had accepted them without question and had not bothered one's soul about them any longer, the year passed well with Henry. But those troublesome students who kept harping about unfairness, injustice, and inhumane requirements were bound for wretched defeat.

These strictures represented the "posture of the Real World," maintained Henry, and it was better that his students first met with reality under his benevolent tutelage than to face head-on the totally unsympathetic demands of an employer upon graduation.

Henry also required rigid ethics. Any stray eyes, whispers, ill-timed guffaws, and the student's work was crumpled and thrown away. Those who entered the classroom after the bell sounded were clocked in, and for each thirty seconds late, a numerical point would be deducted from the next test grade. No handholding, or, indeed, socializing of any kind was permitted inside his door.

There were a few, of course, who found the adjustment difficult, and one or two who found it impossible.

After the close of school on Monday of the second week of classes, Henry was sorting through his homework papers to make certain all his charges had understood the requirements and the assignment. He was one of the few teachers who marked every paper every day. He lived alone in a somberly decorated but meticulously maintained second floor apartment in the two family home of an elderly retired police sergeant and his wife. The highest decibels reached in either apartment were generally on Sunday nights when the elderly pair hung over the TV to watch Ed Sullivan.

This night as Henry was sorting and sifting through his homework stack, he came across the greatest affront to his scientific sensibilities that he could remember. On a sheet without a heading except for the name, Bob (perhaps a fraud), and, the date, was, instead of the assignment, the following poem:

NUMBERS, NUMBERS, WONDERFUL NUMBERS

One is amorphous; everyone is one.
 Don't try to divide it,
But you sure can multiply it.
Two is a twin, a pair.
One pushes and one pulls.
Two is identical.
Three is feminine with ruffles,
Capricious and sentimental,
 Usually colored yellow.
Four is a boy, tall and thin,
Sitting in a chair, ready for a track meet,
Agile and strong.
Five is portly, a middle-aged gent,
Wise and determined,
Like Richard Nixon ... a little.
Six is sexy ... either or both,
It swims and dances,
And does great handsprings.
Seven is smooth, dashing, stylish,
Never hangs around

Very long.
Eight is fat and jolly, another man,
Not very predictable,
But fun.
Nine is a queen, wife to Eight,
Determined and rules
The behavior of Eight.
Ten is absolute; nobody questions ten.
It is both man and woman and
Nobody goes any further than ten ...
If you're smart.

What to make of it? The submission was more than a violation. It was a mockery of the science of numbers, and, as far as Henry could fathom, a distinct message of defiance to him and all he had been trying to get across last week.

But from whom did it come? Henry could remember few of his students after only several days. There was that tall girl with long, brown hair named Susan who could do no work and who wept whenever he pressed her for papers. She hadn't been in class for the past two days. He'd have to track her down.

There was a blond-haired boy who sat in the last row and always had a funny smile across his face, especially when Zimmerman was demonstrating the importance of his requirements. He would go to his seating chart to see if he could spot the name. There he was, in third period Algebra I. Bob West --- could that be the one? He'd have to wait to see if Bob claimed his paper at the end of class. Punish him. It must be done. He might need support in case this West's parents were belligerent people like their son and complained that he was punishing him for his creativity. He'd show it to Duffer, that's what he'd do.

He finished his stack of submissions and turned in, hoping to catch Duffer early the next morning. Go in at seven, just to be sure, for he had three straight classes.

Early that next morning Henry was found sitting in the outer office in one of the straight-backed chairs against the wall, feeling comfortable dealing from this position of humility. He had never, contrary to the custom of most of the other faculty, addressed either Jimmy or Noah by their first names. They refused to offer him the same distance. He tap-tapped his right foot upon the asphalt tile, filled with a rare nervousness. His classroom requirements of exactness and reliability were seldom challenged. But this submission was quite another problem. Henry's nervousness was born by the fear that for once, even though the student had blatantly refused to submit the required assignment, his display of wit may have bettered Henry's.

Jimmy Duffer and Noah Leonard had driven into the parking lot, one right after the other, and greeted each other upon alighting. They entered the building and the general offices together, thus both turned, surprised, to see Henry awaiting them at such an early hour.

"Henry, good morning. What can we do for you?" greeted Jimmy.

"I have a matter, a matter with a student here, that I think you ought to know about before I discipline him, so that, just in case there are any repercussions …" Henry was now on shaky ground, he felt, in the presence of Noah Leonard. He and Noah seldom spoke the same language. Noah's wit left Henry befuddled and frustrated. Noah was a brilliant man, so everyone said. How was it, then that nothing Noah said seemed to make any sense to Henry? So now Henry reasonably deduced that what he had to show would seem quite sensible to Noah, as absurd as it seemed to Henry.

But there he was with the paper, and he had to go on with it.

"Come in, come in Henry, glad to have you so concerned," Jimmy beckoned him into the inner office, genial as he could be, but secretly disappointed that this early morning visit might spoil his Venetian blind ritual.

They sat around Jimmy's desk and waited for Henry to speak. "I have a remarkable paper here," he began, "that was submitted to me by a student in my third period Algebra I class in place of a homework paper. You know my exact requirements, and you have always supported my classroom ethics," he cleared his throat. Noah glanced briefly at Jimmy and rolled his chin up to signal that he was going to have trouble taking this one straight. Jimmy, mindful that Noah might cause some needless confusion, intervened. "Of course, Henry, we all appreciate your high standards and support your requirements. Now what exactly did this young fellow, I take it it's a fellow, do?"

Noah winced at Jimmy's condescending response. "He gave me THIS," and Henry produced the troubling missive and placed it in front of Jimmy with a ceremonious flick of the wrist.

Jimmy began to read. "This is amazing. The boy has quite a sense of humor," and then, forgetting the delicate tension among Henry, Noah, and the matter, he added, "Noah, you've got to see this. It's almost lyrical." Jimmy sprang to his feet to deliver the paper to Noah, tripping on the wastebasket but catching himself on the desk, preventing another early morning injury.

Henry's heart sank. These two were not to be trusted. His values, his standards, all he worked for were to be made a mockery.

Noah read carefully, deadly serious, and turned to Henry without smiling. "Henry, do you know what we have here? This is a freshman student's writing, you said?"

"Yes, yes it is; but he was supposed to turn in a homework paper. He hasn't handed in anything yet this term, and this is what he finally gave me, and he doesn't even have a heading on the paper. And I wanted you to see it before I sent a letter home because if his parents are as absurd as he is, they'll complain; I'm sure they will." Henry had it all out, and he settled back a bit now; if Noah agreed, fine. If not, then he'd just have to try to cope with their judgment in a sensible way.

"Henry, I have no idea who this Bob is, but I see that whoever he is, we've got to recognize his talent in some way. This is great stuff from a kid. You can't categorize this kind of material here...ever hear of Einstein's problems in elementary math?"

"I know all about Einstein," stormed Henry as he rose from his chair, "and thank God he was never in my Algebra class. I can't let this boy ruin my ability to keep up class standards. I can't reward this misbehavior, Leonard. It's fine for you to get excited over this sort of thing. You people in history, English, and so on...you deal with fairy stories, with what people imagine in their little fantasies. I am a mathematician. I deal with fact. And if this Bob---West, I believe, keeps doing this kind of thing all term, he'll fail the regents flat, never mind what he'll get on his report cards; and if I permit him to continue to write these things, the rest of the class will consider the lessons and requirements valueless."

"Henry, Henry, sit down, Henry. Noah didn't mean that we're going to ignore this boy's duty to his math studies. There's a way to get around all of this."

Henry sat down, his fury coldly subsiding.

"Henry, we've got to have some humor about this sort of thing," Jimmy continued. "Tell this West that you were highly entertained by this off-beat submission of his, that he has remarkable talent, and that he really should give it to his English teacher, don't you think, Noah, but that he must, of course, turn in all your assignments as directed."

"You mean to suggest that's ALL I should do?" Henry was still incredulous.

"I'm saying that's the kind of thing I would do myself and recommend to you. It's your class, Henry."

Henry settled back as though getting ready to make his own pronouncement. "I---I can't do that. I've got to do just as I've done in the past with my students. I've got to give him zeros for all the days he's missed handing in his work and tell him firmly that he must meet all requirements or, that's it for the marking period."

"Henry, how DO you 'average in ZEROS?'" Now Noah was incredulous.

"Mathematically, exactly, just as I would any other digit." Henry was now belligerent and punctuated every word with exaggerated enunciation. "If I have fifty percent and a zero, the average is twenty five percent. If I have even three one hundred's and a zero, the average is seventy-five percent."

"Incredible," Noah tipped back his chair, folded his hands prayerfully under his chin and closed his eyes.

"If you don't mind, gentlemen," spoke Henry as he rose, "I've got to get down to my classroom." He turned precisely on his heel, his chin set high, paced directly to the door, closing it quietly behind him.

"Noah, I think you did him in," Jimmy pronounced gravely.

"Did HIM in? What the fuck do you think he tried to do to us? And what is he going to do to that poor kid?"

"Henry is going to have his work cut out for him. The kid's not exactly an Einstein, but do you know the West family?"

"No. Big cheeses?"

"His parents speak with some authority. His mother's a book editor and his father's a research chemist."

"And Henry can't manage their errant son. Now I am beginning to worry about Henry."

"I don't believe we'll hear any more about this. Henry's pride is already shattered, and he'll have no balm from the West parents. He won't want to return to us with news of their reaction to the failure of their son. I expect that Bob will tease old Henry for a few more days and then begin to produce. If Henry checks the files, he'll find that West comes to us from the junior high with a straight A average. He must have found a way to deal with his teachers there. Say, Noah, we missed our game this morning."

"Shame, and after Sylvia got Ole Bill to fix the blind, too. Say, Jim, how about you and Selma joining us this Saturday?"

"I'd love to, Noah, but I've got a big dinner set up for Saturday. An old friend of mine is dropping by. He's the father of one of our new teachers. That's right, you were here when I hired the Mackenzie girl, and I mentioned to you that I had known her father years ago."

Noah reddened slightly at the mention of Lucy. "Gee, I'd forgotten that, Jim, what was the connection there?"

"My buddy, Pete, from the Navy, young attorney then, now a judge in Queens, is coming out. We'll be swapping stories late into the night, I guess. Hope the women get along."

"Oh, Selma's a great hostess, Jim. She'll be up to it."

"Funny thing. You know my problems, Noah. Selma is a woman who just can't relax."

"That's an artless diagnosis, but you're absolutely correct. I've never seen Selma at ease. Efficient, hard working, conscientious, but never...relaxed. She'll flutter about 'till she's gone," finished Noah, suddenly aware that he might have gone a bit too far. But Jim seemed not to have noticed.

"I say, Noah, I'd have you and Marge over to our place too, but I don't think you'd want to listen to Navy yarns all night." Jim's voice rose hopefully on the "night."

"I wouldn't mind hearing the stories, but you know it takes a lot of gin to put up with your Mantovani, and I wouldn't want to disgrace you, kid, in front of your old pal."

*   *   *

Henry stormed down the hall, his pale face florid. He swept up a pile of rexo masters from his desk that he had prepared for distribution and made off in a fast trot for the duplicator room.

Their backs were toward him. They could have been bending over a duplicator machine, but, yet again, they were in a strange posture for that. All he really could recall was the white lab coat smeared with paint and the taller, longhaired girl.

He closed the door and walked away. He was annoyed, but he felt he could do nothing but make some noise and wait for a minute or two. He turned into an empty classroom, as he heard the door of the duplicator room open, close, and two pairs of footsteps echo down the hall. Fair is fair. He entered the duplicator room.

Right behind him came Phyllis Slavin and Lucy Mackenzie.

"Hi, Henry, how's tricks?" joked Phyllis.

"Fine, fine, a good day to you," he could scarcely sustain ill humor with Phyllis. "I'll be only a minute---five pages today."

"This is the Rexo King of the school," Phyllis introduced Henry to Lucy. "Henry Zimmerman, of the Math Department---mostly Algebra."

"ALL algebra," emphasized Henry. "The basis for all higher math. The foundation for the study of the mysteries of the universe."

"Hey, I thought that was Shakespeare."

"Miss Slavin, you need some serious tutoring, I see," Henry was finally smiling again, but as he spoke, his mind jogged along another track to the vision he had seen a few moments earlier. That tall, longhaired girl had borne a remarkable resemblance to his missing student, Susan … he tried to remember her last name. He'd have to look it up immediately.

Susan had decided to bring her animal drawings to school before all the other students arrived. She had been saving them as she drew them so that she could present the whole lot to Nick together.

She spread them out over the floor of the art room so that he could see them as they might be hung: the deathly frightened wide-eyed doe, the bunny in midair, shades of brown and white so delicately rubbed that it looked as though he could bury his fingers in the fur, the exquisite colorations of the wild grouse in flight, all of them, perfect. Nick clapped his hands together in delight, "Susan, Susan, they are wonderful. We must take them to the office to Duffer. We must display these somewhere so that everyone can enjoy them."

"No, please, they're not good enough for that. People will laugh. I'm not ready."

Nonsense, my darling. They are fine, fine. Will you allow me to put them in my closet until we decide?" She nodded as he gathered them up and secured them. "Now, I've got to run off some rexos for my classes, so why don't you come along and learn to use the machine. You might enjoy giving me a hand occasionally?" Susan brightened.

It was ironic. They were merely using the rexo machine. Whatever was going on in their hearts was expressed in the simple lesson of feeding and shuffling papers under the inked form of the master. Zimmerman saw only what he thought he could see. There was only the lesson at the machine. But, of course, they were alone.

WINDS FROM ABROAD
Chapter Seven

"The bigger the word the more magic it holds, the better cover it makes for human ignorance." Carl Jung

"The Mackenzie's and the Leonard's too?" chirped Selma nervously, as she met Jimmy at the door Friday evening. "Oh, I just hope we all get along together. It's been such a long time since you've seen Peter."

Jimmy was touched with her worry. Like an anxious mother sparrow that was worried that her chick might not show off well with finches, she moved in quick, birdlike steps and gestures, her long, thin arms and legs jerking about, picking her best dishes and crystal, her eyes darting over the house for that errant dustball or cobweb. Without children to tend, she fluttered about him and over all his interests. Jimmy was anxious too. Bringing two worlds together might not work well.

Peter knew him in another time, Paris, the Navy days. Jimmy reflected that his life on Long Island might look too homely.

"Last week I asked Noah to be with us. He declined at first, but today, he wanted to come. I think he and Marge have lost touch with a lot of their friends in Manhattan. Noah seems lonely, and I sometimes wonder how someone so sophisticated can be satisfied here in the backwoods. Well, we'll do our best."

And Noah? Noah knew only of Jimmy's present life. But Noah, Jimmy hoped, could be trusted to defer to Jimmy's better parts, and Noah and Marge might act as buffers in some delicate social matters. He tried to dispel all disquieting thoughts, to keep Selma calm.

Once the guests arrive, Jimmy knew she will settle back a little and take the visiting in stride and enjoy the time. He hoped that the aftermath with Selma would be more pleasant than usual. He could count on Peter to make the visiting congenial. But Peter's wife was the wild card. He had never met Laura, their marriage having taken place after Peter and Jim had parted at the end of the war. He knew nothing of the dynamics of their relationship, their child-raising, career blazing years. The Mackenzies might find the Leonards' intellectual, artsy world refreshing, but Marge could be at once cleverly amusing and vulgarly audacious. Forget my apprehensions, he told himself. We'll just let it all flow.

Now that Selma was deeply involved in her preparations, Jimmy retired to his den. Selma was inordinately proud of her hostess skills, and early in their marriage had let it be known that she needed no help. He had stacks of household papers to handle, but his mind began to wander to his childhood, before the Navy, before Peter. Living in his little split-level house in this upper-middle class neighborhood on Long Island, officiating at the school, shopping at the mall, dining at parties with faculty and Selma's family on weekends, occasional trips to the latest Broadway shows, this life was replete with enough movement to let him forget, for most of the time, his lost family: his first family, and the family that might be. And that lovely, frightened girl in the convent. Had she survived her youth? His letters had never been answered, his calls rebuffed. Had he taken enough time, spent enough effort? Was he afraid to know more? Was he not capable of managing with the news? But when thoughts of the past arose, there it was, an ache of incompletion, loss, and consequential actions in those very young, traumatic times without wisdom or strength or power.

And then there was his frantic Navy enlistment and Europe, and all the war horrors. Selma was calling him to check the liquor cabinet and mixers, his husbandry duty. How ritualized these dinner parties had become. Noah made fun of this Long Island Saturday night scenario, but he seemed comfortable enough in it. Somehow, although the rules seemed to have become too formalized, there was a Steppenwolf security in their regularity and form. No one, at least at any of the parties Jimmy had ever attended in ten years, had ever insulted anyone else blatantly. Seldom did any of the guests become sloppily drunk, although Jimmy remembered Julia Shawnessey snoring loudly on her own sofa during the last hour of an Al Love fishing story. The snoring effectively ended the party, and Julia was honored ever after for her indiscretion.

But Jimmy preferred, after all, the family gatherings with Selma's family and all the nieces and nephews, and even Selma's crotchety parents. Selma was proud of him, and she was proud of him with her family. Her expressions of pride were almost enough to make her neuroses worth enduring. As he checked out the booze supply, he reflected on her family's dynamics and wondered how so many divergent personalities could ever get along for several hours together without some kind of explosion, and he realized that Selma's family had a kind of metaphysical cohesiveness, predicated on a loyalty that included but also went beyond personality. Taken individually, every third character was a real son of a bitch, but within the family they were respected, supported, and they gave respect and support in kind. Jimmy was accepted and acknowledged as an educational leader in his community. Uncle Al managed cheap nightclub acts, but he was championed as a scion in the entertainment industry. Cousin Jack was a nuclear physicist with Westinghouse in Pittsburgh, and he was duly recognized for his spectacular scientific career, but was not expected to draw any more attention or claim more time in leading table discussions than was Uncle Al, the entertainer. Aunt Rose, having fallen from grace in her teens when she ran away to Cuba for a weekend with a college beau, had redeemed herself by going to law school and now represented her district in Brooklyn in the State Assembly in Albany. She had also married that same college beau who was also an attorney, working in Manhattan on corporation law. The tribe all managed to get together at someone's wedding, bar mitzvah, funeral or Thanksgiving at least once or twice a year, and it was good, especially for Jimmy. It seemed to be good for Selma too, even though she had married far out of her tribe, an Anglo-Irish Christian, albeit un-churched. She seemed content at these gatherings, seemed satisfied that she had done as well as most of them, in spite of her personal frustrations.

Jimmy had lied a little to them about his origins. His Navy career was easy to brag about. His parents were dead. What more was necessary to say? He had his education, his youthful energy. It all passed.

"Marriage. So demoralizing. None of my married friends have first-rate wine," Noah, first to arrive, grumbled into Jimmy's liquor cabinet.

"You're really all talk, all the time, yakety yak, Mr. Ripple himself," chided Marge.

"Terrible consequences of blatant misunderstandings, these Long Island marriages."

"How can you stand this guy?" laughed Jimmy to Marge. "Why haven't you left him?"

"Hah. And compound his misery? He never had it so good."

Noah curled cross-legged on the carpet in his uniform of black turtleneck and beige cords with a week's new growth of beard trimmed to a point under the chin. Marge perched on a hassock, resplendent in a lavender and purple caftan, her hair drawn up in twisted strands, fastened with combs sewn with tiny emerald spangles and her earrings, cascades of multicolored stones and pearls. She appeared in wildly theatrical contrast to Noah's black severity and Selma's Peter Pan, aproned tearoom austerity. Jimmy shuffled about in brogues and an Irish fisherman's sweater; He was glad his more familiar friends had arrived early. They understood him and his life now. They would be here, too, after Peter and the unknown woman he had married were gone. He was gratified that Noah had decided to help him. With all Noah's gaff there was a warmth in the man that Jimmy treasured, a sense of kindness that knew when he was needed, and a loyalty that surmounted their different professional positions, their lifestyles, and tastes.

"Do the music, Noah," Jimmy pleaded. "I hid the Mantovoni in the back of my closet for tonight."

"I can hardly wait to see what a tin ear keeps in his record collection," Noah hunched over another small cabinet. "What's this, the Clancy's? We'll have to high tail it into the Whitehorse one of these nights where they be crawling. Didn't know you were into Irish revolutionaries."

Jimmy was flattered by Noah's indirect praise for his cultural panache. "Tommy Makem sings a lot of songs I used to know as a kid. You know my background, Noah. The sodden sod of Newfieland. Not much rock and roll up there even yet, eh?"

"I forget. You've got your own brand of cold exotica, Jim. I want to hear more, a lot more about that country when we have the time."

"Not much to tell. Not much more than rocks and fish and lots of lonely, drinking, rag-tag people."

"No beautiful women, Jim? Come on, they're mostly Irish now. They be long-legged, fine featured, firm breasted, red haired colleens, Jim. They be Gaelic masterpieces, and their men are too fagged out with work and liquor to fuck 'em. What a treasure-trove. We must go up there sometime, Jim, some long weekend, or week off. Will you take me, Jimmy?"

Marge was busying herself in the kitchen with Selma who had deigned to let her help with the last preparations.

"It's been so long, Noah. I don't know if I'd know where to go. It'd be a kind of a sad trip for me, you know. But…" and he paused in thought, "it would probably be a good thing to exorcise the ghosts. There are people I should see, and there are questions that I have to ask, and maybe then I'll sleep better," and then another pause as he remembered more, "that is if Selma will let me go."

"Of course, she will. Let's go over the winter holidays."

"Winter---it's so dreary and foggy. We won't want to travel about in that kind of cold. We'll have to wait 'till spring. April this year is our Spring Break. You'll see some green appearing, and the ice will be just beginning to break up in Conception Bay. It'll be cold still, but with warm clothing we can climb up to the Signal Hill and see the harbor and the land all around. We kids used to love it when Daddy would take us up there. Oh, well, yes I guess it could be a good thing, but you'll have to put up with a bit of melancholy from me, you know." And Jimmy turned away for a moment to hide his feelings. "I don't know if I really can, Noah. I'll have to think hard about it." The door chimes sounded, and Selma fluttered through.

"You're so slow, Jimmy. Don't keep your guests waiting."

It was a different-looking Peter who reentered Jimmy's life. His youthful auburn hair was all white now, and the deep-set cerulean eyes were rimmed with gold-framed glasses. His walk was still bravely aggressive, his broad shoulders still leading him into the room with unquestionable authority, but with the most disarming smile and hearty handshake, and the two old friends embraced for longer than it was customary for two men anywhere.

"And you must be Laura," welcomed Selma with an eager shake to a cold, gloved hand, "and these are our good friends, Marge and Noah Leonard."

The tall, slim wife stood expressionless in the doorframe in a violet, single-breasted wool suit with a white ruffled collar and a small pearl circle pin. She nodded to Noah and Marge and Selma with a taunt mouth. Her neutral blond hair was pulled away from her face into a tight chignon at the nape of her neck, flattering her small, pale, face and features. Looking several years younger in age but many years older in temperament than her husband, she followed Selma to shake hands with Marge and Noah, and her presence transformed the gathering into an entirely new French scene of self consciousness where all, except Peter and Jimmy, were waiting for some move or word from this new prodigious character to define the mood of the gathering.

"It's delightful to meet you all," she spoke from the Queen Anne chair by the fireplace, and Marge thought that her deep tones and clear, studied inflections belied the innocent gaze of her eyes. Jimmy hoped that Noah wasn't after her psyche already. He remarked to Jimmy later in the kitchen, "That frozen woman misses 'stunning' by an eighth-inch of a smile."

Jimmy was full of questions about Peter's past from the time that they had parted at war's end till now, but knew that he'd have to wait to ask anything meaningful or appear rude in all this company. First he had to give time for the conventional superficialities, or was it the positioning for combat, as Noah liked to laugh. "A hardening of the social arteries."

"You're lucky to be closer to the city," remarked Marge. "We have to organize ourselves weeks in advance before we can enjoy an evening on The Town." Noah bit his lip to keep from smiling at his wife's newfound formality.

The conversation kept to innocuous topics such as the rising and falling populations of Long Island communities, commuting problems on the Long Island Railroad, beach erosion and seagull control, and, finally as Selma ushered them all to dinner, Peter turned warmly to Jimmy, his arms around his shoulders. "How in the hell did you decide to become a high school principal, Jim? That's got to be one of the most frustrating jobs in the world."

Noah, seeing some discomfort in Jimmy's face and worrying that Peter's question implied an accidental condescension, interjected, "Jim has designed an intricate set of defense mechanisms that would make the toughest corporate executive envious."

Jimmy smiled thankfully at Noah's transforming of Jim's Venetian blind sessions into psychological games. "Well, Peter, it was a natural step from underpaid history teacher, and the Island schools don't have the same pressures as your city schools do. The constituents are different here ... parents concerned about American values, hair lengths, closet communists, teachers with beards (directed at Noah), those superficial issues."

"But we do have rumbles," chimed in Selma, proudly.

"Yes, but the parents of the rumblers are the quietest because they're never home. That's why their kids go out to Amityville with our faculty car antennas for weapons, and why there's sometimes an eye or two lost on weekends. Their ideas of ethnic superiority are excuses to fight---the same kind of gangs you have in the city, letting out their teenage frustrations."

"A gruesome problem," put in Laura. "But what can the school do? Isn't a weekend caper out of the school's jurisdiction?"

"Anything our kids do reflects on the school," Jimmy began to fight to control his facial twitch as he thought of his job pressures. "The more powerful parents don't want anything negative to reflect on the community. And they expect us to provide some kind of positive instructional panacea."

"The school is society's last hope for stability," added Noah. "No one really believes that religions can effect responsibility anymore, and most parents are frightened because they can't really control or even persuade their children, so they lean on the schools; and most of the parents turn their anger and frustration with themselves on us, but know they've abrogated their own responsibilities."

"Heavy, heavy," croaked Marge who had been sipping her claret steadily. "Let's get on to some lighter stuff. Jimmy and Noah here are going up to Newfoundland in the spring. I want to talk about the northland, icebergs, and jolly Eskimos. Are you really going, Jim?"

Jim flushed, not ready for this intrusion, and realizing that Marge and Selma had overheard his words with Noah before dinner.

"I haven't been there for years, Marge, and St. Johns must be greatly changed. I was pretty young when I left---nineteen. And I don't know what has happened to my family."

"You've lost touch with them all?" Marge pursued.

"It's a complicated story," Jimmy tried to excuse rather than really begin. "My family was very poor, and my little sister and I were taken to a convent school when I was twelve," as he spoke he took a deep breath and seemed to relax into himself. although a part of him wanted to go on, to get it all out. Selma was listening intently, and as soon as Jimmy mentioned the word "family," Laura leaned forward, her lips parted.

"But your parents ... are they both gone?"

"I don't know. My aunt took me to the convent alter my mother left---something of a mystery---to Nova Scotia, and two or three years later my aunt came up to see us, my little brother and sister and me, to tell us our mother was dead. I never got any papers or proof. I was just a kid and didn't know to ask. Oh, I guess I didn't want proof then, and I left the country for New York as soon as I graduated from the convent school. And then I tried to write to my sister, but after she graduated the next year, I lost track of her."

"Your father?"

"I don't know. I'd really like to know about him, now that you mention it. He was never home much, a sailor, but I remembered him as a damn nice guy---maybe a bit shiftless, who must have given my mother some worries. If I went up there, I'd probably be able to trace them---he really loved my mother, and there was a lot of pain for me, with no explanation. And by now, maybe I could take the explanations."

He hadn't been ready for this narrative, but once he began, it had come pouring out, as he felt himself protected, supported.

"Then you should go. Noah, you should go with him. Plan on it. I'd love to see it up there too, but I'm terrified of flying anywhere. He hates the water, I hate the air." And as though on an aside to the rest, "When Noah and I go to Europe, I take the boat and meet him."

Selma was looking frightened of something threatening coming out of Jimmy's past because he never spoke of it, never had shared a word of it with her, and what little he had spoken tonight was all she had ever been given of his early years. She rose to attend to clearing the dishes and preparing the dessert course on knees weakened by sitting so long and by the heady wine she had been gulping while Jimmy was telling his story.

"Well, Jim, aren't you going to ask me where I met this ravishing woman to my left?" Peter interrupted the topic of Jimmy's origins to Marge's displeasure. She felt that she had just been getting into the heart of Jimmy's mysteries. Peter had been drinking heartily as well, but his sturdy frame assured him of more stability and judgment than did Marge's. Laura smiled evenly, even as she flinched, Noah observed, with amusement.

"How did you ever get into that officers' club in Norfolk? I don't think you ever explained your spectacular appearance that night."

"A friend asked me to go," Laura offered unsteadily. "She knew one of the officers, an old friend from her high school. I wasn't anxious," she went on, warming a bit to her subject, "but it turned out to be kind of fun. I'd never been to an officer's club before, and the atmosphere was not exactly what I'd expected." The wine was loosening her tongue. Peter looked on his wife with new interest. They were unaccustomed to attending dinner parties away from their established law set in Queens. Laura was becoming unlike her politically guarded self. "And then you were there, Peter. I … I guess I was bowled right over," she gave a little giggle. "Peter was so handsome," she turned to Noah and then to Marge. "He asked me to dance right away, and that was just the end of it."

"The end, I like that," laughed Peter. "What did I finish, darling?"

"Her precious innocence," broke in Marge, thick-tongued now with a hearty laugh. "Well, we women all have our breaking point, don't we, Selmer," she parodied Selma's Brooklyn twang in the direction of the kitchen where Selma stood, staring at her lineup of mousse sherbet glasses arranged on a tray for serving, fear welling up at thoughts of Jimmy's past, a past she had grown to fear but had kept down, way down with other fears of Jimmy's otherworldliness, his unexplained distances from her that matched the sadness of their own early days together when their hopes had been dashed for having children after so many attempts and failures. What women had he before her? What beginnings had he made in the north? In the Navy? These people might know, or might imagine, and could evoke more from him more than she could, and she was afraid.

Jimmy spoke, without guile, "That's a great story, Laura. I'm glad we can put all this together tonight, here at my house."

Marge clearly wanted something more devilish to happen. Her blue eyes were gleaming, and Noah wanted her to stay quiet because he sensed Jimmy's vulnerability. He knew that Marge was finding Laura's propriety irksome. Marge was known to be able to clear out a room with her comments when she was in her cups.

"Let's all talk about our old loves, now." She laughed. "Everyone we knew before we got together---knew very VERY well."

"You're really out of turn, my love," murmured Noah gently, trying.

"Don't get us into trouble, Marge." Peter laughed, with his good-natured self-confidence. "None of us were kids when we met, except perhaps, Laura, here, so what's past is past."

"Yea, Noah, here's a real ex-is-ten-tial-ist," kept up Marge. "So I don't worry none. He found me on a stool at the San Remo, didn't you, love? In the roaring fifties. But I looked real good beside that prin-cess wife of his he left on the upper West Side of apple-town. Ha ha, some set of officers that was. Officers of the peace pipe full of Montezuma's gold, they were," and she cracked Noah across the shoulders.

"Our salad days," mused Noah, relieved that Marge had turned her jibes away from the others.

Laura sat sternly. As Selma served the mousse, she clattered the sherbets on the china plates.

Jimmy was feeling desperate. He knew assuredly what was to come after they all would leave.

Peter saw Jimmy shrinking before Selma, who had apparently been touched in some unknown way, as she served the mouse without trying to speak or smile, with Jimmy obviously avoiding her gaze.

"You all know that Jim and I were great buddies in the war and that's why we're here tonight, but you might not know that he was the bravest most dependable officer on my brig. Couldn't have gotten by with any less than Jim."

"Thanks, Pete. It's funny, war. It lasts for such a short time in the grand scheme of things, but it changes your life forever, and it's out of life, unreal. Friends you know dying all around you, so that all other features of life at home, your present, your future, are suspended. You don't plan, you don't remember much, you come right out of it, and none of the values that you had before fit. None of the lessons that seemed to mean so much work for you quite the same way anymore. And you're grateful for being alive, but you wonder what you were saved to do. It takes awhile to gather yourself together again." Jim breathed deeply, unburdened.

Peter picked up the thread. "I didn't know you felt that way too, Jim. When we were on that ship, I not only had no memory of my law training, I had no idea what I was going to do when the war was over. And then I just fell into this practice here in New York. My father knew someone, you know how it is, and I had met Laura---that was after we said goodbye, Jim, in Newport---and it was natural to find a home in Queens and settle down."

"And then Lucy was born?" interjected Selma, partly at ease again beside Jimmy.

Peter looked away. "No, Lucy wasn't born to us. We weren't lucky that way." There was a pause. "We adopted Lucy."

That explains the lack of resemblance to either of them, the rest of them thought instantly. And further that she couldn't be Laura's daughter. Peter's maybe, Jimmy thought, but it was hard to reexamine his features behind those glasses and white mustache.

"Well, you have a prize, you two," smiled Jimmy. "She's going to be a great teacher, one of our best. I knew at our first interview that we couldn't let her get away. I hope she likes Suppogue."

"Unfortunately, she likes it so well she's left our bed and board," continued Peter.

"She's a willful child," interpreted Laura, clinically. "One never knows the full temperament and inclinations of an adopted child."

"She's all I'd ever hoped for, even if she isn't fully ours," announced Peter as if to cover for Laura's judgment. "I hope her earlier traumas are over."

"Then you didn't get her as an infant?" Selma was alive with curiosity now, as she had hoped earlier to follow the same route.

"No, Selma, we took her...out of an orphanage when she was already four years old. Actually, Jim, when we first thought of adopting, I remembered how you spoke of the quality of the convent school where you stayed in Halifax, so we called there first, and they recommended their sister school in Connecticut. Laura and I visited the place, but no babies. A lovely little girl was there already helping with the younger children. After we left our names and let them know our wishes to adopt an infant as soon as one became available, we came home and got a call from the Mother Superior. Seems as though this girl, Lucy, had taken a liking to us and pleaded with the Mother to ask us if we'd take her. Laura didn't know, a girl that old, but I remembered her so well; she had a softness about her that most kids in homes didn't have, for there is so much competition for attention in a place like that. I wanted to try her, and she had said something so pathetic to the Mother. She said, 'If they don't like me, I'll come back.' Imagine. She was offering herself as a kind of bargain."

"Why hadn't a girl like that been placed before?" Selma was so curious.

"Something about her birth mother stipulating that she not be placed for awhile because she wanted to come for her as soon as she could get settled. The mother never came, and efforts to find her were fruitless. The girl wearied of people at the home telling her, "Your mother is coming for you soon." I suppose they meant to be kind, but she says that her longing was hard. By the time we showed up, the time limit for adoption was up, and she was free to go She had given up waiting for a mother she could hardly remember and was dying to get out of the restrictions of the convent."

"It must have been hard, getting a girl that old," broke in Selma. "You were brave."

"But lucky," continued Peter. "She's been a joy every day of her life with us."

Noah noted that Marge was suddenly quiet. Marge's longings were not Laura's or Selma's. Marge, given to thinly veiled mockery---was more complex. What did Marge want? He was spending his life wondering, without judgment, what could ever satisfy this woman.

Laura showed her amazement at Peter's story. She had come here, Noah expected, because Peter was bent on seeing his old navy friend, but she hadn't bargained for hearing of hers and Peter's ghostly passages. This 50's wife looked upon her barren marriage as an indication of her shameful inadequacy, scarcely ameliorated by Peter's loyalty and good-natured enthusiasm.

"Peter," Laura suddenly exclaimed. "Let's not turn our grand adoption into an event of Biblical proportions. It's just a story of two lonely people and a little girl who needed us."

There were notes in Laura's speech that caused to rest to stir. Something resentful.

"Did you learn anything about her family.. or did you want to know?" Selma asked for more of a story that spoke to her childless needs.

"Seems her mother was from Canada. Wanted the child placed in an orphanage in the States, and the Church found an opening in Connecticut for her. I think she was sent here after she grew up a little."

"Another Canadian story, Jimmy. Good grief, Jim, maybe you and Lucy are re-lated," Marge had to add a silly non sequitur.

"It's a big, wide country, dear," Jimmy smiled. "But we've certainly got plenty of extra kiddies up in Newfieland. Big families there for Mother Church."

Laura's pained demeanor fascinated Marge. When she had first entered with her prim suit and strained greetings, Marge wanted to nail her. But now she saw something that touched her. This lady was terrified---she couldn't tell of what. And Selma, a lady with secret problems, now had become as transparent as cellophane. Selma ached for a family, was unable to conceive, and Jimmy was implacably against adoption. There were stories about Jimmy that still needed told. This evening was electric with memories.

And Peter. Peter was magnanimous. He could spell out every detail of his past and chart it with salt and pepper on the tablecloth for examination: Prep school here, Princeton, then Yale law, Navy, rise to Admiralty, late marriage, retirement to law practice, adoption of daughter, supreme court case won, comfortable late middle age-into-retirement.

She looked around her at faces beginning to show the strain of too much alcohol and food, without movement, and a not-so-guarded conversation among relative strangers about the most important moments of their lives.

"It's time we were to go," she began, for once serious.

"Oh, not yet, really. You must sit awhile in the living room while I bring schnapps," ordered Selma, sincerely wishing that they all might stay longer and sounding like it, although the dinner talk had gone on longer than anyone had imagined. She was gaining strength from the Mackenzie story. She could relate to Laura, she could see her pain, could imagine what trials she had had as a barren wife of such a scion of society. She rose and whisked them all back to the living room as she gestured for Jimmy to take the tray of aperitifs and glasses.

The pause in their dialogue offered them time to reconnoiter and reflect on the purpose of the evening: to reassure each other that though many years had passed, friendships endure and sustain. Selma had to lead in. She was flushed with wine and confidence in contrast to Laura's drained pallor. The blood that had been drained from Laura had revived Selma. Jimmy and Noah could see all this. The rest were distracted. Noah wanted to turn to another lighter world of books or theatre or jazz---anything to dispel the maudlin emotions that he felt were blanketing the gathering, so he knelt again by the record cabinet.

"What do we play for a grace note, Captain," he looked up toward Jimmy standing by the fireplace.

"Do you still have those speakers wired out to the terrace?" Marge broke in. "I'd love to dance out there. Put on some Ella---'Old Black Magic'. I know you have that one, Jim. You played it at your last Christmas party. It's warm tonight. I'd like some air and exercise to finish off."

"Yes, and you old geezers could say your goodbye without foreign intrusions."

"Just fine, Noah, just fine," Selma approved, not needing to be tactful with him.

As the music wafted through the French doors, the four remaining collected themselves in a modified dynamic. Laura, glad to be rid of the clamorous Marge, Selma, cozying up to Jimmy on the sofa as Peter stood, elbow propped on the mantel, glass in hand, gesturing as he spoke.

"The years certainly take some of the wind out of our sails, but they do mellow us, don't they, Jimbo? Can't say they haven't been good to me ... and I hope Laura here, my lucky star, feels the same way."

Some of the tension left Laura's shoulders, and as she gazed for the first time that evening into her husband's eyes, a new softness appeared. His gracious cliches made up for his earlier untoward revelations. She could love him again. He just couldn't relate to her earlier agony. Be generous, she spanked herself.

Jimmy was beginning to feel that the evening had been especially good for him and Selma, even though it had opened up old wounds, but perhaps the sacrifice of enduring his ancient pain would ease his current struggle with Selma. She sat now, so grateful for these magnanimous guests who had freed her from the necessity of having to appear the complete and perfect wife.

"Selma, you've made us a delightful evening," Peter continued his oblations. "I imagine we all came into this night with a bit of anxiety, but you and Jimmy have to be the grandest hosts on all Long Island." Only a man of Peter's definition could make such a conceit acceptable.

"We've had a wonderful time," Laura conceded, "and you must come to us one evening soon."

"Our pleasure, Peter," Jimmy smiled thankfully. "God willing we'll see many evenings more, and maybe some city shows and a beach picnic."

"We'll keep in touch," and Peter gestured to Laura, who rose. "Let's say goodnight to the Leonard's, and then we'll have to be off. It's funny though, going home to an empty house. Lucy's friends used to be all over the place on a Saturday night before she escaped out here to her independent little cottage. That wasn't in her mother's plan, was it, Laura?"

"No, it certainly wasn't. It doesn't seem so long that we had a daughter," Laura murmured.

Jimmy rose to open the French doors to call to Noah and Marge. The two were shamelessly wrapped around each other in floating ecstasy to the dulcet tones of Billy Holiday con brilo. "I don't think we'll bother them," he chuckled to Peter and Laura. "They'll say goodbye when they say hello again."

"Agreed," laughed Peter. "Just how young are those two?"

"Thirty-Six years young this April, by my calculation. Old enough to know better."

As the car door slammed, Noah and Marge were roused from their reverie enough to run to the edge of the terrace to wave goodbye. Inside, Selma began the ritual cleaning of plates and glasses, torn between old pangs of inadequacy and new strengths from unexpected revelations.

Jimmy, from years of caution over such a time, approached her with a tentative smile and open arms of gratitude. Selma, characteristically, turned aside, "Not now, Jimmy. Let's clean up first."

"I just wanted to thank you," he began, "for all this effort tonight. It means so much."

Her own discords were so loud that she couldn't hear his gratitude. He shrank back, then hoped, as always, for better from her later.

Noah and Marge came through the French doors. "Say Selma, you really outdid yourself tonight, old girl," Noah hugged her shamelessly. Selma had to smile, even though she was on drive to tidy up.

"Sit a moment longer, Noah. Let's recoup before you leave. It's been quite an evening. Can't say I'm not glad you were here. I didn't know how I'd find my old Admiral."

Noah perched on the edge of the piano bench. "Your old buddy is a great guy, Jim. But he's got some up tight wifey there. Poor woman. Guess she didn't know what to make of us deviates out here in beer-barrel land."

"Oh, I think she's lovely," warbled Selma, ready to defend her newfound fellow sufferer of the unfulfilled wife syndrome.

"She is that," put in Marge. "I should be so put together, but I never will be, thank God. Well, babe, let's split and much thanks to you both for including us."

After they drove away Selma went through her chores wordlessly as Jimmy dutifully stacked dishes and swept up crumbs, not wishing to provoke another rejection. He waited for her lead. She was sorting out her feelings, he could sense, for on most other occasions she had drunk much more and had begun the torturous withdrawal minutes after the door closed on the last guest. It was a rhythm he had come to dread: the anxious preparations which she always insisted she wanted to do, the perfect hostessing, the slow drinking into the explosion as soon as they were alone, with the accusations of how he had ignored her all evening, how he had shown more deference to his guests, especially his lady guests, than to her, how unappreciative he was of her efforts, as if he hadn't taken every opportunity to ask to help which she, time and again, refused: and the cries of what a loveless, fruitless marriage they had and after all her efforts, what had she to show, compared to all those others who walked through their home and their lives. And the worst time of all several years ago was when Jimmy had proposed that she seek some professional help --- together with him of course. But this was only the end of the fifties, and any kind of psychoanalysis was shameful to her.

But this night was different. First the acknowledgement of Jimmy's hard past---she had suddenly seen his torture, had been able to help her recognize that this man of hers had come from a despair that she had never seen, that perhaps she needn't fear after all. Then Peter's and Laura's strange story of Lucy. The notion that the perfect couple had a kind of unnatural incident in their lives---far more exotic than anything she and Jimmy had ever contemplated and with hints of difficulties still in Laura's closing comments about Lucy's current flight. She hadn't expected such a straightforward evening. Most Long Island dinner parties were superficial, charged with competition. Well, maybe they were getting older and mellower, as Peter said, and maybe old friends didn't need to be so careful with one another.

She was finished loading the dishwasher now, and her discordant emotions were evening out into a slow, steady blend of easy listening melody---Their familiar Mantovani had come out of Jimmy's closet and onto the hi fi. She didn't hurt tonight. Something very good had happened. She suddenly remembered Jimmy, now in the living room, and remembering his open arms, was filled with a new sense of guilt. How selfish I have been with him, she stood stunned. Why, I don't know anything about his needs or his losses. He's never spoken to me of his past before because he was afraid to bother me, afraid that I couldn't take what he had to handle. The least I could do is hug him back, at least for tonight.

She dried her hands on her crinoline party apron and moved toward her husband, standing, looking out onto the terrace. She moved slowly, deliberately, wrapping her arms around his chest from behind his back, and laying her head silently against his warm shoulder. He was overwhelmed by her great change, hardly knowing how long to prolong this long-awaited embrace.

"Quite a night," he finally stammered.

But they lay separately in their wide bed, each fearing to go further on such a night, each not wanting to risk disrupting this era of unique good feeling in their lives.

As Noah and Marge drove home wordlessly, Marge's head on Noah's shoulder as they sat on the wide front seat of their '56 Pontiac, Noah's late night mellowness was interrupted with a flash of his terrible discovery last month, the slashed face of Fawn staring at her ceiling with the hideously mindless stare of death, her mouth pulled into an open smile, such as he had never seen on her face while she was alive.

He had found the door slightly ajar and called her name, at first softly, then louder and louder and then heard the dog whimpering. She had been dead for thirteen hours, the examiner had said. What had made him run to the neighbor's phone? Nothing rational. That had been a lucky impulse---none of his fingerprints left on the phone to confuse the police. They didn't seem to suspect him at all of any involvement, but he supposed they could. After all, he was apparently the first on the scene, but he certainly didn't need any of that kind of trouble. And what of Nick? What had he said to the police? But Noah had really loved her. He had, for awhile, loved her intensely, and maybe even more than he loved Marge, and certainly very differently from the way he loved Marge. But he had never made love to her.

This had been the first time that he had looked on someone he had loved who had been a victim of outrageous violence. It had the effect of numbing him emotionally for some time afterward. He had returned to the school after dealing with the police, unable to describe any details to anyone there except, finally, Jimmy, but he had asked Jimmy to tell no one how he had found her. It was too horrible a secret. Let the police who have to deal with it keep in among themselves. How had the police kept the physical details from the press? Had the police interceded or had the press just missed an opportunity, or had someone from the fourth estate finally shown some taste and respect. Not a chance. They must have thought that a murdered schoolteacher was pale news.

At any rate, her privacy in death had not been compromised, and only a lover and the disinterested had seen her, as is fitting and proper as such a scene could be in this time of tasteless glitz and obscene delights. But even through this ugly horror of her murder, he could still feel the love in that house, in the little whimpering dog who had licked her wounds almost clean except for the gushing gash in her heart that had poured out her lifeblood. What monster had done this? What hideous insanity had prompted this destruction of so beautiful a soul, one of the rarest stars in all the heavens?

Marge nuzzled her cheek against his chest, and he could not respond with even a tightening of his arm, for his whole mind was frozen on Fawn's essence.

INTO THE POTTING SHED
Chapter Eight

Weapons used in commission of a crime: *pistol, automatic revolver, rifle, knife, poison, garrote, bayonet, bola, bomb, brass knuckles, zip gun, shotgun, sawed-off shotgun, six-shooter, bow and arrow, dart, poison dart, slingshot, rock or hard object, fire, sword, chain, rope, gas, gasoline, flame thrower, grenade, Molotov cocktail, machine gun, acid, drug o.d., billy club, cutlass, air gun, ax, tomahawk, ice pick, hammer, gaff, hook, blackjack, bazooka, javelin, broadsword, vehicle, fist, trowel.*

The Fawn Whitney investigation went on, but most of the school in its frantic fall pace buried thoughts of the murder. It was easy and comfortable to assume that a burglar from the highway had come upon a solitary woman's house. Only Jimmy and Noah had been told the details that masses of prints had been found on the front doorknob of Fawn's house with no discreet outlines that the police could follow. No weapon had been unearthed, nor had Fawn's body been sexually molested. The police had cut the ribbons from around the property, obtained the only known key from Fawn's parents, who had left the state and put the house up for sale with a local realtor who had not, as yet, bothered to show the premises because he was vacationing out on Fire Island. Only a week had passed, and so much had been forgotten, except for those who could not find closure, who still felt the presence of Fawn so real in their lives.

So it was that Noah persuaded Jimmy to come with him to the little house on the Monday after their dinner together. They drove down to the section named, obliquely, *American Venice,* several blocks east from Noah's and Lucy's places, to the house which sat in a grove of birches twenty yards up a hill from one of the narrower canals. Noah carried a key Fawn had given him when he cared for her animals on the numerous occasions when she visited out of town. He felt at home, walking to the front door of the cottage. Jimmy was all nerves. "This isn't a smart move, Noah. The neighbors will be looking. The police will know. I don't know why we're doing this today. Can't it wait longer 'till this thing cools down?"

"She's got a book of mine that I need for my lessons. We're clean. The police know that." He turned the key confidently; he was about to embark on an errand of mercy for a friend.

He opened the front door onto a broad living room lined with bookcases. In a corner under the eastern windows she had placed her writing desk, and in the opposite corner south of the western kitchen entrance her baby grand piano. Noah slowly walked to the door of her kitchen, a long, narrow room with a table and three chairs on the northern end and a sewing machine on the south. The length of the kitchen ceiling was hung with drying herbs and flowers suspended from hooks. He touched a bunch tenderly, and some crackly petals wafted to the floor. "Don't touch things!" whispered Jimmy.

"The police found the place spotless except for what we see now; those two china teacups on the counter there. They haven't even put away the teapot. Her parents haven't touched anything either. Those teacups made the papers. Funny no one's moved them yet. Do you suppose that someone besides the police took away the ribbons and put these teacups back where they were at the time of the crime?"

"Noah, You've a head full of intrigue, but you're talking nonsense, and you're making me very nervous," Jimmy paced back and forth.

"I can't believe that the investigation and Fawn's parents' involvement could be so incomplete. Why isn't someone still out here? Why did we get in so easily two weeks after the murder? Are the Suffolk police such bunglers that they leave a murder scene so quickly, and so carelessly?"

"She was just a poor schoolteacher, Noah."

"Yea."

"And we're prowlers right now."

"Not at all. We're close friends, visiting the home of a close friend. Anyway, aren't you at all thrilled by the idea of getting caught in here by the bunglers? Wouldn't they look stupid dragging both of us in for additional questioning? The best they could do on a dull day at the eminent county seat in Patchogue? Fawn trusted me with a key. No one asked me for it. Shhh there's a boat pulling up to the dock." Noah squinted out the kitchen window to see.

"You fool, let's get out of here."

"Will you stop and be quiet?"

"I know that face. It's Jake Sutherland, Chief of Police. He's getting out of his boat. He's coming up here. Now, let's get out fast, Noah. We can't let him see us here."

"Why not? He's got no business here alone either."

"Then let's hide ourselves and see what he's up to. She's got a potting shed attached to the kitchen."

The two sidestepped through the narrow door and down two steps into a tiny room which held two high stools and two sets of shelves on three sides, filled with pots and planters. One small window faced the lake, but was nearly opaque with dust and cobwebs. Noah could make out Jake climbing the hill from the canal. Jimmy found a loose plank on the floor and jammed it against the small door, further fortifying it with several cement blocks.

"Are we expecting the Gestapo?" Noah chuckled.

"What the hell are we doing here, Noah?"

"I don't really know. I just had some strong feelings today that I had to satisfy. I was up all night Saturday thinking about this crime and this house, and I had to get back here to see if there just wasn't something someone had overlooked and that we could see. And we haven't even had a chance to look yet. I wonder what the hell John is doing here now. Maybe he's trying to outdo the rest of the force at detective work."

"Wouldn't be surprised. I understand Jake's not the most popular chief around the island."

They heard him let himself into the house as easily as they had … with a key, and he stood for a moment inside the front door as though stopping to think about where he wanted to go next. Then they could hear heavy feet tramping towards what sounded like the direction of the bedroom. Drawers opening and slamming closed. A scraping sound as though something was being dragged across the pine floor, but no, the scraping stayed in the bedroom.

"He's looking under the bed for something. That's his back and boots on the floor. He's up again. He didn't find it."

The footsteps returned to the living room. Sounds of books being taken and replaced. Then into the kitchen. In spite of their fortifications, Jimmy braced himself against the door. "He'll think it's bolted," he explained, terrified.

Noah was suddenly disappointed at their stupidity. Why, after all, were they hiding? If Jake came toward this room, if he did get the door opened, they would look terrible. If he had merely found them in the house, they might have concocted any number of stories to justify their presence.

They could hear Jake rummaging through a cabinet by the kitchen table where Fawn stored files. Finally he slammed it shut. His steps came directly toward the door to the potting shed. He jiggled the latch and pushed several times.

"Damn. Aw, nothin there anyway." He turned and retraced his steps to the living room. Nothing was heard for several minutes.

"I think he's resting."

"But I don't think he'll be back here," breathed Jimmy.

"Wish we'd confronted him letting himself into the house."

"Then who would file the report?"

"Well, we could do some asinine routine of 'don't tell on us and we won't tell on you.' He'd really love that game, and be so trustworthy too."

"He's not supposed to be here alone without some kind of authorization from the sheriff, even if he's the chief. Who knows but what we've caught Fawn's murderer?"

"Not a chance. He's too smart to come back here after creating a scene like that. Remember, I saw the mess. That was the work of a homicidal maniac, not a slightly aberrant local police chief."

"Listen, he's getting up now."

The footsteps shuffled out, and the door was slammed shut.

"He's not even locking the door behind him. What a cop! No one that dumb can be counted on for any extensive planning or foresight."

"Wait. Don't move until you see that boat leave. He may have forgotten something. Noah! He'll see your car. Why didn't we think of that?"

"I did. Remember, I left it in the road, not the drive. I was thinking of the neighbors." Noah peered out the dusty window and saw Jake sidestepping down the hill to the canal. He was holding what appeared to be a paper folder in his left hand.

"Jimmy, he did find something! He didn't come in with that folder."

"Fawn must have had something that he wanted. But something personal? This may be interesting."

"As interesting as our visit may seem to him."

"Maybe so."

"He's getting something out of the boat. It's a pipe wrench."

"What in the devil will he do with that. Maybe he's coming back."

"Get out of here, Jimmy. Now. Stand in the living room like we've just come in and mean business."

Noah had pulled away the board and blocks and was out the little door. Jimmy had no choice but to follow him back into the living room.

"Close that door behind you!"

Jimmy did as he was told, not knowing at all what Noah was about.

"The front door is hidden from the canal. We've just come in, that's all. We're here on official business. Fawn's parents gave us the key to retrieve her school supplies. He's not supposed to be here at all. He'll never tell that he's seen us. That pipe wrench is for that door on the potting shed."

Jake stood in the doorway, his hands fallen to his sides, the pipe wrench dangling from his left hand. "Whaaa, Mr. Duffer? Mr. Leonard? I ... I just came to fix the pipes. The neighbors said they thought they heard water running somewhere. You see anything?"

Jimmy let Noah take the lead. "Well, hi there, Jake. No. The water pipes seem to be tight as they can be right now. Good of you to come, though. Nice day, Jake. See you tomorrow!"

Jake nodded, gave them a half-frown, as if to say that he was one horsehair short of trusting their own motives, and slouched away from the door and down the hillside. They saw him give one glance back at the house before he pushed the dinghy out into the canal.

"That's the murderer. He was so frightened to see us he didn't even ask why we were here."

"How do you know it isn't me, Jimmy?"

Jimmy just shook his head and smiled sadly. "People I love can't commit murders." And as his gaze fell to the floor he saw something that jogged his memory. Large, dusty boot marks from the door to the bedroom, to the kitchen, and back out the door again. "Look, Noah. Those bootmarks weren't there when we came in. They're his"

"Of course. He's a careless, worthless bastard."

"He may be much more. Don't you remember?"

"What are you talking about?"

"The police report. They gave me a copy and I showed it to you last week. The only sign of a visitor after the murder was muddy, man-sized boot marks from the door to Fawn's body and back again out to the driveway."

"There could be any number of big men with muddy boots."

"The police must see these."

"One of their own made then, and we're not supposed to be here."

"Let's clean up our own mess, get out, and find some way to get some other authority back here again."

"There's something else I want to check on."

"Don't take time. We've been here too long already."

"Don't you ever yearn for the THRILL of getting caught?"

"You're becoming entirely too crazy for me."

"Crazy for a wholly loving person. She didn't hurt anyone. The kids all loved her. There was no malice in her soul---ever. Jake Sutherland has no motive for this."

"I'm looking at big footprints that we ought to know more about."

"And I'm going into Fawn's bedroom for a minute."

Noah felt his heart pounding, and he tried to pull himself together. The last time he had been in this house he had experienced the sweetest beauty his soul had ever known. Now this great memory was kindled with fear and wonder and hope that something he would see or hear would tell him how this wonderful friend had been so hurt. He gazed at the soft watercolors framed lovingly in lightly stained wood, surrounding the room. Her bed was draped with a quilt of pastel silk scarves sewn together with a pale pink ribbon over a frosty embroidered bed skirt. Pale, jonquil-colored curtains cascaded from the casement windows. The smell of jasmine and eucalyptus. A spotless room, save for the boot marks which came in at the door and retraced themselves out again after leaving a few small clods of earth on the right side of the bed where Jake had knelt.

Noah felt faint. Her essence was all around: her mood, her love, and her joy.

"Is it a woman I love," he breathed to himself, "or is it womanhood? This woman was all any man could ever hope for, no one ever really had taken her for his own, and now she is gone, hideously gone, slain by a maniac with no thought for her wholesome, gentle gift to the world. We've got to find him and stop his evil. There was nothing material to steal here, just her life. This murderer has to be the most twisted soul in the world."

"It's time, Noah,"

"Coming, Pal," reluctantly.

"How are we going to bring the police here again?"

"Admit that we were already here for some papers that we couldn't find for the next Middlestates session. We'd like to revisit the place to get them, and ask if they would come along so that the neighbors won't get suspicious."

"Good. Leave the door unlocked."

"Why?"

"Jake did."

*   *   *

That evening Lucy sat at her kitchen table reviewing the first paragraphs her students had submitted, scanning them for class placement before grading them. In most cases their placement in General, Regents, or Honors English were valid. On the topic, "An Event in My Life I Would Like To Live Over," Joey Falconi of the G's wrote the following:

When I stule that there blue racing bike in brooklyn and I got cot I wud lik to have tuk it an put it undr my bed so's no one wud find it fur a long tim so's noone wud tak it bak agin an I wud stil hav it.

Joyce Smith of the R's wrote:

One of the times I liked in my life the best was when Shirley and me met these two boys who asked us out for root beer and we went to the A&W stand and they talked about there school. I would like to have not been so dumb and talked more and asked his phone number and maybe he would have asked me out again.

Lucy Pepitone of the H's wrote:

I would like to have one more class with Miss Whitney She was a beautiful person who made all we read seem very real to each one of us. I really felt as though I were living in Charlotte Bronte's time, as though I could feel the horror of the discovery of Mr. Rochester's mad wife. I felt as though I were on the deck of the Pequod when the white whale was sighted, and afterwards when Ahab held up the gold coin. One more lesson with Miss Whitney would be my wish for a time to live over again.

Lucy put aside the papers and held her head in her hands for awhile, then gazed sightlessly at the kitchen table top, her thoughts suspended, for she, too, could not think too precisely upon the tragedy that had been thrust upon her so abruptly at the beginning of her career, as she was placed so cruelly into the room and the position of this victim of some terrible kind of --- what was it--- a mistake, a plot, or a mad passion? There were, as yet, no known clues. The school had let the horror pass a day after the funeral, and only from time to time when duties that Fawn had handled in the department were found undone, when her students who needed college recommendations and had to find someone new to trust to write them came shyly in to beg a letter from another teacher did her memory reappear. The contemplation of the act of her murder was so dreadful that people had to push it back, out of the way of their everyday feelings.

Lucy rose to relieve her tension and poured herself a soft drink from the refrigerator, her mind wandering to the presence of Fawn Whitney. She had seen her photograph in last year's yearbook: large, almond-shaped eyes set low in a thin oval face, firm mouth and small upturned nose, hair swept back into a low bun at the nape of her neck. A handsome woman in a plain business suit with white open collar, small silver tear-drop earrings, lightly shadowed eyes, and a natural darkness under the high cheekbones. There was a kindness in her smile that was reflected in her students' accolades that gave to Lucy an inspiration so profound that she would remember it years later. The gentle name of Fawn---teacher emerita--- struck down in a prime of loveliness and kindness.

There was one more paper that she wanted to examine before she gathered up the work and prepared for bed. She had been looking forward to reading the manuscript that wide-eyed Harper Jaffee had "entrusted" to her. It was in its own manila folder, typed on heavy bond paper, entitled presumptuously enough, "The Raison D'Etre of Harper Jaffee."

This statement is only the first in a series of blunt truths from my pen. I am saddened and tormented by the insensitive manner in which most of my classmates regard each other. They seem to want only recognition for themselves---to be what they call POPULAR, which seems to have a good deal to do with looking well in expensive clothes, and making good grades to get into the right schools.

Hardly do I ever see a person either popular with classmates or praised by faculty for his altruism or kindness. I do not mean to say that I see none of these qualities about; rather that few seem to take note of them to any important degree. There seems no reason to compete for being the kindest or most altruistic.

I propose the following system to be instituted in the school at once: A certain number of "kindness" chits or coupons should be given to each student and teacher, and when an unsolicited favor is given, which the favored deems appropriately selfless, the giver shall be rewarded with a chit. Then, simply, the holders of the most chits at the end of the term should be recognized in some appropriate manner that reinforces their positive behavior. Hopefully, the practice can be discontinued when both students and teachers recognize the satisfaction one can gain simply from being kind to others, a Pavlovian experiment, if you will.

Lucy would have laughed at the pontifical tone, but there was something sad in Harper's earnestness as there was in his isolation. His audacious formality was seldom received warmly by either students or faculty. And that was the point. Had he felt warmth or tenderness from anyone, she would not be reading this hurt and anger in his writing. She was here to identify that pain and to ease it and to free him from himself somehow. A tall order. How does a teacher approach a student like this without soliciting inappropriate emotions, which exceed, even betray, the teacher-student relationship that must remain respectably distant? She could not tell, yet she must find a way.

*   *   *

Early the next morning Saul Razzler scheduled The Great Suppogue High School Trial of Karl Marx in his plan book. One of Saul's more imaginative students, Joe Lopez-Shapiro had suggested that the trial would be a "revelation for everyone in Suppogue."

Joe was the brightest student at Suppogue High, the most threatening to a conventional image of "smart student." When he passed James Duffer in the hall, Jimmy's facial spasm twitched, as he wondered what Joe was going to try next. Joe sat in Lucy Mackenzie's English Honors with three books open on his desk. One he was reading, one Lucy was reviewing, and one he used for notes from both of the others. Early in the semester when another student, cantankerous Bob Robinson, complained aloud about Joe's "reading" in class, the following exchange ensued:

"How come you let Joe get away with that, Miss Mackenzie?"

"When Joe stops pulling A's on all his tests, I'll ask him to close the extra book, Bob."

No one else ever challenged Joe or Lucy on the subject of Joe's classroom habits again. He loaned his own books to Lucy after he finished with them … from Nabokov to Kierkegaard.

So when Joe suggested to Saul that he arrange the trial, Saul listened, thrilled that a student was so dedicated. He had already astounded his social studies class by writing and producing a play about a utopian society among some aboriginal peoples of North America, a group who had supposedly populated Long Island before the American Indians. He called them simply, "Risers," because men, women, and children rose together at dawn each morning to plant, cultivate, and harvest their crops. All worked together except the old women who happily cared for the infants and the infirm. There were community meetings each full moon to plan the next month's work, and every night after a communal meal, there was singing and dancing.

Their lives were not particularly original, as lives in such communes go, but Joe had invented a climactic activity to make his little story unique. When all males reached the age of thirty, they were stunned by a rock, sacrificed to the god Izzo, boiled in a pot, and eaten by the rest of the clan. Males over thirty in that ancient time were considered to be too old to be of physical use to the community, but were still pretty enough to please the gods.

The practice was not as severe nor as frequently practiced as one might suppose. In those days only one male in twenty actually lived so long, what with rampant diseases, wild, voracious animals, and monthly tribal battles. So the lucky male who was thus dispatched was greatly celebrated, honored, and revered. They called him the Looki, or enchanted one, and in the year before his death, he was allowed to enjoy as many women of the tribe as he chose.

Still the tale was not so original, but one year the practice ended dramatically when one such Looki demanded not only young, beautiful women but also old hags and men alike for his pleasures. He went wildly mad, and before his lusts were satisfied, he had converted a baker's dozen of the young men to rape and sodomy and founded a new clan of pillaging nomads. Joe noted in his text with glee that this new clan populated the southern shore of Long Island, welcomed the Dutch settlers warmly, and were soon inbreeding with the Dutch. Their blood is to be found in some of the town's older residents, which he deigned to name in this first episode. He planned to write this legend into a musical comedy for an assembly program, if he could get the cooperation and the collaboration of the music department.

Such were Joe's interests anthropological that he and several of his friends also extolled the virtues of Socialism; and so when Saul's class in comparative government took on Marxism, and the John Birchers of the class threatened to walk out, Joe insisted that the good Karl be given a fair an honest trial.

After much research into the life of Karl and the histories of trials of famous communists, would-be communists, accidental communists, and, by suspicious association with altruism, even a few Christian martyrs, the class began the trial and continued for a week.

Both students and teachers were called upon to testify. Some historical and literary roles were assigned for the defense. Phyllis Slavin was called to play Simone de Beauvoir; Noah Leonard was to portray Henry Miller: Lucy, a Russian peasant: and the Owl Prince was asked to impersonate Lenin. Saul considered bringing in Jimmy Duffer as Joseph McCarthy for the prosecution, but then thought better of that casting.

Noah was carried away in the excitement of his cross-examination: "You say, Mr. Miller, that you and most of your friends support a socialistic philosophy," intoned Joe, the mock-serious defense attorney.

Having recently reviewed his dusty copy of Tropic of Capricorn, Noah replied, "Support, hell, EMBRACE. What the fuck do you know about the suffering of the downtrodden workers of the world of 1905 here in the 1950's anyway?"

Instead of the bedlam one might expect as the assistant principal fell into his role with gusto, the room went dead silent. Saul Razzler grew pale with fear as he thought of the effect Noah's words might have on the simpler souls sitting with open mouths. The students were amazed. Only one or two laughed quietly, but most were confused as to how they were expected to react. Joe, delighted with the progress of his examination, fell out of his role for the moment to instruct the audience.

"You see, the author, Mr. Miller, was often given to strong idioms of one kind or another, both in his stories and in his speech. May we proceed more discreetly now, Mr. Miller?"

The Come From Aways

Noah did not forget himself again, as he saw that many of the students had not taken his brief departure from acceptable teacher-talk as comic. He had a vision of Jimmy's nervous collapse at the hands of the Board of Education, The Veterans of Foreign Wars, and the D.A.R. He saw himself in court as his own defense attorney. He knew that in that kind of situation it would be difficult to find friendly witnesses. Even genius Joe would not be reliable. Joe, with all his intellectual panache, had his eyes cast toward Harvard, and he knew he needed faculty and administrative recommendation. Would Joe give up Harvard for Berkley in 1960? Not on his life.

Mr. Miller's witness for Karl Marx took on a decidedly pedestrian tone from that point onward.

Next called to the stand was the Owl Prince in the determined characterization of the Great Lenin. Nick had done his reading and was ready for Joe.

"The Great Marx speaks: 'I want all to have a share of everything and all property to be in common; there will no longer be either rich or poor; no longer shall we see one man harvesting vast tracts of land, while another has not ground enough to be buried in, nor one man surround himself with a whole army of slaves while another has not a single attendant; I intend that there shall only be one and the same condition of life for all.'"

"But do you not advocate violence to achieve these ends, Mr. Lenin?" Joe suggested.

"Our vision is, as Mr. Sartre has interpreted, most natural, as changing and as regenerative as nature. Nature is sometimes violent when it is necessary for some species to survive. Your own founding father states. 'Let the tree of liberty be refreshed from time to time with the blood of patriots and tyrants.'"

"Some of us do not understand nor care to remember those words of Thomas Jefferson, Mr. Lenin."

"But one must also remember," and Nick shook his brilloed head, "that the tyrant with the sword is followed by the historian with the sponge."

"Would you start a revolution here in this school, Mr. Lenin?" asked the bedeviled Joe.

"If they give me a room to hold it in."

"What kind of revolution would you plan, Mr. Lenin?"

"I'm good at peasant uprisings, but I can't find anyone who wants to be a peasant."

"I will, I will," offered Lucy. The judge, Sophie Tushwinkle, struck her gavel.

"If you could find more likely peasants, how would you begin?"

"We could call a hunger strike, but the cafeteria staff can't be trusted. They'll always sneak food to the kids."

"Your influence on the students in this school is notorious. The administration may now think that you are even more dangerous."

"Why don't you ask the students what they think of me and my Marx?"

Joe had asked Saul Razzler himself to play Karl Marx, and when called upon to defend himself, Saul recited the phrase, which nobody understood, "The general formula for the circuit of commodity capital is the following:

$$C1 - M1 - C \ldots P \ldots C1 \text{ then}$$
$$C - M - C \text{ yields } L \text{ and } M P$$

He scribbled the formula on the chalkboard and continued, "Commodities become Commodity Capital as the functional form of existence of the already valorized capital value that has arisen directly from the production process itself. If commodity production were carried out on a capitalist basis throughout the whole society, then every commodity would be from the start the element of a commodity capital …"

"Bravo, Bravo," shouted Lenin from his desk.

Phyllis, as De Beauvoir, read portions of Das Capital and made succinct comments about Marxian philosophical integrity and Marx's religious devotion to humankind. She introduced the group to Kantean Marxism which "assumes that socialism is a moral objective determined by the conscience in the face of our capitalist reality." Her presentation was later said to have cinched the case for Karl, but before Joe was to end the trial, at least one witness had to add some verisimilitude to the performance, a witness against Karl Marx totally scripted, Roy Jerko from Peoria appeared, a second performance from the Owl Prince:

"I, Roy Jerko from Peoria, Iowa come to tell you all that you sound like New Yorkers and some are just a little bit pinko if not downright left handed and maybe just a little bit slippery handed too and that I am from the Great American center and maybe a little bit to the right of center too, and I cannot stand to hear you talk with such great levitation of what you plan to do with your innocent young fillies and rams. No, ah, chicks and studs … ah, I nearly forgot myself, boys and lassies, that's right. If we had these little darlings in good, wholesome farm country, we could just put them out into a great big healthy pasture to romp and play and then bring them in and let them listen to Oral Roberts and Billy Graham and GREAT IKE EISENHOWER'S SPEECHES and they'll never listen to these pinko teachers again or sniff your rexograph fluid that is a fluid prepared by the communists of New York to numb young minds and make them open for communist influence in the classroom, for this poison from Karl Marx who wants to overthrow the entire American system of government. How dare you equate the patriot Thomas Jefferson with such a scoundrel? Off with your heads!" The Owl Prince scraped and bowed with several flourishes amid crescendos of laughter, retiring reluctantly from his second stellar act.

Lucy made a very nervous peasant. She was agreeable to everything that Joe suggested about her love for the young, passionate Trotsky, working hard from his cell in Minsk to convert the field laborers and factory workers to follow the bolshevism of her saint, and how he and the philosophy had transformed her life.

"All this and ya not een Chuish?" from Noah.

On Friday the jury of students voted unanimously to acquit.

Three days later the school newspaper, The *Pontovecchio*, ran the headlines: KARL MARX ACQUITTED OF CRIMES AGAINST HUMANITY. The next morning the small tabloid found its way to a seat on the Long Island Railroad, which seat the President of the Suppogue Chapter of the American Legion took to ride to his work in Brooklyn.

That evening the school board president received a call: "What the hell's going on at your school, Max?"

"Why what do you mean, Bill?"

"I got hold of this here school paper that says Karl Marx isn't guilty... and it was sponsored by Saul Razzler and the whole damn Jew social studies department."

"What paper, what Karl Marx? What does he teach?"

*   *   *

When Jimmy Duffer's phone rang the next morning, the good man was found to be at his station by, or rather under, the Venetian blind. He had learned after his last accident to support the blind with his shoulder so that the jangling of the phone, even at this early hour, did not catch him with his nose unprotected; rather since he had to lean backward with one arm stiff against the floor for support, he lost his balance and sat down very hard on the tile The phone continued, insistently. Dr. Duffer, on his knees, reached for the receiver and fell back against the wall.

"Hello, Jimmy, Max Reynolds here. Look, Jim, Bill Prior is pretty upset by what he calls Communist infiltration into your social studies department. Seems he saw the last school newspaper about some kind of trial you had." A new facial twitch began in Jim's left jaw, "I haven't seen the paper, of course." Silence from Jim. "Well, anyway, Jim, the paper said something about Karl Marx being innocent, you know, a whitewash kind of thing, I guess, and in these days you know that kind of thing is dangerous, yessir, and then Bill's kid is in Tony Nappa's class and Bill suspects that Tony IS a communist."

"Tony? of all people! What gives him that idea?" Jim was twitching again. Tony Nappa, one of his best teachers, who never sends anyone to the office, who has a perfect attendance record, who never says a word of criticism in faculty meetings, and who even refused to join the union?

"Well, Bill always tries to get his kid to find out what the teachers ARE---I mean what religion and political party they subscribe to, and when he asks Sammy about Mr. Nappa, Sammy just gets very nervous and won't say a word. The other day when Bill asked him again, asked if he ever had any suspicions about him, the kid said, 'Oh, once I WAS very suspicious, but I know now that he's a Republican because he told us that he was, but I'm not supposed to talk about Mr. Nappa's politics because he won't ever let me out of his class if I do...he'll keep me locked in there all day!' Now what kind of trick is THAT, Jim? What the devil is Tony Nappa DOING in there?"

"I don't know, Max, but believe me, I'll get right on to it right away. I'll get right to the bottom of the whole thing and you'll hear from me immediately today, yes, today. Today I'll call and let you know. No, sir, I don't want anything queer like that in my school."

"Now, don't get upset, Jim," Max saw that he had to proceed carefully. "We both know that Bill Prior can get a little heavy on politics sometimes, and we both know that his kid is a sad little sop who is so scared of his father that he might say anything he's forced into, so don't go to Tony with accusations. Just see what you can find out indirectly, O.K.?"

"Sure thing, Max. I'll get right on it. Don't worry about a thing, Max."

"I'll call you back at home this evening, Jim. Have a good stiff drink, and I'll call you about eight."

A sigh emerged from the doorway.

"If you're finished on the phone, I have some records for you to see, Mr. Duffer."

Kathy Blythe stood shyly, waiting. Jimmy still sat on the floor with his back against the wall.

"Are you hurt? Can I help you?" Kathy breathed, with very little meaning or discernible emotion, a prototype of the beautiful office robot, she padded slowly across the office and bent over Jimmy, her arms outstretched. Waves of Prince Matchabelli poured over Jimmy, his eyes glazed over as a blur of two mounds of breasts lightly covered by a pale blue cashmere sweater fell three inches from his mouth. Her long fingers slid under his armpits. He couldn't see her beautiful knees; she was too close and braced against the desk. "Here, let me help you. Whatever happened? Did you hit your head on the wall? I'll get the nurse again. Oh, Mr. Duffer, you do worry me so very much."

He was on eye level with her now, her gorgeous violet eyes with long brown lashes, her soft pink lips, his right hand free to caress what he knew was less than an inch from his side, at this never-to-be-repeated moment.

"There now," he was at his desk chair.

"I just slipped on the floor when the phone rang and ...didn't take the time to get up, a very important call. I'm… fine. No problem, no problem at all," he began and was furious with himself. He tried to hide his head behind the filing cabinet while ostensibly reaching for a paper on the shelf.

"Oh, I'm so glad to be here to help, Dr. Duffer. Please buzz me if there's anything, anything I can do."

"Thank you, Kathy, I will. I know I can count on you, I really do. I don't know what I would do without you, Kathy."

It was Kathy's turn to blush. "Thank you so very, very much, Dr. Duffer," she quickly exited.

Jimmy was happier than he had been in months. She blushed! There's something there. God! Maybe she does care a little. Maybe I AM more than an authority figure. Do I dare go further? What if Selma suspected anything? It could ruin me--- no it would save me. Save my mind from this crazy school. If they fired me, I could leave with Kathy and start a new life. We could open our own school...she as Dean, I as Principal. We would be free, free of all this torture. Would she go? Do I dare? But I am mad, mad. No, he remembered a line from somewhere in a book, just terribly, terribly nervous.

*   *   *

The following afternoon Tony Nappa, in the sartorial splendor of his exquisite Italian suit, strode briskly down Corridor 2, eyes flashing blue fire, all six-feet four 190 pounds taunt with energy. He did not have all his wits about him. Those he had left behind in his classroom. For a man who lived so dangerously, Tony couldn't take the heat calmly. The commotion over Karl Marx had taken a peculiar turn. The superintendent had referred the entire matter to the PTA .The PTA President was none other than the school's Owl Prince, who had been elected at one of those meetings where all teachers were required to attend and only five parents showed up. With one eye in heaven and the other in the funnier place, Nick had devised a panel discussion for the next general meeting on "Sex, Politics, and Religion in the Classroom." Julius Martino, who came to school an hour early every day to read his Bible, was to handle religion. Lucy Mackenzie, whose nouveau interpretation of the Scarlet Letter was eliciting all sorts of perplexed reactions among the students and parents, would speak about sex, and Tony was asked to be the spokesperson for politics. Noah Leonard would chair this panel.

At this "free and open" presentation of the teacher's views, Tony was to demonstrate to all what a patriotic, loyal and upright American he really was. Lucy would focus on the morality in such novels of scandal as *Scarlet Letter and Catcher in the Rye*. A group of irate but chicken-hearted parents had burned both books last year in a symbolic private ceremony behind the Baptist Church.

The parents could ask any questions of the panel members they wanted.

Tony was calling this arrangement a "dirty little tokenistic trick." Why couldn't his accuser come directly to him? Dr. Duffer had muttered things about the school's protecting itself. Duffer's afraid of what I will say, face to face, Tony knew. He thinks his miserable, clumsy apologies are subtle and clever, but no one understands anyone else around here. He thinks I'll perform more discreetly in public. I hope they do question me hard. I'm more than ready. Duffer will be damn sorry he wouldn't let me handle this my way.

He strode into the open door of Noah Leonard's office where Noah stood hunched behind his desk with a faraway stare.

"Noah, do you know anything about this panel scheme?"

"Panel? Oh, yes. Jim mentioned it to me this morning. Sounds like some fun."

"FUN!" Tony exploded. "You're the moderator, and you can afford some fun. You don't have to worry about the kids running home from class to mommy and daddy with ridiculous stories."

"Tony, who are you trying to shark? Everyone knows how you tease those poor kids with your little commie acts."

"Little acts? MOTIVATING...like no one else in this crazy place ever tried. That's the reason some of the weaker kids can't take it. They're so used to sitting in a stupor, listening to lessons that sound like recorded announcements that they go into withdrawal fits when someone gives them an opportunity to open their minds and think. But my God, then the status quo might be disturbed and all hell break loose. What could the dangerous Mr. Nappa be doing in there? And Mr. Razzler? Holding a trial in a classroom? Never heard of such a thing. Do you know that one parent called Saul and screamed, didn't he know that the American government had hanged Karl Marx in 1940 for selling the atom bomb to the Communists?

And we have to justify ourselves to this crowd by fawning around in a silly little tea-and-crumpets panel discussion?"

"Ask the Owl Prince about it, Tony."

"I'm afraid of the Prince."

"You're kidding."

"He doesn't speak the language. He's from Calabria."

"He will tell you why the panel."

"Maybe at this point I don't want to know why. How come Lucy got dragged into this?"

"Balance. She's also the only woman who would do it, we had to have another department represented, she's the only woman who will work with the Prince, and she's had some difficulty with a parent about The Scarlet Letter."

"O.K. Noah, I guess I can't get out of this so quickly. I hope my tenure is still good."

"Are you now or have you ever been a member of the Communist Party?"

"For forty-five class minutes a year only."

"You sex life?"

"Decidedly monogamous."

"Your daughters?"

"Still in training bras."

"Your son?"

"At seven he wants to be a bus driver. No complaints from neighbors."

"Your wife?"

"Still orders her housedresses from G.U.M., but her sports clothes are all Bloomingdale's."

"You could almost be President if you fixed that fancy vowel at the end of your name. Just hold off on the classroom dramatics till after the panel. I'm sure everything will be just groovy."

"Terrific. You sound like a tape of Duffer's closing remarks from a faculty meeting."

"That's why I'm here---to serve, Tony."

Tony shook his head disgustedly and turned away, still burning.

NIGGER-LOVING TEACHER
Chapter Nine

> *"...thou wilt quarrel with a man that hath a hair more or a hair less in his beard than thou hast. Thou wilt quarrel with a man for cracking nuts having no other reason but because thou hast hazel eyes. What eye but such an eye would spy out such a quarrel? Thy head is as full of quarrels as an egg is full of meat; And yet thy head hath been beaten as addle as an egg for quarreling."*
> Mercutio, *Romeo and Juliet*, by William Shakespeare

Honors English Eleven. A very big deal. Some of the greatest American writers here.

Moby Dick, Huckleberry Finn, The Scarlet Letter, Grapes of Wrath, Uncle Tom's Cabin, Let Us Now Praise Famous Men, Black Boy, The Autobiography of Frederick Douglas.

"Miss Mackenzie, why do we have all this crap from crazy liberal and nigger writers? Are we gonna read some real American lit-ra-ture before the year is out?"

"I don't understand."

"O.K. I'll spell it out for ya. In *Moby Dick* we spent too much time with that wild Indian Tash-te-go whats-his-name. Then in *Huck Finn* we read pages and pages about a nigger-lovin' kid who'd rather die than see that nigger caught. In *The Scarlet Letter* we see that cat Hawthorne fall in love with his own character, that lady who was dumb enough to get herself knocked up by a lily-livered priest, and then wasn't smart enough to tell and get the old man busted. Every book after those has been the same. Those poor slobs in *Grapes of Wrath* weren't men enough to get an education and find real jobs instead of wallowing about on the desert hoping someone would take pity on them and find them jobs picking somethin, and *Uncle Tom's Cabin*, what trash!

Do ya think those plantation owners really behaved like that? Nomam. They were gentlemen Englishmen who wouldn't harm ladies or children if their lives depended on it. The rest are about or by black writers who probably couldn't spell good enough to write so had someone write those books for them. My dad says we ought to be reading books like the Horatio Alger ones like he read, or *Little Men*, or maybe President Eisenhower's speeches. And what about poetry? Longfellow, we haven't even looked at, nor James Fenimore Cooper, nor some good political speeches like Henry Clay's or Patrick Henry's."

Lucy could see that Kurt Sutherland had taken some notes for this presentation. He had mentioned his father, the local chief of police. She must be careful to treat this outburst gently.

"The books we're studying have all been suggested and approved by the English Department here ... " she began. "If you and your father wish, you can get in touch with Dr. Perkins about your interests and see if he's agreeable to discussing changes in the curriculum. I'm not sure that others in the class entirely share your views, so why don't we have a little discussion now that you've raised some interesting questions."

"Hey, Miss Mackenzie, Kurt here represents a very personal point-of-view, if you know what I mean. That is, we don't all think like Kurt about the books."

"That's alright, Clark, we can work with all kinds of viewpoints here. After all, this is a literature class, not an indoctrination session," she responded to a more even-tempered student.

"Yea, Kurt's a Nazi."

Kurt rose from his seat, his scowl fixed determinedly on Ralph, the latest speaker. "You want to meet me outside, Ralph?"

"It's true," Ralph pursued, doggedly. "Miss Mackenzie, Kurt and his gang want to kill all the Jews, Negroes, and anyone who likes them. His mom got killed by a black man, Miss Mackenzie, and that's what drove him crazy."

Kurt was on him in a second. The girls shrieked, and the boys dived for the strugglers. Kurt was pulled away by several heftier lads as he snarled and wrestled, stronger than any of them, and broke away to land on Ralph again. Suddenly Noah streaked into the room and jumped on the pair as Kurt was beginning to beat the indiscreet Ralph on the head. He quickly overpowered Kurt and laid him out on the floor with his foot on his chest. Now Noah looked quizzically at Lucy.

"We were having a little discussion about the English curriculum," Lucy shrugged, "and things got very personal."

"On your feet, Mr. Sutherland," ordered Noah. "Let's take a long walk." Kurt rose feebly from the floor. "And one of you boys please escort Ralph to the nurse's office. I'll take care of this gentleman, Miss Mackenzie. I hope you can proceed with your discussion more peacefully with us gone."

Lucy saw them walk outside to the field beyond the parking lot. Kurt, walking with bowed head, and Noah, gesturing animatedly. He's going to try to walk off Kurt's anger, thought Lucy.

The class was too broken up to try anything organized for the rest of the period. "Just try to read if you can," suggested Lucy, "or you can talk quietly at your seats. We'll try to work this out reasonably when we're all together again."

"You think those two can talk reasonably, you're mistaken," Jeff Collier offered.

"We'll have to try, Jeff."

"Kurt's even into Klan ceremonies. Last year it was animal sacrifices."

Lucy gasped. "But how can he be? His father is the chief of police."

There were shrugs and smiles exchanged.

"And Ralph just likes to fight him. Ralph doesn't know when to keep his mouth shut. But Kurt doesn't have any friends in this class, Miss Mackenzie. His gang is over in the next town, where he usually isn't spotted so easily. They're quite a group. But he's really smart, and that's part of the trouble."

The class opted to talk quietly among themselves, and Lucy went to the back of the room to stack books in the shelves and work off her nervous frustration.

"You couldn't have stopped that, Miss Mackenzie," one of the girls suddenly spoke out, as if she were reading Lucy's thoughts. "There's just some things a teacher can't predict. Kurt's just crazy. We all know that. We feel sorry for him...up to a point. But then we have to stop him from hurting other people. Ralph was stupid. He should just keep his mouth shut around Kurt."

"Yea, you don't antagonize a maniac," put in Jill Rowland. "Don't feel bad, Miss Mackenzie. Not even Miss Whitney could do anything with Kurt." And then, as though on second thought, "Especially not Miss Whitney."

"Thanks so much. You must know what I was thinking, and you make me feel much better. You know, I think Kurt must miss so much in life now because of his tragedy. Ralph shouldn't have blurted it out like that, but it does help us to understand his anger. You don't think, do you, that his father feels as he does?" And immediately after she spoke, she realized that she had been unwise. Do not engage the students in a discussion of local adult affairs, ever, she knew.

"I don't think so, Miss Mackenzie. Mr. Sutherland is a very dignified man. He's the Chief of Police, you know. He wouldn't ever act like Kurt does. Kurt used to say the same kinds of things to Miss Whitney to upset her. Mr. Sutherland will be very upset about today, if he finds out."

"Thank you all. You've made a terrible day a little more bearable. And now, have a great weekend."

The students rose happily, shoving their books into their bags, and leaving the room excitedly, chatting about the school dance that night and the game on Saturday. Lucy saw Noah standing by the door.

"What a way to prepare yourself for a strenuous night ahead," he chuckled.

"Oh, I'd forgotten all about it," sighed Lucy. The big PTA panel is upon us. But first, what did you do with Kurt?"

"He's a tough kid. I hated to have to overpower him, but in an emergency, I guess that's not a time for pacifists. He's strong for a seventeen-year-old and so crazed that poor Ralph there didn't stand a chance; and he told me that they were all on him at one point. What's your version?"

Lucy reviewed the altercation.

"He was unable to show any remorse. Said you mocked him and invited the class to do him in."

"I'd really be happy to have you speak with some other members of the class about it."

"I don't think I have to do that, Lucy. Kurt's obviously a troubled boy. I told him that I was going to have to speak to his father, and I'll try to discover how best to proceed. He promised to refrain from violence, but only if you and the kids stayed off him. I told him that promise wasn't good enough. He seemed to understand my position. Didn't seem to blame me for playing the heavy, but he still justified his idea that you and the whole English Department were dealing in some kind of necromancy. He calls it 'liberal poison.' Here we are again. We may see some of this kind of thing come out tonight at the meeting if Kurt's attitude reflects rumblings in the community."

"It's 1959, Noah. I know a good many people my parents' age who think that Senator Joe McCarthy is a great hero. They don't see the sinister, devious side of the hearings. Was any one of those people deserving of prosecution?"

"On the grounds of attempting to overthrow the government of the United States? No. As far as I know all of the defendants McCarthy grabbed were the most famous personalities in the arts so that he could grandstand and play the great white knight. Joe McCarthy wanted to be President."

"He sneered too much."

"Yes, and eventually enough thinking people saw him for what he was. He became his own worst enemy. No. The McCarthy hearings were an 100% American spectacle...all the glitter and glamour were there: Hollywood, Broadway, Harvard, the Jews, the intellectuals, the stars, and the people that all the good, simple, moral men and women want to identify as evil so that they can tie themselves to a crusade to defend the American Way of Life with pure hearts and a just cause. It was a classic battle, and had very little to do with communism. Socrates was a victim of a similar kind of purge. Get the guys we envy and can't ever understand."

"But aren't the American Communists supported by the Soviet Union … at all?"

"Yes, I think they are … the officers get money. They provide PR for the USSR, but I don't know how much that means in substance. The American Commies are still the idealists, real different from the Soviet brand. Of course they might involve themselves in a little espionage, but for the most part the Russians have all our secrets anyway. They have more effective moles within our system that they can manage more directly than they can any of these intellectuals who busy themselves with club communism. The Russians loved McCarthy. He showed them how scared we were, and perhaps how vulnerable. And our government permitted the jerk to go out and grab some of the most harmless artists, people who had no idea that they were contributing to a national threat."

"How do we interpret all this for the kids?"

"Leave that to social studies. You're having enough trouble with Huck and Jim."

"Oh, so you heard about all of that? Well, if I had trouble with Mark Twain, think what will happen when we work with Frederick Douglas and Richard Wright. How do all these issues get tied together anyway?"

"Mr. Kurt, here, seems to see that liberal spirit of many artists, especially those whom Joshua Perkins chooses to have you teach, supports the cause of Negro rights. Reading these writers touches a frazzled nerve in Kurt. Ask Joshua if you can introduce some writers who look at life a little differently. Give them Frost's "Two Tramps in Mudtime" or some of Ayn Rand's stuff. There are certainly enough reactionary writers in American literature to keep him happy for the rest of the year. Give the kids alternative selections. They don't have to read everything you like to read. Let them thrash out the ideas in small groups. Maybe we are too heavy on the liberal line here."

"I though you see yourself as liberal, Noah."

"I see myself as a wannabe intellectual. Don't ever tie me down to a philosophy. I don't want to have to accept anyone else's dogma. There's room in a gentle world for all kinds of thinking."

"What are you going to be doing tonight? Do you know that this conversation has me scared to death about what may happen at the meeting?"

"I'm going to be the moderator. Don't worry. I'll try to deflect the most troublesome questions. The less you say, the better. Remember, we are speaking of our students as impressionable children. As far as the parents are concerned, they're all brilliant and sensitive. We do best to agree. We do not teach the books, we help the students to understand them. None of the literary authors are advocating anything political, social, or sexual. Nothing except human sympathy and understanding. You support the literary choices of your department because those books help the students to understand human behavior. You are oh so sad to learn that Johnny Simpleton misunderstood what you were trying to explain. If he would only come to you after class, you would be delighted to discuss the matter. That's the line. Anything more you refer to Joshua or to me or to Jimmy. Most of the parents who speak just want the opportunity to sound off in public. But we'll see. We may get a few impassioned idealists out there, but my guess is that the ferment, if there is any, is underground. They don't want to go public. It would weaken their cause, to risk losing a round, and this is our turf, and we're ready for them, and they know it. How about some dinner?"

Lucy blanched. She was drained from the events of the class, and the intensity of the conversation. She was scarcely ready for a reckless social proposal.

"Aren't you going home?"

"Oh, don't worry. Marge is in the city with friends, and I just thought I'd like some company. If you like, we can find a third party to make the hour respectable."

Lucy recoiled from the ridicule, but was provoked enough to want to call his bluff. "That won't be necessary. If the arrangement doesn't bother you, why should it bother me? But Dutch?"

"O.K., Dutch it is. Meet you at the side door in, say, twenty minutes?"

Friends? Anyway, he went to lunch with Mina last week too. I saw them together at the Greeks. Now is this different? We don't have that blameless a history, but what's the protocol for this? Should I be worrying about protocol? After all, we're colleagues. But he's my superior here, so that adds another dimension. Oh, stop this, she cautioned herself finally. In the context of this last encounter, dinner together seemed practical sense. And we need to discuss the program tonight. All right, silly, so you know he admires you. Go as a friend. Forget the first night after the swim. We were both stupid that night. Start over.

* * *

"Did you know that I had dinner with your parents a few weeks ago," Noah began over clams. Lucy was genuinely surprised.

"No. They never mentioned it at all. Funny the subject never came up. What on earth was the occasion?"

"Jim and Selma, that is Jim, is an old friend of your father from Navy days. The two of them just realized that they were living twenty miles from each other. In fact, Jim found out through you...your name when you were interviewed rang a bell, and he phoned Peter and invited them to dinner."

"I remember his asking me about my father at my interview. What an amazing coincidence. How did it go?"

"Wonderfully. I guess Marge and I were invited as buffers in case there was some awkwardness after all those years, but we weren't needed. Seems the women, especially, grew to really appreciate each other, your mother and Selma, that is. You look surprised now."

"My mother doesn't make friends so easily. Now I'm curious about the conversation."

"You mean to ask, did it involve you?"

"Of course I wonder if my name ever came up, especially since I was the catalyst of the occasion."

"As a matter of fact, you, or rather the subject of your adoption, did occupy some time that night. It seems that your mother wanted to be discreet about it, but after she realized that the audience was warm and accepting, she grew easy with the subject and relaxed. Jimmy's an awfully kind, caring person, and your Dad's a real trump."

"I wonder that no one said anything to me, but then I don't see my parents often these days, and they may have found it awkward to speak of seeing my boss in a social way," Lucy was perplexed.

"Jimmy's roots are in Canada too. He was raised in Newfoundland. Seems he had a lot of pain in his early years and has broken all ties with relatives there, but he seems to want to resolve some family mysteries, so we may go back up there together next spring."

"That's exciting. Where will you go?"

"Jim's from St. Johns, way over on the East Coast. I'm selfish about the idea. I really want to see that country. Cold, stark, rock hewn land, so different from anything I've seen. I'd like to see how people live up there and learn how they think."

"I'm not from so exotic a land," Lucy mused, as though in answer to his next question. "The orphanage I first remember was in Nova Scotia, but that was just for a few months, I think. I remember one visit from my mother."

"What do you remember about her?" Noah asked kindly, as he saw that she wanted to talk.

"I just remember a beautiful woman with dark red hair sitting with me for awhile and then hugging me and kissing me good bye. It's like a dream, really, and after she didn't come back, and after everyone kept telling me that I would have to stay with them until she came, I started to hate her. No one ever offered an explanation, an answer. No one seemed to know, even. And then they told me that she wanted me to go to Connecticut...that she would meet me there. Of course she never came there either, and it seemed that the people in the home there used me to help with the younger children. I never knew whether I was sent there on her orders or their wishes. Anyway, when Peter and Laura came for a baby, they looked so kind and loving, and I wanted so to belong to somebody. I became very aggressive."

"That kind of life in an orphanage doesn't shape a docile child."

"Maybe I'm a little hard that way---a survivor. I think my mother, Laura, sees that in me. That's why we don't always get along. My father sees me as someone to always forgive and protect. My mother ... well, she's regretful that she couldn't shape me like she thinks she could have a child of her own, or a baby she could have adopted from the nursery."

"And how do you feel now about the adoption?"

"Very grateful to them for taking me. They educated me, clothed me, gave me all kinds of social opportunities. And my father loves me so much. My mother seems to want more from me than I can ever give. I'll never be like her, and I guess that's the problem. No matter how much tension there is between a mother and a daughter ... or a father and a son, for that matter, the mother can see some of herself in the daughter, if it's her own, and remember what life was like when she was her age. My mother can't do that, and I can't imagine what her life was like when she was my age, nor can I think that I'd ever want to be like she was then. And that doesn't help her very much, as a mother. I guess there's a part of parenting that has to do with identifying with your child that is both painful and soothing---that life is lived over through your children, and that part is missing for my mother. The same-sex parent must have it stronger than the other-sex parent. Dad can love me without understanding me, as a needy little girl he can imagine me to be. What Mother sees is my resilience, and my boldness, and my willingness to shove her damnable propriety aside to unmask the truth about people."

"How did you learn so much so young?"

"I had good teachers and I saw a lot of sadness in that orphanage. Do you know there were a lot of children who were returned when parents, both birth parents and adoptive parents, couldn't handle them?"

"We don't hear much about those cases."

"Do you know what that does to the children? Do you know what happens to these children when they reach maturity?"

"You mean that they're out there, here, in the world, with all that rejection and pain to work off on society?"

"You bet. And they must form the largest pool of drug and alcohol addicts and criminals and prostitutes. I have heard of rare cases who became obsessed with social salvation work, who stay with the church and work with the homes and try to make the lives of other children better. I don't know what produces that sort, whether it is their body chemistry, or a special gift from the gods."

"Like you?"

"No, not like me. I was saved. I was lucky, and I'm thankful."

"Are you Catholic?"

"Yes."

"What kind of Catholic?"

"I think I'm the right kind. The kind that questions everything."

"Did the Jews kill Jesus?"

She finally had to smile. "Now what in the world does it matter? He was crucified like all the other criminals. If it hadn't been the Jews, it would have been someone else. If Christ had been a Moslem, the Moslems would have killed him. If he had been Roman, the Romans would have fed him to the lions. Christ was too dangerous a man for any group to tolerate."

"I love you."

"Stop it. You're being outrageous." Her head dropped.

"I'm utterly serious. You are amazing."

"Yes. And how many others do you love?"

"Damnit, don't spoil it."

"Spoil what, a fantasy?"

"Now I see you're not as grownup as I thought."

"And what does that insult mean?"

"It means that you don't understand that we can love more than one person at a time, and it isn't bad, and don't blame my ideas on my Jewishness because thousands of men have known the truth of what I say, from all walks of life and religions and philosophies. You are beautiful inside and out and I love you and that's that."

112

"Thousands of men ..." she couldn't complete the thought, "That is a wonderful freedom from sexuality that you're talking about."

"Sorry, but try reading some of your more liberated women's writings on the subject, like Phyllis's Simone de Beauvoir, and come back and we'll talk more about this another day. Right now we've got to get to school. The PTA awaits."

She hardly noticed that he had grabbed the check and was off with it. His audacity and his strength of commitment frightened her. Her head was swimming with contradictions she could not reconcile.

She was tough, yes, she knew she was resilient and hard, but she had counted on several maxims that seemed to her so significant. That people needed to be faithful to each other, to be utterly honest and steadfast and secure. That married men didn't go around declaring love to a number of women outside their families. And now she had to be put on the stand in front of a community of irate parents with this man in charge.

She was sorry that she had left her car back at the school and had to ride the three miles back with him. What was left to say? And the more distressing thought: was he really laughing at her naiveté? Was he merely having fun at her expense? She was more shaken now than she had been during the scene with Kurt. Why did all this have to happen in one day? And how was she to get through the evening? She felt utterly alone.

They drove to the school wordlessly. At least, she reasoned, he did not taunt her. What was he thinking now? At least his silence meant that he was serious about something that they had said. This dinner had been a mistake. She had probably said too much about herself. He had wanted her to know about his evening with her parents. Was he demonstrating his power over her with this knowledge of her life?

Oh, she was tired of trying to think it through. And why was he worth all this consideration? He shouldn't even be a part of her life right now. If good Sam Rose had been the right sort of companion, if she could become involved with someone younger, someone unattached, someone with ideas more like hers, it would all be so much easier. What if her parents knew that she had dinner with Noah, alone? Someone in their own generation, who had dinner with them, accompanied by his wife? Her mother would swoon.

The long table for the panel was decorated with baskets of flowers and appointed with pitchers of ice water and glasses and white place cards identifying the speakers. The Owl Prince appeared in a suit, peculiar attire for the Prince whom Lucy had never seen in anything but his artist's frock coat. He strutted and stomped across the stage, making certain that all the arrangements were complete.

Julius Martino was already in his chair when Lucy reached the stage, his curly dark locks sparkling in the footlights, his social studies text and Bible stacked on the table in front of him, at the ready.

Lucy sat down nervously beside him. "I think you're supposed to be on the other side of the moderator, Lucy," he offered politely.

"Well, I can sit here for a little, can't I? I want to ask you what you know about all this, and how you happened to be chosen. I'm not completely certain why I'm here."

"If you want to know what I really think," began Julius in a querulous voice, "I think they asked the youngest, most innocent of us to be up here. I think that the administration is looking to present its faculty without a history."

"But what about Tony Nappa?"

"He's the perpetrator. He has to be here. He's the one that started all the commotion with his lesson on communism when he pretends to be a communist and scares some of the more simpleminded kids about what he really believes. Kids don't listen very carefully. They just take a few words out of a lesson and interpret them the way they want. Often they think just the opposite of what we're trying to teach them. Tony's a terrific teacher---for college students, maybe, but high school kids aren't so complex. Most of them don't understand irony. That's why he's in trouble here. Little Sammy Prior went home and told his dad that Tony locked them in the classroom, and Bill Prior's furious. He really took it out on Jimmy, I hear. So Tony has been asked to explain himself tonight. Noah is here to deflect some of the rancor, and I hope he's successful."

"Thanks for filling me in, pal," Lucy shook Julius' cool hand. "Where'm I sitting?"

"On the other side of Noah. Be careful. But I know you'll say the tactful thing, Lucy. You're circumspect."

"Thanks again for the vote of confidence, Julius. I dunno---I've never been through a tribunal like this. Why didn't we refuse? But it all sounded so harmless when Noah first told me about it."

"That's his job, to make things like this sound harmless, and he's good at his job."

In other words, to deceive, thought Lucy. Just as he was working on her emotions. No way, mister. I won't play into your hands any longer. Just don't come to me again with your bold declarations.

The Owl Prince bent over Lucy.

"The time is out of joint.

O cursed spite; that ever I was born to set it right."

"Just to give me confidence?"

"A piece of cake, my love." He glanced over his shoulder at the audience with one hand still supporting his weight on the table. "Ah, here comes the goddess of love, Kathy Blythe with her latest fling, Mr. Franchot Smiddling, owner of six used car lots from Amityville to the Outer Moriches. Why would she want to bring such a date to a droll old PTA meeting?"

Julius overheard. "His son is in my American history class, Nick. He's the one with the trouble over evolution."

"Geewhillikers. We should have had the science department here for that one. Are all the American counter-cultures coming out of the woodwork tonight in our modest auditorium? I'm surprised no one called the press."

"Don't bet they didn't, offered Noah, arriving in place. "Look your most respectable, Mr. Bruno, or we'll see blood on the stage before we're through."

"I'm out of original lines," spoke the Prince modestly. "I used them all on my sixth period class. I hope you're warmed up for this Noah."

"Bring 'em on, bring 'em on."

The audience was filling up with a grande melange of teachers and parents, some mothers still in hair curlers. One woman had brought a Great Dane who sat peacefully in a side aisle, pointing at the stage.

"Isn't there some rule about animals in the auditorium?" queried Julius.

No one thought that deserved an answer.

Tony Nappa strode briskly to his seat beside Lucy, his eyes glowing, his silk suit perfectly pressed, his grimace obvious. A murmur passed among the crowd. The participants fell silent. It was time to get to business.

Lucy wondered where the curlered moms were going after this show that they had to prepare for so unsightfully. The supermarket monsters. A piece of the South Shore culture that drew ridicule from the sophisticates of the more affluent communities in the north and east.

She spotted some students in the crowd. There was Harper Jaffee, alone, as far as she could tell, and of course Simon Finch. Next to Simon was Bob Robinson, and there with his parents was little Sammy Prior. The movers and the shakers. Could she see Kurt? Would he dare to come out tonight? Yes, by golly, there he was standing in the back by a pillar. She didn't know his father. Noah will. She saw Joshua Perkins, met his eyes, as he sent her a warm smile. Over to his left was Phyllis Slavin. Oh, Phyllis, how I need to talk to you --- maybe tonight. You have all the answers, Phyllis. And I really need some now.

Noah was rapping with the gavel. "Good evening ladies and gentlemen. For this evening's er ... ah ... program (a short breathy sigh/laugh from somewhere in the audience) we have with us three of our most respected teachers from Suppogue High to present to you their stories of problematic classroom situations, which have puzzled many of us. We have asked the participants to be as candid and fair as they can be with you. We must all appreciate that their high level of academic preparation permits THEM to understand complex texts far better than you or I, and that some of US may be puzzled about the more subtle interpretations THEIR EXPERTISE permits.

"But tonight I have asked them to try to reach out and help us understand some of the more challenging concepts they deal with in the classrooms in this high school, one of the most AMERICAN of high schools in which I have ever been privileged to serve."

"I don't believe him," breathed Tony in Lucy's ear. "Will they swallow all that?"

"Because our time is naturally so limited tonight, and because this is so public an occasion, we ask that you hold your questions until everyone on the panel is finished with their presentations, and then to keep your questions as succinct as possible. We also ask that you limit yourselves to ONE question for each speaker so that as many of the audience as possible will have a chance to speak in the fifteen minutes we have for questioning."

"Good. Good. Good, so far," muttered Tony. "He's being careful. But where's the riot police?"

Lucy thought about how they all looked up there. She hadn't planned in advance what she was going to wear this evening. That morning all that she had considered was dressing for her classes. She was wearing the colors that she knew kept the kids alert in the classroom: a dress of bright greens and yellow, but the full skirt made it easy for her to adjust her legs under the table. She hadn't been on a stage in this position before an audience of parents and students before. She remembered not to cross her legs and keep her feet together and off to one side, but this meant an unnatural concentration on her posture, and she wanted to focus on her words, so she slid one toe back of the front leg to her chair. I don't care how awkward this looks, she thought. I'm not going to worry over appearances and hope that they concentrate on what I'm saying.

Julius was first with his explanation about the religious question. He took the matter head on, a relief to many, for Julius was irreproachable, his devotion to holy writ assured. The community was at least fifty percent Roman Catholic, the newest members of the community, with a few Bavarians and Irish Catholics of the older stock. He made several references to Genesis, then diverted to the Epic of Gilgemish and explained that it echoed many of the same notions he found in Genesis. Then he worked around Darwin to make his theories seem to agree with the days, months,

The Come From Aways

and years of the ancient prophets. "So we really have little to differ over," he concluded happily. "The noises that came out of the Scopes trial were more the swords of political warfare than the thunder of religious battle the press wanted to make of it. Our students suffer now from their forefather's misconceptions. Darwin's book was a collection of theories. There is still so much we don't understand about the formation of the Universe, let alone our finite world. We try to show students what we think may have happened, what we think the ancients may have meant as well as what our scientists are trying to discover. The ideas in both sources don't have to contradict each other. In many cases we're just reading different words for the same occurrences. God never has to take a back seat to science anywhere in our curriculum, so far as I can see."

Several hands shot up.

"We would like to take your questions now, but our plan calls for all our speakers to present before we can open the floor to questions," announced Noah, firmly.

"Mr. Leonard, just one question, please," pled a gentleman from the third row.

"Take it, Noah, take it," whispered the Prince from the wings.

"It's hard to refuse such a passionate request," continued Noah. He saw what the Prince might be trying to do. If he spent more time with Julius, the audience might be worn out over the innocuous and be easier on a zealous presentation from Tony.

"Alright, one question apiece after each presentation."

"Who wrote Genesis, Mr. Martino?"

"The scholarly answer to your question, Sir, is that it is a matter of some debate."

"GOD wrote Genesis, Mr. Martino. How can you speak of this book, Gilgeshus, and the stuff of Darwin in the same breath with the sacred writ of the ALMIGHTY?"

"We have in our school, Sir, Christians, Jews, and devout students of several Asian religions. We consider only what we have at hand and what the New York State Regents approves for us to teach. We do not advocate here, Sir, we only try to interpret writings the Board of Regents finds significant in our shared cultures. We also consider the Koran, ancient Chinese creation stories, and the stories of the Swahili and the Native Americans. This is a public school, Sir."

"Some Catholic you are," grumbled the man audibly. But he sat.

Lucy caught her breath. This might not be so easy. But Noah was smiling. Could this kind of outburst be common at such Long Island meetings? She felt so unprepared, so naive.

"Miss Mackenzie is going to address tonight some misconceptions about *The Scarlet Letter.* Miss Mackenzie, by the way, has done extensive graduate work on the writings of our great American writer, Nathaniel Hawthorne, and is well prepared to work with this fine novel. Miss Mackenzie."

As Lucy rose, her eyes caught a familiar figure gathering herself into one of the rear center seats. It was Marge Leonard. Lucy reached for her notes, and in the process her hand grazed the side of the pitcher of ice water to her left. Down it fell, sloshing the cold liquid all over Noah's trousers. The auditorium was in an uproar. Noah shot up on his feet, bravely trying to flick the water from his pants.

"This is just one of the vaudeville routines my father taught me. And I hope that this is one of my scotch guarded suits, or Miss Mackenzie's going to have some big cleaning bill."

"Under the circumstances," Tony rose to the occasion, "I think I'd better go next while Miss Mackenzie and Mr. Leonard recover." The audience was with them all. Tony had seized the perfect moment when the impromptu comedy had broken through the hostility.

"I wish to say before I begin my formal presentation," announced Tony, "that we teachers know that it is impossible for any one of us to reach every student in our classes in the way we want. There will always be misunderstandings, even under the very best of circumstances. We try, year after year, to repeat lessons that seem to have succeeded in the past, and to introduce new approaches to see if they'll work as well. I have several lessons that seemed to have been consistently effective. I have never had any negative repercussions from them, but I realize that there's always a first time for everything. Perhaps that's what happened this year in my lesson on communism."

The audience stirred. Several hands went up.

"Mr. Nappa has just begun. We'll be glad to take your questions later," Noah said agreeably. Fortunately the hands went down, obediently.

"One of our hardest jobs is to keep our students awake in the classroom on warm autumn days," continued Tony, adapting a whimsical tone, which came to him so naturally that he even seemed surprised himself, Lucy thought. "Especially at two-thirty in the afternoon I like to add a little drama to my work." There were a few nervous laughs. "I always hope that when I tell the students in this particular lesson that they must not leave the classroom, that they know me well enough by now to buy into the joke. And that when I whisper to them that I am a communist and pull down the blinds, they won't be afraid of Mr. Nappa.

"Unfortunately, this year there were several whose trust I had not secured. I will not take this chance again. I realize that there is a possibility

The Come From Aways

that some of your fine sons and daughters have been raised to respect and hold such trust in authority that they cannot understand a foolish teacher's little pageant, and I apologize. I am also aware that this lesson has provoked a great deal of controversy this year and has, indeed, precipitated the plans for this evening's meeting.

"I am truly sorry to have caused so much anxiety among the students, parents, and teachers of our fine school community, and I will do whatever is in my power to make amends. I am most assuredly not a communist, I know of no communist within our school, and I hope that you will all now think better of me and my department than you may have when you walked in here tonight. Thank you very much for allowing me this time."

The auditorium was dead silent. No one raised a hand. Noah let the mood play itself out for a moment, but then felt obliged to speak.

"We are grateful to Mr. Nappa for being so direct in his remarks. If you have any questions to ask him, you certainly may do so after our next speaker, Miss Mackenzie, makes her presentation, that is if she is sufficiently recovered and is in appropriate remorse for the attack she launched on the moderator a few minutes ago."

Lucy, fully recovered and in good spirits from Tony's brave delivery, was now glad to carry on. With the same direct tone the other two had adopted, she began, "I wouldn't have known what to say to you tonight if it hadn't been for an exchange we entertained just today in my classroom." Without mentioning his name she went on to elaborate on Kurt's accusations, modifying them carefully to avoid sounding defensive and unkind.

"The question seems to be how Nathaniel Hawthorne saw both the actions of his characters and the society in which they lived. Because Hawthorne speaks as an omniscient observer, he is able to transmit both the feelings of his characters and the attitude of a narrator, but it is not always easy to tell if his words are to be taken as a straightforward declaration, an ironic satire of the times, or as thoughts of the characters themselves.

"When the meaning of the letter on Hester's breast seems to change from "Adulterer" to "Able," is the change a reflection of the attitude of the townspeople, or is it an apprehension of the author himself?

"We do not tell the students what to make of Hawthorne's writing, rather we ask them to try to come to their own conclusions. We do not invite them to form judgments, rather we ask them to try to understand what the author is trying to say. They will not all come to the same conclusions, but we try to see that they do not miss significant possibilities. We show them that the interpretations are complex, that Hawthorne's thinking about the times and the characters is complex, and that he seems to want to convey the agony that the people in that time suffered, rather than to form his own judgments about their actions. Because of these complexities it is a more magnificent novel than many of us realize on the first reading. It is tempting to try to dismiss the story as a simple narrative of a woman who made a terrible mistake and suffered great hardship as a result. It is a story of the many facets of human nature and how they interact in a strict, hypocritical, and dangerously punitive social setting.

"I hope if you have any really lengthy questions about the text or about our curriculum that you see me someday at school, for it is hard to address some of these problems in detail with so limited a time restriction," she finished.

"We'll take just a few questions now," Noah remarked after the brief but unexpected applause.

"Are you all dried off yet, Mr. Leonard," came the first unsolicited question from one of the ladies in curlers. Much laughter.

"No, and I'm glad it's such a warm night," he shot back, grateful that the mood was so lighthearted. "I'll take care not to sit next to Miss Mackenzie at the next meeting."

"My son said that you told them that communists wear pin striped suits. Is that true, Mr. Nappa?"

"Yes. One of the UN delegates even wears a crew cut. They don't look at all like beatniks. They're bureaucrats, just trying to compete with the rest of the international power brokers."

"Can we come to your next lesson on communism, Mr. Nappa?" queried a little man in Bermuda shorts.

"That lesson won't happen again until next October," offered Tony, "and as I promised, the next one will probably be a real sleeper."

"Thank you all for coming. I hate to hurry things along, but I've got to get home and into some dry clothes," was Noah's wrap-up.

Suddenly everyone was applauding. And the one important person that Lucy hadn't noticed was on the stage, beaming. Jimmy Duffer had been in the front row, but the footlights had obliterated his face. He hugged everyone on the stage, even Tony. "That was splendid, Julius, Noah, Lucy, and especially, Tony. I just wish I could hear that communism lesson once before you pack it up for good."

"Don't tempt him, Jim. Remember, he made a promise."

"I was expecting the sky to fall," remarked Julius.

"They didn't touch the Karl Marx trial."

"Let's not be sorry. I think we satisfied the troops for awhile. There's been a lot of excitement in old Suppogue lately... enough for a month of Sundays. Let's go home and unwind and get ready for another day."

"You really know how to cool a fellow down," whispered Noah to Lucy as they left the stage. Lucy avoided his eyes, and seeing Phyllis waiting in the aisle looking straight at her, went directly to speak to her friend.

"You did such a fine job up there, Lucy, just like an old trooper. I think you talked yourself into tenure in one quick speech."

"Thanks, pal. I needed to hear that from you. I've got so much to speak to you about ... but not tonight. I'm wrung out."

"Have you heard the latest about the Fawn Whitney investigation. I must tell you this much."

"Please tell me."

"They have someone in custody. Some truck driver from New Jersey. Seems like they found some footprints of someone who was in the neighborhood at the time of the murder."

"Just a truck driver ... oh, but Phyllis, we'll speak tomorrow. I'm dead tired. Thanks again, dear. Goodnight."

She was all but falling over when she entered her little bungalow. But she remembered that she had not been home since that morning to empty her mailbox. There was an unmarked envelope, the only mail. In it, she read:

Dear Miss Mackenzie,
I think you should be very sorry for what you did to me today.
Kurt

SAM, KURT, AND HARPER
Chapter Ten

We never know how high we are
Till we are called to rise.
And then, if we are true to plan,
Our statures touch the skies.
The heroism we recite
Would be a daily thing,
Did not ourselves the cubits warp
For fear to be a king.

Emily Dickinson

Sam Rose, English teacher from room 203, erstwhile dinner companion of Lucy Mackenzie, was proctoring Wednesday morning study hall, surrounded by several stacks of unmarked compositions and a pile of vocabulary quizzes, and was neglecting them all, hunched over his stenographer's notebook. He was attempting for the thousandth time to begin a short story.
"He came upstairs and found his roommate in the arms of another man ... "
No. That's much too confusing for the general reader. He began again:
"He came downstairs and found his lover in the arms of another roommate." No. Impossible.
He tried several more opening lines, inserting "wife," "friend," and "paramour" here and there and rested with a sigh. I don't really know what I want the character to be. I write and revise this roommate line as I do with so many others, put them away for a week, perhaps a month, and reread them. One month I am amazed at their ironic genius; the next month depressed by their cliches. Sometimes I am afraid that not only my sexual preferences but also my immense talent may be mauled by the brutal masses, regurgitated by spiteful critics, rendered sterile by self-righteous priests, or, quite worse, ignored by them all, proving that I have utterly no talent at all.

These paralytic fears are enough to madden me as I write. So instead I return to the deceptive freedom of the classroom to play with children's stories.

The story Sam thought he had to write was the story that, if he signed his name to it, would force him out of the closet and out of his job simultaneously. He had tried to put together other kinds of episodes; one about the New Jersey banker who had joined the KKK when he had thought all his life that he was born an Episcopalian. Upon the discovery that his parents had been German Jews hanged in Germany for treason and that he had been adopted in infancy by an English physician, he hanged himself with his bed sheet.

This account had made a deep impact upon Sam. He thought that the self-hatred the Jew had felt upon the discovery of his identity must have resembled the self-loathing Sam had experienced when, as a young man, he had heard his father speaking of those "damn filthy faggots."

But he had gotten a quarter into the story about the New Jersey Jew and had to stop and come back to his own story, the only real story for him at this time.

As he sat, staring at the fidgeting students, he repeatedly scratched his right ear with his left hand draped over his head, one of his recently developed nervous compulsions. Of course the students had noticed and were having great schoolyard fun with it. He had also begun to write his name beginning with lower-case letters, an indication of pretentious humility in the confident, but a constriction of the emotions in Sam. He had also begun to dot his i's with circles, a painstaking procrastination.

Only one other male homosexual taught in the school. Sam and John Williams hated each other's voices, bodies, and souls. John was a fancy screamer who taught speech and coached the drama club. He staged such 16th Century delights as Gammer Gurton's Needle and Ralph Roister Doister, keeping away from most of the rest of the faculty, hiding at his desk in the green room behind the stage, and keeping his hands off the children; but last year he had approached two young male music teachers, attempting to draw them back to his office. Very shortly they knew what he was about and carefully avoided him.

Whenever John met Sam, he would slap him violently on his backside and chortle, "How the hell ARE you, you old fart?"

Sam would scuttle silently away.

He was quietly sociable and enjoyed gathering with the faculty and listening to the banter in the lounge, especially to the witty interchanges of the social studies teachers.

He was sexually inactive. Except for a teenage seduction by his mother's brother, three subsequent encounters with the same gentleman, and a brief college tryst with a baseball player from a visiting fraternity, he had confined all his puerile activity to his imagination. He enjoyed the brown flexing of dark, hairy hands. The soft, fair curves of women imposed upon him a curious fear. Their very delicacy, their dependency both repelled and excited him. He hoped someday he would meet a woman he could trust and feel a new attraction to because he did not want to be what he now seemed to be. He did not enjoy being different from most of the people whom he admired. He had liked a girl who had sung with him in the University of Wisconsin choir. He had even kissed her several times, a pleasant enough experience, but she had been a year older than he and had left for graduate school in the East without any memorable farewell or answers to his letters. It had not been difficult to forget her.

He enjoyed thinking about a line from W.H. Auden about the human personality: "as secret and inconsistent as a limestone landscape." He liked the "inconsistent." He wanted to feel that his life was just beginning, that his personality was still developing.

But Sam's compulsion to write was bound to destroy his self-image if he did not soon complete his thoughts, find definition, see himself wholly, and accept his own image. The cocoon was ripping. This writer should be metamorphosed by his gut-clenching aches. He must write because of the remembered pain of his youth and the later agonies of disappointment, guilt, and fear of the hatred and jealousy of those who cannot accept the poetry in life, the snubs of the simple, the ordinary. He must write to extend, to play out, to convince himself that the sweet people who flowed in and out of his life in a vapor of joy, never staying long enough to demand or question, can be made to stay; that their friendship is limitless; that this joy that came from this sweet person, who fled before guilt came, is eternity, and that he can make eternity with his pen and press it out for every other human being with his typewriter so that they, too, can believe his fantasies. This is the meaning of writing, of human creativity, and this is what he had to do for himself and for the world. He believed.

Today, as he thought of Auden, his musings were becoming a little different. Sam was beginning again to feel that perhaps he could make a significant break with his old, painful lines, his old beginnings of stories about roommates and KKK leaders. In September he had come across a student in one of his classes whose essays were increasingly puzzling. Shelly Clawson, straight A cheerleader, first woman President of Student Council, President of Girls' Leader's Club, choir secretary, Snow Queen, Junior Prom Queen, nicknamed "Shelly the Tease" by the football squad had begun to worry Sam when, after several weeks in his class, she had asked if perhaps the students could write numbers on their compositions instead of their names so that he would not know whose paper he was reading. Her papers dealt repeatedly with the victims of vague illnesses that had no cure. Sam, although hithertofore never questioned the students' topics, asked her please to find some other subjects for her writing. Each time he tried to vary the assignments, she somehow twisted the direction of the topics and called up images of suffering and death.

Then one day there had been a revelation. Shelly had entered his classroom with her chin high in the air, tears streaming down her face.

"Mr. Rose," she choked. "I must be able to go to the office, possibly for the entire class period."

"Of course, Shelly, anything you need to do, you just DO."

A blank-faced boy, unusually handsome in an innocent, delicate way, who also sat in Sam's class, seemingly uninvolved with any of the other students, was just about to be reported by Shelly, eight other hysterical girls, and the health committee for infecting twenty-two students and, it was learned much later one teacher, with gonorrhea. As was reported, upon fiery examination, the boy could only repeat, "What did I do? Will someone please tell me what I did?" even after the matter was explained in vivid detail by the head nurse and a private physician, and the young man was released into parental custody.

Shelly's manner changed remarkably after the incident, and her papers finally reflected the normal "hopes, aspirations, and dreams," as the college circulars describe their coeds, of the normally bright, successful teenage girl. She wished fervently to continue her cheerleading performances at the State University of New York in New Paltz.

But the incident served to remind Sam that he should perhaps have something more to write about than his own problems and frustrations. The horrors of Shelly's emotional entanglements and physical fears should be documented by some responsible adult writer. What writer before had ever tried to measure the myriad social miseries of the adolescent? Surely one that young was generally incapable of fathoming the words to use to share her pain. So, Sam tried a new beginning: "I could understand the fear of this young girl, her ambivalence about her body ..." But he found himself continuing, "because I too ..."

Lucy Mackenzie stood in the doorway.

"I have to talk to you, Sam."

"Well, Lucy, it's three o'clock." His free foot swung up and down, while he worked a pencil between two fingers.

"Three o'clock. Does that mean you have to leave?"

"Yes, yes, I was thinking of running into the office to get my mail, then vamoosing straightway out of here, but I guess ..."

"I won't bother you if you're eager to go. I just wondered if you'd like to come over to dinner some night with, ah, maybe Phyllis and me."

"Oh, yes I'd like that. Oh, Phyllis. She's a lot of fun, Phyllis. Can I bring something, for dinner I mean?"

"Oh, some cheap champagne will be fine thanks --- oh, and how about some bitter herbs? We could celebrate the plagues of our respective childhoods---here's rue for you and here's some for me. You must wear your rue with a difference," and she swept her right hand around her head, resting with upturned palm on Sam's desk. He sat, transfixed.

"Lucy, I don't know what you're doing. I'm not sure I like it."

"What's not to like? I'm just plain old Lucy. Awfully young and naive, I'll admit, compared with your tweedy maturity and your impeccable tastes and unblemished past, and all your dignity---your recognition of the brilliance of Monsieur Leonard and his show-biz wife. I envy it all, and especially your deference to the female sex, and your self-control. Why you don't give a girl much of a chance, do you? You know it's all right to kiss a girl on a first date in 1959, even if her grandmother hasn't formally introduced you. It doesn't mean she's a whore, or that you're a cad. You know you've got to shake those Presbyterian ideas loose, Sam. You're in New York in 1959, Sam."

He would have bolted, but he saw some tears sparkling in her eyes, and he knew the tirade for what it was.

"Wait just a minute now, you just wait," he commanded. "Sit down." He rose briskly and strode over to shut the door. Lucy sat, still and quiet.

"You sit and you listen, Lucy, and then perhaps you'll stop torturing us both. You're not going to like what you hear, but apparently the gossipmongers haven't gotten to you yet. It's taken me a long time to admit this even to myself, Lucy, but I see that I've got to face up to it now and do what I have to do, and stop hurting everyone, especially myself."

He was looking out at the darkening eastern sky, as far away from her as he could be. She waited. He glanced back to her and then to the far wall.

"I'm a homosexual, Lucy. May have been all my life. Nothing I seem to be able to do about it. I keep trying to be normal, but as you saw for yourself, there isn't any use. I'm cooked." He looked out the window again. "Just your old, average, jerk-o-Faggot, as they say in the Village. Can't help himself. Was born that way. They find out around here, I'll be out in a day. They'll think I seduce all the little boys and am guilty of all kinds of nameless perversions."

"So when we went out, you, you. were trying to be sure?"

"No, yes, no, it was more than that, Lucy. You're very attractive. Look here, this isn't an absolute condition. You have to realize, it's an individual thing. I just can't ... follow through with anyone. And I'm no psychologist. I can't figure this thing out either. All I know is that I want to identify myself by now, and then maybe I'll find some kind of psychic stability. Yes, a man seduced me when I was a kid. And I can't get that out of my head. I probably require heavy shrinkage, and maybe I'll have to get that somewhere other than Suppogue." He looked toward her now. "No, Lucy, I wasn't trying to use you. I really wanted to be with you, and I still want to be with you, only I can't be with you like you want, like you should want."

Lucy took a deep breath, rose, and walked to the window.

"I think you're very brave, and I think I want to be your friend," she moved toward him, a little nervous because she'd never heard a confession like this before, and she didn't know what else to say except the guileless words she had just spoken. "And I don't want you to go away from Suppogue. Please stay."

Now it was Sam's turn to tear up. "You're a wonderful, kind person, Lucy. I wish, 1 wish I could love you."

"Maybe someday, after you go through all that shrinkage," she smiled as tearfully as Sam; "and in the meantime, stop wearing all that damn great aftershave."

The two stood, far apart, heads down, blubbering into Kleenex from Sam's desktop.

"Can I still come to dinner?" Sam broke the ice.

*   *   *

The sun dipped lower and lower over the Great South Bay. Formations of thousands of birds flying south dipped and swirled against the gray skies, and the water in Lucy's canal grew chillier and chillier so that finally she had to abandon her evening swim across and back. The leaves rustled and fell in a myriad of northeastern colors all over her little yard, and the wild ducks huddled against her bulkhead and padded, quacking aggressively, up to her backdoor in the twilight for the scraps of bread she threw to them. Their tufts of eiderdown mingled with the leaves and grass like the giant flakes of an early snowfall. One crippled duck stayed on the lawn all season, not moving far from her door, never venturing back into the water. "Lucy's Duck Pen," she called her home, affectionately. It comforted her to think of the place as a safe haven.

She wanted to make the same kind of comforting place for her 11th grade students, to try to make amends for all the consternation of Kurt's commotion over the curriculum---to try to bring them all together in a more congenial, gentler setting.

"Why don't you all come over to my house someday after school this week, say, Wednesday? We can cook out and sit around on the dock and talk? It's not too cold yet to be outdoors."

Her eager invitation was met with puzzled stares.

"Oh, gee, Miss Mackenzie, we've got football all week."

"Yea, and play practice, and Wednesday the fall track team's running."

"And some of the rest of us work."

"Well," she sighed, "who's left?" About six hands went up slowly. "Harper, Jesse, Julie, Crissy, Maude, and (slowly), Kurt.

"Good. A small group, but maybe more of you can join us later. Maybe some of you can come after practice?"

Wednesday came and Harper was the first to appear with flowers and candy. He drove his father's silver Bentley up to her little door and presented the gifts with great solemnity.

"Harper, how delightful. I'm thrilled. But you must understand that you are trading flowers and bon-bons for hot dogs and Cheetos."

"I'll take that trade, Miss Mackenzie," he returned, with the faintest hint of a smile.

They assembled around the barbecue grill on benches and a blanket in the backyard, the ducks having retired to the empty launching ramp to sit it out and wait for the leftover buns.

The small group who came to Lucy's home that evening were mostly the social leftovers---the kids who didn't have any of the after-school activities that all the mainstream kids always have like football or track or theatre practice or publications meetings or even a hangout time at Pete's Pizza. But they were not the slowest in the class, by far. Maude was possibly the most striking looking of the five with straight dark brown hair pulled severely back from a pale ivory face that could be called beautiful were its expression more serene. Instead Maude's demeanor changed slowly throughout the day from a quizzical frown to an ironic eyebrow-elevated disdain. She usually wore black or dark brown dresses with black oxfords, very seriously. As though in deliberate contrast, Little Crissy sported a head full of ill managed, short golden curls tied in an unfashionable bow of blue satin. Neither she nor Maude ran with any of the regular crowds, entering and leaving the classroom always alone. Lucy was afraid that both of them had come to her home as though on another assignment.

Crissy's appearance was on the far side of neat, her frizzy hair seldom combed, her mouth smeared with bright lipstick. She often wore the same sweater three or four days in a row. Lucy had heard that she came from a wealthy family who neglected her but who indulged her with clothes which she didn't care to wear and a horse to which she was utterly devoted.

Julie was often seen with one or two friends who were at school meetings today, and Julie just happened to be free between appointments. Different in that way from the others assembled, she was a self-confident, tall, attractive leader who could hold her own in most settings. She now assumed a superior attitude and deferred only slightly to Lucy as she tried to gather them all into conversation

Jesse was relatively inarticulate, compared to the others, who sat alone, but who tried very hard in class, always dropping off extra credit reports to win Lucy's favor. His parents had begged the administration to put him into the honors section, and Mina had relented.

"He'll surprise you," his mother had chortled. "Just you wait, he'll be the star of the class."

Kurt had not yet appeared, and Lucy did not intend to wait for him, so she prepared the grill and arranged the meal, and with Harper's help she tried to get the group going.

"Would you like to play some games after dinner, or just sit and talk?"

"Oh, talk's fine with me," Crissy giggled self-consciously. No one disagreed.

"We really don't know each other very well, Miss Mackenzie, so this would be a good time for us to begin. I think we ought to talk, in this least threatening of social environments, about religion. That's something we all can say something revealing about, and we'll get to know each other very quickly---that is, if we're all honest," offered Harper, sententiously.

"Well, O.K., you start, Harper, since you brought it up."

"Well, surprise. I'm not GOING to be very interesting---because I'm an atheist!"

Crissy gasped. "You mean you don't believe in God...or anything? That IS what you mean, isn't it?"

"Yes, I really do mean it."

"Are you sure? Aren't you afraid of going to hell?" This from Maude.

"No. The whole idea of hell is only part of the cosmology of the religious. If I reject religion, and I do, then I also reject the ideas of heaven and hell. Anyway, people just invented hell to force other people into subsidizing one religion or another. It's the ultimate threat or promise---life after death---horrible or pleasurable---what else? Perfect."

"I don't know if we should talk about religion anymore. Why not … art?" Lucy floundered.

"I like this subject," said Julie. "I think we're all learning something. Let's keep it up awhile. What religion are you, Jesse?"

"Catholic---like my mother, but I don't think much about it."

"Do you go to church?"

"Every Sunday."

"Confession?"

"Every Saturday."

"What happens in those booths? I never really knew. All my close friends are Protestant."

"Not much. Your priest says a prayer to forgive you, and then the priest asks you to pray and then he asks how long it's been since your last confession, and if there are sins you would like to confess. You say your sins, like, bless me Father for I have sinned it has been one week since my last confession I cursed out my father for telling me to mow the lawn, and I didn't do all my penance last week, and I looked on Mary Lou with lust in my heart. Like that. And then he gives you a penance. It's always so many Our Fathers and Hail Marys. I hear that some people are told to come to early morning mass for so many days, but that's for really big sins, and if you are doing something all the time, that's bad, you have a big penance, and if you can't promise to stop it, that's really bad---you are told that you might be excommunicated. That's really serious."

"Like drinking or gambling?"

"No, that's not so bad. It's worse to read Dante or date a Protestant."

"That's funny. What's so terrible about Dante?"

"Dante wrote bad things against the church. At least that's what my father told me---he's a Lutheran---but I never read about it."

Someone was landing at the bulkhead, for they could hear the crunch of oars against wood. It was getting dark at seven thirty now, and the lengthening shadows cast most of the yard in shade. As Kurt approached against the orange setting sun, he was a black outline of a figure, but they could not mistake him.

"What's up, Kurt? You missed a good meal," picked up Julie, their fearless spokesperson.

"Didn't come for dinner," drawled Kurt. "Just wanted to see Miss Mackenzie, and her house."

"Well, sit down here and have a coke, Kurt," Lucy tried to respond cheerily. "We're just going around the group, sharing ideas."

"Yea, Kurt, we're reviewing everyone's religion. What's yours?"

"I don't think you all would be interested in what I believe."

Lucy wanted to avoid Kurt's sensational interests, especially with these several timid souls in her charge.

"Let's explore something different now ... like hobbies," she offered, this time more forcefully. "I know Harper writes a lot---at least that's what he was doing a week or so ago. Won't you share some of your ideas with us, Harper?"

"I'm working now on a libretto for a modern opera based on Camus' *The Stranger*. It's going to be a stranger stranger than even Camus ever thought of. This stranger might even metamorphose into some kind of animal for awhile."

"That's like Kafka!"

"That's it. Like Kafka"

Kurt snorted.

"What's the matter with you, Kurt? Jealous or something?" got up Julie.

The others looked frightened. There was no Mr. Leonard patrolling a hallway tonight, and Harper and Jesse were no match for Kurt's rage.

"Jaffe's just trying to impress us with his perverted mind. You want to know what animals are for? I'll tell you what animals are good for."

Julie was up to him. "We don't want to hear what you think about animals, Mr. Sutherland. Why don't you just sit down and join in with good spirits instead of standing over us like some kind of judge or something."

Kurt, miraculously, sat down.

"I have a hobby," offered the serious Maude. "I make Christmas wreathes from pine cones and grape vines with a glue gun and walnuts."

"I've always wanted to know how to do that," eagerly picked up Lucy. "If I get you paper and pen, can you draw us a diagram so that we can copy it?"

Maude was ecstatic. Questions came about the source of cones and grapevines and the various uses of glue guns. Harper asked Kurt and Jesse to help him clean up the yard, and the group finally folded into the house, for it was now dark. Julie called her parents who offered to drive everyone home who needed a ride.

The students were massed in the living room now, chatting together. Crissy was telling about some hikes her family had taken on the Appalachian Trail, and the rest were asking questions and remarking on hiking they had enjoyed. Lucy was happy that these quiet kids had found a way to come out and hoped that there could be a residual effect on their classroom interactions, so that the popular, garrulous ones wouldn't swallow them.

Kurt lingered by the back doorway to the kitchen and watched Lucy's every move. She burned with his eyes on her. Finally, she had had enough. She dropped a heavy pan into the sink with a clatter, and sped into the living room and over to Harper and Jesse who were standing side by side. She spoke to them in a whisper with her back to the kitchen. "Please don't leave until I can get Kurt out of the house, and quietly ask Julie to speak to me in my bedroom." She walked over to her bedroom as casually as she could, and Julie soon followed.

"Julie, can you do me a big favor. When your parents come, can you have your father come inside for a few minutes? I'm uncomfortable with Kurt still here. Does your father know what happened in class?"

"Yes, he does. Yes he will. Oh, Miss Mackenzie, do you think he's going to try anything?"

"I don't think so. I just don't want to deal with him alone, and it's not exactly appropriate for me to tell a student to leave. Maybe your father's presence might help me."

"Don't worry, Miss Mackenzie. I'm going along now. Didn't want to mess up your little party. You don't have to call out the troops, or your boyfriend Mr. Leonard." Kurt sneered as Julie and Lucy emerged from the bedroom. They all turned to face him as he lolled backwards out the kitchen door, eyes glittering, mouth sneering. Suddenly he turned, and was gone as stealthily as he had come.

Julie ran to the back door and reported that she could see him climbing into his boat.

"I'm so sorry I had to ask you all to help," began Lucy, feeling embarrassed at her awkwardness in front of her students.

"Please, Miss Mackenzie. We understand. And we all had a great time tonight. Thanks so much for everything."

"You don't need to ask your parents to come in now, Julie. Please don't alarm them. Just have a safe trip home, everyone."

"Can we come back sometime?" spoke shy Jesse, suddenly.

"I'd love it," signed Lucy, gratefully.

"When Kurt Sutherland learns to act like a decent human being, then the class can meet and really have fun together," pronounced Julie.

And then they were all gone except for Harper. Lucy was discomforted in a different way now as she gazed at Harper sitting alone on the edge of her sofa. If Harper's brilliant mind hadn't set him apart, his appearance would have done a great deal to assert his uniqueness. Huge eyes so dark that the edge of the pupils merged with the iris into one black disk set in two caverns in a skull, markedly smaller than average, over a small, pointed nose and generous, sensuous mouth, the face capped by a shaft of straight, oily, coarse black hair. His complexion was pale ivory with a faint pinkish tinge over his high cheekbones. His shoulders were broad, much broader than they should be for a young man of five foot two.

What could she do for this needy student? She imagined a thousand mysteries in him. It seemed that the inner and the outer person were incommensurable, and that contradictions warring in his nature kept his soul in perpetual combat, as the sea storms against the land in the midst of a typhoon.

She said, "Harper, I want to thank you for your discretion and your help. I found tonight very difficult, and you helped me get through it."

"You know, Miss Mackenzie, tonight was important to me. I felt, for the first time, that people really listened to me ... and didn't laugh."

"I had that feeling too, Harper. There was something about our little group. We went from your deep religious discussion to Maude's wreathes, and no one blinked. Do you think we can recapture the best of the evening ever again?"

"No. Were you ever on the stage, Miss Mackenzie?"

"Why, yes. As a matter of fact, I've done a lot of theatre ... at college, then in a summer theatre in Pennsylvania. I used to want to be a professional actress ... until I found how difficult it was to find good work, and until I knew I wanted to be a teacher."

"I was on stage once. My mother got me into a play in one of her acting groups out in Sag Harbor. Do you remember how you felt when the set was struck?"

"I know where you're leading."

"Yes. That never again will these same people meet and have the same kind of experience together."

"But that's theatre. And this is life. If we bring the same people, real people playing themselves, together in my house again, we might at least capture the tone of tonight, of the best of tonight."

"No. Time will have passed, and people will have changed. Besides, some of what went on happened because of the threat of Kurt. Some of us became desperate towards the end, even though we seemed to be sparkling with sociability. We were making a diversion. I'm not saying that we can't try. It might even be better. We might go further. Maude and Chrisy have much more to offer, and they might, given enough support, bring all kinds of meaning to us and to themselves by opening up. But it won't be the same, naturally."

"You do, ultimately, give me hope, Harper. Harper, what makes you so full of insight?"

There was a moment as Harper looked at the faded yellow rug. "Being alone, I guess. I have so much time to think and read. The maid never interrupts me, and no one's ever home except us."

"Where do you live, Harper?"

"I stay, at night, in the gray stucco mansion at 102 South Second Street with the Jaffe family, my grandfather and my adoptive parents, when they're home. My grandfather is there only three months out of the year. Other times he's in Bridgehampton or Palm Beach. The family's wealthy. They, they took me in."

"But you're adopted. Just like me!"

Harper's eyes widened. "Like you? Oh, Miss Mackenzie, are we then the same like this?" He gazed delightedly at her. "I never guessed that we were both foundlings!"

She could have laughed at his eagerness, but she was too overwhelmed with his gratitude and restrained her strong urge to embrace him. They both sat poised, she on the edge of the wrought iron chair she had pulled from the dining table.

She told him of her memories of Nova Scotia, of Connecticut, and how Laura and Peter had consented to take her. "I actually had to sell myself to them, a little kid," she chuckled sadly, "but it all worked out fine. I'm not much like either of my parents, but my father, at least, is proud of me. My mother wanted a girl a little closer to her idea of femininity."

"You mean she has trouble with your independent spirit?"

"Yes. She sent me to cotillion to try to get me a Yalie boyfriend, but no one seemed interested in me with my sharp tongue. She'd like me to sit home and do needlepoint with her."

"Maybe both of us are children hard-to-match with parents," Harper mused, "My father's younger brother was not yet married, and my parents wanted to produce an heir before he did. They contracted some doctor from Virginia who could present an infant candidate in a few months and make it available straight from the hospital with papers to sign right there---less trouble than registering a pedigreed dog with the A.K.C." He took a deep breath. "My father is heir to Bolivian tin mines through his mother. He is used to acquiring what he wants quickly. I often fantasize that I am the product of the assault of some poor mountain girl by her imbecilic stepfather to be the heir to the Jaffe family fortune. But it's a good thing that they didn't try a reliable adoption agency that might ask for family psychological profiles."

"Why. What's wrong?"

"My father has been manic with hostility ever since I can remember. He's always been half-deaf and ridiculed by his stupid father for that imperfection. He tries to repress his feelings of rejection, which, of course, makes them worse, and he unleashes them at mother and me when we least expect it. Of course, when he looks at me, the strange, ugly insurgent from the Virginia Mountains, he has quite a time restraining himself.. They thought they were coming home with a precious prize, a great deal, a perfectly packaged American commodity. Almost every time I see them now their disappointment is impossible for them to hide."

"You know, Harper, if you were not so talented and rare, I would weep for you. But I can't." Lucy spoke carefully. He was aching for love. But she could appreciate only his talent; she must stop cold there.

"Fortunately I have few regrets about not having been born from them. I have been under the care of a series of despairing nursemaids since infancy who dressed me formally for painful interviews with my parents after dinner in the early evening. They always asked me what new 'thing' I had accomplished that day to present to them: a drawing, an artistic construction from found objects, or a short reading (notice how I have memorized the scenario)." Lucy laughed. "I mastered the art of monologue by three-and-a-half, and became somewhat of a curiosity, if not a joy."

"Then your parents do appreciate your intelligence and your pluck?"

"Yes, but they're not equipped to handle me. They have too many mixed emotions of their own to sort out. Dad always did well academically, but he's not especially creative. He never tries to make any imaginative leaps away from the world of school or corporation. He's a careful plugger, but he hires others to make choices. They both worship good looks. I could at least have been tall and rugged. They hide me from their friends.

"My mother should know what to do. She is the product of a social science curriculum at Columbia and worked for the Mayor's staff on psychological support for public assistance cases for several years, but she's completely sublimated her old life with her new role as society matron here on Long Island and dabbles in all kinds of charity luncheons and the like. It's terrible what our culture does to women, especially wealthy women. She's so impressed with her own social position that she felt secure in doing right by me in hiring proper British nannies; as though those surrogates provided all the intellectual food I needed. Meg Mullin was sweet and supportive, but I can't say the same for Geraldine Brockington or Agnes Fleigel.

I found a letter that my mother wrote to a friend and forgot to seal and mail but left it with some old magazines. It said something like this:

Every time I hold him, he either spits up on me or passes wind like a toy cannon. His huge eyes loll around in his head, and his skin reddens so deeply that I'm constantly afraid he's feverish and call the nurse to take his temperature. He's better off with his nanny. I just don't understand what we do to each other when we're together.

"I would hear her cry to my father about me, and he would grunt and change the subject. They never seemed to think I heard or understood anything. But every Sunday they would dress me up and take me to church. At least that pageant is over. They've given up on church for me."

"What happened in church?"

"Well, the last time we went I remember distinctly as the worst time I ever had with them. Grandfather insisted that we go every Sunday, and since there were few couples in our church who had young children to bring, there was no cradle roll and I had to sit with my parents, between my mother and my nannie-of-the-moment. At least three-quarters of the parishioners are over fifty-five, pretty dull for me, and the nurse brought a satchel full of snacks for bribes to keep me quiet. She used to dole them out one-by-one, quiet gumdrops, so that they couldn't be 'pinged' onto the floor during the service. Actually, I really listened to the silly service, and nobody counted on that. The worst part was at the restaurant after the service."

"What happened there?"

"The last time I remember was one Sunday when I asked my father why we really go to church. As usual, he looked to my mother for an answer. This time she threw the question back to him. 'Go ahead, Richard, tell him why we go to church.'" Harper mimicked his mother scornfully.

Lucy didn't like this part of Harper's narrative. She was beginning to feel that she was hearing very private confessions, and that she was now in an inappropriate role. But Harper continued.

"My mother asked him twice, and I think she was trying in a way to get back at him for something. 'That's a very good question to ask your father, Harper. Go ahead, Richard, tell him why we go to church.' She was chiding him to say that we went because his father bullied us all into common propriety. She knew he couldn't say this, but she was reminding him that she resented his meekness to his father. Our family dynamics are horrible.

"I remember my father taking a deep breath---isn't it funny how we can remember the sharpest details of a scene we either delight in or abhor---and came out with the answer he was programmed to produce for the moment, 'Harper, we go to church on Sunday because we believe that God is there.'

"I think my mother was still trying to love me then. I can see her smiling benevolently, hoping somehow that his ridiculous abstraction would appeal to my imagination, but I kept on questioning relentlessly, 'But isn't He at home too, and in the garden, and right here in this restaurant?'

"Mother said that God is in church all the time, and that we are always sure to find him THERE, and I insisted then that God should want to go where it was fun, like Coney Island instead of that dark, damp church where nothing happens. Dad was almost understanding then. I remember his saying that God probably does go to Coney Island, and even that he might like to go there more often himself. My mother said that she didn't like Coney very much, but that church was like God's bedroom. That was such a great slip that my father might have made much of later. But my grandfather would say that only the lower classes sublimate their sexual desires through religion.

"But the worst was hearing the tone of their voices talking to me in that 'tell-the-baby-some-more-lies way, that fairy-story-telling-way, and I got angrier and angrier at their smugness so that I can remember screaming out, 'So Dad, you're making all this up because I can hear you and mummy laughing at me while you're talking, and I really don't want to go to church anymore,' and then I jumped up from the table and ran as fast as I could out of the restaurant and down the street with everyone after me."

Lucy pictured their catching him, this hysterical, wriggling mass of arms and legs and troubled sobbing soul.

"And I remember that horrible scene. Dad had never even rebuked me before, but something had gotten into him, and all his hostility came out, and he struck me again and again until my nurse and my mother pulled me away from him. I was in bed a long time, and I remember my father never came near me when I was sick, and he's kept his distance ever since."

"Do you know why, Harper?" began Lucy, tentatively.

"Oh, yes. I understand why. But it doesn't make it any easier. He was beating himself. He was out of control, and he was beating himself."

"And now? How does he treat you now?"

"He mostly keeps his distance, as I said, but I think he appreciates me a little. When my perfect College Board scores came back last month, he came to my room, beaming. Oh, I think he sometimes even brags about me to his friends, but he's so afraid of me, and he sometimes behaves as though he's a little jealous."

"How can you tell?"

"He sometimes snorts at my statements, as though to say that they couldn't possibly be true when he knows they are. He tries to put me down, but it doesn't get to me anymore because I know my mother understands, and because I know he can't stand to be buffaloed by a kid. I try to understand that he is doing the best he can with a difficult situation. My grandfather is old and sick now, but he gets excited sometimes about me because he thinks I can go to Harvard or Yale."

"What do you think?"

"That I can. But I hate the thought of being anywhere as a Jaffee. I want to know where I came from, even if it's gruesome. I want to know who I really am, and then I can go anywhere. I'm tired of playing a role, even though I haven't been able to play it well. Then, after I make things straight with whoever my mother and father are, I'll borrow some money from the Jaffees, take five long years of reading time, and then see what I want to do...maybe go on a cargo ship for a year or two; but there's this system that

Jaffees are supposed to follow, and the family would not understand giving me that kind of freedom. What would they say to their friends? 'Why, our Harper refused to go to Harvard and is being a stevedore for now.' They'd think me queerer than they already do. And distant as it is, I need their approval. That's the damnable thing."

"What is, Harper?"

"That we can't live without someone's approval. That's what makes them what they are, and damn it, that's what makes me what I am too. If we could just, say, go chuck it all and do exactly what we want, but there's always someone else to please, someone else, or someone else's standard. That's what makes us move, somebody else's clockworks. But what do the real genius's do, Miss Mackenzie? How do so many of them break away?"

"I don't know if they do, Harper. I think, sometimes, that we're all acting either to please or, sometimes, to revenge someone else, or a whole lot of people."

"Do you know, Miss Mackenzie, that this is the first time I've ever talked like this to anyone?"

Lucy was uneasy again. It had gone too far. Why couldn't she be a counselor in an office now instead of an inexperienced, very young teacher in her own living room late at night on a lonely road on Long Island.

"You know, you should try hard to confide in one of your classmates. Someone you find that you can trust, and who will trust you. That would be the finest thing, Harper," and the healthiest, she thought. "There were a few here tonight that really appreciated your mind, you know. Did you hear what Crissy said, that she learned a lot and didn't want to give up the conversation?"

"It wouldn't be the same," he ventured, "but it would be nice, trusting one of the students, if I could ever get that far with them. You have to know what some of them called me once when I overheard them in the hall. At first it upset me terribly, but then I thought, "What do they know of the real Harper, and it was a group of the stupidest ones who don't care what people hear. They called me SNAKE Jaffee. 'There goes SNAKE Jaffee," he laughed disdainfully. "I guess my big eyes got to them. I even got them back once. I went right up to them in the hall and told them, 'I see you've finally found a more suitable name for me than my parents could. That stopped them dead in their tracks, and I've never heard it again. And at least now that we're older, they're accepting more and more of what I have to say in class."

"They respect your mind, Harper," Lucy offered gently. "Do you know that it's eleven o'clock now? We've had such a wonderful conversation that

I've completely forgotten to look at the time, and now we've both got to get some sleep for tomorrow."

"Miss Mackenzie," Harper continued in a pleading tone as he rose from the sofa. "I hope that all I've said doesn't make you disrespect me and my family. We all do mean the best, and my parents THINK they're doing the right thing, all the time."

"Harper, I can only follow your lead. You speak with integrity, and I think that ultimately you all love each other over there," she gestured toward an amorphous Second Street.

"Yes, but we all need more, much much more, Miss Mackenzie. Maybe someday, we'll all find a way to come to terms with our disappointments."

"And Miss Mackenzie," as he was standing with the door ajar, "why did Kurt say that about you and Mr. Leonard?"

He was a child again, brash, indiscreet. Lucy blanched.

"Mr. Leonard is a happily married man, and I'm proud to be his friend."

"Oh, good. Because some of the kids saw you out to dinner with him the other night, and there's talk around school. You know how kids are."

Lucy caught her breath. "Oh, yes, I remember, teachers are always on display. Well, that's it. We were out to dinner, talking about the PTA meeting. That's that," she smiled.

"Well, O.K. then. Thanks so much. For everything."

"Oh, yes, and Harper, thank you for the beautiful flowers and candy, and for all your understanding."

"Goodnight," he whispered dramatically, and was gone into his huge car.

Lucy ached from a piece of self-discovery. Harper dreamed of finding his real parents. He was brave enough to say it. She had never spoken of her own longing to anyone. She had spoken of her mother's visit, but the pain of her never returning had been far too much to dwell upon, and so she kept it buried.

This small student's own longing had drawn out her own. She was suddenly forced to reckon with a very real need, a need, if she were to function tomorrow, would have to be buried again, perhaps until a time when she might try to satisfy her longings with the help of Peter and Laura, if they could understand and be so totally unselfish for her sake.

MURDER, MY LOVE
Chapter Eleven

*"If thou rememb'rest not the slightest folly
That ever love did make thee run into
Thou hast not loved."*
Silvius in *As You Like It* by William Shakespeare

"What time is it? Six thirty. What date is it? The twenty-ninth of December. What day is it, worst of all? Oh, yes. It has to be Saturday. And what sort of day? A beautiful winter day with the sun sparkling on the new fallen snow? Not at all. It is gloomy, damp, chilly because it is raining, my pet, and I am shivering and sad. I might as well be in a damp cellar because I have just gotten up and have had nothing to eat yet. The hot water heater is not working well enough to produce even just enough for my tiny little shower. I am not really awake. I am in a frightful humor, and yet you must choose this moment to propose lovemaking, the lovemaking that I have desired all week and that I vainly attempted to kindle into flame over dinner with wild enthusiasm and which was repeatedly rejected and scorned at the most auspicious times when I had even laid a cozy fire crackling in the grate and cooked you a hearty meal. On Tuesday I even lay on the sofa dressed in my sheerest negligee."

She saw that even though he was not looking directly in her direction, he was smiling grimly, so she continued. "Now you blunder grievously. You are like the man who, after investing your entire fortune unwisely, waits two years and then suddenly demands it back with compound interest. Your capital is lost. In a single moment you have spoiled everything."

"Oh, wonderful. If you hadn't added those last lines, I would have believed every word. You're paraphrasing Molnar, by damn, and you almost had me going. You don't mean a word of it, you know, and you also know that I've been completely out of it all week with this wretched investigation. Oh, Marge, what are we to do? They're calling me in again."

"Piece of cake. You know that Sutherland's messed up everything royally. That interlude with the truck driver from Jersey almost did him in. Now the FBI is on it, and they'll have to check out the entire faculty all over again and anyone else whose ever been in Fawn's house or driven her anywhere or belonged to any of her organizations. Her life reads like a celebrity's with her monies going to every kind of left-wing gathering on Long Island and New York City. They're canvassing the roles of all her clubs. They have to. They have to ask you back, especially after your little trip to the house. What's Jimmy doing about it?"

"Jimmy's going crazy. Selma's worse. She's so insecure she's trying to imagine that maybe either Jimmy or I really had something to do with Fawn's murder. Not that we actually murdered her, but that we know who the murderer is and aren't telling. That it might have been a demented faculty member or student that we're protecting."

"How in the devil did you manage to go to her house at the very time that Jake was spying? And what was his excuse for being there? You never took the time to tell me."

"It was a dumb thing. I had a key that Fawn had given me several years ago when I was taking care of her dog. And Fawn had some important books of mine ... those on Bertrand Russell. I could have told Sutherland and gotten his permission to go in, but I just didn't want to deal with him again, he's so thick-headed, and Jimmy, like another fool, went with me."

"And what was Jake doing in the neighborhood?"

"That's a mystery. He had his key too. We, stupidly, hid when we saw him coming, and then when he decided to come back the second time, we pretended that we had just entered on an official mission and that he was the culprit. Jimmy was right; we should have stayed hidden or gotten away, because he finally outsmarted us. He maintained that the neighbors had heard water running in the house and had come to investigate."

"He's lame-headed about some things, but he's looking hard for someone to pin this on."

"That's part of the problem."

"Well, you had a key legitimately."

"Of course, but I wasn't in there with anyone's official permission. I can't say that Fawn told me to return."

"No, but you can speak the truth. That should be enough to get you some kind of marks. They have nothing to connect you with the crime. You have alibis for all the time between the possible hours of the murder, and you have absolutely no motives, nor has Jimmy."

"But I don't want to get into all that."

"Anyway, we'd better call a lawyer."

"You're right."

"Noah, could there be any connection at all between Jake Sutherland and Fawn? Did they know each other before the murder?"

"Not that I know, but it's an interesting speculation. Jimmy smelled out something like you're thinking when we were with him in the house, but it's a very long shot. Why would Fawn want anything personal to do with Jake?"

"Josie Farinelli knows Jake from the country western clubs. I'm going to ring up Josie today, after I get back from the theatre. Max is preparing me for another audition."

"What is it this time?"

"Don't laugh. A Portia for the Roundabout's next *Julius Caesar*."

"I do laugh. You'll be screaming over a thousand school children's matinees."

"I don't think they take them to the Roundabout, do they? Anyway, it's better than vegetating any more out here in Deadsville."

Noah flinched. "Will you not be embarrassed to introduce me to all your new artist friends, your husband, the assistant principal?"

"Come on, Noah, that's not funny."

"I know it's not. I, who dragged you out here to decompose on this salt flat."

"We'll make a game of it. You'll be my big Saturday night date again."

"Just don't bump into any more sugar daddies."

As soon as he had said it, he knew he had made a big mistake. Her whole demeanor changed, and she pushed away her chair and vanished into their bedroom to dress. His stomach turned over. Was this play thing going to be a more serious interlude than he had first envisioned? He had thought that it would be good for her, for the marriage. Now he had reminded her of other times, other challenges for which she may have been mourning all these years. What was to come of it?

*   *   *

It was now January, and back at the school the gusts of wind from the bay piled the snow in tufts around the cars in the parking lot and sent the faculty and students shivering from busses and cars into the warm hallways and classrooms. Football season was over, and the students were preparing for their January exams, so there were only a few brief meetings after school. The halls were quiet.

Nick Bruno had fought his desire for Susan Morand and tried to maintain a formal distance, but she was always there, escaping from her torturers. Ever since she had found sanctuary in the art room, she had clung to him for safety and strength. And the more security she derived from the haven he provided, the weaker his position became regarding her.

He feared most from the reaction of the other students. Now, whenever Susan approached him, they seemed to sense a private encounter and excused themselves and walked away. He sensed danger, and feared her presence, but still his heart pounded whenever he thought of her, even as he tried to avoid those solitary moments.

Late one day Susan could not leave the school. The matter of her drawings had not yet been settled. Besides, she had cut algebra for the third straight day, Zimmerman was still in his room, and she would have to pass that room to leave school by the main entrance, as all other doors had been fastened for the night with chain locks. She returned to the art lab after English. The Prince was in his closet, she could see, as the double doors were ajar, and she could hear a rustling and a sliding, it seemed, of jars. "I'm here again," she announced. There was a sound like a jar crashing to the floor and a splattering of paint and a flow of bright red under the closet door. "Awww, lovely," ejaculated the Prince.

"I'm so sorry," she cried, and hastened to the closet.

"No, no," he threw both doors together behind him angrily.

"I'll go then," she was insulted, rejected. She hadn't meant to pry, and she was sorry for having startled him. She had closed the door behind her for fear of Zimmerman's passing and catching her. "Please ... but I don't know where to go."

"What do you mean you don't know where to go?"

"I have to hide ... until Mr. Zimmerman leaves." She was standing against the counter by the door. There were tears in her eyes again. Her hair lay in soft strands over her shoulders and fell over her breasts. Nick came to her.

"What are you afraid of? That wimp downstairs with the slide rule? He's nothing. He's nothing better than my nephew's Cupie doll. Don't worry about him." He couldn't stand to see her cry again. "Come here, if you really have to see. "He threw the inside bolt on his closet door. Come here and see. No more secrets."

Susan gasped. He took her arm and led her over to the doors behind which the large smear of spilled paint flowed and held her arm gently but firmly with his left hand, opening the doors with his right.

The figures stood and lay in a multitude of graceful, dance-like positions of coitus, gray clay against a sapphire velvet background. Some were lying in poses on the shelf, while others were suspended by thin wires, entwined, copulating in mid air. There were several in artful positions of fellatio, some men with men and women with women, and at the heart of the display on the wide center shelf were a dozen or so miniature figures, all entwined with one another, fondling and loving each other in an exciting variety of embraces and expressions. He had been touching up several of those figures in a surreal light red when Susan came.

"I don't expect you'll understand much of this," spoke Nick softly, as Susan gaped. "I just couldn't bear to think that you felt rejected by me. This is my secret closet. If you can't understand, if it seems hateful to you---I know you said you can't stand sex ---then please try to forget about it and try not to wonder about it and about me."

"It's not that I hate… ALL of it. I know there's something beautiful in it somewhere," she tried. "I thank you." She looked away from the figures to Nick. "Thank you for showing me. Maybe I'll look at it again sometime and I'll understand it better."

He could see that she was shocked, but he could also feel the great warmth that she felt in appreciation of his sharing. Suddenly the child drew him to her and put her lips against his. It was not much of a kiss. She hadn't really learned how to yet. He tried not to respond. Then, as if some frantic sense of despair overwhelmed her, she pressed her lips harder, with a little sob. He automatically opened his mouth gently, and his arms folded around her. "I want to try… everything … with you," she pulled away for an instant and gasped.

"You don't know what you're doing," he sputtered, but then drew her again into the embrace. His hands felt the soft mounds of her buttocks; she allowed his tongue to explore her mouth, her hands stroking his back, his arms. He kissed her ears, her long hair falling back. She groaned with, it seemed to him, a hint of fear. He drew back again, sensing her reluctance.

"Do you really, really know what is happening?" he held her by the shoulders, shuddering as he looked at her flushed beauty.

"I want it to be you. It has to be you. I want it to happen now," she pleaded.

As he drew her to the floor, as he fit his mouth to her taunt, throbbing white abdomen and down to her tight pink lips, he thought over and over that he must make it absolutely perfect for her this first time. Absolutely perfect.

She slowly opened to him and rose to him and moved with him as though she had been in rhythm with him for centuries and would be in rhythm with him till the end of centuries, and all he could wonder was if there ever, ever had been a beginning and an ending and how there ever would be. She cried out as he entered her, but her cry was followed by a deep sigh which urged him on, and when they locked in shuddering climax, and when they fell against each other, still clinging fast but falling into relaxation, he could see an incredibly beautiful smile spreading across her mouth, a smile that he had never even dreamed could be on the mouth of Susan. He touched her again, his hand cupping her lips. "Don't ever take your hand away," she gasped.

"Are you happy? Please be happy about this."

"I am very, very happy. I don't want this to ever end."

Suddenly his mind filled with a retching fear. The moment had ended. The day was about to end. The windows were darkening in the January sunset.

"We must put on our clothes and go home now."

"Help me."

He did not want to help her. As he began to dress himself, he was suddenly horribly ashamed of his feelings. He did not want her any more at all ... this child ... what could he do with her?

"We have to get up and go home." She stared at him with wonder. She silently put on her clothes. When she was dressed, she stood before him again without trying to touch him. She stood unquestioning, respectful of the great change that had taken place in both of them.

"I will take you home," he announced. He locked his closet and threw several rags over the paint spill, drew together the papers strewn over his desk, and beckoned for her to come through the door, which he locked behind them. Coming through the hall, they met and greeted Noah Leonard, just leaving the main office behind Jimmy Duffer and a policeman. Noah merely raised his eyebrows ambiguously to Nick. "Still on the Whitney thing?" Nick muttered in low tones as they drew close to Noah. Noah, instead of answering, frowned and swept his hand back and forth to indicate to say nothing more. Nick drew Susan back and waited while the trio left the building.

They drove to Susan's home in silence. Her face was a blank. As they approached, she began to give directions in a monotone, but when the car stopped, she sat and waited, then turned and looked at him. He turned to her, intent, studying her face for a clue as to what he should say to her now. She broke the silence. "I don't know what to say now, Mr. Bruno," she began. "I have felt so much in so short a time that I guess I'll have to think about it all for awhile."

The "Mister Bruno" was too much for Nick, and now his eyes began to fill with tears. He was amazed at the mysterious strength that had emerged from this gamine. And he felt his desire returning, like a wave of some fiery chemical through his blood. He took her hand. The move was uncalculated and senseless. "I want you now, even more than before," he began, "but you must know that what we have done and what we may do again may be very, very beautiful and even very, very good," he risked, "but the rest of the world won't see it that way, and, too, he felt he had to add, " if I ever get impatient or rough with you, it's just because I'm afraid, O.K.?" He looked over at her now because he had been speaking to the steering wheel for awhile so that his feelings wouldn't interrupt his thoughts. He wanted to take her right at that moment again, here in the car.   "Do you understand? I'm very much afraid of this?"

She looked back, longingly, her lower lip trembling. "I don't want us to be afraid."

"Can we go over there for awhile?" he motioned to a pull-off beside the road, surrounded by tell reeds of the canal banks and light enough to see only car tracks and room for one car.

This time they lay in each other's arms for what seemed to be hours. And this time there was no desire to pull away for either of them, and they lay naked, fondling and caressing, Susan in wonder and Nick in a new world of ecstasy with this tender, wise child with a miraculously lovely body. What had been the character of her fear? Had she been afraid of not feeling? How had he erased the source of it? His mind wondered as he lapped up the delight of moment after exquisite moment lost in the misty outline of the end of the day and the hazy moon of the January night beside the rumbling waves of the ocean bay.

At ten p.m. he opened the door to the lighted foyer of his home and the light from the large room upstairs where all their work was done where he could hear muffled scrapings. Joanna was still busy on her large canvas. She had built layer upon layer of plaster and clay and sand, and the enormous three-dimensional beachscape was almost ready for painting.

"Fantastic," he stood over her work. She rose to embrace him. They were artists. They often worked all night, had meals when they thought about it, and made love when they felt like it. A late homecoming meant that someone had just felt like staying out late. Nick adored her. She worshiped him. They worked, played, loved together with no questions, no suspicions.

"I have wonderful news. The agency called."

"What did they say?"

"They have a little girl they want us to meet. Her name is Sarah, and she's two years old and her grandfather is her only living relative. An explosion in their home killed her family while she was playing at a neighbor's. The grandfather is old and poor and wants desperately for her to have a good home. The director says she seems intelligent, and is beautiful. But we have to meet the grandfather, and the child has to want to go with us, he says."

"When do we see her?"

"Tomorrow morning. Can you call the school early?"

"Of course." He was joyful, but a sick ache dulled that joy as he thought of Susan, her wide eyes filling again with tears. She'll be waiting to see me tomorrow morning, he thought. And I'll be away, and she'll be afraid. She'll be afraid of Zimmerman, and Leonard, and everyone that calls her to account. But most of all, she has more reason to be afraid of me.

He looked into the glimmering eyes of his wife. "I'm so happy, Nick. I hope this one works out. We've waited so long."

"So do I, Joe, so do I."

*   *   *

"I told them everything about our visit," began Noah with Jimmy the next morning in Jimmy's office.

"What ... everything? You didn't tell them about our hiding in the shed? Noah, that's ridiculous, Noah. What good will that do?"

"No. You're right. I didn't tell them about that. I just told the account from Jake's appearance onward."

"Was Sutherland there?"

"No. They left him out of it. The Feds seem to want to do things their way ... alone, and interview Mr. Sutherland the same way they're interviewing us. At least they spoke of him in the context of what he had told them when they questioned him."

"Do you think they believed that we were merely unwise and awkward... like we were?"

"I can't tell. They're much too shrewd to second guess. We're dealing with the big time here."

"Did you mention the footprints?"

"Of course. And they were mighty interested. But they're also interested in something they found in Fawn's desk. It seems that they found a crazy letter from Nick Bruno to Fawn---something he probably wrote at school as a joke. They questioned me about him and his relationship with Fawn. You'll hear about it when they talk to you tomorrow. You know how Nick jokes. I can just imagine the letter. They wanted to know if any of the faculty had any reason to want to revenge themselves on Fawn, any professional jealousies, any known love affairs she might have had, any men she may have scorned. Nick can say outrageous things, and Fawn might have saved the letter for a memento. She loved Nick as a dear friend. She loved us all. She used to have him over to her house with students for special art and literature projects, and they ate together with Jo and sometimes with her friends from the city. She might have all kinds of Nick's mementos floating around. Jake Sutherland would never have gone deeply into her life. I have a feeling, though, that they'll finally find Fawn's murderer, but with the details they're examining, the job will take awhile."

"There's another thing," Noah continued. "It's a rumor, but an interesting piece. Phyllis Slavin said that Jake hung out at the bar at Cap'n Joe's, and Fawn used to take a few breaks there herself. Jake tried to put the make on her at least a couple of times."

"That must have been a wild scene. Jake's not in her league at all."

"I dunno---Fawn could be ... eclectic in her preferences."

"Couldn't be much there. Jake should have been home working on his kid's head instead of hanging out in bars. Anyway, let's just hope that this Nick thing will be over quickly. How do you think he'll hold up in an interview?"

"Wow, that's a hard one. Nick has so many facets to his personality. He appears to lead an impeccably normal life with Jo, prances and jokes around like the wildest, happiest clown just to make the world laugh, and yet he has the inwardness of a Hamlet, as melancholy as a clam. Don't try to talk with him when he's depressed. He'll cut you off like you've stabbed him---pardon the imagery."

"I'm also haunted by the sight of Jake Sutherland sneaking into that house with a pipe wrench. What in the hell did he want? Is he capable of such a crime?"

"I don't think so, but I'm no psychologist."

Jimmy smiled, then grew serious again. "I'm worried about something concerning Jake's son, Kurt. Lucy was in the other day to say that Kurt came to her house with some other students for a meeting of some sort, but he came by boat in the middle of the evening and behaved badly. She was going to have Julie Levitan's parents in to help her with him, but Kurt saw her concern and decided to leave after ridiculing her and the other students, and she says, following her around the house in an objectionable way. I told her never ever to let him in again, and if she should see him near her house, to call the police."

"Great. And his father would come?"

"She'd have to take that chance. His father will have to begin to control that kid. And I haven't heard about your scene with him after he disrupted her class."

"I'm sorry I forgot to tell you with all this commotion over the investigation. He was sullen and moderately agreeable to behaving, but I didn't think for one minute that he was penitent. She hasn't had any outbursts from him recently, at least, not that she's told any of us. But your story of this little visit really disturbs me. I think I'll go myself to John Sutherland and let him know what his son's been up to."

The Come From Aways

"I've already called him. He's very defensive of Kurt's behavior. Says he has no trouble with him at home, and that he's never done anything rash before. It seems that Big Jake agrees with his son that the curriculum is biased and maintains that Kurt was tormented in class by another boy. Do you know about that?"

"Yes. But the other boy slung taunts, not fists. Kurt elected to begin the violence. More like a junior high salvo than something that happens in a senior honors section. I remember that Kurt precipitated a few incidents on the grounds of the junior high, but this is his first big problem here that we know about."

"You know we still don't know why Jake was alone at Fawn's that day."

"Maybe he decided to conduct his own investigation; find something before the FBI had to be called. After all, they're coming in partly because Jake hasn't done much of a job, and he knows that and maybe wanted to be sure the place was clean."

"The footprints?"

"The murderer had boots just like Jake's? It's too circumstantial."

"His kid haunts me, and his behavior with Lucy has me furious. I'd hate to have her scared away from the classroom. She's a prize, that girl. The kids love her, and I do too, if you want to know the truth. Peter Mackenzie is a damn lucky guy to have a daughter like that."

"There are so many other leads opening up now, disregarding the story with Nick. The FBI is going down the lists of members of Fawn's organizations. There are all kinds of possibilities. Fawn is, was, a woman who inspired awe, and, quite possibly, jealousy and resentment from evil-minded crazies. It'll take time, but, again, I think they'll find the culprit before the school year is out, and it won't be any of our own."

"Please God."

"Now, on a brighter note, have you heard about Sam Rose?"

"No."

"Got a short story coming out in the Kenyon Review. Phyllis Slavin says it's wonderful, but won't tell anyone about it, only that it's going to be in a June issue and that Sam's got a new career. Sam scuttles by in the hall, smiling like a lunatic, but embarrassingly shooing people away who want to congratulate him and ask him about his story. He wouldn't even show the manuscript to me, as if I'd be judgmental of anything like that. I marvel at the ambition it must take to produce a finished manuscript."

"But you always wanted to write too, Noah."

"I know, Jim. And I have a novel, in my studio. I get the first six chapters out and look them over and type a few more lines every vacation, but I just don't have the gumption to make a really good effort to finish it. Someone's always wanting me to come out and play stickball."

"That can't be the reason. You certainly wrote enough for your graduate classes--- mounds of research."

"No, I think that I'm really afraid to finish it. Someone might actually want to publish the thing, and then everyone would know so much about me that I have hidden so successfully from the world for so long, and then so many of my greater human relationships would be destroyed, like yours and mine, pal."

"You put so much of yourself into your writing?"

"Doesn't every writer? But most of them must hide their thoughts more successfully than I hide mine. At any rate, if they would publish my story, then I'd have to promise to write another, and another. I couldn't stand such a lonely life. I belong here, torturing you, Jim."

"That's my boy."

"But I think we ought to talk with Lucy again...about Kurt."

"'Now you're worried'"

"Damn straight I am. You're not the only one who loves that girl."

"Say, Jimmy," he began again as he was leaving, "I haven't seen you at the window lately."

"Life's getting too serious these days, Noah. It's funny with me. When the big problems come along, I seem to forget the trivia."

Selma was not at peace with herself, or with Jimmy. His interviews with the FBI had left her in a constant state of upheaval and vexation with Jimmy for going to Fawn's house with Noah.

"You crazy idiots," she stormed that night. "Why did Noah have to take you over there, and you agree to go? What happens if they decide to take you to trial? Who pays our legal fees? What happens to our retirement? Our old age, down the tube. And what if there's a false conviction? It happens every day. You could go to prison. Noah too. That Fawn! What was she doing with all those pinko groups anyway? She should know better. She was so smart. Too smart, and always wanting to help people who should have been able to help themselves. Who knows what weirdoes she was hanging around with? Probably some black communist killed her who decided she knew too much about what was really going on."

"Selma, you're talking nonsense. Fawn's chief interest was civil rights. And civil rights just happens to mean rights for blacks, Jews, and all powerless minorities, as well as socialists and ... women, I might add. Noah and I are not suspects. They have absolutely nothing on us, and you're talking like ... a reactionary!"

He decided to try a new tack. He had been worrying too much around her lately. It was time to present another air at home, now that he was feeling more secure.

"Let's go to bed. I want to make love to you."

"Jimmy Duffer, you pick the most outrageous times."

"I mean it, Selma. You've been holding out on me too long, and I am sick of your evasions. I have my rights as a husband. I know, yes, that you have your nerves, but I also have my irrepressible needs, and not too many years ago you promised to fulfill them."

Selma gasped. What had come over him? He didn't seem at all worried anymore about the investigation. Well, if he wasn't worried, that labyrinth of worriers, then maybe she could relax. Some kind of strange relief, or was it a manic reaction---she knew a lot about those---a psychotic reaction to sheer terror? But should she pause to delve now? After all, her role as a good wife had been defined and reviewed for her since she was a tiny thing standing on a stool in the kitchen baking kitsch. She gazed up at Jimmy fondly. "I'm so sorry, Jimmy, that it's been so long. It's just that we had so many problems, and I thought, well, that you had lost interest in making love with me, and I didn't want to force myself on you or make you feel guilty or anything. I do love you, Jimmy ... you MUST know that."

"Then don't touch one more dish. Let the dog lick every one on the table and don't even think about cleaning up one more minute because I want you, NOW!"

"Oh, Jimmy, shouldn't we lock the doors first?"

"No, damn it. Takes too much time," and he scooped her fragile body into his arms and made off with her down the steps from the dining room and onto the sofa in a production that was half-drama, half-passion. But the performance had a residual effect. He found that he wanted more and more. Selma was in ecstasy. It had been ages since she had found him to be so ardent, and she was only left to wonder how it all had come about.

* * *

Phyllis blustered in from the cold and apologized to Lucy for shaking snow all over her rug.

"Don't worry. I'm so glad to see you finally. We have such a hard time trying to talk privately at school. I just had to ask you so much. I've got stuffed mushrooms to nosh on before dinner. Come on into the kitchen, and I'll mix you a great martini."

"Make that a double. It's been a fierce day. I hope you've gotten used to these tight schedules by now. The paper work is enough to make us all defect and go to stewardess school."

"Really now. But I would miss these kids so much. And we might make some little difference in their lives, give them some confidence."

"It's good to hear you say that in March. You've made it all of seven months in the school with the biggest JD record on Lawn Guyland."

"Now, let's get down to business," began Phyllis determinedly after a healthy swig of her martini.

"Let's take Harper first."

"O.K., Harper. What's the problem? I don't know Harper very well. He sat in my seventh grade class, but he never spoke. He took notes. Voluminous notes. And then wrote with great zeal and talent. A tiny boy with a perpetually serious demeanor. I never could get him to laugh, and that's my deepest commitment to my students. To show them that both literature and life ultimately produce something we have to laugh at. But I'm going off here on my own tangent. Harper. He's grown up now, I should think, and is after loftier goals. And let me guess; he's come to you with some extraordinary paper, or plea for advice, or confidence, or all three. Which? What? Tell old Phyllis."

"He's quite a case," Lucy began. "I hardly know what to make of him. He's brilliant and sensitive and terribly needy of some kind of parental love, which he denies, but knows all to well what he's after, and he's come to me, and Phyllis, I think it's inappropriate for me to encourage him, but there he is, and I don't want to hurt his feelings, but I know that his importunings are going to become more and more of a trial for me, and a self-deception for him. Honestly, I don't know how to handle this one."

"I think you've given me the toughest case first, girl, and I've never had a student lolling around after me that way. Maybe I'm just not the right type to inspire confidence in needy children, but, honey, I guess I would just say that all you can do is to maintain a friendly distance, keep him OUT OF YOUR HOUSE, and gently let this thing play itself out. He's got only one more year in the school, and you won't have him in class next year, and then he's off to college and you'll never see him again. There's only one thing, and I don't want to hurt your feelings, but you've got to hear it."

"My feelings are tough, Phyllis. Go on."

"No they aren't. I know you well enough for that. O.K, here goes. He flatters you. You're just as much involved with him as he is with you right now. This is your very first year as a full-time teacher. He's possibly the brightest kid in the school, and he's come to you. Yes, you're bright enough, but you're also warm, friendly, young, vulnerable, and he'll be like a parasite if you don't watch out. You'll be running every which way from him all over school. He's going to get hurt. But you should never, never blame yourself. He's come to you, and you must naturally, inevitably, rebuff him. You cannot be his mother or his lover or his confidante. He knows that. He's smart enough. Don't let him use you."

"Phyllis!"

"I know what I'm talking about. I've seen so many cases like this before. It always happens with these needy kids, and some teachers fall for it, excuse me, I know you said you were tough, but this is how I have to see it, and then feel guilty as hell when they have to put the students off, finally, and the students are crushed. That's why I never get too involved. All business. All at a distance. They know I care for them when they see their college recommendations. That's all folks. Let the counselors do their thing, and let the kids find affection from other adults that can support those relationships, but we're just the teachers, the kind teachers, the encouraging teachers, but not their emotional bulwarks against the world."

"I hardly know what to say. You've said it all. I did say to Harper that last night at my house that he should find a confidante in some sympathetic student, and he agreed. The students who were with us that night really showed an appreciation for some of the things he was saying."

"There you go. Good girl. Now ask him when he comes to you if he's made any headway with any of the others, and for heavens sake, stage your next student gathering right in your classroom. Don't bring anything home … ever."

"That brings us to my next problem. Are you ready for another martini?"

"You're taking me home?"

"You can even sleep over. Tomorrow's Saturday."

"Great idea. We can slosh our way into the night…through martinis instead of snow. Your next problem?"

"Kurt. Kurt Sutherland. He's becoming a real menace." And Lucy reviewed the Kurt Sutherland history.

"My God, you need help here. He should be removed from your class, for starters."

"Absolutely, I agree. But do you know what the school psychiatrist tells Noah?"

"Don't tell me. Let me guess. 'He's done nothing really violent to anyone; merely responded like a normal boy to a taunt. Until the young man initiates seriously violent behavior, we would have to have a court order recommended by a psychiatrist to have him taken out of your class. The only other option would be to convince him that he might enjoy another class better, but it's the middle of the Spring semester, and that would be against school policy,' and on and on. Yes, I once had a student who couldn't compose a straight composition to save his soul. He drew pictures of people being hanged, people in electric chairs, and people with guns to their heads. He listed all his hatreds: Wops, Kikes, Polaks, Niggahs, and, remarkably, Cunts, with my name attached. Without my solicitation several male students approached me and promised that if he laid a hand on anyone in the class, they would be on him in a second. I took the matter to our psychiatrist with all of these remarkable papers, and was given the same recommendation I have just related to you. The following summer he stole a shotgun and wiped out his entire family in their own garage. Ever hear of Bob Connery, the Hempstead killer? That's him. We serve the loveliest and the most monstrous, and at their ages it's sometimes difficult to know what they're going to do or be, but Kid, we have to protect ourselves, and I think you'd better get Jim to talk to old Jake himself about all this."

"He has. Jake was defensive. Says his son was unduly provoked. Says I must not be handling the class right. After all, I'm so new at this game. He says that Joshua had better review the curriculum, that it's all left wing biased, and his son is smart to notice. Not much help there."

"Not good. Well, just treat him like Harper. Keep your distance. Be on the defensive. And lock your doors and windows. Tightly."

"Now the biggie."

"Oh, aren't we finished yet? This drink is getting to me, and we haven't even started dinner. Have you no mercy?"

"I'm sorry. The stew is just finished. Let me take this in to the other table. No more questions till we eat. I don't mean to exhaust you."

"Exhaust, no. Get me soused, yes? These drinks are devilish strong, my girl … ummm, and this stew smells delicious. Is this what you fed your little student group? No wonder Harper is ardent."

"Au contraire. They got hot dogs and potato chips."

"Have you heard about Sam Rose?"

"Yes. Isn't it wonderful? But he won't let anyone see the manuscript. He's being modest, or something else. Everyone is dying to read it."

"I can understand his not wanting to show it around before it's published," Phyllis mused. "First of all, the editors will be changing it, and then, authors put so much of themselves into a story. I'm even a little surprised he's told anyone here at all if he didn't want us to ask questions. A lot of people write under pseudonyms and stay underground all their lives, especially with business colleagues. There are always jealousies, and cruelties, and callous remarks. And authors are such sensitive people, especially Sam. You do know that he's homosexual, don't you? Oh, that sounds like gossip, and I never should have said it, but we're getting into such heavy stuff here that it just came out. I didn't ever mean to ridicule. He's a wonderful man, Sam is."

Lucy was careful. "Are you sure? I mean does everyone know? Did he tell anyone, Phyllis?"

"Yes, I know. He tries to be straight. No, he's never made a formal announcement. But all the indications are there, Lucy. It's not hard to guess it. But then maybe you haven't … but then, why should you have? It's not something that he's proud of, that's for sure. Not the way they're treated. And it could cost him his job. The general climate isn't warm to them, not yet, and I doubt if it ever will be. Especially not in this Nazi community."

"What do you mean, this Nazi community? I don't know any Nazis, except, maybe, Kurt there. But that's all a fantasy now, this far away from World War II."

"Don't bet on it. Their only real regret is that they lost the war."

"You're serious."

"Yes I am. There are thousands, maybe millions, who are still thinking that even though what they did might have been a bit extreme, at least they were getting at the right people."

"Heavens."

"Yes. And this community was one of the Bundt strongholds on the East Coast. The name of this town, by the way, used to be Breslav, before the war. Check out the Board of Education, and the Veterans of Foreign Wars. What do you think that PTA meeting was all about? Noah managed to diffuse a lot of the immediate complaints, thank God, but the hatred is still around and treacherous, and we all have to walk a fine line. Some of them have transferred their hatred to communists and Negroes, but that wild isolationism is a classic disease, and they gassed thousands of homosexuals too. Those DAMN fascists," she shuddered. "But then I'm sounding almost like them, and we can't let them push our buttons. Oh, yes, Lucy, Sam will have to resign if he's written any kind of confessional. The politics of any community has an undeniable effect on the workings of its school. And teachers who the town perceives to be different will be scooted out with a heavy hand. They will assume immediately that Sam is out to seduce their little boys. It's a sick assumption, and wrong thinking, and society will have to deal rationally with its prejudice one day soon, but right now the homosexual men…and women, for that matter, are politically and socially powerless."

"Now you are anxious about another problem. Can I guess this one? Noah? What's going on?"

"We went to dinner."

"So. Big deal."

"It was a big deal."

"For him ... or for you?"

"For me for sure. I don't know about him."

"Lucy. Noah Leonard is bananas over his wife."

"I know that. He told me he loves her. But that people can love more than one person at a time in different ways."

"Gadzillikers, girl, he's right, but he's a royal cad."

"Why, Phyllis?"

"Because he's leading you on so, whether he wants to admit it or not. You're twenty-two. He's thirty-eight and been married twice. There's a world of difference in perceptions. He's flattering you and wanting you to flatter him back and that's it. NO MORE. FINIS."

"He's so entertaining, and brilliant, and suave."

"Yes, and damnably attractive. I can see how Marge gave up her big career and trudged way out here for him, but you know that marriage has its problems too. Oh, but here again I speak too foolishly out of turn. Marge is bored to death with Suppogue, and Noah is as comfortable as a clam here. Likes his work, likes the school, Jimmy, his great house on the water. Marriages are changing. Women aren't satisfied anymore to give up everything else they love for a man. Traditional marriage is one of the lies that the fifties tied a strangle hold around. We're going to see some social explosions one day soon."

"Are you saying that she might leave him?"

"No, Lucykins, I'm NOT saying that, and don't get any high ideas. I believe that Noah would even move back to the city for her, and he'd probably be as miserable there as she is here. So there. Marge is from Minnesota. The city represents her revealed personality. Long Island, Suppogue, more specifically, is more like the Duluth she left, only a lot warmer. Noah, on the other hand, is originally a city kid who loves the freedom of movement and quiet on the Island. He's still afraid of the water, but then, that doesn't stop him from liking to look at it and dream."

"How do you know so much about all these people?"

"We've all been here together for at least eight years, and we're very attached to one another. You know the faculty room? Of course there are always a few who can't fit in, who shy away from intimacy of any kind. There's Henry Zimmerman."

"A timid, wistful man."

"He may be timid and wistful, but he sure as hell strikes the fear of God, or the Devil, into our kids. A frighteningly literal mind, if I ever saw one. He doesn't belong in the classroom, and I don't bandy that phrase about lightly."

"I guess you've given me your best on Noah."

"Yes, as best as I can read it now, Lucy. Gosh, That was a great meal. Where'd you learn to cook?"

"I just putter around between student papers."

"Don't let it get out. You'll be even more dangerous than you are. Hey, what's the scoop on dashing Julius Martino? There's a catch if I ever saw one. Rumors are, and here I go again, that his whole family's into the mob... except Julius. He brings his Bible to school every morning and pours over it feverishly. Too much St. Johns. A wondrous case of overcompensation."

"What's that?"

"Guilt, my dear. Julius has it bad. Seems like a fine person, but I think he's scared of what his family's doing. His mother had to go back to Italy for safety last year, and Julius is the pride of his father's eye. But he won't go near his family home in South Ozone Park. Even had his name legally changed, but wouldn't give up the Italian. He's pretending he's someone else's son and carrying the name of some uncle who is a priest."

"What does his family do, Phyllis?"

"Everything illegal. They finally went into drugs when they couldn't stand the competition, and I've heard rumors that there are some links lately, some dependency, by the federal government. You know the kind of tricks that some of our ambassadors pull? Well, the mob is mixed up in all kinds of international dealings in many countries. The government sometimes can't function without their cooperation. But when a revelation becomes a possibility, somebody, or a whole lot of people, get bumped off. And there's so much money in racketeering that once they get used to the lifestyle, they can't give it up. I guess it's an addiction. Julius could have a great career ahead of him if he'd forget about going to Hell and go to his Dad," she smiled wryly.

"My big Saturday night date," Lucy groaned.

"Oh, Julius is quite the dapper gentleman. He'll show you a wonderful time, and I really should keep my big mouth shut. But you'll hear all this in the faculty room sooner or later. Everyone's past is explored in the faculty room. Someone should write a song about it."

"And you, Phyllis. What sort of great secrets are you carrying around with you?"

"Foul, foul. You'll have to find out about me from someone else with too loose a tongue. It's more fun that way. Besides, my slate is so clean and boring you'll be yawning before you're halfway through the life of Phyllis Slavin. Raised on small farm upstate. Father into radishes. Model student at

Binghamton. And working right here afterwards with an MA from Queens College. Fell madly for another English teacher my first year here who ran off with a far prettier, far richer art teacher to California. And nothing that interesting has happened to me since. I'm biding my time, writing poetry for fun, occasionally publishing in little mags and seeing every play On and Off-Broadway that I can afford. If Mr. Right doesn't come along in a year or so---you see I'm still a child of the fifties---I'm packing my bags and taking a job abroad. Why sit around Suppogue any longer? The world's out there waiting. Gad! It's after midnight. I've got to be in the city by noon tomorrow."

"The bed in the second room is all made up. I'll set the alarm for eight?"

"Perfect."

"Maybe we should think about sharing a house next year, Phyllis?"

"And maybe then we won't be such good friends. I'm a lousy housekeeper, won't clean or cook or anything else on schedule. Let's keep separate digs and stay friends, O.K?"

"O.K., but let's see more of each other."

"You bet."

MARGE GONE
Chapter Twelve

*"How long will ye vex my soul,
and break me in pieces with words?"*
The Book of Job, 19:2

"Well, if you can dine with Julius, what's wrong with me?" quipped Noah, in the faculty mail room with at least seven teachers, and a secretary within earshot.

"You have some nerve."

"This life demands nerve, my pet."

"I'm nobody's pet," Lucy grimaced. What was he doing now? Making his advances appear harmless. Well, maybe that's what they are.

"I'm serious." he followed her down the hall.

"I'll just bet you are."

"I have wine, and a deck, and a willow tree."

"Get away from me. I've got a class to teach."

"Can't think about two things at once? Me and Moby Dick?"

"Moby Dick's much less of a nuisance. You're a scoundrel and a cheat and I don't want to know you anymore."

"Hey, don't you remember that first day with your interview in the broken shoe? Don't you remember how I pleaded with Duffer to hire you when you came in so disheveled and nonplussed? All the favors I did for you? And now you treat me like dirt?" He followed her into the classroom.

"I don't believe you today," she whispered as she stacked her papers and adjusted her glasses. The kids were fascinated.

"I'm sorry. I really am sorry. You're taking this all too straight. I'll be a good boy from now on, I promise," in a much lower register.

"Just go now, please. The kids are staring," she spoke into her gradebook. She could see Kurt Sutherland leering at her. Harper was white. The girls wore big smiles. The electricity was sparking.

He turned, bowed to them all, and strode out with a flourish.

"Mr. Leonard needs a stage, not an office," she announced so that he could hear. Most of the kids laughed. Her tone seemed to work, for they busied themselves with the lesson.

*   *   *

"They're questioning Nick today," related Jim to Noah.

"Did you speak with him?"

"Last night on the phone. He's terrified. I didn't think he'd take it so badly. He's sick over it. I hope he holds up under their scrutiny."

"Did he mention the letter?"

"Yes. He said, 'You know, Jim, how I joke. Who would ever think that she'd keep something like that letter? Yes, I threatened murder if she wouldn't come around. Of course it was a big joke. Of course she knew it. Will you explain to them, Jim? Will you tell them?'

"I felt awful. I told him to refer anything to me. They're going to be crawling all over this place. Noah, you'll have to help me ... and Nick."

"I'm standing by. How literal is the F.B.I?"

"They have to be...a lot more than we ever are."

*   *   *

"Did all the American Presidents go to church?" came from the son of a Seventh Day Adventist in the rear of the classroom of Noah's American Culture class.

"They had to. They were politicians." A few giggles.

"What does that mean?"

"History is a story of what someone thinks happened, or wants to think happened. Sometimes one person's history disagrees with another's, and, so, people's perceptions are what matters; not, perhaps, what actually happened. Does that seem to relate to your question?"

"Doesn't make sense to me," cracked Buck Matthews. It all should be written the same so's we know what to believe."

"That's just the point, Buck. Unless we read enough to make some comparisons among all the writers, we can't be too certain about anything. Anyway, quite a few of the earlier Presidents indicated in their writings that they did not hold to a literal interpretation of what most others held as holy writ, so that those traditional religions that they appeared to practice, they generally followed for their political image. Read some of Thomas Jefferson's papers about how he regarded the Almighty. Some of his ideas surprise mainline Christians today. There's a great subject for a term paper, by the way, so I won't give away any more free information."

Only Harper raised his hand. "Why do the people tolerate this hypocrisy?"

"I suppose that people of that time were no different from people today, Harper. Certain forms and traditions lend comfort to many of us. In fact, it seems to me that some of the most outdated, most unreasonable practices are followed the most passionately. There must be something there that we can't see with our intellect. So we expect our Presidents to follow the forms, even if we perceive that they might not believe them religiously."

Harper was horrified. Motives had to be pure. Beliefs had to be genuine, static and immutable. Was there no one he could trust?

*   *   *

The cold March wind struck Lucy as she stepped outside the school, and she remembered that she had left her coat on the hook in her classroom. *I can't go back in there again. I will see him. What's wrong with me? Why do I let him get to me so?*

Now in her white Buick convertible, the engine running, she was waiting to think. Her mind felt as heavy as the leaden March sky. *I've just kept to myself too much. I need to go out more often instead of working away every night with my lessons and reading. Noah is working on me, and I'm trapped in this emotional tornado.*

The steam from her breath had frosted all the windows. She realized that she was breathing too hard; she thought of the scene in the school mailroom today, and a wave of nausea welled up.

Then a new sensation overwhelmed her. She was not alone --- had she heard something from the back seat, or was it her imagination? Dare she turn? Her eyes rose slowly to meet a reflection in the mirror. Two huge eyes, overwhelming a piquant face, met hers. The eyes were frightened, the chin slightly quivering.

"Harper!" She turned and confronted him, the restraint of her classroom broken in an instant.

"Miss Mackenzie, please, please don't be angry. I just had to talk to you and couldn't stand to stay in there anymore, so I waited for you here. Please, you're not angry, are you?"

"No, no Harper," she collected her wits. "I couldn't stand to stay in there much longer either."

Why in heaven was Harper doing this now? What a burden he is becoming, especially at this time, but I can't hurt him.

"I had to see you alone again," and the tears began to well in his sad eyes.

"Harper, Harper, what's wrong? Tell me, tell me." She hugged the back of the seat in a substitute gesture for a physical closeness which his position in the back seat fortunately prevented.

"Miss Mackenzie," he choked, "the kids are saying terrible things about you. They just can't be true."

She could feel that unwelcome rush of warmth flood her cheeks which lately had been flowing much too often. Her words came slowly.

"Harper, I really don't know what you mean."

"About you and Mr. Leonard." A great sob.

She grew angry. She must remind him that his questions were outrageously impudent, even in 1960. That he must never again address her in this way or hide in her car or speak in such familiar tones to any teacher: but she was beginning to realize that dealing with the emotional astigmatism of adolescence when you are yourself barely escaped from it, the tunnel vision of this maniacally moral generation cannot happen without excruciating hurt. No, especially not for Harper.

"Mr. Leonard. Hah! Mr. Leonard and I are friends, Harper, and we clown around like the rest of the faculty. We're just one big family, Harper."

"You're sure that's all?" She didn't want to feel foolish either.

"That's all, Harper. Once again I promise you." Oh, no, Lucy, don't sound condescending either.

Now the rushing, grateful smile that only the blindly inexperienced can produce. He believed her, instantly, and she prayed, completely.

"Those lousy kids. But they're always doing things like this to teachers. I should have known."

Lucy didn't know where to go from here. She must lead Harper away from this intensity.

"I know," she tried to chuckle. "They once had Mr. Duffer linked with Miss Tonka, I hear," believing she spoke the ridiculous.

"Why do they do these things, Miss Mackenzie? Why do kids make such fun of teachers? They might hurt people---a lot."

"Maybe because, because it hurts so much to grow up, Harper, and I think the kids feel that adults have too much over them, that adults have made it, have all the answers, and the kids are a little jealous of that, so they make fun of us who are in authority to try to make themselves seem more important. It's more complex than that---jealousy and fear too---but I think you understand, and maybe see more than I can if you look hard."

"How do you know how much it hurts to grow up, Miss Mackenzie? You are so beautiful and smart."

"Oh, Harper, I was ugly and skinny with huge braces on my teeth, and I thought the world hated me. I never really believed I'd be an adult. It seemed just as likely that I'd become an orangutan, or maybe I'd be lucky and God would strike me dead for my wretchedness. I hated pretty people."

"I don't really feel anything special about growing up---as opposed to just having to survive. Maybe it's because I'm with adults so much of the time anyway. I know the kids think I'm queer, but it really doesn't bother me so much anymore. I feel adult already. I guess I am in some ways."

"Yes, I think you are, Harper, in some ways," she lied again with a sigh.

"You don't like that?"

"I didn't say I don't like it. It's not something to like or dislike. I know that you are a very special person, and you are wonderful to know."

Harper beamed. He had been assured that his Miss Mackenzie still lived a pure life of the mind, a life he could share.

And Lucy flushed as she thought simply of Noah and how it might feel to be with Noah, close with Noah, and how she had to play so many different roles. She should try to tell Harper about that sometime, that being adult means you have to be a chameleon, be ... he'll call it being "hypocritical."

What a strange trio: brilliant, precocious but sentimental Harper; frustrated, naive, defensive Lucy; and Noah. What was Noah? A mystical lover? An emotionally unstable thirty-plus balding neurotic? A devious sexual wildcat, or, as he appeared in his office, implacable as a TV anchorman? Oh, yes, then there was Marge. That really makes four. I must not forget Marge.

"And now," she directed to Harper, "Let's do something very daring and very brave. I'm freezing without my coat. Let's go back into that school."

*   *   *

"I'm glad we went to the Kirch's for dinner tonight," Noah began as Marge pulled the car onto the approach to the Merritt Parkway. "How else would I have known about your plans?"

"Well how else am I to be at the theatre till eleven thirty every night? Oh, Noah, don't make this hard for me."

"There's always the Long Island Railroad. You could get cabs to and from the stations, I can pick you up there, and at least we can maintain some semblance of a marriage."

"The show's only running for three months, Noah. You can come into the city with me any time you like. Why should I have to be the one to commute?"

"I like it on the Island," he responded with no lack of self-pity. "Besides, there's the house and the dog and the cat and my job too."

"Noah, I know I'm not thinking of you right now one little bit. I can't stand it in Suppogue one more week. I want you, but I want myself more."

"This sounds serious, very serious."

"It is."

A long pause ensued while he counted birches on his side of the car. Then, "Please don't tell me there's anyone else attached to all of this."

She didn't respond.

"Come on, Marge. Good God, shouldn't you be able to level with me at all. I didn't even know about your apartment, and now... what ELSE Marge?"

"It's nothing."

"I'll bet it's nothing."

"Just thank me," she began, "for now you can spend as much time as you like with that Lucy what's-her-name. Don't you think that the gossip isn't all over school? Have you been to bed with her yet, Noah, or is she too pure for that kind of involvement?"

"Oh, no. This is getting cheap and silly. A game of tit for tat. Marge, I never thought we'd be this way. No one can compete with you, you know that, Marge. You're being silly and tormenting me. Now, tell me, is there really someone else in your life now? Answer me, and I'll try to accept it, and then we'll try to work things out."

Silence.

"Alright. It's Max Kellerman. It started as a friendship, and maybe it's all about what he represents for me, I don't know, but I do know that you and I just can't make it anymore, Noah; I can't keep living with you out in all that godforsaken sand and water. I have to be with creative people in the city, and, love or not, Max goes along with all of that."

As she drove, she could feel his rhythmic sobs shake the car bench seat. After about a minute, the sobs stopped. "You can't do this. You can't wreck our lives, Marge." His face was uncharacteristically flushed with beads of sweat on his forehead, and his hair around the nape of his neck was stringy with sweat on a cool April evening.

"I want to kill you," he stated flatly now. "By God, I want to kill us both. How can you do this to us? We've had such beautiful times, such exquisitely wonderful times together ... and you've wrecked it all---all over---all over." He paused for a moment, and then pleaded, "Let me out of this car, now, anywhere."

"I can't do that."

"Yes, you can. Drop me anywhere, but if it pleases you more, you can stop at the next Savarin and feel less guilty. I'll get a ride, you know I will. Just leave me there, please. I can't stand to drive another mile with you."

She did as she was told. She was relinquishing her responsibility for him, and she was surprised that she didn't want to do that, but she was not in charge now. He had taken control by demanding to be let out.

She drove into the next station and over to the restaurant entrance.

"Will you come home tonight?"

"Well, where will you be?" he answered.

"I'll probably be there."

"I don't know. This all happened so suddenly," he waved her off wryly now, only a few tears left. He closed the car door slowly and firmly. She hesitated a minute to see him walk over and stand by the restaurant door. Then, as she pulled away, she looked back. He looked smaller than he ever had to her, small, but defiant. She knew that she was being seriously bidden to leave, so turned and moved the car slowly out of the drive to merge back into the highway.

*   *   *

"It's Lucy on the phone," cried Laura upstairs to Peter who was shaving before leaving for court. "She wants to know if we'll be home tonight. She's off a day early before spring break and will come to dinner if we're free."

"Absolutely," roared Peter from the bathroom. "Haven't seen that girl in a month. Ask her where she wants to go. I'll get home early."

"Lucy, your father ..."

"I heard him, Mom. That voice carries for miles."

"We're so glad to hear from you, Lucy," Laura almost stammered. She had missed her daughter more than she knew. She had been thinking about her daily, every time she passed her room, every time she prepared a meal or saw the empty space where her car used to be parked in the drive. It was heart wrenching, this leave-taking. And she knew that she had made so many mistakes...maybe not terrible mistakes, but how was one to know?

Nothing ever prepares us for these relationships, these times, she reflected. No matter how busy I keep, she's always there with me, and we had her for such a short time. She was always so much of her own person. I could be so angry with her because I didn't understand her. Could I have done better with my own child? But that's a foolish thought. My own would not have been all my own either; they never are. Oh, foolishness, let us enjoy this evening and try to talk together as adults.

Then she was plagued with thoughts she hadn't had for a long time. What if something happens to one of us before we see each other this evening? What if one of us has an accident, and what if we never speak again to try to say some of the things we should have tried to say for years, some things that sometimes aren't ever said between children and parents, and then we die, and so many wounds could have been healed? I know she had to escape us. Why does that have to happen? Have we made her do anything rash that she wouldn't have done if she hadn't been resentful? Children do rash things sometimes when they're frustrated or upset with their parents. I know she likes Peter more than she likes me. Why shouldn't she? Peter is never judgmental. Anything she does is fine with him. He just takes her as she is ... high spirited, quick with retorts, careless of her appearance sometimes when she is working hard at something artful or intelligent, biting her nails down to the quick, and always restlessly moving about as though she's driven.

She must think about her real parents sometimes and wonder. I wonder where she came from. They weren't stupid people, that's certain, and they were fine looking people, but were they refined, educated, ethical people? Why did they abandon her? Is she resentful of them? Does that resentment fall back on us, on me, because of what her mother did, made all those promises? I can't solve all these mysteries by myself. I just need courage to ask her some of this. And I've never had much courage to do that. We've never ever talked about it at all, and Peter thought we never should. But I know how I'd feel, and we're all three adults now. I think she might want to talk, to get it off her mind. She's probably talked about it with someone else by now, some confidante, someone at the school. Maybe with those nice people, the Duffers. Maybe with Selma. She seemed like such a good person, for a Jewess, that is. But I can't ask her if Lucy ever spoke with her. That would be rude and tactless and...sneaky. I'll just have to do my best tonight to make her feel how much we really love her, just as she is, and maybe then she'll come to us more, more than just these monthly phone calls and occasionally running in for something she forgot.

The little restaurant off Queens Boulevard was nearly deserted on Wednesday evening, perfect for a quiet meal and conversation. But Lucy was hardly hungry. She was too full of news and problems at the school that she was anxious to tell her father. Had he heard about the murder investigation?

Did he know how the FBI worked? Her friends were in danger. Might Peter help?

"They'll never indict him," pronounced Peter firmly when she told him about the Nick Bruno trouble. "They'll see through something that foolish in a second. Trust me. He'll be in for questioning, and that's it, dear."

"Poor Nick is so shaken. They took him in, but they haven't told him anything. There's been no indictment, but he's certain that they'll consider him a prime suspect. He's such a funny guy. Writes and says the most outrageous things."

"Not great behavior for a schoolteacher ... you say he's an artist?"

"And a fine teacher too. The kids adore him. He's very charismatic. They even elected him president of the PTA last year, and he puts good programs together. He can be quite serious and effective when he's in the mood. He doesn't deserve this."

"We don't always get what we deserve in this life, my dear."

"Did you know this Fawn Whitney, Lucy?" her mother queried.

"No. Only by reputation. I was given her eleven honors section to teach, along with my other classes. That's one of the reasons I've been so harried this year. There's so much to adjust to, but I love the students, I really do."

"I understand that this Fawn Whitney was involved in civil rights organizations. I can bet that the FBI is poking around with that angle and will soon leave you at the high school very much alone. Such a person can represent some terrifying symbols to certain kinds of people. If she had the blameless social reputation you say she had, there must be a political motive for someone. But why would they come into her home like that, and no records were taken, nothing was disturbed?"

"Well, Dad, you certainly make me feel better about Nick, and the others. Mr. Duffer and Mr. Leonard have been questioned too."

"They have to examine and cross-examine everyone, Lucy. That's their job. If there were some personal motive, usually the murderer lurks around, trying to find out what effect the murder had on the friends, associates of the victim. It's funny, and I don't mean to sound maudlin about the old notion of the murderer always revisiting the scene of the crime, but it seems that if there's been anything psychological about the act, if there were hatred, or guilt, especially, the murderer wants more than the life of the victim ... he wants to destroy everything the victim represents."

"So what do you suppose someone like that might do next?"

"Oh, it's hard to say. He, of course it might be a women, might show up at the house again. Sometimes they take pride in what they've done and want to see, gruesome as it may sound, if they've left any blood, or if they can see the crime all over again. That's the real psychos, not the burglar killers. Of course, if there were cold political motives, she might have had a hit on her, but this murder that you describe doesn't sound like a professional job."

Lucy had other worries too. She had heard that certain forces within the federal government were in league with the Mafia, some dark mischief that involved the elimination of key civil rights leaders. Suppose that Fawn, little English teacher from Long Island, were a significant power in her particular associations? Suppose that she ... God forbid ... had been some kind of spy? She communicated those ideas now to her father, dramatic ideas that Julius Martino had whispered to her on their date last month as he was trying to entice her to go with him to Canarsie Pier, the makeout capitol of Brooklyn.

"If this were true, I think the case would have ended ... but then ..." her father hesitated ..."there would have to be someone on the investigation to keep that information absolutely quiet. The government would see to it that the FBI itself would never find out what it was looking for. That's a wild speculation, Lucy. Who suggested all this to you?"

"I'm sworn to utter secrecy," pleaded Lucy. "But it doesn't matter, does it... who has these ideas?"

"Certainly not to us ... nor, for that matter, to poor Fawn anymore. But it must matter a great deal to the federal government if it is anywhere close to the truth. And it would be good if the case were closed soon for your friends out there who are worried about the FBI crawling all over the school. I'll bet Jimmy Duffer's having a cat fit. Poor Jim. He's such a fine man. He spoke highly of you too, and I think it's wonderful that you're out there in his school. And it was just by accident that you went there for an interview. Do you know we're seeing them again for dinner? It's silly. We couldn't set up a date until early June, both our calendars are so full, but they're coming to us this time. Laura has it all arranged, don't you, dear?"

Lucy's mother had been markedly silent while all this conversation was going on about the school and the murder. Now she finally got a chance to speak.

"I found Selma and Jim delightful people. I'm glad too that you're in his school, Lucy. And there was another interesting couple there too that you must know. Noah and Marge Leonard. Noah's a brilliant man, and he must be your assistant principal."

""Yes, I know them well." Lucy wondered at the irony of her mother thinking that they were "interesting." Was that as opposed to "delightful" ... or what?

"Well, I hope that I wasn't the object of much discussion," Lucy had to say slyly.

"Only that everyone praised you in several ways," her father took up.

"That's consoling. So you think I'll have a job next September?"

"Undoubtedly," her mother laughed.

Laura was unusually ebullient. What was up? Lucy had never seen her quite so enthusiastic and positive before. There had been no questions about her living arrangements, her social life. Maybe she hasn't had time for that yet, she mused.

"I hate to run off like this," her father began, "but just today I got a call from a client who is in terrible trouble, and I have to see him. I hope you're staying over tonight with us?"

"Yes I am. Tomorrow's the first day of spring break, as a matter of fact, so I'll stay over and sleep late."

"Wonderful. Then I'll try to skip home for lunch. And your mother and you can have a good visit tonight. Well, dinner's over, so why don't I drop you at home?"

Laura hadn't heard before of any client. Was Peter reading her mind this morning and knew that she was yearning to visit with Lucy alone? He could be that perceptive.

"You seem to be very happy at Suppogue, dear," her mother began when they were alone at home and Lucy was curled up in the den, sipping her mother's lemonade.

"I am, mother, very happy. It's a hard job, though. I've got a lot to learn about how to manage some very troubled students."

"Oh, I thought you had normal classes."

"They are ... at least they're supposed to be, but I'm learning that there's no such condition as normal when it comes to high school students. Some of their problems can rip you apart if you let them get to you. I think I'm mostly in control, but I still say some of the craziest things and sometimes get myself into some unnecessary circumstances that I might have avoided if I weren't so ... stupid."

"Not stupid, Lucy. You've never been stupid."

"Or some other more polite euphemism you might use, Mother."

Laura flinched. She was determined not to find irony in Lucy's retort and move on.

"This murder investigation ... it doesn't touch you in any way, does it?"

"In a way, because my friends are so upset and have been questioned so often, and because I'm in Fawn's classroom and I am getting to know her so well from the things the kids say about her. I feel sometimes that I'm dealing with her ghost every time I hear her name spoken. Her students were distraught early in the year. They had so counted on her being their teacher, and then I walked in, a really disappointing neophyte. But they were polite, and we've managed. Except for one boy who thinks the curriculum is biased and left wing and, oh, Mother, he's a mean one. I don't think I want to talk about him much, though."

"Are there many nice young men out there?"

"Yes, several." And some not so young, she wanted to add to her mother's dismay, but she bit her tongue. Why spoil tonight by provoking unfortunate questions?

"I've kept as busy as I want to be for now. I've had good companionship with both men and women in Suppogue."

"That's fine, Lucy." Laura was warming to her more receptive listener now, because this was the longest talk she could remember their ever having together alone. "I want you to know that after that dinner we had with Selma and Jim Duffer, I suddenly began to realize how very, very fortunate we are to have you as a daughter. I pitied poor Selma so. She's never had a child and wanted one so badly, and now she's almost past that age I would expect. I don't know why they didn't adopt like we did. Perhaps Jimmy ... but it isn't fair to judge other's motives ... repressed the idea of adoption, but did you know that Mr. Duffer's from Canada, just like you? Newfoundland, originally, he said. And he and Mr. Leonard are going to return there soon, I think...Memorial Day weekend and maybe longer so that Jimmy can trace some of his roots. He left his family at an early age too, just like you."

Lucy thought, I hope he has better luck than I've had, but kept it to herself. Instead, she said, "Sounds like our school is chock full of foundlings, like some soap opera. I hope he gets lucky. Newfoundland's a wild place, I hear. Kind of romantic, actually, I guess if you don't live there. The kids in the convent school used to joke about Newfies. They're supposed to be pale, white, brainless things who swim in ice water all year. But Jimmy Duffer certainly doesn't fit that description. He's a perfectly insightful principal, as far as I know. Always supportive, and never intruding. The city fathers try to drive him crazy. Too many political reactionaries around there."

Laura suddenly thought how fine it was to relax with an adult daughter and be relieved of the need to correct, to protect. She remembered some history of Lucy's new town. "Suppogue, I've heard some fascinating stories about Suppogue that I wanted to tell you about. During the twenties that town used to be the spot on the South Shore where all the liquor came in for New York City during prohibition, of course. There was a big speakeasy there...the authorities left it pretty much alone, of course. The police would stage a raid every once in a while, but they would warn the owners to make themselves scarce, and then they would make mock arrests and release everyone the next day. Baloney Johns, they called it."

"Mother you're a font of information. You with your town histories and genealogies. Any more dirt on Suppogue?"

"Yes. Annie Oakley used to live there. Grew up in a little house on the bay."

"I have news for you. Her house is at the end of my block. I...swam there once!"

"Delightful! Now I hope I can garner an invitation to see your place. I promise not to scrape my fingers over your picture frames for dirt, or worry over anything. Please let me come sometime."

This was indeed a new Laura Lucy heard. I really think she's reformed, Lucy thought. I will invite her. I'll take that chance now. It sounds like we can be almost friends.

"Tell you what. When all my exams are over and I have time to clean and set things up the way I want, I'm going to have you and Dad over to dinner."

Laura was thrilled. She'd done it, and it wasn't so hard to forget to try to be a mom for just this once. Could she continue this kind of behavior? She'd try her hardest, for it meant keeping a daughter.

"And Mom, if it's alright, I think I'll go to bed now. It's been a rough week."

"Well, sleep late, and I'll fix a good lunch for you and your father."

"Luv you, Mom."

The two embraced in such a genuinely affectionate way, that both were overwhelmed. "It's just wonderful to have you here," sighed Laura. "I think I've found you by losing you to Suppogue."

"Maybe ... that could be true, Mom."

HENRY'S SOLUTION
Chapter Thirteen

A narrow fellow in the grass
Occasionally rides;
You may have met him...did you not,
His notice sudden is.
The grass divides as with a comb,
A spotted shaft is seen:
And then it closes at your feet
And opens further on.
Several of nature's people
I know and they know me;
I feel for them a transport
Of cordiality;
But never met this fellow,
Attended or alone,
Without a tighter breathing
And zero at the bone.
Emily Dickinson

"I want you to know, Mr. Bruno, that I'm pleased and thankful that the Federal Bureau of Investigation did not see fit to indict you yesterday," Henry Zimmerman stood over Nick who sat, pale and shrunken, in a lounge chair in the faculty room, the last afternoon before spring break. "It is a good thing for you and for our school that this little case is finally closed on our faculty."

"Henry, I don't think that Nick wants to talk about it, please," put in Phyllis Slavin.

"Of course. One can understand that completely. Miss Slavin, I have a very high opinion of your judgment within the scope of your understanding, that is, but I must speak to Mr. Bruno privately about another matter, if you don't mind." He turned again to Nick, "Can we go to my classroom?" Nick looked up, weary, and puzzled. "Can't it wait, Henry. I'm just trying to get through this day so I can go home and plotz."

"I don't think it should, Mr. Bruno. The matter carries with it a kind of urgency ... about a student, you see, that I've been waiting to broach to you when I knew your mind would be more receptive, after all this commotion over Miss Whitney's murder, ahem."

Phyllis detected something sinister in Henry's tone.

"Alright, can I come after this last class, Henry?"

"Certainly, I'll be waiting," he strode briskly out the door.

"What a pretentious pain-in-the-ass," broke in Nina Cordoza. "He doesn't belong with adolescents. He's dangerous to fragile minds."

"Whoever gave him tenure ought to be shot," from Saul Razzler, "but it was so long ago I can't even remember who it was."

Nick, as though summoning his last ounce of energy, rose and stood in a rumpled silhouette before the soft golden afternoon light of the western windows. "This bastard has me. He's got me wedged tighter than those damn feds who just had me through two lie detectors and a psychiatrist's exam. He's going to get me, and after what he's going to do to me, this old Nick might not be around anymore." He paused, gave Phyllis a taunt moue, and slouched toward the door.

"Wait a minute, Nick. You don't have to take anything from that creep. Do you want me to go with you ... Nick?" But he was gone.

"It's nothing. He's exaggerating again. He's just in a state from all his hassles with the feds."

"He always lets whatever he thinks all hang out --- too far sometimes."

"What in the devil is going on between him and Henry?"

A note from Henry had reached Nick's school mailbox earlier in the week, but he had tried to ignore it in the throes of the FBI trauma. It had read, "I must, as a point of conscience and duty, speak to you about Susan Morand."

Yesterday afternoon Joe had been waiting for him outside the Suffolk courthouse with little Sarah in her arms. He saw the beautiful tableau through the car windows as he approached: the ecstatic mother, the tumbling, happy child. They might have been so lucky, they three.

He felt a sharp pang of anxiety for Susan. He was trying to keep away, but at the same time, not appear to reject her. Thank heaven she seemed to understand that this affair had to end. And possibly to help matters, Simon Finch had found Susan ever so interesting lately. If she can now go to Simon and be happy there, and by next fall after a long summer of separation, she will have cooled off to me, but last night he had seen her one more time again in his car. This had to stop. Now.

He dragged heavily into Henry's room after his last class was over.

"I'm so glad you came right down, Mr. Bruno. We have to talk about a very serious matter, and it's important that you take this in the right frame of mind... that you be prepared."

"What are you talking about?" Nick was furious with Henry's tone, his devilishly provocative presumptions, and his insistence on ridiculing their equality with the "Mr. Bruno."

"I know everything. I saw everything."

"What?"

"The afternoon you took advantage of Susan Morand in your art room. I came up to try to find her. She constantly hides from me, and I know where all those students go ... to you, Nick Bruno. And now I know why. You have been molesting heaven knows how many innocent children up there in your den of iniquity, and now we must put a stop to it all."

Nick was transfixed. He was hearing, through this agent of the absurd, the horror of horrors finally come true in his own world.

"I thought it was the most honorable thing to do to tell you what I am going to do this afternoon. I had to wait until this hearing was over with the police to go to Mr. Duffer and the Board of Education to tell them about you and Miss Morand and to tell them to investigate what else ..."

"Look, Henry. It's not all like that. You can't do this to me. Susan ... she is ... it's not really what you think it is ... not so terribly bad. It can be undone. I ...Henry ... I don't know what more to say."

"There's nothing more to say, Nick, I'm afraid." Henry put his hands together on top of his desk at which he sat with the mouth of a wooden rabbit: tense, tightly sealed lips, oval pate, side-tufted with gray, pig eyes rimmed with gray spectacles.

"You've got to listen to me, Henry, as a man you've got to try to understand. Yes, what you saw was wrong, very wrong, and I'm trying to make amends and help us all out of this, but before you speak, you've got to know that even though what you saw was wrong, if you speak now, you'll wreck four lives. Count them, Henry, four. I'm not pleading just for myself, Henry, but think about the shame this disclosure will cause Susan, and my Joanna and my child. Please, please Henry, I promise you that I'm trying to work myself out of this mess as honestly as possible with as little hurt as possible. It's just Susan. No other students, just her. She came to me. I was foolishly vulnerable, and I hate myself for it, but we're both trying to work it out. I love my wife, my new child. Please try to understand, Henry, and wait. Please wait."

"How do I know you're telling me the truth. That Susan's the only one?"

"Henry, you don't know. You just have to trust me for a little while. Please, Henry!"

"I have to think about all this. I don't know exactly what my responsibility should be now. It's a matter of duty and conscience. And you are complicating the matter considerably, Nick. But you are doing a terrible thing, and such secrets should not be kept inside. They can destroy us and ultimately destroy all we touch."

"Yes, yes, Henry, I know. But just please wait and I'll find some way to prove to you that I can mend matters. I respect and adore my students, Henry, and I respect and adore my wife and child. Don't destroy it all for me and my family and my students because of my one mistake."

"You should have thought of all that before ..."

"It's not a question of thinking, Henry. Good God, haven't you ever done something that you hated yourself for but couldn't help doing it? A desire so strong and so overwhelming that your whole being was on fire or ..." he stopped as he looked at Henry's face, so obtuse, so composed, so utterly passionless. "I guess not. I guess I'm just at your mercy."

He was spent. He looked one more time at Henry's pitying eyes, for now, at least, they seemed to contain a glimmer of sorrow for him and shrank away and out the door.

Somehow he reached his car, engaged the engine, and drove slowly out of the parking lot, turning at the end of the block toward his home in East Patchogue.

* * *

Lucy awakened the next morning with a feeling of ease she had not felt for some time in her parents' home. Her visit with her mother had been enervating and hopeful. She was looking forward to talking with both her parents that day and enlisting their help in what she had decided she must do to put her mind at rest; the kind of quest that little Harper himself had shared with her at her cottage that autumn evening which now seemed so long ago.

She glanced around at her room, the room she had grown to love that she had been given as a young girl, fresh from the convent home in Connecticut. Laura had decorated it, of course, and even though Lucy had yearned to make drastic changes in the decor as she moved through one growing stage to another, she was afraid of insulting them by asking.

Now, as she returned from another place of her own, she found herself cherishing the ruffles and the embroidered pillows and pinks and lavenders of her mother's choices. She was glad that she had left the room as it was over all the years as a kind of monument to their gift of a new life, of the best of what they could give her. There were photographs stuck around the rim of the mirror of her with Laura and Peter and her cocker spaniel "Vous" that they had given her that first Christmas in Queens, and who was curled still at the bottom of her bed, even though she was now so arthritic that Lucy had to help her up onto the comforter.

The apple tree outside her window was in blossom, and Lucy remembered how she had climbed up and down that tree and in and out through her window to the consternation of Laura who thought that she would take a terrible fall, but it was Peter who insisted that Laura not forbid her to climb. "That girl's as coordinated as a gazelle. We can't always be sheltering her and scared to death that she'll hurt herself, or she'll hate us forever, and, worse, still, never know how to face the world."

She could smell the fresh funny cake, her father's favorite, warm from the oven, and knew that it was time to join them in the kitchen. How can I falter from any kind of news about my first parents, she mused, with this wonderful sheltering and loving from these thoroughly decent people? Yes, I fled from Laura, but we've both learned a lot since then, and it's all worked out fine. We're different in our mannerisms and tastes, but that's all to be expected. And they really treat me like an adult now. I surely hope what I have to say to them today won't change anything.

Peter was warming up with coffee and a piece of the funny cake when Lucy put in her appearance. "Whoa, girl, you must have been very tired. It's eleven o'clock. Just in time for brunch!"

"I haven't been able to sleep like this for months. It felt so good not to have to jump out of bed to an alarm clock, and those spring breezes in at the window!"

Laura, delighted to have them all in the kitchen together again, made a great deal to do with several intricately presented dishes of meats and breads. "I see Vous was back at her old spot on your bed last night. She didn't waste any time showing you how she remembers," laughed her mother. "I've been stuffing her full of vitamins and aspirin to keep her going. She still likes to go out to the park with us on Sundays and chase the squirrels."

"I'd take her to the cottage," mused Lucy, "but I don't think my ducks would appreciate her, and anyway, she's probably too old to adjust to new surroundings. And I guess you'd miss her too."

"You can let her stay here, Lucy," her dad put in. "You hardly have time for dog walking with your schedule, do you?"

"I guess I could work it out," and she thought of Sludge. "But I don't know where I'll be this summer yet. The owners will be moving back as soon as school is over, and I have to make other plans."

"Oh, you'll come back here for the summer, won't you dear?" Laura put in, and then wondered if she had sounded too eager.

"I haven't gotten that far in my plans yet," Lucy spoke out honestly, not wanting to offend her mother, but realizing that her life was, as yet, unsettled. She hadn't been thinking more than a few days in advance all year, even though she knew she would be invited back to teach at Suppogue ever since her last observation and interview with Joshua Perkins. She though also of Phyllis and her ideas about seeing more of the world than the school community of Suppogue. But somehow there was so much of the Island living that appealed to her for the time being at least, and there was still so much for her to learn where she was.

"I'll let you know what I've decided as soon as I know myself," she smiled at them both. "I might continue my graduate work at Columbia this summer, and then, if you don't mind a cloistered student hanging out around here again, I'd love to stay."

"Delighted, darling," from Laura. "Let us know anytime you're ready."

"There's something else I have to do this summer," she began tentatively. "I want to talk to you both about an idea that has been with me for quite some time, and it won't go away. It's probably not the best of ideas, but it's come to mean a great deal to me, especially since I've been living on my own and wondering about my past and if I should know more. I keep thinking that perhaps there are some people in my family in Canada that should know me and that I should know. I guess it's not exactly an identity crisis, but I really want to know if there's any way we can find out if anyone of them is alive."

Laura grasped the sides of the table and looked imploringly at Peter. He seemed comfortable with Lucy's words, ready to respond.

"I don't see why we shouldn't make inquiries. I don't know how much the place in Connecticut knows or how much they have the authority to tell, but we certainly can make the effort to discover as much as we can. There seemed to be no need when you were a little girl. You were eligible for adoption, and we were more than ready to take you. At that time the place hadn't heard from your mother in over five years, and that was the time designated by the state that permitted them to let you go. We weren't told if they had any records of addresses or telephone numbers, but they must have had names in their files. Frankly, we didn't want them at the time. We wanted you all to ourselves, like most adoptive parents do. I suppose that's the worst fear, that somehow you might have been taken away from us.

But you're an adult now, on your own, and we love you and want you to be satisfied that we've done our best."

"Lucy, are you sure that you want to know? What if it isn't pleasant?"

"Laura, stop. It's her decision to make. She's got a brain that can sort out all the possibilities. If she wants to go ahead, we've got to help her. Adoption isn't what it used to be. There are all kinds of dimensions to this kind of thing."

"Yes," put in Lucy. "There are several agencies now that help adopted children find their birth parents."

"And some of them aren't legal." added Peter. "Let's see first what the convent in Connecticut will tell us. We may be pleasantly surprised that they have helpful records. Then we'll go from there."

Laura was distraught but trying to contain herself. Lucy knew she was having a hard time, and sought for some way to console her for the present.

"Mother, this concern of mine has nothing to do with my wishing for more than you and Dad have given me," she tried. "It's just wanting to know about a part of my life that is right now an utter void. You must be able to understand how empty a feeling it is not to have any inkling of where I was or whom I was with as a baby. It would just fill in my perceptions of who I am and where I came from, that's all. I think I could be healthier …"

"You're wonderfully healthy now, dear, and so smart and strong …"

"Laura, let's do as she asks. I will call that convent today, and also I'll ask Ben Polanski, who put me in touch with the mother superior, what their Canadian connections are and what their policies are on privileged information. Laura, you're great at solving genealogical puzzles. When we get a name, maybe you can trace all the connections in the Canadian Maritimes. If the orphanage doesn't have complete records, maybe we can be our own sleuths. Maybe we'll even take a trip up there to your first home, Lucy."

*   *   *

"The Babylon line of the Long Island Railroad was shut down for several hours from five until eight o'clock this evening when a thirty year old man was stuck and killed near the station by the four forty-two express train from Jamaica. The engineer on this limited express train claimed that the figure appeared from a clump of bushes beside the track directly in the path of the train so that it was impossible to apply the emergency brakes in time. Identification of the victim is being withheld until the family has been notified."

Poor devil, thought Noah, as he listened to the evening news while downing another can of Bud. Wonder who in the world could summon up the temerity to take his life away like that?

The phone pierced his thoughts. It was Jimmy. "Joanna called me. Nick isn't home. She says it's late for him on a Friday night, and she wonders if he's with you."

"No, Jim. I'm all alone by the telephone."

"Where's Marge?"

"Gone. Gone. Gone."

"Why the chorus?"

"It's pretty final."

"Noah. What are you saying to me?"

"She's back in the city. She wants a separation. Like that."

"Noah, can you come over here?"

"You bet. I'm lonely as hell. I'm in my car now."

Henry Zimmerman was at a late supper in his kitchen with a cold plate of tuna and onions when the news came over his radio, but by the time it was read to his station, the ID had been cleared, Joanna notified, and the name Nicholas Bruno read by the announcer. Henry paled and stared transfixed for several seconds, then left his dinner, rose, and began to pace to and fro in the small kitchen of his apartment as the news broadcast turned to the international report, but Henry did not hear anything further. Finally, after several minutes of pacing, he turned to his telephone. I've got to do my duty. They've got to know, he reasoned as he dialed Jimmy Duffer's number.

Noah held Joanna as she shuddered against him until her exhaustion overcame her emotions, and she fell into a chair. Jimmy sat with them until her sister and husband arrived.

"He's been so worried about the investigation, so unlike him. He usually didn't let anything to do with the law upset him. He's been out late, very late lately. I don't think he wanted to bring his anxieties home to me." Noah sensed a dedication in their relationship, the trust, and now the excruciating pain for Joanna.

"Joanna, you should know that the FBI have excused us all from further questioning," Jimmy put in.

After a moment, Joanna frowned and looked deeply into Jimmy's eyes. "Then what ... what was it? Was it really an accident? Could he have just been crossing those tracks and not heard? Maybe he was deep in thought and just didn't see."

The phone rang mercifully. Joanna's sister delivered the message. "It's Selma, Dr. Duffer. She says that she just received a call from Henry Zimmerman who says that it's urgent that he speak with you."

"Let me take it then, thanks."

"Jim," Selma's voice was shaky. "Henry Zimmerman says that he's got to speak with you. Says he may be the last person to have talked with Nick."

"Selma, can you return his call and tell him that we'll meet him at the school in half an hour?"

"Certainly."

Jim nodded to Noah, who could sense the necessity and was ready to follow Jimmy's lead. "Joanna, we're standing by with anything you need, any time, day or night," Jimmy embraced her as they left her in the care of her family.

"Jim, why is Henry calling us instead of the police, or Joanna?" Noah queried as soon as they were in Jim's car.

"I think we can be thankful we're the ones he's called first. We know the limitations of his understanding, and his temperament, at least to me, is gravely unfathomable. He hated Nick, and even though the man's dead, he could blow his reputation sky-high, and for what purpose? I think we're in for …"

"Deep shit."

"Eloquently put."

Henry was waiting for them in his blue sedan in the parking lot.

"Wise to meet him here. I wouldn't want him in my house, either."

"Always good to keep these things out of our homes. And I'm glad we're on break. Strange. Nick was just exonerated, and then, this. Wonder what this grim bastard has to tell us."

"Maybe nothing. Maybe he's just eager to exercise his own sense of importance again. You'll have to watch me, Jim. I'm not discreet around Henry."

"You'll be fine. Henry can use a little flaying. Wonder if that guy has bone marrow?"

"There's definitely some physiological void."

"God. Joanna. What terrible grief," Noah went on. "Certainly puts lesser concerns in prospective."

Jim imagined he was thinking of Marge's defection.

"It's amazing, the commonalties of our human tragedies of separation, Noah. We all get to know about it in different forms, sooner or later."

"You bet," rejoined Noah through clenched teeth. "Now it's on to St. Wunderlicht."

"Yes, we can't make him wait any longer. He'll wonder why we're sitting in here so long."

"Because we're so eager for his company," finished Noah as they left the car and walked toward the south door of the new wing where Jim had his offices.

Henry scurried after them and was upon them as Jim turned his key in the lock of the big door.

"I wanted to come to you first," he began, "before the police came to me."

"Let's wait a minute, Henry, 'till we all sit down," cautioned Jim.

After they were settled in Jim's office chairs, Henry continued.

"I invited Mr. Bruno into my classroom late in the afternoon yesterday to discuss with him his behavior with the students in his classes," began Henry. "And some of that conversation I think best to relate to you, as it concerns what I must perceive to be your responsibility."

"Whatever can you mean, Henry?" Jimmy, though immediately put off by Henry's obnoxious presumptions, was listening to his words carefully, under the critical circumstances.

"Mr. Bruno consistently drew some of our most aberrant students away from their scheduled classes and into the art room to, to dally with him. To waste their precious time when these same students needed to keep up with their responsibilities in math, and science and, well, they even cut their gym classes."

"Henry, what is the point of all this? The man's dead. What was it you said to him yesterday, and how could it have affected him in any way?"

"He was not contrite when I confronted him with his indiscretions, but he was most concerned when I told him that I was ready to go to you and to the Board of Education with my charges."

"I'm surprised, Henry, that he would be so concerned. The students went to him voluntarily, as far as I know, and certainly I've never heard of any real recklessness in the art room."

Henry drew his lips tighter together, and, Noah thought, his mind seemed to be searching for the proper way to say something significant.

"I am most regretful that my poor power of language cannot express my sorrow over what I believe to be Mr. Bruno's very real guilt over his, that is what I perceive to be, licentiousness of behavior with his students, and," he took a deep breath, "I cannot but believe that these practices of his have proceeded from a faulty degree of indulgence on the part of the administration of this school. You are to be blamed, Mr. Duffer, for all this misfortune."

"What in the hell are you insinuating, Henry?" Noah rose, flushed and furious.

Henry was in no way intimidated. He was empowered by his newfound magnanimity.

"The result of this excessive latitude which you have given Nick Bruno shows that you must rein in many of the rest of the faculty who may have exceeded the limits of discretion in their inter-personal relationships, and, it may follow along, their business with their students."

"Henry. You'd better get your pretentious ass out of this office right now, or they'll be another faculty death before the sun comes up in the morning."

"Noah. Sit down. Henry, if you have nothing further to say, no other way to enlighten us, perhaps we'd best speak about this matter sometime again. If you have nothing more definitive to say to us or to the authorities, I would appreciate it if you keep silent until we can speak when classes resume. I appreciate your concerns, and wish you good evening."

"I will, under the circumstances, leave now," Henry replied to Jim. "And I do not intend to go to the authorities. I realize that as concerns this matter of Mr. Bruno, that nothing that would help either they or Mrs. Bruno was exchanged between him and me this afternoon. The other matters concern only you. And I hope that some of this ugliness will be dispelled from your mind when you rejoice later in the spring at my unusually high mathematics regent's scores. But now there is another matter," and Henry glared at Noah. "I will never set foot in this school again if you do not promise to keep that man," he gestured with a dramatic sweep of his right hand to Noah, "out of my sight."

"Well, now, Jim," Noah rejoined. "A most difficult decision lies before you. From what Henry says, you must now be rid of one or the other of us. Henry will resign if you refuse to restrain me, and I will certainly be gone tomorrow if you do. I am a free spirit, Mr. Zimmerman, and am wont to roam about the school wherever I choose, as befits the nature of my position."

Henry was perplexed beyond his understanding at this retort. He was certain that if either Noah or James had all the information that he had, they would make the matter of Nick Bruno and Susan public immediately. But some ambivalence about his own motives, perhaps some small voice deep within his conscience, prevented him from making this final disclosure.

"I can only be consoled," he extended his parting words, "that this unexpected tragedy has made us all indiscreet and inarticulate for the time being. Good day." And with a little bounce, he turned and was out the door.

"God save us!" sighed Jim. "That was all I needed to finish me off for the semester. Tell me that we can survive the next ten weeks before summer."

Noah, slumped in his chair, suddenly was roused by a memory. "Jim, we forget. We have a trip to take."

"Whatever are you talking about?"

"It's almost May. Memorial Day weekend. Remember? We're going to the frozen north. St. Johns. You promised to take me to meet all those Gaelic wenches. Pack those bags, Jim. Tell Selma it's time to visit her aunt in Sheboygan."

*   *   *

When Susan Morand first received the news she fled to the phone to ring up Simon Fitch. Together they ran to the school, and sneaked in by a janitor's back door. Simon had keys to all the rooms important to him, so they entered Nick's classroom easily and found his secret closet key on the big ring he always kept behind his lab coat hook on the back wall. While Susan held a large plastic garbage bag, Simon took a sledgehammer from the sculpture shelves and smashed every figure from the closet into powder against the wooden counter. When the cleaners found the bag beside the closet, there was less left of the remains of the figures than there had been of Nick on the railroad tracks. Afterward, the two huddled together for awhile, surveying the art room in one final goodbye.

Susan never came near the art room again. After the spring break she began to attend all of her other classes that she had fled for so long. She even appeared in Henry's room, ready, as Henry announced, to "be done with past offenses and try her best to understand at least some of the material before the end of the term."

*   *   *

Lucy spent the afternoon after Nick's tragedy in the garden. She had always loved this precious plot behind the big house on top of the hill, the terraces and circular walk surrounded by varieties of daisies, phlox and roses cornered with fern and, on one side, an herb garden. She trimmed and pruned and clipped some spring shoots of basil and chive to use in a sauce for tonight's meats and vegetables. She had missed being home, and she hadn't admitted to it. She was still lonely in her cottage, even though the independence was refreshing. It was a time for her to be on her own, she felt, but also a time to look forward to new companionship.

Peter and Laura lingered in the kitchen. "We'll have to tell her soon, Laura. Otherwise she'll hear it first on the radio or television."

When Lucy returned from the garden, happy with her herbs to cook, she found them still waiting in the kitchen.

"We've heard some sad news on the radio," Peter began. "One of your friends from Suppogue, whom you spoke of last night, was struck and killed by a train in Babylon. I expect you'll want to make some phone calls. It was Nick Bruno."

*   *   *

"The act was not unlike Nick, I can't help but think," mused Phyllis. "So much of what he did was so marginally tenable. Once when we were discussing Kierkegaard, he seemed so entranced by the idea of angels, and I asked him if he believed that they really existed. He lit up and announced that anything we could imagine, anything our minds could conjure up, MUST exist. I only hope that there is a glorious side to all of this that he did imagine."

"Phyllis, we have to go to see Joanna. Not at the wake but before … now."

The three women huddled together long into the night, pondering the mysteries of deepest sorrows. Earlier in the evening Joanna had received a call from Henry Zimmerman, expressing his condolences and offering help.

*   *   *

The wake was crowded. There were relatives from up and down the eastern seaboard surrounding Joanna who clutched her child in her arms for much of the evening. With many endorsements of her stability and character, the adoption agency had consented to permit her to keep the child, at least for a year while she was given a chance to re-form her life.

Students were in and out, their grief wholly apparent. Susan and Simon stood at the edge of the crowd, holding hands. Noah and Jimmy and Selma were with the group when Lucy and Phyllis arrived together, Noah all formality to them both. Lucy wondered at Marge's absence and remarked the same to Phyllis.

"I don't know. Noah isn't himself. He's drawn and unusually taciturn. He and Nick were close, and the Whitney investigation has exhausted them all, but Marge? I heard she's involved with a new play in the city. That might put her out of touch with anything here."

And as the days went on and classes resumed the horrors of the past month muted into the warm days of the later springtime, and the students and teachers began their heavy concentrations into studies before regent's exams. The seniors, dreaming of college, had all they could do to remember to come to class, but for some, there had been a transformation. The heavenly hiatus of the art room experience was gone. In Nick's place was installed a former student-teacher, newly graduated from Hofstra University, who was anxious to make a circumspect beginning, and so followed all regulations to the letter, ensuring an efficient but barely creative experience in the fine arts.

One day Noah approached Lucy as she was dismissing her honors class. Unsmiling, he asked how Kurt had been deporting himself.

"Sullen but generally cooperative," she replied, guardedly.

"Well, just let us know if he does anything unusual. Jimmy, especially, wants us to keep an eye on that kid," and he was down the hall.

Lucy again wondered at Noah's change. His behavior was so markedly different, that her curiosity prompted her to raise the question again to Phyllis.

"It's apparently not for public discussion," Phyllis responded, "but Marge has left him. They're arranging a separation. She's permanently in New York, rehearsing for a new musical. She's doing well, but apparently has abandoned her life out here."

Lucy felt a deep sadness. That pair was so brilliant together. Why did life do these things to people?

*   *   *

"Would you take a little drive with me this afternoon, out along the ocean?" He was at her door again, this time without any of the gaff, the old lightheartedness. She thought it scary.

"Noah, I don't think I can go now. I have all these papers ..."

"Please. I'll have you back before dinnertime. I just want to get out of Suppogue for awhile, get some salt air in my lungs." He didn't sound inveigling or intimidating. He looked, instead, vulnerable, nearly contrite.

She finally smiled. "I guess I could use a break too."

"Great. Meet you outside at my car?"

The long drive over the causeway was exhilarating, and seeing the land fall away behind them as they sped toward Jones Island was relieving after the long weeks of winter work and anxieties and recent sorrow.

The fishing center of Captree rose on their left as they turned west on to the Ocean Parkway which led to the town beaches, and, finally to the John Paul Jones Monument and the beach parks beyond it.

Noah drew up into a parking lot behind the high dunes of Gilgo Beach, nearly deserted now except for a few early beach goers who had remained into the late afternoon. "Would you like to walk?"

They left their shoes in the car and climbed out over the dunes until they could see the rolling Atlantic, sparkling in the late sunlight. "I love this ocean," began Noah, "and, funny thing, I can't venture into it, but I love to watch it come in and go out, and I think if I had learned to swim as a child, I would spend my days floating through those waves."

"You speak of early times," Lucy took up. "I have so many mysteries that I can't solve about myself."

"Some things you talked about the last time we spoke? Why don't you try to find the answers? That's what Jim and I plan to do ... just in a few weeks. Hey, here's a dry ledge. Let's sit here for awhile, it's so warm today."

They sat on the ledge of hard sand overlooking the sea.

"Jim and I are flying up to Newfoundland over the Memorial Day weekend. He's ambivalent about going, but I think no matter what he finds, it'll be a good thing. So often our fears are so much worse to bear than the reality is to face, and his past seems to have had its poignancy. There seems to have been some kind of lost family up there that he was too young or too disempowered to search for. But now he's worried about Selma. She doesn't understand, is afraid for him to go."

"Why doesn't he just tell her everything he knows and feels. She'll be better off if she thinks he isn't holding back on anything."

"I think you're right, and I think I'll suggest it if he hasn't told her already. If she loves him like she should, she'll understand, and if she doesn't, well, he's done his best, at least."

"I spoke to Laura and Peter about looking into my family just last week," Lucy responded, "and it's going to happen...this summer."

"And they're going to help you? That's the best way, Lucy. That's the wisest way for all of you."

"I know it's a great sacrifice for my mother too. It makes me sad to think how I have resented her."

"Big problem with kids ... they just never know when to appreciate their parents." Noah teased gently. "Seems they have to spend too much time embarrassing each other. Lucy?" Noah turned to look at her; "I want you to forgive me for any anxiety I've caused you." he looked away again at the sea. "I probably didn't conduct myself as I should have before with you. I didn't always know what got into me, but it's been a confusing year."

"I heard about Marge, Noah, and I am very, very sorry."

"Well, that's that." he pronounced gravely, and rose. "I think we should go back now."

Lucy rose with him, and they walked slowly back to his car in the topaz sunlight. They exchanged few words as they drove back to her house, but before she left the car, he paused and took her hand. "I would like to see you again. At least before we go to Canada?"

Lucy found herself slipping into feelings she had about him long before the days of the investigation, before the introduction of Marge, 'way back to that evening after her long swim.

"Noah, I'm very confused. There has been so much, so very many crises in our lives this year. I don't know what to say."

"You've been a good friend, Lucy. We haven't talked all that much, but I've sensed that you've been a kind of sturdy, steady influence on a lot of us all along. It's kind of remarkable," he smiled, "that a beginner like you could make such a difference." He reddened. "I guess it would be good of me to go now."

*   *   *

Lucy wandered around the little cottage, making superficial tasks for herself, dusting the books, making coffee that she didn't drink, feeding the ducks for the third time that day, and, finally, walking out to sit on the dock to watch the sun set over the rows of little houses across the canal. She feared that if Noah had made one other gesture toward her person, she might have responded with discomforting fervor. She recollected that she had spent a wholly chaste year, filled only with internal passions and anxieties. She thought of her days with the football coach, those halcyon moments of carefree infatuation. What worlds away have I traveled from that adventure, she mused.

The phone jangled, cutting into her memories. "Lucy, its Phyllis. Are you free? I've got some news that I don't know how to handle, and I've got to talk it out with someone. Can I come over? We can't do this over the phone."

After they were settled comfortably in Lucy's living room, Phyllis began. "Lucy, your father's a judge. Maybe he'll tell us where to go with this information. Marge Leonard just called me, probably because she isn't calling Noah these days. Before she left Noah, she was in touch with her friend Josie Farinelli, who has frequented Capt'n Tony's for years. Josie told her that Jake Sutherland and Fawn Whitney did have a relationship --- very serious. She says no one really knows Jake very well, that he's obtuse and taciturn, but brilliant, far from the bungler we've all made him out to be in this investigation. Guess it's easy to assume our small towns all have Mickey Mouse police forces. Anyway, Jake was beginning to spend a lot of time at Fawn's in the weeks before the murder. Fawn confided a little to Josie. It was a hot, intense romance. And the something strange occurred one night in Cap'n Tony's. It was early on a Friday, and just a few people were there. Fawn was meeting with one of her political buddies. You know she was active in several leftist organizations from around the Island, but Jake may not have appreciated these groups. Anyway, he usually never came into Tony's that early, but this evening he did, and whether it was out of jealousy or some other political motive, the two men got to arguing so loudly that Tony had to ask them to leave."

"Not a way for a police chief to behave in a public restaurant on his beat."

"Hardly."

"The argument turned into a fight in the parking lot, and both left a bit bloodied, according to Josie's story."

"Does this tell us anything about the murder?"

"I don't know, but Marge wasn't certain that any of the other investigators knows about Fawn's relationship with Jake. At any rate, after this fight, neither Fawn nor Jake met at Cap'n Tony's again, and that was just two weeks before the murder."

"Surely anyone that's into this investigation would find out quickly who she was seeing during her last few weeks alive."

"You'd think so, but Josie says that Jake is everyone's friend at Cap't Tony's. She doesn't think that anyone wants to implicate him in any way."

"What's Josie's motive for talking?"

"Sounds like some jealousy there too."

"Passion blurts it out."

"Damn straight. Do you think we should ask your father where to go with this information?"

"Yes, he'd be the first one I'd call. But you have all the details, Phyllis. We need to talk to him together. Come in to Jamaica with me tomorrow night after school and we'll tell him all we know."

*   *   *

At one am Jake Sutherland was fixing himself a ham sandwich in his small kitchen. He had just returned from his office in Town Hall, there having been some overdue paperwork to complete, and Jake's time was his own these days, although he was a singularly lonely man.

The kitchen door of their bungalow rattled and opened as his son Kurt entered, disheveled, eyes avoiding his father as he shuffled through the kitchen towards the TV, which he flicked on to a favorite channel and then retreated to slump in an overstuffed chair.

"Good evening, sir," Jake tried.

No answer.

Jake's anger rose like the heat from ignited coals. "I said good evening," he stood framed in his kitchen door, a dark silhouette to his son in the chair.

"Leave me alone. Just leave me alone."

"Damnit Kurt, all I ask is for small courtesies. After all, we do have to live together," his voice almost pleaded.

"I don't need to speak to you right now. I'm tired. I want to be alone."

A sickness tightened in Jake's stomach. "Alright, I'll arrange that for you." He turned and dumped the sandwich in the garbage can, grabbed his jacket from the peg by the door and slammed the door after him as he headed towards his car.

Parking several blocks north of his destination, he made his way slowly and carefully toward the cottage. The neighbor's lights were all out, and tall pine shrubs protected the entrance as he quietly let himself into Fawn's living room.

This is the last night I'll spend here, he reasoned. No one will want to believe that this is a stake-out anymore.

HARPER, NOAH, UNBOUND
Chapter Fourteen

"...my behavior to you at the time had merited the severest reproof. It was unpardonable. I cannot think of it without abhorrence."

"We will not quarrel for the greater share of blame annexed to that evening," said Elizabeth. "The conduct of neither, if strictly examined, will be irreproachable; but since then, we have both, I hope, improved in civility."

from *Pride and Prejudice* by Jane Austen

"That Susan Morand and Simon Fitch are certainly an inseparable item," commented Nina Cordozo in the faculty lounge one afternoon in May. "He's working so hard to get her through her classes, and she's blossoming into such a self-assured young woman."

"Simon's done more for her than any of us could, that's certain," continued Mina, who had joined them for a rare visit. "He shows us something. We can help them to help themselves, but no more."

"And to help each other; their better mentors are each other," smiled Sam Rose from his seat by the window.

"But Nick's class is where it all began," remembered Phyllis.

"Yes, it's hard to say how much he did, and how. We'll never know it all, will we?" Saul put in.

Henry Zimmerman, in a chair by another window, finally looked their way, opened his mouth as if to speak, then turned away.

"Excuse the swift change of subject," began Nina again, "but I overheard a curious conversation recently among several of the seniors. Seems that a pair of junior girls have acquired an old clam boat and are having some pretty wild parties out on the bay on Friday nights."

"Would it be indiscreet to ask the identities of the young ladies in question?" asked Saul.

"The names I heard were a great surprise to me," continued Nina, "and I really wonder at the truth of it. Jennifer Story and Irene Lock."

"My very best regents students!" exploded Henry, as he rose with a flourish. "There's got to be an error here. Jennifer and Irene. Never."

"Well, Henry," Nina played it out, "you can be a super sleuth and find out for yourself. It's all innocent fun, I'm sure. They probably dock at the pier by the town beach. That's where all the older kids go in the spring before the water in the ocean warms up. Friday night's the action time, Henry."

Phyllis hid her face behind her plan book.

Henry was exasperated. He flounced around in his seat, looking back ominously at the gossipy trio at the lounge table. Finally he grasped both arms of his chair, rose again, and addressed the room. "If there is anything in what you say, it should be brought to the immediate attention of their parents," and marched out of the room.

"Oh, oh, Nina. You've set him off this time. Our most ardent wolf of morality is after the luckless sheep."

"I wonder if he'll show up at the pier on Friday? It would be worth the trip to watch. Do you think he'd actively confront them?"

"Not on your life. He'd be terrified to face those kids. He'll drive us all crazy, but you can bet he'll keep away from that whole teenage scene."

"But he'll go down to spy ... in his tweed suit and oxfords. I don't know who will be in for the greater shock if they come face to face, him or the kids."

*   *   *

One night in the middle of May Jimmy found a moment after dinner to approach Selma about his plans for his trip with Noah.

"How are you getting up there? Will you fly all the way? I'd go with you, you know, but I can't endure airplane flights, and I hear that ferry trip across the North Atlantic is a fierce one. One of my friends ..."

"Selma, it should be an easy flight. We'll take a large 727 to Halifax. From there it's only another five hundred miles or so, and there are smaller planes into St. Johns."

"I don't like those smaller planes. Why don't you just fly all the way to Gander? Then drive down to St. Johns?"

"This way is supposed to be faster. And we only have the weekend."

He omitted his reasons for stopping at Halifax. That part of his past was something he needed to omit, at least for now; and if he found nothing there, then the subject would be closed forever and there would never be a need to explain.

"Do you think you'll find either of your parents alive, Jim?"

"It's possible. My mother may well have returned to St. Johns, and I never received news of my father, not even from my aunt who kept in touch with my cousin Ned for years before she died just a year ago. I think she would have sent word of his death to Ned, who assured me that she had written to him of her sister's death. They think I'm the one who deserted, and, in a way, it's true."

Selma, for the first time in her life with him, was easing into a new self-confidence. She was beginning to feel that he really loved and valued her. Now she looked at him with new understanding. "You had to talk yourself into this trip, didn't you? Don't go up there if you have to force yourself to get on that plane, Jim."

He smiled sadly. "I've had some anxious moments, but Noah's right. No matter what I find, I'll feel better afterward that I tried. I think I owe them that much, even though my mother's actions were always a puzzle. No telling what made her run away. But my father … it's hard to think that his was a case of desertion. I remember him as such a kind, gentle guy. We couldn't wait 'till he came home, but of course his drinking may have taken its toll. He'd be in his late sixties now, if he reached that far. I really have to know. Strange. That country isn't so far away anymore, but I've made it as far away in my mind as the moon."

*   *   *

Noah came upon Lucy as she was drawing down her classroom blinds for the day.

"You promised me a dinner before we left for our journey," he smiled, with much of the melancholy of the last few weeks dissolved from his eyes.

"Dinner? Why dinner at all? Why not just lunch?"

"Here we go again. Why? What's wrong with dinner this time? Is it the hour, or the formality, or … what?"

"Well, I've just been thinking about the reality of so many of our social customs," she went on, "and I wonder if we should perpetuate the whole sexist tradition of observing the formal restaurant scene. Nowhere are women more debased than by sycophantic waiters in restaurants. Furthermore, the man is expected to decide everything in a restaurant. He tastes the wine, and he even checks out the bloody soup to make sure it's cool enough, and, finally, the gravest insult of all…he insists on paying the check so that the woman is ever more beholden to him and …"

"Lucy, stop, Lucy, you're absolutely bewitching, and now that you've pulled your last blind and the door is closed, I can't wait for you another minute and …"

He caught her in his arms and pulled her so tight against him that her first fierce struggles were for naught, and he kissed her so heartily that she nearly swooned, but felt herself melt into him shamelessly.

I can't think at all anymore, she thought, and I don't know how this will come out, but my resistance is gone now, for sure.

As they finally drew apart, the door clicked as though someone had begun to enter and then thought better of it.

"Well, if we've an observer, let it be. They've no business here at this hour anyway," Noah grinned. "I want more than anything in the world right now to see you home, but I've got to go up to Jim's to make some final plans. We're leaving day after tomorrow, you know, so, damn it, won't you please see me tomorrow night? I'll even bring a picnic LUNCH, and we can forget all about your bloody restaurant."

"Of course."

He gathered her in his arms again. "I can't wait. See you around seven thirty at your house?"

And he was out the door.

There were still so many questions. Outside a light rain was beginning to fall, and Lucy felt a pang of fear. Her heart was racing, and she knew her behavior was thoroughly out of control, but she would have to know more before she let herself go into this devotion completely. Where was Noah's heart? He had a happy marriage. Phyllis had told her as much, and she could see it in his home that night she'd come with Sam, and even in his treatment of her---as something of a lark when he didn't think carefully enough of her perceptions, so could she trust him now?

She gathered up her papers and notes and sped briskly down the corridor and out to her car. Most of the faculty and students had left for the day, but several familiar cars were still in the lot. One familiar Bentley was pulled off on the side opposite her own car. In it she could see Harper huddled behind the wheel.

"Oh, no, could he possibly have been spying on us?" she shuddered. At first she was as angry as she had been when he confronted her in her car. Then fear for him overcame her anger as she remembered how shaken he was. I can't presume anything now and approach him, she reasoned. How responsible am I for this young person? Phyllis warned me to stay my distance. She said that I've done all I could for him.

She went to her car and backed slowly out to the street, wondering if there were anything she could do to reassure him that the world was indeed a mystery, but that he had the talent for a wonderfully satisfying life if he would only try to overcome his ... literal thinking? Tunnel vision? No, Lucy, you're just not equipped to handle that kind of lecture.

* * *

Later that evening Harper found himself alone at dinner in the large dining room of his home. The heavy draperies were drawn against the heat of the late spring sunlight, and the lack of light from outdoors gave the room a still deeper sense of isolation.

The family maid, Carry, set his dinner before him wordlessly and escaped into the kitchen. She had very little to say to him for a long time, possibly sensing that his disdain for his family included her shortcomings; and so he was left alone again to finish his dinner.

He was surprisingly hungry. It had been against his nature to take comfort in food, but tonight his appetite was kindled by some new sense of determination. Now he ate thoughtlessly, and with relish.

After his meal was done, he quietly left the table and went directly to his room. His autobiography was nearly finished, the introduction to the last chapter waiting for one final episode. He sat and typed, meticulously, and when he was satisfied with those last ten pages, he stacked the whole story neatly in a shirtwaist box and drew one last sheet of paper into his typewriter. The dedication page, "To Lucy Mackenzie, who has taught me, finally, the deepest pangs of despised love." He was even able to smile at the irony he felt he was the first ever to recognize.

But it wasn't quite enough. He sat for a time, gazing out at the carefully manicured lawn of his mansion. And after awhile he began to type, slowly,

Time is punctuated by man. Nature has given us the unalterable flow of seasons, tides and light years, but man alone has drawn the calendar, harnessed the energy of the sun, and spanned the world with his knowledge. When each man knows his work is done and can work no more, it is up to man to dispose of himself, rather than be a burden to other men who would otherwise be offering their own tributes to humanity.

I leave you with love and hope.
Harper Jaffee (or whatever)
May 29, 1960

* * *

"Our last class before our last break," Lucy announced wearily. "It's been a hard year for me, but you've made it worth it all. I want to thank you now before the end-of-term rush is upon us in June, and I might forget to tell you how much I've appreciated your making do with me as a substitute for someone we all know was a very special human being. I know I can't fill her shoes, but I've tried to make something out of the year, and I hope at least you'll remember the class for the effort."

"Miss Mackenzie, we've had a great year with you," spoke up Buck. "In fact, I wish there was another course we could take from you. Why don't you think about designing a new elective, like, say," he thought for a moment, "Controversial Love Affairs in Western Literature?"

"Oh, hey, we can do better than that," prompted Simon Fitch. "Let's make it really specific, say, 'Bawdy Language in Somali Poetry.'"

Lucy was delighted. "Tell you what, guys. Write down all your ideas, and I'll submit them to Mr. Perkins. He might even buy one or two of them. I know there are any number of you who want to reform the curriculum."

"Yea, but would you teach anything crazy, Miss Mackenzie?"

"Try me."

The class hour was coming to an end. There had been no comments from Harper, one of her most faithful contributors. She saw him fumbling with a large box as the rest of the students bustled out the door. He finally came forward with the package.

"Miss Mackenzie, this is my autobiography. Finally finished. I want you to be the first to read it. And, if you think it has any merit at all, would you please send it off to someone who might want to publish it?"

"Why, Harper, I'm more than flattered. But do you have another copy? Wouldn't you want to handle the submission of your own work?"

"I don't think I could, Miss Mackenzie. And I want you to be the first judge of what I have to say anyway. Of course if there are any charges for postage, my family will take care of all that," and he was out the door. He had not met her eyes throughout this encounter, so unlike Harper.

Lucy picked up all the work she had saved for the long weekend. She thought of leaving Harper's manuscript in her desk. *Oh, but he'll be certain to ask me about it as soon as we return. I'll have to scan it, at least, so I can say something intelligent about it, or he'll be defeated again.*

She pushed the big box into a shopping bag and dragged it out with all her other goodies.

* * *

The afternoon was warm and muggy, and Lucy began to think of the evening before her. Noah was to come for her around seven-thirty, so she had time to relax, even to nap before she showered and changed. She fell onto her bed in the little cottage, but she couldn't sleep with thoughts of what she could say to him that night.

Oh, I can't plan this. I'll just have to let the words come out as I feel them. Maybe I'll just look over Harper's writing for awhile before I take my shower.

She unearthed the box from the heap of material she had brought from school and stacked on her dining room table. Fastened to the top of the box was the note he had typed after he had finished the manuscript the night before.

"Oh, my God!" she spoke out loud. "Oh, Harper. Oh, what shall I do?"

She ran to the phone and grasped the faculty phone list from the shelf above her table. She had never called the Leonard house before, so had to find the number. Noah answered on the first ring.

"Noah. We've got to go somewhere quickly. I just found a suicide note from Harper Jaffee. If we get over to his house, maybe we can find him in time. I can't handle this alone. Can we go in your car? I don't want him to recognize mine."

"I have to dress. Come right over, and I'll be ready."

She felt there might not be a minute to lose. She grabbed her keys and then, thinking that he might have left other clues, the box with his manuscript, and was out the door and into her car to drive around the block to Noah's. He was just closing the door with his shirt in his hand as she approached and motioned for her to leave her car in his driveway. His car was in the street.

"Get in. Where do the Jaffes live?"

"On Second Avenue. The western end. The last house on the block."

As they approached the middle of Harper's street, Lucy saw the Bentley pulling out of the drive.

"That's Harper. His parents drive a red Rolls."

"What's next?"

"Let's just follow him, discreetly."

"What's in the bundle?"

"His autobiography. He had a note pinned to the front, announcing his intentions. He gave me big hints today after class, but I had no idea what they were about until I just read this."

"He's turning East on Merrick Road. Where do you think he's going?"

"I have no idea. Do you think he wrote anything more in the manuscript?"

"It's possible. Let me look at the last chapter."

She raced over the contents and tossed the first pages into the back seat as they rode. It was hard to read, as the afternoon light was growing dimmer.

"We did it. We did this thing to him, however innocently, and we've got to prevent it."

"What are you talking about?"

"I'm reading. He was at the door yesterday; when we heard it click, that was Harper. It's not the first time. He's been shadowing us. He's been crazily infatuated with me, Noah. I'm not boasting. He's in deep need of affection, and he chose me for his attention. He writes that now that I'm gone from him, his last hopes are over, and that he will take his mercenary parents' most sanctimonious gift and drive himself into the sea."

"Good God, where do you think he's going?"

"As he says he is, 'into the sea' somewhere."

"Well, he's not there yet, so we'll follow as carefully as we can."

"Do you have much gas?"

"Filled up this morning."

"It could be just a cry for attention. He may stop before it's too late."

"Could be, but we can't take that chance."

"Noah. Thank you."

"Why? This is every bit my job as much as yours."

She thought of all the anger she had spent toward him over the months for his teasing and his indiscretions. Somehow it all paled in the fervor with which he was pursuing this lost child.

"He's turning off the highway now down Deauville Parkway. What's at the end of the road here?"

"There's the remains of an old causeway. It's blocked off, but some fishermen use it as a pier."

"We'd better hurry. It doesn't matter if he sees us now. We've got to stop him before he gets to the water. How long is the parkway before the pier?"

"About six blocks, with stop signs."

"I hope he stops at them. Maybe we can grab him out of the car. Oh, Noah, he's running the first stop sign."

"He's speeding up. We've got only one hope now. I've got to force him off the road; take a chance."

The Bentley was a block and a half in front of them. Noah leaned on the accelerator, and his car sped forward. There were few houses near the road at this point, so the only impediments to Noah's next maneuver were trees and deep ditches on either side of the road.

"I'll have to hit him on his right side. Hold on tight." He pulled alongside the Bentley, turning into the door just behind the front fender. Both cars collided, and the Bentley leaned and rolled neatly into the ditch.

When they found him, he was drawn into a fetal position against the wheel of the car, sobbing, but not in mortal pain. "Go to that house right there," Noah commanded Lucy, "and call his home. Leave a message with whomever that we're headed right to the hospital."

When Lucy returned, Noah had Harper in his car, which, miraculously, had only a front fender missing. Harper was speechless and docile. When Lucy climbed in, he shuddered and fell against her, and, as Noah drove, she cradled his bead in her lap.

At the hospital as soon as Noah explained the matter to the triage nurse, Harper was delivered post haste to children's psychiatric. Noah and Lucy followed.

"We're not going to stay here one moment too long," Noah cautioned. "This is the business of his parents now. We've done our job."

"But shouldn't we stay so that Harper knows how much we care for him now?" puzzled Lucy.

"Not at all. We're not the ones he should be caring about. He's misplaced his affections too long. I expect we're going to see some appropriate response from the Jaffees before long, once these guys here take charge of the matter."

The maid had managed to contact Harper's mother who was merely out at another social affair and alerted her to Harper's whereabouts. She was on the scene only a few minutes after Noah and Lucy ascended to the psychiatric floor.

"What in the world ... ?" she came upon Noah and Lucy in the waiting room.

"Harper just made an unsuccessful suicide attempt, Mrs. Jaffee," Noah began. "I'm not a doctor, so I'll leave the rest of the explanations up to them and Harper, when you can see him."

"What should I do?" Lucy saw how helpless the woman felt. "Why don't you get in touch with Mr. Jaffee so you don't have to handle this alone," she put in.

"Yes, that's a good first idea," added Noah. "And I have to tell you that we had to interfere with Harper's plans to drive into the ocean. He wrote about what he was going to do, to Lucy, his English teacher here. If there's any trouble, we'll be glad to show you the manuscript."

"No, no. I'm just so grateful ..."

"So, Mrs. Jaffee, you son's car is in a ditch a few blocks south of Merrick on Deauville Parkway. I don't think it's badly damaged, but if the police have questions, here's my card. I'm going out of the country for a few days tomorrow, but I should be back next week."

"Whatever led to this ... what happened to Harper for him to do such a thing?"

"I think that's best left to whatever the doctors determine and what you can learn from Harper, Mrs. Jaffee. You have an extremely brilliant, but sensitive son who, just like the rest of us, needs very badly to feel loved and appreciated."

A doctor arrived just at that moment to speak to them all. After he was apprised of the recent events concerning Harper's actions, he assured Mrs. Jaffee that her son was lucid and could speak with her. "I think, if you have nothing further to ask us now, Miss Mackenzie and I would like to leave," concluded Noah.

"You can reach me tomorrow," Lucy offered, "at my home in Suppogue. I'm listed in the directory."

Harper's mother, leaving for Harper's room, scarcely noticed that they were going.

"Well, let's hope for the best now," Noah spoke as they descended in the elevator. "She seems appropriately distraught."

"Maybe this terrible emergency will work to bring that family together in a good way," offered Lucy.

"Maybe yes, maybe no," Noah evaluated simply. "I don't know those folks at all, but I do know that we've done all we can right now. And I also know that a trauma's easier to heal in the young. We'll have to give those doctors time to work and hope that Harper will be back with us in a refreshed state of mind in the fall."

"You sound like you've handled things like this before."

"A few. Some didn't come out so well. Teenage suicide is no joke. There are thousands that never even get reported. Psychiatrists say that the ones who try don't really believe that they're going to die, that something will save them at the last minute, or that death isn't really permanent. They work themselves into a kind of hypnotic state before the act."

"You say some didn't come out well. Here in Suppogue?"

"We had an awful scene here two years ago, a young fellow much like Harper. Only his parents were too much a presence. They brow beat that kid into behaving like an intellectual robot. Over vacation he finally took himself into the chemistry lab and sniffed carbolic acid. Probably died instantly, but his body wasn't found for days until the custodians noticed that natural reactions had taken place in the air around the room. It took a crew of four working six days to clean up that room. Tiles had to be replaced, furniture discarded. Such a pitiful but senseless, desperate act."

"Thank God we caught this one ... you did. Noah. You handled this so well. I was helpless."

"Oh, no. We did this together, lady. You got me going from the beginning. He certainly was not going to write me that suicide note."

"I almost didn't read it. I was going to put the whole package away till much later in the weekend. Part of it was just plain luck."

"Well, let's wish all troubled teenage souls the same luck, Lucy girl. Say, I hate to say it after such a ruckus, but I'm starved. Is it DINNER? I'm much too fagged to pack a picnic now."

"It's gotta be casual. I just had time to pull on these blue jeans."

"Well, hey, just the thing for Popeye's. Ever been there?"

"Never yet. You'll have the pleasure of introducing me."

"I can assure you, the waiters are not going to dazzle you with their charm. They have a fashion of slinging clams over their shoulders. But let's head for the bar first. I'm ready for a double Rosy on ice."

"Please tell, what's that?"

"A strawberry daiquiri, ladies' drink, they say, but I'm not ashamed. Attracts slightly less attention than cross-dressing, and hey, it's almost summertime!"

"I see behind those piercing Irish eyes of yours. You're full of more questions," Noah teased when they were finally halfway through their mounds of clams and fries, and a few light drinks had chased the monsters of the afternoon away. "You want to know just where I am with Marge. And where we are, and if you should really think of continuing to hang around with this old geezer."

"You're not old. You're younger than a lot of the kids in my tenth grade class."

"I'll try to take that as a compliment, but seriously, Lucy, I can appreciate what's going on in your head right now. Truth to tell, I have to stop myself every day to sort things out for myself, so maybe if I try to articulate some of my feelings, it will help us both tonight."

"I don't ask to pry into your mind, Noah. But we have had a…. frayed … history over this year, and there are some things that you must understand, leave me wondering if …"

"If I'm being imprudent?"

"That's an appropriate word."

Noah took a deep breath. "I'm going to be as clinical as I can be tonight, after demobilizing a Bentley and three drinks," he began. "Simply, I tried to ensconce a fetching, damnably attractive actress out here in the cultural wasteland of southern Long Island while I dabbled in the fine art of secondary education. She was at first compliant, even enthusiastic when we built the house, and enjoyed decorating and cooking and entertaining, but it all soon---took just about a year---wore off, and she took to booze and crying fits and hating me for wanting her to stay. Her guilt kept her going for awhile, but then even I encouraged her to look around for some theatre work. There's nothing challenging for her level of talent on the island, and she was dying to go back to Manhattan." He took a deep breath and plunged on.

"She told me early on that she had no interest in raising a family. She didn't hate children, but she had no need for them for herself. This was a big sacrifice for me, but I tried to make up for it by working with them at school, even though I've always longed for some in my own home."

Lucy's eyes were down now, her thoughts busy with feelings of her own.

"Then finally there was this opportunity for a big role. I foolishly thought that she would want to join me at least on weekends, that we could preserve the marriage. But last month she let the bomb fall. There was someone else in the picture, connected to the theatre. I wouldn't even want to try to compete with him, Lucy. And when she told me where her new affections lay, my feelings for her died so completely that I really hope we never have to see each other ever again. I was a fool for trying to keep things alive as long as I did."

Lucy winced at the notion of deadened affections in one who had seemed so consumed with love.

"You know I never expected to be going through a separation, then a divorce, ever again after my first experience, which, by the way, was so long ago, and I was such a different person, that it's hardly worth recounting. Briefly, as to that affair, it was parentally arranged and mutually dissolved, for the good of us both ... no children, no heartache, just in case you hear later from other sources."

"Anyway, Marge couldn't understand my longing to stay with my job here, my happiness in old Suppogue, my affection for my little deck out over the grand old ocean bay, so much so that she's leaving flat. She's even told her attorney that she wants me to have the house and everything in it. From what I hear she's earning at the theatre, she'll be able to build a place three times this elegant soon for her and Max, but then I really don't want to talk about her anymore. I was just trying to fill you in with my version of the story so that you could sort things out for yourself. I don't know how to make up for all the awkward moments between us this year, but for my part I can chalk my stupidity up to one big giant frustration with my failed marriage, and a deeply growing appreciation for you and your crystal clear judgment, and your infuriating sharp-tongued banter."

"I thank you for trying to tell me so much in so little time," she began, then shook her head as if trying to clear cobwebs away, "and what you did tonight for Harper has meant so much to me. You have to understand, I've never had a really big love affair. I'm probably right where you were when you had your first marriage. How good am I for you?"

"Lucy, you're worlds away from what I was then. Believe me, I may still be in the cradle emotionally compared to you, from the kinds of things I've heard you say."

Suddenly she had the presence of mind to glance at her watch. "Noah. You have to catch a plane in the morning. It's eleven o'clock. Are you packed? How are you getting to the airport? Do you need to talk to Jimmy?"

"I know it's eleven. I am packed. I'll meet Jim at the airport, and I've said all I want to say to that bloke before we take off. We'll be together for five days, so I guess we'll have time enough to chat. I don't need to hurry off to sleep because I love to doze in airplanes, and right now I want to spend some more time with you. I've been lonely enough for ten men for the last month or more, and I want to show you the scene from my deck at night. Interested? Just a little bit?"

"Noah, please. Can't we go more slowly?"

"No. Speed is of the essence. I'm jetting away tomorrow. What if the plane crashes on the rocks of the Grand Banks? What if Jimmy's long-lost sister turns out to be another Maureen O'Sullivan, and I never come back to you? What if ... silly woman. I'm not going to beg."

But he did stop in front of his house. "You have to get your car, you know."

"Maybe ... first ... I would like to see your view."

They never reached the deck, nor was the house itself illuminated that night at all. In it were two people who were engaged in the tenderest kind of lovemaking.

Lucy awakened first with a salty canine tongue caressing her nose. "Noah, it's seven o'clock. You have to be at the airport in forty-five minutes."

They bounded up, pulled on their jeans again, and Noah grabbed his duffel.

"Our neighbor's coming in for Sludge, so just pull the door to," and they were gone in Lucy's car.

Jimmy and Selma were surprised to see Lucy drive up with Noah, but were not about to make comments about the sight of the pair in an amusing state of dishevelment.

"There's something I have to ask you before I go," were Noah's last words before they left the car. "I want you to move in with me ... as soon as I get back. Make plans. Get packed. Remember, it's 1960, and, as the beatniks say, It's love-in time... move-in time too?"

"I'm not quite there yet. What kind of proposal are you making?"

"Everything. The works. As soon as I'm free. I'm honest and fair and yours. Let Jimmy and Selma see, so there," and he caught her in his arms again so there would be no dispute. "Call you as soon as we reach the frozen north," and he was away up the escalator to the plane.

Jimmy stood poised at the door of the aircraft. "Well, Noah. You're certainly full of surprises this morning. I thought you'd never make the flight."

"I have much to tell, Jimbo. Much to tell. Lucy and I had several kinds of adventures last night, and at least one of them I can relate to you. You'll have to use your imagination about the rest."

Jimmy looked back at Selma and then Lucy, waving goodbye. "I can't say she doesn't look happy, Noah. At least some of it must be good."

"Selma looks O.K. too, Jim. Now how was YOUR evening?"

After the men entered the craft, Selma acknowledged Lucy's presence. "I don't believe we've met. But I remember you from the PTA forum. You made a wonderful speech, dear. And you are Peter and Laura's daughter, aren't you? Well, we're going to visit them soon. How delightful to meet you here. Let's go and have coffee. Jim and I didn't take time for breakfast."

Lucy was grateful to have someone to share a bit of the morning with some comforting words, and Selma had found a fortunate distraction, for she was terrified of Jim's flying away. They waited until the plane left the ground safely and was obscured by the fluffy morning clouds.

"Why are they going up there? I wish Jim would just let things be."

"I guess we just have to take a few things on faith," were the only words Lucy could think of to say. "And they're both sensible, don't you think?"

*   *   *

Jake Sutherland double-locked the door of Fawn's cottage behind him, "For the last time," he announced out loud to the wind in the beach pines, and strode purposefully toward his unmarked car way down the street. His hand on the car door handle, he took one last glimpse of the cottage, and as he stood there he could hear her deep throated laugh, see her sweet smiling face; but as he looked down at his hand holding the handle of the car door, he saw the blood of her wounds on his hands. He kicked the side of the car with deep self-loathing, fell into the driver's seat, and began to sob uncontrollably.

THE COME FROM AWAYS
Chapter Fifteen

"O brave new world
That has such people in it."
Miranda *in* The Tempest

"You've been sleeping deeper than an ol' marsh dog after his last feed," grumbled Jimmy as he jostled Noah's shoulder. "Wake up now. They're bringing lunch, we'll be landing soon in Halifax, and we haven't spoken a word about where we're going."

"What's this about a dog?" murmured Noah as he roused himself slowly. "What's all this about lunch? I don't want lunch. I want to sleep."

"Noah, you said you were coming along to help me. And so far all I've gotten from you are snores and grunts so loud it's embarrassing. You nearly got a pillow over your mouth a minute ago. No one sleeps like this on airplanes."

"If we'd taken a boat, you'd hear me screaming for mercy." laughed Noah, almost fully awake now.

"Look out there. We're over the Maine islands."

Below they could make out the tiny Isles of Shoals dotting the flat gray sea. White rocks appeared like flecks of dandruff on a suit shoulder. They were flying particularly low, lining up to the southern shoreline of Nova Scotia just beyond the horizon at a hundred miles.

The flight attendant was pushing the cart through the aisle, dispensing plastic-wrapped cold sandwiches of ham and cheese and a tiny fruit salad in a cardboard cup. Noah winced at the package.

"Just enjoy the fruit and ham, Noah. From now on, all you'll get is fried fish and chips if we're lucky."

"Now Jim, you didn't warn me about starvation."

"Not starvation --- frugality, me boy."

"I can hear you're into your old brogue already. What's next? A drunken brawl in the tavern tonight?"

"I'm forgettin' I'm hearin' that nasty jibe at my ethnicity and will concentrate on beginnin' to educate ye. Are ya certain you're awake now? I don't want ye to choke on y'er sandwich."

They finished their meager Air Canada fare, and Noah leaned into Jimmy's left ear. "Now, whar ye tak'in me, ye ol' sea rat?"

"We can't try that lingo after we land, or they'll think we're mocking them," Jimmy was more serious now, easing into the business of the day. "For starters, we're about to visit the scene of my older youth, working backwards, you might say, into my younger days in Newfoundland."

"You've said nothing before about this part of your life, you know."

"Well, maybe I'd better spare you this part until we make our visit. We have to see a Mother Superior at the Convent School of St. Mary of the Mount in Halifax. This was my last stop of significance before I left for the states. At least, this is the scene of my last connection with anyone of importance."

Jimmy was lost in thought now, and Noah could tell that he should ask no more for awhile. His head was in his hands, and his eyes closed as the plane began its decent into the airport at Halifax. The bright green of the Nova Scotia farmlands soon became visible out the right window of the aircraft. They flew over the rock-strewn harbor of Peggy's Cove, where the monoliths jutted far out into what was now an azure sea in the brighter noon sunlight.

"Pretty land. Different from Maine."

"Yes, they're more affluent on these farms than on the land of the northern states. The soil here is rich and accommodating, which probably tells us more about the motives of the loyalists than does their claim to an affinity for the crown. They threw in their hats with England because they were sure they would be on the winning side, and they were eager to stay right where they were."

"Not for love of George, eh?"

"More for love of a different kind of independence. From the clamorous South. Oh, we're almost on the ground, Noah. Let's hope our car's ready."

The granite buildings bordered by tall poplars stood atop a windy hill overlooking the Bay of Fundy. Bright blue sky gleamed against the sharp white limestone rocks set in russet clay in the harbor beneath them.

"We're a long way from Long Island, Jim, but this is striking scenery here."

"A little too cold for my bones now, Noah, but it was my element years ago." He wrapped his trench coat tighter around him against the wind. "But

I did forget how beautiful it can be on a day like this. You're seeing it at its best. Look at that ketch out there in the sunlight," and he pointed to a distant white sail against the sparkling sea. "I could fancy a turn at that tiller."

Noah shuddered. Give me the dry land or a high flying Sesna."

"We'd better go in and hear what we can of what we came for now. I probably should have phoned ahead, but visits of this kind go better in person, don't you guess?"

Young wimpled novitiates bustled to and fro in the lofty stone corridors off the lobby in the main hall. A small, childlike hooded woman occupied the desk in the center of the room opposite the doorway. When Jimmy asked to see the Mother Superior, she looked surprised. "Mother doesn't see anyone without an appointment. Can you tell me what is your business here?"

Jimmy explained that it had been difficult to make an appointment with the Mother whose name and contacts he had not known; that he had not even known if the convent school where he had spent a significant portion of his life was still in existence until he had come upon it today. Would she please prevail upon any authority to ask that he be able to make inquiries about a dear old acquaintance?

The little lady at the desk bustled away after summoning one of her passing sisters to guard the desk.

Jimmy and Noah took straight-backed chairs against a stone pillar in the lobby.

"I feel like I'm waiting for the inquisition," remarked Noah.

"Don't begin to holler until you feel the spikes," kidded Jim, nervous as a trapped monkey. "They're adept at psychological intimidation in these places. But there's a motive of kindness here and there."

"You mean the fire and brimstone sin-and-damnation scenarios didn't originate with the Calvinists?"

"Hardly. Anywhere fundamental religious law is applied, fear is the dominant operative. I don't have to lecture you on the varieties of religious experience."

"Just checking you out. How do you feel?"

"Deathly frightened myself. I feel like I felt over thirty years ago when I first set foot in this place with my brother and sister. Can you imagine it as a home for a little kid? Granite and shrouded women and no soft place to cuddle up to anyone except myself on a narrow hard cot in a vast hall. Certainly makes me appreciate my bonny home."

"Selma would appreciate those words."

The small woman was back with a stern look. The mother was involved in a terribly important business and could not be disturbed until tomorrow morning. Would the gentlemen be so kind as to return then or call?

"We've compelling reasons for seeing her as soon as possible. Is there no way now?"

"Not in the least. She is taking care of an emergency with a student. Please call back early tomorrow and she will be glad to see you."

"I guess that's it," Jim turned to Noah. "I'll have to stop back here, even if it's a wild goose chase. I've come this far, and I've got to see this part through. Somehow I didn't expect to gain admittance this first time. In a way, I'm relieved to postpone this part."

"Obedient as ever. Well, then, it's heave to for Newfieland, Old Jimbo. I'm with you all the way."

Aloft again in a small plane, they flew low over the dark green vistas of the mountains of Cape Breton, then climbed to a much higher altitude for the flight across the Cabot Strait, the narrow entrance to the Gulf of St. Lawrence, which flows between Cape Breton and the Southwestern tip of New Foundland, where sits the little city of Port Au Basque. "Someday I'll treat you to the ferry ride. It can be delightful in calm weather."

"And when not calm?"

"There are the north Atlantic storms. But our ferries are well equipped to handle almost anything."

"Even bergs?"

"The ferries turn into ice breakers in the winter. They can't get enough supplies in by air. It's a magnificent sight, seeing those huge vessels crunch through several feet of frozen sea."

"So you do have challenging winters up here? You told me the Gulf Stream keeps these waters temperate."

"Fair by inland standards. We don't, as a rule, go down much lower than thirty-five below in February."

"Happy days. I'm glad to be airborne in late May."

"Look, there's the coastline."

Thousand-foot palisades of multicolored rock stood out before them under a brilliant green carpet of moss. As they drew nearer, Jimmy pointed to some little boats gathered in a cove. "Those are the lobstermen's rigs. Can you see those dots out in the harbor? They're marking the nets. it's off season for the lobsters now here --- each area has it's season, so off times they catch what fish they can to supplement their income."

"How are they doing now? Do you keep up with their commerce?"

"The lobsters for the last five years have been plentiful. Some of these fellows are hauling them in by the hundreds, and if they've made the right connections with the shipping companies, are doing so well they'd never think of any other employment. The cod take, sad to say, is getting slimmer by the year. No one knows exactly why. Some blame the shifting winds from the southwest, others, the Japanese, who are allowed out beyond the twelve mile limit, but I hear they've found other waters near Iceland to use. No one is sure. It may be cyclical, and in a few more years the fish'll come back again. At any rate, the lobsters are keeping these fellers going strong for a good bit yet, and they're building salmon runs all over, especially in the west."

"Your dad, was he a lobsterman?"

Jim smiled. "Pap shipped out on the bigguns, on someone else's rig who hired twenty or so flunkies to do the oiling and the greasing and the pulling and the harvesting. He hadn't the gaff to stand with the responsibility of his own business. Poor Mum had to put up with his long absences, and it was only because she had a deal with the ship's chandler that she got his wages attached and received a regular income for herself and us kids. She wasn't always certain even what rig he was on or where he was to come into port. His absences were a neighborhood joke in a place which took husband's long absences as a matter of course. I can remember words, you see I was old enough before I left to recall a lot, that the only times Mildred Duffer was certain to have seen Tom were the six nights he fathered his children. And she was a beautiful woman, too. Folks called him as homely as a wharf rat, but we kids remembered him, we sure did. We couldn't wait till he was there, full of all kinds of jokes and relics from the sea. Surprises they dragged up in the nets. He even brought home a skull once that mother wouldn't allow inside the house, so we kids hung it on a pole out from the back shed. He said it was from the Spanish Main, and was probably the skull of a very important pirate we'd read about someday."

"I guess your mother must have been a strong woman, Jim."

"One of the strongest, for awhile, at least, before something, God knows what, got into her. Anyway, I remember she had to put up with her man coming blustering home for one or two nights and then going off to the taverns until the next ship went out. She and the rest of the women spent their days laboring heavily with household chores and their nights huddled around pot-bellied stoves in their small kitchens mending and sewing and spinning yarns from their childhood. Fantasies, mostly. Fairy stories that could be versions she was handed down from her mother. They had to keep telling those stories to keep their minds from going mad from the harsh life here. Some of the women took to drink. Some were institutionalized who couldn't control their limits, and then all the work fell upon their older children. Newfoundland is a beautiful but hard place with lots of desperation, if you're not hard as the rock itself to survive the North Atlantic."

They were now crossing the desolate interior of the island. "Not much here besides swamp, mosquitoes and caribou on the higher elevations. But the caribou herd is thinning more and more. The moose are taking over, over forty thousand by now, they say. That's not what the government intended when they brought them here."

"Why moose?"

"To attract the wealthy hunters, especially from Toronto and the States. But we hate to lose the caribou to the bigger animals, and the moose can be a problem if they're cornered."

"I wouldn't want to mess with them."

"They're amazing swimmers. Maybe we'll see a few before we leave." He squinted and leaned into the window of the aircraft as if to get closer to the land he was feeling into, as if there was something powerful drawing him to the place where he had known a strange coexistence of happiness and despair.

"What happened to your mother?"

He squirmed in his seat and closed his eyes again for a moment. "It's a strange story. I never got whole answers. But I so clearly remember that morning when we found her gone," and he looked away and out the window again for a moment.

"I remember that the big yearly revival meeting was the most important event in the world to Mum and her friends. I guess with all her pain and loneliness the one place she could vent her passion legitimately was in the church. She was a woman of great personal pride, Noah, and I don't think she could ever be given to plead with my father for any more attention than he was wont to give her. I can remember her crying though, every time that Tom, my dad, would leap over our white picket fence at the edge of our hill and yell, 'Be see'n ya ever sa soon, Millie.'

"She'd run back into the house to her bedroom to sob away. I followed her one day, and then I avoided it after that, it hurt me so. The insult of him must have churned away inside her, and gradually eroded so much of the strength there. But she never missed a prayer meeting, and she wrote many of the Sunday school lessons we kids had read to us. They even used them in many other of the churches all over the province. And she was musically gifted. She could play by ear on any stringed instrument and composed hymns of her own on the small pipe organ we had in the sanctuary. We adored her. She was never unduly cross with us, and enjoyed it when we brought our friends home ... unlike a lot of other mothers who were eager to get rid of the noise. She made all kinds of special puddings and cakes for all our guests and us. The house was always full of her own and everyone else's kids in the neighborhood.

"As I grew older, she spent more and more time down at the church discussing programs with the rector and at meetings at night which became more and more frequent until we started to hate the church for pulling her away.

"One night when she was all dressed to go to another meeting, we pleaded with her not to go. She was so much fun for us at home with her story telling and her reading and her playing on the fiddle, but this one night we asked her to stay home and she got kind of gruff and said that it was a most important meeting, that a new minister from Toronto was visiting, and that she was obliged to the minister to be there. And we felt guilty for asking her to stay away from church. I remember her promising that was the last time she's leave us on a weeknight, and she'd even skip the prayer meeting on Friday to stay with us." He drew a huge sigh.

"And that was the last we ever saw of her."

"What in the world did she do?"

"I've suffered so long over this," said Jim slowly. "I don't know what kind of moral arrangement she had to make, or what wild kind of mood she was in to desert her children, but I guess we all have a selfish, self-pitying core that takes over us when we've been pushed or pulled too far to bear beyond the limits of our control. That night she took the ferry to Sidney with the visiting minister of the Canadian Church of God. She sent a message to her aunt Winnie to please take care of the children, and was never heard from again that I know about. When I got up that next morning, I could hear sobbing downstairs, and when I dressed and went down, my aunt was seated at the kitchen table with my brothers and sisters, and they were all being told that we would have to go to an orphanage, except for the littlest, Susie and Perry and Joey, because Aunt Winnie was too old to take care of us all."

"Jim, you've had to carry this with you for so long without sharing it?"

"No .I told this part to Selma. That's why she warmed at last to the idea of my coming up here. She realized that I had to make some attempt to find a closure to the story of my family. And Peter too. He knew about my early life from our conversations in the Navy. They'll both be concerned with what I find here. It's not too ordinary a tale, is it? Such mothers don't take off so regularly without so much as a goodbye."

"No. But you've done some profound philosophizing about her state of mind. We never know how much we can take, and that woman seems to have suffered grievously."

"We're almost there. We're over Placentia Bay. See the icebergs?"

"They're blue! I've never seen one in person before."

"They seldom speak, unless they're disturbed by a steamship. They break up in Greenland and float down here in the early spring and get caught in Placentia and Conception Bay ... over east nearer St. Johns," he pointed.

"Right there is Heart's Content, the village where the first transatlantic cable message was received in 1866. We'll visit the headland where Marconi received the first wireless message from Europe too, in 1901, right in St. Johns. You're approaching an historic city, Noah."

"Looks like the moon. See those little craters."

"Yes, there's just so much wind atop those hills that no tall vegetation has a chance. Don't know where the craters came from. Glaciers, maybe."

The plane banked to the left, then the right, and settled in on a long glide down to a single runway atop a mountain covered with the same green mossy cover that they had seen on their approach to the island. Noah could see little children waving from a fence along the strip.

"Some of the locals are greeting us."

"It's a friendly place, that's for certain. They'll love you to death here, they're so eager for visitors."

Wind so strong Noah had to lean against it buffeted the ten passengers as they climbed down the several steps to the tarmac. The temperature had dropped about fifteen more degrees since they had left Nova Scotia, but the air was dry and scented with flowers. They buttoned their jackets and slung their grips over their shoulders and grabbed a little cab at the curb by the low building used for a ticketing office and waiting room. The big airport, thanks to American investments during the war, was up at Gander, as Selma had noted. But this little place was bustling and growing with construction starts in several places around them. They were high on a hill and could see the town as they approached and descended.

"Look at that magnificent harbor! Wonderful bottleneck. Terrible challenge for invaders."

"Close to the very words John Cabot spoke as be rounded the bend and saw those cliffs laid out before him. It's the closest port to Europe in North America."

"I wouldn't know where to put up, so I didn't try to make reservations. Why don't we just take one night at the Holiday Inn until we find out if anyone I know's around?"

"Straight down Dunk'urth and up tha hill ye'l find the Stel Battery hotel. If y'r think'in of spend'in a passel a change, ye myte t'is well doo it ryte. Ye be CFA's frum Neu Yawk, are ye?" and before they had time to answer, "Bet ye din't cain wha a CFA is, don ye?"

"I sure do. I was born here, Cabbie. He's not insulting us, Noah. A CFA is a come-from-away, and the Stel Battery is a great place to stay, but I forgot about it. It's right on top of Signal Hill with a view of the whole city and harbor. Right beside the meadow where the English fought the French for the last decisive time in North America."

"Say, how long ye been away? So good to 'av ye return now, eh? Don ye know anyone round here na more?"

"Not for sure," Jimmy laughed with a bit of embarrassment. "Say, it's a small town. Why don't I start right here? Do ya know any people around by the name of Duffer?"

"Duffer? Duffer. D'ers a Joe Duffer down east in Petty Harbour. Caint says I knows any t'other, but d'ers prob'ly at least several mor if d'ers one, eh?"

"Joe. Maybe my little brother Joe. What's this Joe do for a living?"

"Why, he's a schoolteacher, he be. Got hisself an edikashun over at Toronto, he did. But I tink nows I'm on it, dat Joe's got a sister too. Married to a fisherman, she is. Can't say's I member that gal's name na mor. Duffer. Duffer. Let me jist tink on dis a little mor."

"Do most of the houses have telephones now up here?" Jim didn't know how to put this any more tactfully.

"Why yes, ther be telephones in 'mos evry place, dese days, sir. Say, if you be from dese parts, what's yer name, if ya don mine me ask'in?"

"I don't mind at all. My name's Duffer too. James Duffer. And I was separated from my family years ago, and I'm here to find as many of them as I can."

"Wall, thas wonerful. I wish ye the best of luck, mon. And if ye find yerselves lonely tanight, come pass de time down at Charlie's on Duck'urth. Dere's quite gud musicians pla'in thar, and a good many kind of beer on tap. And lovely lassies too," he winked at Noah.

"You've been more helpful than you know, man. And good luck to you."

"Where do all those wonderful words come from, Jim?" Noah could hardly wait 'till he was out of the cab to ask.

"Depends on who you're speaking to, Noah. Down around St. Johns here there's lots of Irish and English dialects that go back hundreds of years. And up north they claim it's a Devon speech near to Shakespeare's that isn't even found in England today. And of course there's the French and Basque on the West Coast, mixed with a little Beotuck, I hear."

The Battery Hotel was not crowded this time of year, and they had their pick of rooms. The view was astonishing.

"See, Noah, how the houses become fancier the further up the hill you go. Practically this whole town was wiped out by fire only a hundred years ago. Everything that wasn't stone or brick burned, and the whole place's been rebuilt."

"What's that strange looking rig in the harbor nearest us?"

"Oh, that must be an oil digger. They're starting to work the black stuff out of the sea around here that's supposed to be more plentiful than in all the rest of Canada combined. No telling what that industry will do to the place once they begin harvesting in earnest."

"Noah, should I call? Or should we eat first?"

"That depends on how you want to feel at dinner."

"How's that?" as he was already thumbing through the directory for Petty Harbour.

"If he isn't your brother, you'll be anxious and depressed. If he doesn't want to talk to you, you'll be wanting to get on the next plane out and not even try again. Anyway, I don't like to give advice on these matters---but call anyway."

Jimmy was already dialing. The phone rang and rang and finally quit on its own. "It's seven o'clock. We'd better get to the restaurant and call from there if we're to get in touch tonight."

They walked down to the 290 on Duckworth, recommended by the tourist guide Noah had picked up at the airport.

"For your first meal here, I'd suggest the cod tongues," Jimmy ventured. "After awhile, you'll be ready for the seal flipper pie, kind of between a duck and a fish. And for dessert, there's nothing better than partridge berry pudding."

"I'm at your mercy."

"I'm almost glad he didn't answer right away. Gives me some breathing time." But he ran to the phone again before the dessert course.

"Good Gawd, Mary, it's my lost brother Jimmy. JIMMY! Whar ye be? We'll be right up to get ye! Stay put there. Twenty minutes, not a minute later, eh?"

A ten-year younger, thirty pounds heavier Jimmy burst into the door of the 290 Restaurant with his arms outstretched, bellowing for his brother. The whole restaurant turned in amazement to see the two men embrace, and the bartender left his post to add his support to the reunion.

There was no staying on at the Battery now. After accepting a complimentary sip of "screech" from the bartender, the party was ushered to Joey's wagon to return to Petty Harbour, after a quick pick-up of the men's gear from the hotel. Accompanying Joe at a shy distance was his teenage son Mark, who was laid speechless at the scene in the restaurant, and never moved but a few nods during their journey down the coast. Joe's wife, Betty, was waiting at home with the younger brood, and Joe assured them that their sister Sue was on her way down from Quidi Vidi up ta north. "Wall, thar'll be a hollerin tanight, eh? What in the divil tuk ya sa lang?"

The family gathering in the generously appointed but rustic kitchen was noisy and warm. Everyone talked at once for awhile. Betty insisted that the 290 "nevr sarved enuf far a bawk," and set out to put before them mounds of turkey and ham.

Jim later explained to Noah that the locals felt that serving fish, especially lobster, their plentiful catch, was too humble a fare for respected guests. Sue and her three children and husband arrived amid squeals of delight from all the welcoming cousins who set out for the hillside to play while the adults had their visit. And most of the big questions were answered in a hurry. Pa was gone these five years. He had lived with Sue for a good while after his legs grew too weak to carry him onto another boat, and had passed out and died of a coronary very quickly one day down on the docks while visiting with old friends. They'd had some good times with him too, 'fore he died. He tinkered around Sue's house and built boats and toys for the kids.

And Mom? Never heard a word for a long while. Then Winnie got a letter from Vancouver. A big check for "the children" from the minister friend and word that Mom had been carried away with a stroke.

"Ye can't blame her, Jimmy. She must ha' been dad near trammeled wit pain from Pa's philanderin'. We jist put it out'n ar minds."

"I guess it's much harder to live with something like that from far away, folks," Jim offered. "I wish I'd had the strength of character to come back to see you all before now, but the pain I had myself was too hard to bear. It took my friend Noah here, to give me the gumption to come, and you can bet, I'm thankful."

Noah had been listening to the group while watching the kids play on the hillside, and peeping out the windows at the town. The harbor he could see was unique. Huge rocks surrounded the crescent, and, at the southern side, high cliffs rose where thousands of birds soared and roosted in the crevices. The little houses were curiously flat roofed and seemed to bend towards the sea.

"Sue, here, didn't want to take the money from the minister. Said it was guilt money. But I say, why wreck your life over an empty principle. That money will give at least one of each of our kids some extra education, and all of us some extra life insurance." Noah noted that Sue's husband spoke without the brogue. It turned out that he was the teacher, Joe a fisherman, and the cabbie had been confused. Sue drank her whiskey straight from a glass, with no evidence of intoxication.

Plans were made for tomorrow's trip on the high seas.

"Ye'll av to gow on me private yacht to see some whales," Joe insisted. Jimmy looked amusedly at Noah. He was not going to save him from this adventure. "And be up at five," Joe warned. "Otherwise, we'll jist see the ittle tyke porpoises in thar afternoon romp." Sue would be down to join them again for fun in the evening.

"And Perry?"

"He be a single man and lumbering over by Corner Brook in the West. Don think I kin catch him 'fore you go, but then yull av to cum back now that you've found yur way, eh Jim?"

Jim knew from a card or two that his two older siblings were in the states and had apparently been just as wary of returning as he had, for no one knew of them. But they all decided that now was the time to track everyone down.

"A big reunion next year, right here in Petty Harbour," Joe raised his glass, and everyone loudly assented. Noah thought of Lucy. How she would enjoy this fun.

They spent the night in the boy's room under the eaves of the only room in Petty Harbour with a sloping roofline. The edges of the roof came within a few inches of their heads, and the rain's rat-a-tat lulled them both into a deep sleep until Betty called in at a wicked hour to warn them that they had to dress for the outing. Nothing but fog could be seen around the little house, and Noah pondered upon the doom that was about to descend upon him. He was terrified of this adventure at sea, but knew of no way to refuse the invitation without risking an insult to these wonderful hosts.

Betty had fried up an ample breakfast of fish and potatoes, which they both had trouble stuffing in at five-thirty a.m. She then equipped them with heavy woolen pants and sweaters and yellow slickers and boots. "Ye'll doff these out thar when the fog do lift," she assured them, "but thar nice ta 'av in the arly mornin."

Joey was waiting in his boat when they came to the dock, so proud of his rig. It was the most modern boat in all of Petty Harbour, he announced. All new ship-to-shore radio equipment, a spacious head, and two bunks for overnight cruises. He spied the nervousness that Noah was wearing so thick it shuddered through his sweater and windbreaker. "Noah, me baye, this rig has enouf lead in 'er bottom to lay the Queen Mary low in the water. We could 'it a 'berg, and it'll topple first afore us."

Noah was ashamed that his feelings were so obvious and with an ever-so-forced grin took a seat inside next to the tiller.

"War go-in' out first ta sae da bawks, den we'll go fur da bigguns."

"He means the puffins and then the whales," translated Jimmy. "Don't worry if we go pitching and hawing after we get out of the harbor, and don't worry if you feel a bit queasy. Everyone has his first time at sea, and after awhile, you'll like it a lot. The return trip's always easier, and, meanwhile, if it gets too bad, just heave over to the starboard side there. It's downwind of us." Noah winced and paled, but was determined to stick. "Just think, Noah, tourists are paying upwards of a hundred dollars for this kind of tour."

"Are we keeping you from your work today?" Noah tried to make pleasant conversation with Joey.

"Naw, I'll jist check de ol' nets whan we git back dis afternoon." He stirred up the engine, turned the ship around in the wide bay while Jimmy handled the lines like an able seaman, and putted slowly out toward the open sea.

The fog was slowly lifting, and the sky was rosy in the East with promise of a fine day ahead. The temperature was a temperate fifty, and the wool sweaters were already feeling a little heavy when all at once they rounded the bend past the cliffs and the sea wind thrust it's full force against them. The waves thundered against the bow of the boat, and Noah felt his first full thrust of sea motion, way up and down.

"Come outside the cabin, Noah; it's really better if you breathe in the open air," beckoned Jimmy from the stern.

Noah tried to obey, walking gingerly, holding on to the side of the boat all along, treading with bent knees to catch the roll and pitch, and looking greener and greener. He soon was back by Jim on bent knees with his head over the side, heaving and sweating and groaning.

"He'll fail betr soon enuf," Joey pronounced with a twinkle. "Hae's a ral CFA, he is."

"Joe, he's fought getting into a boat all the time I've known him," Jim laughed. "You're being greatly honored today."

"A'll tak dat as a compliment, den, al right Jim. Lookie thar … thar's the island wit de bawks." Noah lifted his head to see. All over the cliffs were the little birds, terns right there, but on top were the nests of the Puffin, Joey's "bawks."

"Look, Noah, they nurse only one egg a season. And they are like the Ganets of Gaspe. They look for the same mate and the same nest. If an old female comes back to find a younger in her place in late spring, she kicks her out to find a new roost, if she's strong enough, and a male will search and search for his old mate."

"Touching. So that cove I saw on the map wasn't named for the birds. Did you er see such names? Cuckhold Harbor?"

Joey laughed. "Dats named for humans sure. Ders some wonderful legends about that Cove, none of dem true, eh?" He was relieved to see that Noah had recovered.

The tourists' boats were cruising around the island.

"They're not allowed to land. You have to apply for a special permit from the forestry service, for they don't want the birds disturbed. It's a smart move. One careless tourist can wreck the happy homes of hundreds of those beautiful creatures."

Joey turned the boat out to sea. "I think he's telling us we're going out to see the big Balline."

"Whales?"

"You bet. That's what we're after now."

"Do they ever capsize boats?" Noah was still tentative.

"Naw, that story was a myth of Melville's about an enraged whale in pursuit of men. These great creatures don't want to hurt us. They know we're protecting them now."

The sun was thoroughly up, and the sea was settling into its mid-morning roll with steady winds from the northwest. Joey put the boat on full speed, and the spray from the foam made the slickers most comfortable back at sternside. Noah was almost easing into it now, and tilted his head back to feel the warm rays in his face.

"You look almost as if you like it now, pal."

"I'm getting there. To think I was afraid of a sailboat on the bay at home."

"Maybe when we get back we'll buy a little rig together and take a sail on Sundays past your deck?"

"Let's think about that one for awhile," he laughed. "I tell you, that beautiful breakfast sure was wasted on me."

"You enjoyed it for an hour anyway, and that's good enough for a lot of things. Now you can look forward to dinner."

"Aww, let's not talk about food 'till this cruise is over."

An iceberg loomed in the distance. "Gawn ta steer clear of dat one over dar," remarked the captain. "Keep a look off yur bow side now, and yull see some action pretty soon."

They had not long to wait. Alongside the starboard side came the deepest sigh as though the whole ocean was expiring at once. Silver spraying into thin air, then a sparkling fin, a glistening back gliding faster than double speed of the boat. They all stared, dumb with the beauty. Then another profound sigh and spray, then slipping down. The boat was bathed in white light. Noah was entranced.

"I don't care if I ever go back now. I didn't know. I didn't know at all about this."

Jim was enjoying the thrill that come only to those who can revisit a childhood scene and marvel at the beauty that had been theirs from the beginning, like no other.

Minutes later the spectacle was repeated, and again and again until the huge mystery seemed to have drifted into other waters, and it was time to turn about. The party doffed their heavy wraps and basked in the full noon sun. "War gwan ta 'av a party tanight fur sure," announced Joey. "Johnny Matthews, ar fiddler from Witless Bay is comm' ta da fishermens' hall, and they'rl be dancin' and singin' 'til the wee. Yur stayun the week, eh?"

"Oh, Joe, we're just on a three-day hike up here from work," protested Jim. "I never figured we'd be met with all this. I guess I don't have to tell you how I feel, and also that I'll be back again with my wife, and Joe, you'll all just have to come to New York too. This day has to be the happiest of my life."

Joe beamed. "New Yawk? That'd ave to be a wunnerful trip. Wait'll I tell Betty."

Their return was accompanied by a gaggle of dolphins who played all around the boat.

"They seem to know we're here for a holiday," Jim laughed. "I can't remember such a big show." Even Joey laughed at the spectacle.

Betty was instantly on hand when they pulled up at the dock. "Guess what. Sue got ol' Perry who's in town at his gal frens. They'll be over ta here in an hour or two, and we'll al go over ta the hall together."

The fiddler played "Cod-jiggin' Days," and "Wee Small Mary," and the crowd danced and sang till "the wee." Then Jimmy sat up late with the men swapping stories of hundreds of relatives, some of which he had long forgotten but didn't ever say as much in order not to offend.

And then in the morning it was time to go up to Quidi Vidi to Sue's where she was taking them on a "CFA tour" and keeping them for the night. They spent a long time up on Signal Hill, taking in the view, and then over to Gibbet's Hill where long ago the local criminals were hanged and left there wrapped in chains to deter others from law-breaking.

On the pretext of "checking out the local evening establishments," Noah insisted that Jimmy spend that evening alone with his family. Joey would drive Jimmy and Noah to the airport along with Sue and Perry the next morning.

The pub at Charlie's was jammed with both youngsters and a crowd of sailors from several international flags in the harbor. There was good music, a full band, but no less the spirit than in the Fisherman's Hall in Petty Harbour. Noah climbed up to the bar and fell in with some sailors from a Portugese merchant vessel. It seemed not long before Jimmy and Sue joined him. "We weren't going to let you spend your evening alone so quickly," said Jim. And Sue here said she hadn't been to Charlie's for at least a month, so you'll have to put up with us again.

"Just when I though I was lucky enough to shake you."

"Well, it doesn't look like you're making time with any lassies yet. What's the matter?"

"I've got plenty enough to handle on the Guyland now."

"Whoo, so it's that bad, eh, Noah. He's stealing away my teachers now, Sue, can you beat that?"

But then Jim's gaze was fixed on the bartender. There was a cross on a chain around his neck that Jim recognized. He had made one just like it as a boy, and hammered and tacked with a special scallop design. When the man came near, Jim let him know that when he was free, he would like a word with him.

The bar was so busy that the interview seemed unlikely to take place soon, but there was a woman who gave the man a relief, and he motioned to Jim to stand aside with him over in a corner by the door.

"I once made a cross just like the one you're wearing. I know there might be more that look the same, but I had to ask you where you got that one, for I've never seen another."

"I've 'ad dis fer a lang time, sir. Little girl gave it me when I was a kid. A kid in a 'ome in Scotia."

"You don't say."

"I don e'en remember 'er name, mon. Lilly, Louise … dad bye me, but I kint 'member."

"I have to tell you sir, that I gave a cross just like that one to someone long ago, someone that I'm desperately trying to find."

"I've ad it sae lang now, I'd hate to part wit it," the young man saw what Jim was thinking. "But come now, would it 'elp ye to 'av it?"

"I don't know. I don't really know."

"Eere. I'm going to give it to ye. If Y'r back dis way, ye'll bring me another. I'll never see that little lass nae mor, and if I do, I'll tell 'er about ye, and she'll unnerstand."

"I don't know how to thank you, sir. Will you at least give me your name and address so that I can get it back to you?"

He scribbled something on a paper from the bar, and Jim tucked it into his pocket with the cross.

Perry, who joined them later at the table Sue had procured from the establishment since she was such a "reglar," was taller and thinner than the other men with a more serious aspect and shades of tragedy about him. Joey mentioned in an aside to Jim that he had met with marital problems as a very young man, and was suffering over them still. But he had a new gal now, and things seemed to be getting better. "We all cain't be as fortunate as me and Betty 'ere," remarked Joe.

219

It was a tearful parting, and once inside the little aircraft the next morning, Jim hugged Noah breathless. "Oh, Noah, I'll never forget what you've done to make me come up here," he almost whimpered into Noah's sleeve. "My life's nearly complete now. Just one more thing in old Nova, and I'll kiss the Canadian ground, but I can't hope for any more miracles."

JEANNE
Chapter Sixteen

*"He brought me to the banqueting house,
And his banner over me was love."*
The Song of Solomon, 2:4

The plane banked off to the right, and they could see the crowd waving from the airstrip. "So good to look down there and see all those forgiving people. Some very good things came down to them from somewhere. I guess my mother instilled a lot of heart, while she was with us."

"I can't wait to come back here, Jim. I've been to Europe, Asia, and all over the States, but I've never met people like this before. They must ladle out friendliness in the nurseries."

"It's in the screech, lad. Now look at the mountains, will you?"

The pilot announced that they were leaving the St. Johns area and heading north toward Labrador to avoid storms over the Burin Peninsula. Just off their starboard wing was Terra Nova National Park. The mountaintop Jim was pointing to was just a small hill, but atop it, clearly observed for they were still flying low, was a huge Bull Moose.

"Well, if you can't see him in person now, he'll be waiting there for you when you get back."

The pilot followed the Canadian Highway now, keeping south over Gander Lake to avoid the international flight patterns near the greater airport there, then across miles of tundra to the Gros Morne range and down to the western village of Deer Lake.

"People on this side are mor'n likely to have some French blood in 'em," Jimmy put in. "Many of the English stayed to the north, although we're all of some mixture. You hear a lot of the Irish on my side, although my family's mixed too. My father's supposed to have some Beotuk blood in 'em. But the Basques were the first Europeans here, after the Vikings, of course, in 1000

AD. Come back and we'll cross the country by car some day and check out the Northern Peninsula and Labrador too."

"That's where they make paper." Noah could see white smoke belching from the stacks at Corner Brook. "They're robbing the interior of scrub spruce for that plant," finished Jimmy. "I hope there's enough to last for a couple more centuries, or we find something else to write on. Funny, we've got plastic and acrylic for everything else on earth."

He shuffled about in his seat. "I'm going to tell you now a little about where we re going this afternoon so you won't be completely baffled. But I'll have to fill in the story later, because it's a little too complicated to tell all at once and do it right. If you hadn't slept so long on the way up, I'd have had a chance to get my thoughts together and spin the whole thing out right.

"After our family was broken up, we three older kids were shipped out by my Aunt Winnie, who was getting too old to take care of all of us, to the convent school in Halifax. I grew up there, I did well in school, and when I was about sixteen, I met a young acolyte who had just come to the place from New Brunswick."

"Somehow I knew there was a woman involved."

"Not a woman. Just a girl, Noah. A lovely young thing who, well, let's just say we discovered the beauties of life together. She loved art, just as I did, and we spent long hours together in the studio, and the nuns left us pretty much alone, and one thing led to another, and pretty soon we were seldom apart when we were not restricted to our rooms or to classes.

"Well, one day she told me she was in trouble, and I didn't know what to do. I was just sixteen, scared to death. You know that kind of life makes a kid feel so powerless. The nuns have a way of manipulating the children so that they become either viciously rebellious or meek and modest. In those days I was without the strength of will that developed in many of my fellows. I was to graduate the following spring; she was eighteen, also without a family, and working in the convent school as a kind of trial before her senior training back in New Brunswick.

"Before we could even try to make plans of our own, early one winter morning I was looking out my window of the dormitory and saw three figures entering a car drawn up to the front door. There were two nuns and my little love. As they encouraged her into the front passenger seat, she leaned back and looked up at my window with the saddest face. That's the last I ever saw of her, Noah. I raced down to the desk of the Mother Superior who greeted me like a criminal when I asked what had become of Jeannie. No one at the school would give me any accounting of her, and I wept away many nights and grew listless over my work. Finally, after I graduated, I took work at a nearby farm. The long hours and hard harvesting led me to sleep deeply, and I began to allow my pain to subside. But I never forgot, and now, as I grow older, I realize that I must have some responsibility there. There must have been a child. And its mother was an orphan too."

"Would we expect the sisters to place the child in a convent school, the same as you were?"

"Probably. And he would have grown up just like we did, with little or no knowledge of his parents or background. With a mother that age, the church may or may not have encouraged her to separate from the child. I couldn't even find the name of the convent where she was supposed to be going to in New Brunswick, but with just a little effort we should be able to make significant progress now, don't you think?"

"Just as with anything else, Jim, it all depends on how much the particular authorities we approach care to do for us, and how vigorously you intend to pursue the matter. Is this the part you didn't tell Selma?"

"Yes, for if there's no trail, no news, there's no sense in alarming her over an ancient tale that has no ending, and that she might fear is tearing my affections away from her."

They soon saw the cliffs of Cape Breton off the right wing of the plane, and fifteen minutes later they were again approaching the Halifax airport. The weather was milder than on their first visit, and they had no trouble finding a cab and getting out to the convent.

The same small woman who had greeted them two days earlier was back to announce that Mother would indeed see Mr. Duffer in her chambers immediately.

"Do you want me along on this one, Jimbo?"

"Of course. Why do you think you're here? If I swoon, you'll have to catch me."

They were unprepared for the tall, smartly suited gentlewoman, a thoroughly modern Mother Superior, who greeted them in an opulent office. The few clues to her profession were a nearly barren desk top and an absence of decor other than the magnificently carved mahogany furniture and Edson's portrait of Christ, hung on an eastern wall. Long windows draped with damask faced out on the Bay to the view they had recently admired from the hilltop.

Her dark red graying hair was done back in a tight chignon, but the softness in her face belied their reception in the hall and the temperament surrounding this fortress. Jim was staring at her as though he were seeing a ghost.

"I think you remember me, don't you, Jim?" she began softly. "'You've come at last,'" she sighed. "And now it was so long ago. So long."

"Jeanne. What happened to you? What on earth happened?"

Noah let himself out quietly. But it wasn't so long before the doors were opened again.

"Please come back in, Noah. We want you to hear our story. You will scarcely believe your ears," Jimmy was ecstatic.

"Yes, please come back in, Mr. Leonard. We have happy news," the lady beckoned.

"Well, to begin from last weekend," the lovely Mother Superior continued, "my little prioress here confused Jim's name so that I received a message that a Mr. Dufee was here to see me from the States on some matter of an old friend. I was in the middle of a crisis case with one of the students that could not be interrupted. You must know how those things come up at a school, so I sent the message that I could not be disturbed and would the gentlemen kindly return the next morning. I'm afraid she overdid the answer. At any rate, when the crisis eased later in the evening, I called to her again, and she seemed confused about the name. Said it could have been Duffey, or, perhaps, Duffer. As you can imagine, I could hardly contain myself, and have waited so anxiously for your return, for I had no idea how to reach you."

"Then you are ... ?" The question was unnecessary, for Jim's eyes told it all.

"Yes, I was Jeannie Du Bonne, Jim's old friend, Mr. Leonard. And to make the story brief, I was being sent back to New Brunswick when Jim saw me from the window that last morning. The rest of the story I must ask you to keep locked in your memory," she lowered her head ever so slightly, "at least that part of it that might damage my authority here at the school. I am effective here at my work, and there are rules of the church and the convent schools, and the adoption practices that we preserve, we believe are for the good of all our children and the adoptive parents. If news of revealed identities gets out to the public, we will lose face in our noblest duties to those anxious families who want so much to be whole mothers and fathers to our needy clients. I'm sure you can appreciate my position." Noah and Jim nodded, Noah wondering where all this was leading.

She rose and went to the windows, trying hard to put her words together in a way that would fit the delicate story she was about to tell. Then she turned, and drew the cross from her desk top that Jim had been carrying from St. Johns.

"This cross Jim gave me just a few days before I was taken away from this place," she continued tearfully, "and I always wore it. I was wearing it when our child was born. And I wore it until I made my last decision about her, a heart-wrenching decision, but one that Jim tells me has indeed been for the best." She could hardly keep her composure now, but as befitted their present positions, neither man rose.

"I had no means to care for her, and if it had not been for the Church, no means to care for myself at that time. They convinced me to keep her in the convent school while I was assuming my avocation, the calling that I longed to complete, that I seemed wholly suited for. But there came a time when I felt that she needed far more than neither the Church nor I could offer. I knew that I should give her a chance for a normal home and family. She was returned here, to Nova Scotia, to this convent, and then there came an opening at a school in Connecticut where there were so many more applications for older children from parents in affluent, respectable homes. You must guess the rest by now, as you know her history."

Noah could only nod, not yet realizing her point.

"I left her after one last visit here in Nova Scotia. I couldn't tell her that I would perhaps never see her again because she was too young to understand the delicacy of the decision. I gave her this locket then. She was still so young, only four, and certainly would be of an age where keepsakes between close friends were precious to bestow. I can understand why she passed it along to that lad you met in St. Johns. She had no family then; she needed to make an important gesture to the boy, just as we needed each other so very much, Jimmy."

"Then ... her name?" Noah still needed confirmation for what might still be an amazing coincidence.

"She's our Lucy, Noah. She's our daughter," Jimmy broke down.

After the little group had taken time to fit all the mixed pieces together, an important decision was reached.

"She's been aching to know who she is, Jim. We're going to have to find some careful way to relate all this to her."

"I ask only this of you," the lady continued. "That you try some way to explain my singular position with her. I dearly, dearly want to see the child, but even though she is now of age, in the interest of everyone, the request should come jointly from both her and her adoptive parents. Then, to protect the interests of the authorities here and the restrictions of the State of Connecticut, if the request is made sincerely from all parties concerned, I will come to see her on Long Island, but only if all is discreet and proper. I have only the highest respect for the wishes of the adoptive parents."

"We'd better call Peter and Laura now, before we leave this place," Jimmy finally spoke.

"Make it Peter first," cautioned Noah. He left the two alone for another long time then, and when Jimmy rejoined him, he could see that he was collected and filled with a new assurance.

"I spoke with Peter. Then Jeanne spoke. He's taking such amazing news bravely, but I wonder how long it will take him to break the news to Laura. He thinks it wise to delay telling Lucy until we return and are able to speak together."

They took their leave of the lovely lady after she promised to be in close touch with everyone concerned.

*   *   *

"I didn't tell her," Noah remarked with remorse. "I didn't tell her one of the most important pieces of news."

"Whatever are you talking about now?" asked Jimmy, distractedly.

"Jeanne, Mother, whoever she is ... we're getting married. I'm marrying Lucy."

"Well, it would be nice for her father to know too," Jim slapped him heartily on the backside. "Both her fathers. You'd better be making proper plans after what I think I saw last Friday."

"Comeon, Jim, you know I'm an honorable guy."

"Yes I do, but it better be as soon as your divorce is final, or ther'll be hell to pay in Suppogue." Then, after a pause, "I think that shock will wait for Jeanne."

"Do you have a problem leaving her here now, Jim?"

"Not in the least. She's not the same quivering child I knew, Noah. She is a matron of the Church, in the strongest sense. She represents a beautiful time in my life that I'll always have, but I've got a new kind of happiness now. Just think. A wonderful daughter to share with a great friend. I really don't believe that Selma will falter at this news."

"Just one piece of this that I don't follow, Jim. What is that locket all about? You never showed it to me."

Jim slapped his leg. "Ha ha! That was the cross I found on the neck of the bartender in Charlie's. It looked exactly like one I had made myself and given to Jeanne so long ago. And blamed if it wasn't! I took it on a hunch and didn't even look for the inscription on the back, which was there for Jeanne to point out to me today. Won't it be a fine trinket to give Lucy? She gave it away to that boy while they were in the home together---a little seven-year-old's romance."

"Just don't get those two together again, mind you, Jim."

Noah phoned Lucy with news of their success in Newfoundland and could hardly contain himself with the discoveries that concerned her so vitally. Jim was dying to speak to her, but for the sake of discretion forbade himself that happiness until all matters were resolved back on Long Island with Peter and Laura.

"Now when will you land? I want to be out as close to that tarmac as I can get. Selma is phoning me constantly with questions about what I have heard to compare them with what she has heard in case Jim forgot any of the details."

"We should be in at eight o'clock tonight," Noah reported. "Just tell Selma I've taken great care of old Jim, and that he's returning to her one happy piece of man. He's also looking forward to a decent meal. Codfish and potato cakes are turning our New York stomachs inside out."

"I'll call her right away, and we'll both be waiting tonight. Have you said anything to Jim ... about us, I mean."

"Of course. I had to say something after our slipshod arrival at the airport. He's most protective of you, you know."

"He's a dear man. What did he say?"

"He slapped me on the back and said that my life was on the line if I didn't make an honest woman of you a.s.a.p. Take good care, lock your doors, and I'll see you as fast as Air Canada can deliver me tonight."

*   *   *

As their flight from Halifax touched down at La Guardia, a flight attendant strode down the aisle to speak quietly to Noah. "Mr. Noah Leonard, please do not leave the aircraft until all other passengers have disembarked. Some gentlemen have an important message to deliver to you." He turned and began helping other passengers with luggage.

"Do I have a choice here, Jim?"

"It's got to be significantly legal, or the flight attendant would never stop your progress. Sit tight, friend."

As soon as the last passenger disembarked, two FBI agents led by Jake Sutherland came forward and cuffed him. "Noah Leonard, you are under arrest for the murder of Fawn Whitney. You may make your call at any airport telephone."

*   *   *

Lucy hummed snatches of an old song as she shuffled through the remaining papers on her table, sorting and labeling for distribution to her classes tomorrow. She was looking forward to a joyous reunion with Noah, and to seeing Jim, happy with his discoveries: a man who deserves much happiness. A rare kind of leader that hopes only for the success and well being of others. And there's a lot around like that, I've found this year. Now if we could all be relieved of the problem of Fawn's murderer ... why haven't the FBI come up with something after all this time? Is it because it's such a low profile case, or do they want us all to forget about it for some oblique reason, like Vinny suggested?

The heavy knock at the back door in the dark and quiet of the May evening sounded like repeated gunfire. Lucy, startled at so thoroughly unexpected a sound from the door that was seldom used by others than she, sprang from her seat at the table and cautiously made her way back through the kitchen. It wasn't wholly dark yet. No dangerous intruder would be so bold as to visit her house at this hour, making such obvious sounds. She unbolted the door slowly. It was Kurt Sutherland, with a tire iron in his right hand.

"It's your turn, Miss Mackenzie. Don't scream, or you'll get everything Miss Whitney got ... and more."

SHORT CRUISE
Chapter Seventeen

"These hot days is the mad blood stirring."
Benvolio *in Romeo and Juliet* by William Shakespeare

Lucy took in the whole of Kurt. His unnatural leer, harder and, now it seemed, thoroughly demented. His ragged blond hair lying as though caked to his forehead, covered with sweat. Her mind raced to the horror of Fawn in the tub of bloody water, to the threatening words of Kurt in the classroom, to the photos Noah had shown her of the mutilated animals and birds.

"We're going for a little ride, Miss Mackenzie... a little boat ride. Close the door behind you. We don't want to alarm anyone, now, do we? Don't scream, or there'll be a fancy ending to this right now."

She seemed to have no choice for the moment. He was holding the tire iron firmly in his hand, and had braced himself against the door. She must go with him and try to find a way around him. If there really is a boat ride, there must be time to play with.

Down the walk as they approached the still waters of the canal the lightening bugs blinked at them. A crow shrieked, and the ducks scattered from the lawn, diving into the murky waters and swimming away. The acerbic odor of the exhausts from the last boats home wafted from the water. Only a few ripples showed the motion of the incoming tide along the shore, fighting against the midstream current from the underground river. Kurt's dinghy was drawn up to her dock with no signs of life on either side of the canal. The day had been a soggy Memorial Day, discouraging picnickers into parlor reunions. No lingering barbecue parties would be in backyards tonight.

"Sit in the bow," he barked.

Lucy stepped gingerly into the small dingy. She had to sit facing Kurt, so close she could smell his stale beer breath, as he pulled the rope out of the dock loop with an angry jerk. "Good by house. You're going to a party."

As Kurt pulled on the oars downstream he began his heinous recitation:

"Bunch of my friends are sitting out on Captree waiting for us. They're anxious to meet a young, pretty teacher like you. Miss Whitney was nice, for an old gal, too nice, but we wouldn't touch her that way, nossir. Not with her damn nigger-mixed blood. Did you know she was a damn nigger-lover just like you? Her pa was black, and her ma loved that black blood. And now you, Miss Mackenzie. Why dja hav ta be that way? You could have been a nice, sensible woman and taught us some good books and not tried to copy her, a sweet, white copy-cat that deserves just what she'll get."

Lucy gripped the sides of the boat and tried to think, think what to do. Where she was. How could she save her life?

"Now, Miss Mackenzie, I hear from various sources that you've added to your crimes in the classroom. Yes indeedy, you're a Jew-lover now. And I've always wondered. How is it that Jews do it? Do they do it with their hands, Miss Mackenzie, or their feet, or their big, always-talking Jew mouths? Why no, they wouldn't ever do it with their mouths, 'cause they have to keep talking right through all their fuckin'. They never stop talkin. But you know the way us All Americans do it, Miss Mackenzie? Why with what I got right here, what you're gonna get soon, Miss Teach," and he ripped open his fly and demonstrated. That beauty's what you'll get, Miss Mackenzie, the old-fashioned, straight-fuckin American way, and you'll never go back to yur Jew man again."

He's mad, so mad, shuddered Lucy, without a clue as what to do.

"That beauty's what you'll get, Miss Mackenzie, Now. Let's see some of you, 'cause I've showed you a big some of me. Let's see your tits now, Miss. I wanta see your pretty white tits. Show them to me --- take that shirt off, lady, and show me what you got. Comeon now, don't be shy. I can't touch ya or nothin yet while I'm rowing."

Lucy froze. She could not expose herself to this monster. It would show her weakness. She could not victimize herself. But if he could not reach her here, she might prevail somehow. "Take off that blouse, lady, or I'll crush the side of your pretty head," he cradled one oar on the side of the boat and wielded the tire iron, lightly brushing her hair.

Lucy undid her blouse.

"Comeon, off with it, and that fancy bra too. My, oh my, aren't we pretty, and all white 100% American too. Let's see those pretty pink tits. Do you know that nigger ladies have brown tits? Do you know that's what Miss

Whitney had? I wanted to suck 'em 'fore I killed her, but I don't suck black tit. But oh, how I suck pink white tit. You come on to me on that island, and I'll suck you right up so good you won't ever want to go back to that big smart Jew again. Comeon, don't make me pretend I'm going to hurt you again," he brushed her head once more. "Take off that pretty bra."

As she slipped out of her bra, Lucy tried to pretend that it was all a terrible dream that would end soon. She quietly dropped it into the water ... maybe a trail.

"Godalmighty my juices sure are flowing. I can hardly wait. Now if I can stand it, you've got to show me your cunt too so's I can get a head start on the rest on that island. I won't geta yard out of this boat before I have you lady, I swear. Comeon, honey, pull that skirt up and spread your legs wide open for me. It won't hurt a bit. You've got me going here already so's I can hardly row."

Would his ugly passion weaken his resolve? She should play along just a little ... until she saw a chance, for as distasteful as the charade was, it was her life. She now knew that he would never let her go alive.

She saw that the canal was widening as it began emptying into the bay. Her little cove with the sharp rushes and the tiny island and the Oakley house was just around the bend.

"Do you really like this, Kurt?" she ventured, and undid her skirt, dropping it into the water. "Jesus Christ, you're killing me---what'd you do that for so quick? Are you really gone on me now, chick? I can't hurt you now none. Touch me. touch me, baby, or I'll die. Put your hand out and stroke me while I row and pretend I'm rowing you, baby. Just help me through this time, and I'll protect you, baby. Just pick up my dong and stroke me, please." He was panting and full of turgid life.

The boat was rounding the bend and coming nearly alongside the little cove. She could make out Annie's house over the long reeds. Last season's crop stood in spikes out of the water. They were strong and hollow, and the children closed their ends and carved holes along their sides and made whistles of them.

"Please, please," he panted.

The tire iron lay at his feet, not two feet from the edges of her skirt. He was stupid and careless and crazy.

In one quick flowing motion she leaned forward, and as he saw her moving, he closed his eyes, waiting for her touch. She grasped the tire iron in her left hand, rose, and dived into the black water, her naked body cutting through the tangled depths until she reached the clusters of reeds and then the hard bottom by the island. The tide was in, so there was plenty of water to hide her. And a reed could help her breathe and hide.

She stayed under for half a minute with the help of a reed for the last few seconds, and finally surfaced behind a huge clump where she could see the boat circling closer toward her. His cursing and grunting was far enough away so that her breathing could not be detected, but near enough so that even gentle movements might be seen. She had to move further inland before he came closer, and she had to go underwater ever so quietly, remembering that little island had an overhanging rock on the far side nearest the beach. She could swim underwater just that far. Slipping into the water again, she found that she could creep along the bottom. A jostled crayfish picked at her toe, and the icy May water was beginning to numb her feet and hands.

I can't stand much more exposure, she reasoned. I'll have to get away from him on land somehow, soon. Why didn't I think to stun him with the tire iron?

She surfaced on the southern edge of the little island and pulled herself around to the western side. There was the overhang; she could barely make out its shadow, and no one could see its protruding lip unless they had been in these parts before in so intimate a way as she had been that warm September evening just nine months ago. She pulled herself under the rock and tried to keep her feet and hands moving quietly under water to keep her blood flowing. The oars crunched in their locks. He was pulling into shore, guessing that she had landed.

Sure enough, the boat glided past the little promontory and bumped up on the beach. He was out of the boat and up the shallow beach in several quick strides. No time to lose now, she reckoned.

He was behind the Oakley house, thrashing in the tall weeds.

Quick---she lunged at the boat and pushed it as far through the cove as she could wade, then flung herself into the little dingy, still clutching the tire iron, making a clatter as she hurried to take up the oars.

She could see his figure hurrying around the side of the house.

"Goddam." He raced to the shore and dived flat into the water. Not reckoning on its shallowness, he was immediately on his feet, trapped by his heavy clothes and boots, and the thick, muddy bottom of the cove.

She rowed frantically, out of the wide mouth of the canal where he might trap her. Shivering with the cold, she wished for the luxury of her blouse and skirt that she had dropped into the bay. He did me quite a favor to make me strip, she marveled. Now he'll have to take time to get off all his clothes to swim to where I'm going, and he'll be just as cold as I am.

But he swam forcefully. She could soon see his head in the water as she pulled against the incoming tide. It was harder and harder to pull the little dingy that wanted to turn back, first to the left, then to the right to ease out of the canal with all the current against her. He was gaining on her, and one oar slipped out of her bruised and muddy hands. He was coming abreast, and her only hope lay in the bottom of the boat. She drew it to her, and, as his hand desperately grasped the side of the dinghy, his head alongside, she swung the iron as hard as she could against the side of his head. He gave a hideous gasp, and clutched hard at the dinghy, pulling it over his head into the water, sending Lucy flying out into the bay beyond him and the boat.

She tread water weakly, unable to swim. The little boat bobbed in a circle, caught in fighting currents. She was afraid she would see him, feel him come up behind her and claw at her head and face, but no Kurt appeared. She finally decided that she would have to try to get to the boat, for the shore looked too far to swim for.

It was easier stroking back to the boat than she had thought, and instead of wrestling to right the craft, she opted to try to push it back into the canal. It went smoother than she had guessed, for the incoming tide was now helping her. And now there was no Kurt.

The boat butted against a shallow edge of the canal, and she righted it and fell inside. She could not row, but she felt the boat carrying her back up the canal slowly. She could hear herself whimpering and gasping, but was able to push enough with one hand to guide the boat into her ramp.

A dark form stood on the ramp. "Lucy, what in the world?"

"Phyllis. I was attacked by Kurt. I escaped---in the water---and I---I think I killed him, Phyllis." Then she lost consciousness, and Phyllis pulled her onto the lawn.

*   *   *

Lucy's head was tiny under the white sheets of the hospital. "Noah, Jimmy, the airport ... tonight!"

Phyllis was near at hand. "I called Selma. She's going out to get them. She'll explain."

"Oh, Phyllis, what will they think?"

"That you're recovering, and hardly the worse for the time you had."

"Did I kill him, Phyllis? What did I do?"

"Don't you worry about anything. There'll be a few people in to question you soon, but the truth of your experience is pretty obvious."

Phyllis waited for awhile to see how lucid and healthy she was, and decided to tell her the rest.

"They found Kurt's body, Lucy. And they'll have to know more later, but right now you must rest."

"Oh, Phyllis, he tried to kill me. And he confessed to Fawn's murder."

"That's a very helpful piece of information. I don't think you have to worry about being believed, after the way I found you. How on earth did you ever escape?" And Lucy was wide-awake and ready with her tale.

Soon Peter and Laura were by her bedside, and soon thereafter, Jimmy and Selma. "But where is Noah?" she had to ask.

"Lucy, he's been detained by the police," Jimmy began. "It's part of the Fawn Whitney investigation. But it seems your experience will serve to straighten things out."

"How can this be? What has Noah to do with anything?"

"We had to leave him with the police, Lucy. It appears that Jake Sutherland has him as the prime suspect in the murder, with all kinds of circumstantial evidence, because he was first on the scene of the crime and left prints all over the house. He also was an old friend, and then he revisited the crime scene, unauthorized. Jake was desperately looking for someone to indict, and Noah was the closest to the crime that he could get without facing the truth about his son, so he claimed he had given the feds indisputable proof of Noah's guilt, and they're still holding him until they can interview---" Jim looked at Phyllis for the go-ahead, and she nodded, "until they can interview you about tonight."

"Oh, send them in. This is terrible, poor Noah. There must be more to what Jake has done than everyone knows."

"That's what we're thinking now that we know your story. And I think you are going to have those visitors very soon."

Several F.B.I. men waited outside the door until Lucy's doctor gave them permission to enter, and they stayed until she, and then Phyllis, described her ordeal. Later that evening, Noah was released and was at her bedside.

Jake Sutherland was indicted for having withheld substantial evidence that linked his son to the murder of Fawn Whitney. After the news was out about Kurt's death, several of Kurt's acquaintances, who had already gone to Jake but had been suppressed, testified to the FBI about his bragging over the murder.

"Thank God you're alive. To think that maniac was there while we were still in the air coming home."

"To think that you were in a jail cell while I was utterly ... unconscious!"

And finally the rest left the two alone for awhile before her doctor assured the group that she was fit to leave the hospital. Phyllis offered to stay the night with her to be certain that she was comfortable, and Noah and Jim made their plans to speak to Peter and Laura that week to decide how best to break the news to her about her newly discovered family.

MISS MACKENZIE
Chapter Eighteen

"Then thus she says: your behavior hath struck her into amazement and admiration."
Rosencrantz in *Hamlet* by William Shakespeare

Peter and Laura planned a dinner party at their home for the following Sunday. It was decided that they would take Lucy aside quietly before the gathering and explain to Lucy what Jimmy and Noah had learned in the convent.

"This is an awkward but happy time for all of us," Peter began. "Jim and Noah had an amazing trip. Some of it you know about, but we wanted to wait till you had fully recovered from your adventure and till we all had a chance to digest what they discovered to tell you what the implications of it all were for you."

"Me? How could any of it have to do with me? Except that Noah says that we're going to be taking a trip up there ourselves as soon as we …"

"Lucy, Jim and Noah found your birth parents."

The amazement on her face made Peter almost afraid to continue, but he braved it along. And as he came to the part about Jeanne's difficult decision, their bell rang, and Laura ushered Jim and Selma in. As soon as Jim saw her face, he knew, and she was out of her chair to run sobbing into his arms. She then turned to Laura, then Peter, and, finally Selma. "And you're another mother for me now too. I can't believe all this is really coming true. But my … my first mother?"

Peter stepped aside. "I think I'll let Jim tell this part of it."

After Jim stumbled through the story as best he could, Lucy asked, "But will I ever see her? Will she come here, or will I go there?"

"We made a promise to her that we would all be discreet. She wants very badly to see you, but she will have to choose the proper time. She is delighted that you found a home, and will come when the right occasion presents itself."

"I'll trust that she'll come when she can," breathed Lucy. "But where's Noah? We have news too, at least for you," she gestured toward Peter and Laura.

Noah seemed to step right out of the woodwork; actually it was the dining room where he had been waiting so as not to disturb the familial developments.

"I wouldn't have missed this evening for the world," he joked. "But I thought I'd give the principals time to get adjusted." Lucy ran to him, and they wasted no time in announcing their plans to Peter and Laura.

It had been necessary for Jim to advocate strenuously for Noah a few days before this formal announcement to Peter and Laura. Otherwise, their daughter's plans to marry a man whom they had assumed was happily married not so long ago would not have impressed them favorably. Laura was still most dubious, but with so many alterations to her perceptions happening at once, she decided to let herself mull over that more tentative issue until she felt herself back in some semblance of equanimity.

"Relatives, relatives," Lucy laughed. "I'm going to have some time sorting out my family members for awhile. It's a good thing I'm not a little kid. I'd be impossibly confused."

"And you've got a whole passel of aunts and uncles and cousins up north," sighed Jimmy. "You won't believe the broods they raise in that cold country."

*   *   *

A few hours later on Noah's deck, Lucy sighed to him, "I'm glad it's the end of the year ... for us all, and especially for the kids. They won't be spooked by that crime every time they see me. And Harper's so much better. He's had some good headwork with the doctors, and his parents are apparently wise enough to understand what their part is now in his problems. Do you know what his parents are going to do for the school when he graduates? Endow an English chair in the name of Fawn Whitney in gratitude for our efforts to save his life."

"I'm glad neither my name nor yours is on the chair," said Noah. "Somehow I'd feel we were obliged to expire just to be traditional."

"Maybe that's one reason they chose Fawn's name. But also, I insisted on it. I still feel that I'm just the stand-in."

"You're about as much of a stand-in as Niagara Falls."

"OO ... you used to say that about Nick. Speaking of casualties, there's another for the year ... besides Nick. Have you heard about Sam Rose?"

"Only that he's being published soon."

"It's out. The Kenyon Review came out last week, and Sam is resigning his teaching position."

"Why is he resigning? He's not going to be able to support himself on stories in the Kenyon Review."

"You'll have to read it, Noah. It's really not fiction. It's an autobiographical piece about his life as a homosexual high school teacher. Phyllis spoke with him about it yesterday."

"We won't want to lose him. Jim will not accept his resignation. He's a wonderful teacher."

"Yes, but what will he face if he stays on ... especially in this community? He told Phyllis he has friends on the West Coast where he may go for awhile until this article cools off. I think he's published the article to accept himself for what he is ... and the world be hanged."

"And maybe the truth will ultimately save him. If not, his bravery may help others to understand his problems, but society is a long way from accepting that lifestyle for a teacher in 1960."

"But back to big changes," added Noah as they gazed out over the Great South Bay toward the twinkling lights of the causeway, "next year you won't be Miss Mackenzie in the classroom anymore."

"How old fashioned you've suddenly become. I'll always be Miss Mackenzie. Don't take that away from me."

"Well, a thoroughly modern Miss. You could be Duffer, you know, as well as Leonard."

"I've had Miss Mackenzie so long now it fits. And besides, my second parents need some support right now. They've had their knocks through all this. I want them to know that they'll always be a big part of me."

"Good girl. Yes, we all have a wonderful part of you, my brave Canadian lassie. And now, I can't wait for part of my part anymore. Let's go to bed."

"Oh, Noah, not yet. Let's sleep right out here under the stars, near the water that saved me."

Noah chuckled. "Wait right here---I'll be thirty seconds."

He dragged the Castro mattress through the panel doors and out onto the deck.

"And away we go! You know, you're the most aggressive lover I've ever known, and it's delightful. I don't have to work so hard in my old age."

"Oh, ancient man ... twelve years older! The older we grow, the shorter the years."

"Hey, it's cold out here."

"It's getting warmer and warmer."
"Only a genuine Newfie could have survived that icy May bay water."
"You know that awful Kurt was right about one thing."
"Wazzat?"
"You really can't shut up long enough to make love."
"You have your Blarney nerve."

*   *   *

The wedding was set for October, the week after Noah's decree was final and a suitable time for the pair to leave school for a week. Only a few close friends were invited to the ceremony in Peter and Laura's garden where Lucy loved to be. Early in the morning after breakfast, Laura came to Lucy in her room, packing for the happy week ahead. They would stay one night at Noah's house, then fly out to an undisclosed location in a warmer clime.

"There's a lady downstairs to see you," Laura summoned her daughter.

A quietly suited woman, who bore an interesting resemblance to the bride, rose from the sofa as Lucy entered. They regarded each other for only a moment, then embraced for a long time. Few words that were spoken between them could be heard from the other parts of the house, but they stayed together for at least an hour or more until the elder of the two rose.

"But before I go, I have a gift to return to you," she smiled. "It's made a few round-about journeys in its day, but I think it's come home for good now." She pressed the cross into Lucy's hand. "Your father found an old friend of yours wearing it when he visited a place in St. Johns. He'll tell you all about it, and when you go back there with Noah and Jim, you might see him again. He was eager to know that you were well, and wishes you only the best." She drew herself away with a soft dignity.

"I'll be with you someday soon again. And you'll know where to find me if you need me now." And she was out the door.

"John Henry Lorry from Random Sound," Jimmy read. "We'll have to take him a fine gift when we go back to Newfoundland. He jotted his name down for me in Charlie's bar that night, Noah."

"I remember now. I gave him that cross so he would stop crying. Little John Henry, who was always getting beaten up by the big boys."

"Never could resist a babe in need. Well, he didn't look so helpless behind that bar, and I'm your babe now, so don't think of rekindling any interest in little John from … did you say 'Random Sound?' Now there's a name for a song."

"They've already written it, pal," said Jim. "And I bought some records on Water Street of Newfie folksongs with that song in it that I'm giving you for a wedding present. Then you'll be prepared for your trip next summer. Oh, and this time we have to go by the ferry. Selma won't travel in the plane. Comeon, don't look so green. After our whaling trip, how could you be afraid of a huge icebreaker?"

"Just don't feed me cod and fries for breakfast, and I just might make it. You did hear, didn't you Lucy, that I was nearly swallowed by a whale while out on this rickety rig his brother sails? On second thought, I don't think I'd better take you up there. It's much too dangerous a place. Auntie Sue told me that they have black flies so big that they've been known to carry off small children."

"Naa, laddie, y'er gittin' them confused with da bawks!"

"We really ought to go for Christmas. Now there's a tempting idea. Thirty-five below in February, you said?"

"That's only once or twice a year. Don't go exaggerating."

"Sounds perfect for me. I'm the original snow maiden. But don't you think we ought to take some students along. A great field trip. Those folksongs are full of great poetry and wit."

"No students on this trip, lass."

"Well, stop talking about the distant future," interrupted Jim again. "You've been home a week and haven't seen my real wedding present yet. It's out in the backyard, just waiting to be taken home."

A few minutes later Selma joined them in the backyard to see a sparkling new bay runner bobbing at their dock. "You've done too much looking out into that bay for years. Now, if you don't learn to captain this rig on your own, I'll be over to show you how."

"But no whales, Jim? Where will we find the whales?"

Lucy was scrambling up to the deck, ready to take it away.

"There be your captain, boy."

About the Author

Nanette Asher holds a B.A. from Westminster College in English and an M.A. in English language and literature from New York University with concentrations in Shakespeare and literary criticism. She has taught writing, literature, and drama in schools on Long Island and in the City University of New York, and has taken her students from Hunter College High School to perform Shakespearean plays in London at the Globe Theatre. In 2003 Nan was awarded the Blackboard Prize for outstanding teaching in Manhattan schools and recommended three times by parents and students to *Who's Who in American Education*. Her poems are published in several periodicals, recognized by *Pen and Brush*, and she is currently completing an interfaith postmodern interpretation of *The Pentateuch* and another novel. After discovering the beauty of Newfoundland on a Canadian vacation, she returns frequently to visit favorite haunts.

Printed in the United States
35770LVS00005B/58-204